BASTARD!
SUCKI
WHO
LOVE TOO MUCH

Nikki Van Bergen

Pen Press Publishers Ltd

Published in Great Britain by

Pen Press Publishers Ltd

39, Chesham Road

Brighton

BN2 1NB

ISBN 1-905621-09-4

ISBN13: 978-1-905621-10-1

Cover design Jacqueline Abromeit

This book is dedicated to Peter, Pete and Thaddeus

Chapters

In The Beginning

I was in bed with the Vicar, when the ex-love of my life called. Guess I should have slammed the phone back down on him there and then, but I wanted to hear what he'd got to say for himself. Particularly since this was the man who'd taken off to Oman with only the clothes he stood up in the morning after our moving-in party, having neglected to mention he was leaving.

It turned out he had a good deal to say, most of it unsuitable for the ears of a woman long since married to someone else.

'Listen to me very carefully, Zoe,' he told me softly. *'It's time, isn't it? Time for me to say what I want from you. Time to let you know why I never quite let you go.'*

That voice. It's been more than twenty years since we lived under each other's skins, breathed the same air, drank from the same glass. But I'd never forgotten the feel of him under my fingers, the touch of his back beneath my cheek, the taste of him in my mouth. As to what he wanted, I remembered only too well that it was usually his own way with no strings attached. Well this time he'd picked the wrong...

'I want an adventuress, Zoe. An adventuress who needs... an adventure.'

Well maybe so, but it was Monday morning, I was about to try to do some work and though you used to be sex in a CK suit, I'd never forgotten all that trouble you'd got me into the last time. The Vicar, tired of being ignored, nudged me in what my gran used to call the Front Bottom Region. Discouraged him by crossing my legs.

1

'*And you?*' asked That Voice, even more softly than before. '*I expect you're wondering what's in this for you. That's easy. I've always known what you wanted. Haven't I?*' I felt a distinct twinge somewhere gynaecological since this was perfectly true – talk about an Ex who marked the spot, and in this case we were talking G-spot – then eased the fat black and white cat off my midriff, where he was turning in ponderous circles, needling the duvet with his claws. The Vicar hissed irritably and stalked away across the honey-coloured floorboards, showing a tall straight tail and tight little bum button. The white collar of fur marking his neck flared silver in the cold February light which poured in through our dirt-streaked, floor-to-ceiling windows.

'*You know, I could have your most private, intimate fantasy right here in the palm of my hand,*' he continued. '*The one thing you've never admitted to anyone. I already know all about it, because I know all about you, Zoe.*'

I'd hoped he wasn't being so crass as to be talking about – what it sounded like he was talking about (he always did have an ego the size of Brazil). But if he wasn't referring to That, what was it? Kicked off the bedcovers and heaved upright, stepping painfully on a sharp piece from my son's K'Nex kit. Cursed silently and rubbed throbbing foot, reflecting that this was not an appropriate conversation to be having at nine o'clock on a Monday morning. I was meant to be finishing an article about the new Extreme Foot Fetishism that should have been in last Friday, and had just been enjoying a cosy snuggle back in the fusty, unmade bed with a cup of tea after everyone had gone before tackling the day head on. What was all this about, anyway? Last time we spoke, he said he'd be in touch to arrange a lovely lunch.

'*I can set the whole thing up for you. Everything you ever wanted. The more secret it is, the more ashamed you would be to tell anyone about it ever, the more exciting I shall find it and the better I shall like you –*' he would, huh? damn, my instep was really hurting now '*– and we both know just how* *much I've always liked you sweetheart –'* he stopped short, then the hypnotic, creamy cadences drained abruptly from his voice: 'Darlin', what was that noise?'

It had been me, uttering a strangled sort of sheep bleat, which came out as I cleared my throat and tried to retrieve the conversational upper hand. 'Now wait a minute, Shaun. What about that lunch? You told me, you said –'

'A detail. Hush, and be still,' he whispered. *'For I have a deal to offer you. A proposition. You remember how much you always enjoyed propositions?'*

That very much depended on who they were from. Even so, I was alarmed to find that I wanted to hear more. No, stop right there. Arrogant bastard. How dared he, especially at that time in the morning, and particularly after dropping off the face of the planet for so long…

'I don't want a proposition. Look, we're talking about a meal here,' I'd insisted in a tone normally used by teachers instructing six-year-old boys to cease fiddling with their trouser fronts; trying not to remember all those other times, other propositions, other games of dare, bluff and sexual aberration we had once enjoyed. With two children teetering on the cusp of teenagehood and a full time job I no longer had the energy, and anyway my backside's got way too big for the right sort of little outfits…

A lewd, purring growl undulated down the phone. God almighty, he always used to make that sound just before he –

'Cut that out. You should have grown out of this sort of thing by now. I certainly have.' But my knees gave a dangerous wobble, and as the words left my lips I could taste the lie on my tongue.

'Sweetheart, sweetheart: if you do as I tell you – and I mean exactly as I tell you,' he had paused for a moment and I'd heard the soft hush of his exhaled breath: *'I promise that I will take us on the magic carpet ride of our lives.'*

Us.

That clinched it. I'd never forgotten the time when we'd been Us. Tried to reply, but the words got lost somewhere around tonsil level.

'Do you hear me, Zoe? Do you want to play?'

I heard you all right, Shaun. Even now, I can still hear you. For seven magnificent lawless months, I did everything you told me to.

And now look what's happened.

Though it wasn't (strictly speaking) murder, just see what you made me do.

Pants on Fire

The white-knuckle ride of our lives begins on the most ordinary of family days, ushered in by flaming knickers, incontinent pigeons and a routine bullying phone-call from the loathsome features editor at *Yes.*

'Mummy, Mummy my pants are on fire!' yowls Kasha, pounding into the bathroom and ripping back the Psycho shower curtain, wrenching me out of reverie induced by yesterday's abrupt reappearance of the most X-rated of Ex's. Clad in only a pink crop top and navy ankle socks, she is clutching herself and hopping from one foot to another as only an agitated eleven-year-old can.

Jim and I are in the shower stall, bickering with practised marital amicability over who gets to stand under the erratic blasts of hot water. After all our years together, he still looks like Clint Eastwood, though with a weaker chin. Sadly his libido is not so much Dirty Harry these days as Norman Wisdom: all playful ineptitude and egg-stained jumpers, albeit of the black Paul Smith variety.

'Now what am I going to wear to school?' our daughter screeches. 'Those are my best ones, my *Kylie* ones, and now I've got no knickers and I can't go to school without any, I can't possibly –'

'Sssh... keep it down, Kash. You'll wake Angel.' Angel Saint is our lodger and her dim Indian grotto of a room is next door to the bathroom. A slim, gorgeous Kashmiri girl with a broad Cockney accent and deadpan sense of humour, she is the ideal housemate being both solvent, and congenitally nocturnal so rarely encountered. The latter two qualities are down to her regular late and live lap-dancing shifts at Cottonfella's in Piccadilly. By September she will have saved enough to return to her B.Sc. in Applied Maths at Imperial College (she says).

'Mum-eee, my *pants.*'

Once upon a time Jim would have found this funny. Now he merely looks long suffering, rubs hands tiredly over his face and mutters something about not even being able to soap his scrotum in peace.

Vaulting out of the shower and grabbing a damp towel, I thunder downstairs into our battered conservatory kitchen, ducking the outsize spider plants hanging too low from the ceiling. The microwave is on fire and the air thick with the stench of combusting nylon (that's the last time we put wet knickers in there to be dried).

While dithering over whether to throw water on their melting remains or chuck them outside and make the Camden air even more polluted than it already is, there is a blinding flash and all the lights go out. Since this is seven twenty on a gloomy February morning, it plunges the entire house in semi-darkness.

A thunderous knocking at the front door makes our little Victorian house quiver. Two seconds later the fire alarm, finally registering smoke, starts shrilling a warning that would wake sleeping back-benchers in Westminster. Fighting the urge to go lock myself in the garden shed, I start flinging open windows and flapping at the vile-smelling smoke with a tea towel, before scuttling off to answer the front door. A newspaper is emerging slowly through the letterbox, a bill in bright red felt pen peppered with exclamation marks attached.

Cursing freely, having just stubbed a toe on Kasha's metal scooter and managed to step in The Vicar's water bowl, there is an answering roar of frustration from upstairs and shrieks of ghost-train delight from the children. Wearing a soggy *Legally Blonde* towel and an expression of enormous irritation, Jim comes thumping into the kitchen, skidding to a halt on something noxious and green.

'What have you done to the electricity?' His eye falls upon Franklyn the junior tabby, who is trying to drag a fully-grown pigeon out through the cat-flap. 'And what's that winged rat,' he starts scuffing his besmirched foot on the floor, 'doing in our kitchen?'

Its name is Roger, it had hurt a wing, and Tim had rescued it the day before from the attentions of next door's muscular, three-legged tom. Last time we saw Roger, he had been in a cardboard box on top of the dresser, nervous but comfortable. Jim and the pigeon have not yet been formally introduced. Tim, perched on the kitchen work surface eating a standard twelve-year-old's breakfast (fistfuls of Cheerios straight from the box) pipes up: 'It's not an it, it's a he and his name's –'

'Zoe, is this another of your blasted strays?'

'Oh no, look,' wails Kasha, nose pressed against the kitchen window, staring in disbelief at the blackened remains of her knickers on the grass. Tim snickers and continues shovelling cereal into his mouth like a dumper on a deadline. 'Chill out, Kash,' he smirks. 'Who's going to see anyway? Oh, yeah, maybe your *boyfriend* Richie? Dah!' he gasps, as Kasha punches him accurately in the solar plexus. 'You *little minger* –'

Rootling in the stygian depths of the broom cupboard, I try plunging down all the switches on the fuse box simultaneously. The lights come back on, then go straight back off again. Try twice more before giving up and launching into the usual frantic morning gavotte of cajoling the children into school readiness.

'Kasha, Tim, five minutes! Oh, Tim, sweetheart, we're going to be horribly late: do try and hurry.' He's still standing tousle-haired in the kitchen clad in only black boxers and grey socks, lifting another casual handful of cereal to his mouth. In slow motion, he slides a reluctant arm into the school shirt I hold out for him. Over the last few months Tim has become increasingly reluctant to get ready, looks far more cheerful in the holidays and seldom says a word about his day. All enquiries are met with evasion. Jim says I'm being over protective but I'm not so sure. Am going to corner his teacher again this week, though last time she implied that older mothers (who, me?) tend to be over-protective and Tim was just picking up on my own anxieties. Yet the increasing droop of this gentle boy's narrow shoulders is telling a different story – dammit, a pile of dirty clothes in the bathroom is playing *The Marseillaise*. So that's where my mobile is.

Ignore it. It stops, but the downstairs phone starts up almost immediately. Ignore that too. This time in the morning it could only be Jim's overly directive mother, the Camden Animal Refuge Centre with another stray or an irate magazine editor, and I don't want to talk to any of them.

A deceptively girlish little voice comes onto the old answer-phone in the hall.

'Zo-eee. Pick it up would you. I *know* you must be there. School run, and all that. Must have a wordette.'

Please no, it's Katrina Clarke-Erikson, the synthetic Features Editor of *Yes*. Tim, now absorbed doing up his shirt buttons up all wrong on the stairs, sticks a finger down his throat and makes sick noises. *Yes* is aimed at *Good Housekeeping* readers who used to like *Cosmopolitan* but found all the fellatio masterclasses got them down. Every single issue covers the new sex – nouveau celibacy *again* this month – the new black (aubergine, for February) with a little psychology, reiki and life-coaching thrown in. It sells half a million copies a month so somebody out there must be enjoying it, and I wish I could say the same. For my sins, which are many, I am their Health & Relationships Editor, which means I get to write lots about sex despite the fact I've had precious little myself these past two years.

'Sorry if it's a tad early, but you know me,' the little voice continues. 'Busy-busy. Been in since seven thirty. You can get so much done when the office is deserted.' Right, like snooping in drawers and raiding the Fashion cupboard.

Tugging a faded Vivienne Westwood T-shirt over my head (a valued vintage from her *Let It Rock* days in Kings Road) I shoot out a hand to nab Tim as he shuffles back upstairs, shoelaces undone and tucked into his shoes. If only I hadn't left it to my thirties to have babies he'd be at 6th form college by now, and maybe even doing up his own laces...

'Nice little column you sent me on clitoral adornment, by the way. Can't *wait* to read the next (oh, it's due today) on sex during periods,' continues Katrina. 'We're calling it *Love Lies Bleeding* –'

'Catchy title,' mutters Jim, who is also now in the hall, bending over our mountainous coats pile and scrabbling for his motorbike gloves.

'– but anyway, I'm afraid there's Something Else. I felt it would be best if you heard it from me *in person*, since we've worked together for so long.' Jim, now up to his elbows in assorted children's outerwear, goes still.

'I *tried,* Zoe,' her breathy voice echoes round our tiny hallway, Marilyn Monroe on Lithium. 'Heaven *knows* I stood up for you. But the Hadleigh-Medico Group is suing over that piece you did on their frightful liposuction record. Remember, you quoted that poor little property dealer's wife who ended up with one buttock so much bigger than the other?'

I lunge for the phone.

'They're major advertisers. And, well, the thing is sweet pea – you're fired.'

Next morning I wake up at six, doing sums based on the loss of fifty per cent of my salary. From the way he's breathing, I know that Jim's done the same. A large warm hand reaches for my chilly one where it's pleating the duvet cover. 'It's all right, love. You're good, remember? You're experienced. You'll find something else.' In answer, I burrow closer and put my head on his shoulder.

'We're well matched,' he continues sleepily. 'No one's paid me for weeks either, there's no work in and the company's owed money all over London. But you know as well as I do, that's working for yourself – either bugger all or far too much.' He bundles the duvet round our two bodies then starts piling the bed's pillows all around us, ramparts against the urban enemy who these days is neither the Goths nor the Viking hoards, but the ranks of three million unemployed whom we look like joining any day now. Experienced, ha! Who's going to want a sex writer who's (I don't know how it happened) in her forties? Editors increasingly prefer a perky Fern Cotton clone with a dodgy psychology degree, no frown lines and low rates who is happy to be loaned out to *Loaded* for the occasional blindingly explicit 'Ask Fern' letters page.

'There. That's better, isn't it? Like being in a ship,' whispers Jim, putting an arm around me and squinting ahead into the gloaming, a captain at his helm. I feel cosy and cared for, so why is it that the only ship's name springing to mind is the bloody *Titanic*? Again, Jim picks up my thoughts. 'It'll work out, OK? Swallow several strong filter coffees then when you're really buzzing, just get on that phone and make your pitch to a few new commissioning editors.' My heart skinks, remembering which ones they are. 'It's not so hard once you get going, and if they don't want you, well fuck 'em,' he announces with the casual confidence of one who has to do this several times a week and doesn't care. 'Then if all else fails,' he adds, disentangling himself from my arms and putting on his moth-eaten black silk kimono inside out as usual, 'I can always take pictures of your tits and flog them on the net; lie about Tim's age so he can get a paper round, and send Jed out to deliver pizzas for SohoMoe's on that pretty new Vespa of his the dozy sod can't steer.'

Jed is Jim's co director at Seventh Wave Films. He came off his fashionable red scooter yet again two weeks ago and went home to recover leaving Jim to fend off creditors, chase debts, pursue show-reels and schmooze ad agency staff with ten-second attention spans, single-handed. My husband had minded far less before we spotted his partner playing tennis on Hampstead Heath courts last weekend, apparently as spry as a squirrel.

As Jim yawns hugely, supporting himself on the door frame and rubbing sleep-puffed eyes ('We got any decent T bags left? Morning, Tim') our son stamps in, white faced and furious, clutching an armful of styling products which he throws down on the bed. A can of Ben Sherman hair mousse rolls onto the floor, where the Vicar starts to pat it to and fro. 'Bastard stuff doesn't work.'

Indeed, his hair is over-gelled and limp on one side, the spiked fringe is already drooping, and the back looks like a hedgehog's arse. 'I'm not going to school like this. They'll –' he cracks his knuckles nervously. 'They keep saying my hair's dodged up anyway. I'm not going in. I'm not, *I can't –*' Take hysterical son to the shower, remove a ton of hair product then seat him before big round mirror that reflects the bed, Kasha's Ant & Dec towel round his neck and one of Jim's old *Viz* comic books in his hand. 'Just pretend you're at the barbers, darling.'

Wave away Jim, who is now fully dressed, making faces and pointing at his watch. 'Here, let's have a go with that Fudge Wax.'

Between swigs of the tea and furtive glances at the clock, I consult The Client.

'Any better?' He closes his eyes as if in pain.

'How about this, then?'

'Mum, look at the *front*.'

'Like that?' Jim's appeared at the door again mouthing Do You Know What Time It Is, a fully dressed but sniggering Kasha in one hand and his briefcase in the other. A few minutes later, he's gone in a cloud of exhaust but we have achieved a look Tim will consent to leave the house with.

'Sweetheart, you look seriously cool –'

He sniffs, and tugs a single gelled spike further down over his forehead. 'S'all right, I s'pose. But you do take *forever*. I can do it much quicker myself.'

Recreational Filth

Sitting in a heap on the stairs opposite the front door, after a frenzy of domestic displacement activity. Housework has its uses: for the past two hours, it has enabled me to avoid ringing up commissioning editors I don't know to tell them about features ideas they'll turn down.

Our post, which seems to get later every day, splats onto the doormat and I sidle down our dark, narrow hall which the saffron paint and collection of Javanese wooden mirrors only partially manages to enliven, to see if anything nice has arrived. A spiteful draft slithers underneath the door, sneaking round my bare ankles. Scoop up three more bills, two rather red and inflamed looking. One is from BT, giving us a week to cough up before they cut us off.

Cradling the walkabout like a sick baby, I force myself to concentrate on the morning's more urgent unpleasantness and am just screwing up the courage to call back *Yes* and insist they reconsider, when it rings so suddenly that I drop it on my own foot.

Pick it up gingerly. This is about the time that we've been getting those other calls recently. The ones where nobody says anything. Well if it's Them again, they're in for a shock, because hanging on the wall by the phone socket is the football whistle Jim put there yesterday for just such an occasion. Yep, silence. Right you sad little shit, whoever you are let's bust your sneaking eardrums for you – pheeeeeeeep!! *phweeeeeep!!! Pheeeee* –

'Christ, take it easy,' drawls a man's voice whose very speech rhythms are burnt into the circuitry of what passes for my brain. 'Was that absolutely necessary?'

'Oh – it's you! Hell, I am so, so –' Shaun Lyon. My man under the bed (I wish).

'Yes it is. At least I think so, but my ears are now ringing so hard it's difficult to be sure. However, if you could just pocket your rape whistle for a moment, I merely wanted to let you know that something's come up. Something – well, let's just say something that could be right up your street.'

Heart starts trampolining enthusiastically. Ignore it. Sulking, it lodges itself in my throat. 'Has it? Look, it's, er, lovely to hear from you, really it is. But it's just that as of yesterday, I'm semi unemployed and I've got to get it sorted. So, gosh, I'm ever so sorry but –' dammit, how old am I, ten? '– this is not, um, an especially good time.'

'No pressure, you understand,' he continues as if I haven't spoken, a City head-hunter selling a career change to a wavering client. 'Just an idea you might want to think about for the next forty-eight hours. An evening out with a difference. Because, you know, when I heard about it just now, somehow I immediately thought – well, of *you* darlin'.'

'What?'

The man's voice in my ear is heavy with seduction. Slightly bully boy Essex but with intriguing soft Irish edges. There is also a faint but unmistakable quiver of piss-take. Is he kidding? Not on his own at the other end? It would be just like him to –

'It's Master and Margarita's Night on Thursday down at SkinDeep. The club's got an amazing new basement premises in Windmill Street, and they're running their first fetish slave auction alongside the usual House of Correction hour. Remembering how much you used to enjoy that kind of thing?' *No, you used to enjoy it. I used to hover at the back, latex'd to the max and looking at my watch.* 'I've provisionally booked us in. Sweetheart, don't tell me I never took you there?'

I hitch up my jaw, which is now dropping floor-wards. Booked us in? In your dreams, mate. The blatant effrontery of him, the brazen cheek, the arrogance of the man: how *dare* he *even suggest* – yet – can't help wondering who else he's gone with, and what the club's guests get up to these days. Bet he's never taken his white-knickered wife. In the interests of research, since I am supposed to be a sex and health journalist, I suppose (technically that is) it could do little harm to take a peek. Might be quite a laugh, actually. Not that we'd be staying, of course. Goodness, no. I mean, how unsuitable can you get?

'Naturally, you'll need a little outfit, but that's all taken care of. Keep a look out for a bike from *Slippery When Wet* sometime this afternoon. I think I've remembered your size. Who'd forget a body like yours?'

You, that's who. The last piece of clothing you gave me all those years ago was two sizes too big about the bust and two sizes too small around the waist. This is going a bit too fast for me. Sitting down heavily on the chipped orange gloss stairs, I cast frantically about for something grown-up to say. The mounting pressure of him biding his time on the other end of the line is making it difficult to breathe right. Tugging at the fringe of my shoulder-length mop of dark hair, which flips and kinks in all the wrong directions (after a ruinous visit to an exciting new Camden hairdressers – distressed granite flooring, giant cacti and bullet holes in the mirrors – it looks like a psychopath's been at it with a switchblade) I look about the hall for inspiration. The only items in sight are a small pair of lilac *Kate and Ashley* pyjama bottoms, a sliding pile of unopened bank statements, three pairs of rollerblades and a rusty racing bike.

Optimistic as ever, Shaun chooses to interpret the silence as speechless delight.

'You like the idea, don't you sweetheart?'

'Actually, Shaun, I've rather gone off these tribal, audience-as-part-of-the-show things. I mean, the Theatre du Complicite's done it to death don't you think? All that, er, obligatory confrontational involvement and interactive guerrilla drama stuff is really the complete opposite of the spontaneous dramatic anarchy it's trying so hard to achieve. Frankly, the whole genre's getting a bit tired, if you ask me –' now, what was the rest of that bit in *The Guardian*? '– and like I said, I was thinking more about that spot of lunch you mentioned. I mean, the club sounds fascinating, but –' *Why don't you just tell him your husband might be suspicious if he sees you trotting off wearing a rubber cat suit with groin flaps and a furtive expression. Or that the closest my demographic group now gets to dressing up in rubber is a pair of Wellingtons on a muddy walk?* Wandering into the sitting room I start mechanically pulling fluff out of a tear in the arm of the ancient green Chesterfield.

'Ah, c'mon, honey… why not give your relationship some latitude? Let it breathe. Experimentation is the modern marital therapy, darlin', and marital therapy's the new rock n' roll. Or hadn't you heard?'

Well, that makes a change from it being cooking, gardening or interior decoration. 'No. And Jim and I are perfectly all right, thank you.'

This isn't strictly true. We'd sort of reached the stage when I'd catch myself starting wistfully at him in the evenings, wondering if was ever going to turn back into the man I used to know. And him? He'd be wondering why I was staring at him, hoping it wasn't because he'd forgotten 'Monthly Sex with Wife Night'. Again.

Shaun merely laughs in the way he way he used to when we'd had a fight and were just about to make it up in bed. 'That's not what I heard. But hey, why not give us a try? If anyone deserves a second chance, it's you and me. Regard this as, ah, a little test drive if you like, but it could be just what you need to ventilate your marriage –' *what, some Soho designer slave market with drinks at the interval is marital therapy?* '– and I promise you, no strings.' Right, for him. I remember he'd never shown any hesitation in tying other people up in knots. *I don't want a test drive. I want a new job, and I want Jim to be the way he used to be. Oh hell and damnation, that's not the whole story either –*

'Sweetheart, don't you think that you deserve a little adult amusement, or shall we say, a little recreational filth, after so many years of young children and hard work?'

Yes. Yes! Christ, yes!! I mean no, absolutely not. Parents don't do filth. Parents don't even have *sex*. The nerve of the man, the bloody cheek, the swollen-headed presumption of him. And if he thinks I'm going to be fobbed off with some member's-only flesh-fest in lieu of a decent meal, he's got another think coming.

'Yet you do know that this isn't just fun, don't you?' His voice is dropping a further irresistible octave, which up until now you'd have thought would be an acoustic impossibility. 'We could be at the beginning of something special here. All over again. I'm offering you a unique mixture of love and deviance –' *God, did he just say* '– which only we could make work, because you and me are something special. We always have been. The things we got up to. I've never forgotten a single detail of the games we played, or the way we loved.'

Me neither. But I'm married now, and just because I've got a good memory, it doesn't mean we'll –

'Listen to me, Zoe, just listen. For the next forty-eight hours, I'll be here. Right here, waiting for your call. Think about it. We could be us again, *us*. Pushing back the boundaries, playing just the way we used to. What do you say, sweetheart?'

I can think of quite a bit but cannot seem to squeeze a word out. May have been something to do with the cardiac arrest taking place in my larynx, whence my heart had leapt at the sound of his voice. Breath-holding, I try to push the upholstery fluff back in. Won't fit.

'My private mobile's 07523 900822. Write that down. Go *on*, I said write it down. When you've thought about it, you call me –' private mobile, huh? He's done this before '– by

17

tomorrow afternoon, at the latest. The club won't hold our provisional for long.' No pressure, hmm? Kick a smaller defenceless heap of dirty clothes piled up on the floor by the coffee table.

'I don't think so.'

'Darlin', all I'm saying is, don't say yes, but don't say no yet either. You think about it for a little while, OK?'

What's to think about? Just do it.

'Jesus, what's wrong with you? No, OK? No. Thanks for thinking of me and all that, but –'

He cuts right across me. 'Feisty as ever. God, I've missed you sweetheart. So much. All right, I admit I've had dozens of other women since we were together, but you – I tell you, you were always one of the very best. You left all the others standing.'

I stiffen. *What others*?

'Never think it to look at you, butter wouldn't melt... five foot four, body like a statue... I remember it all.'

A bit of soft soap is one thing, a shower of bullshit is quite another. 'Do you, now. Well it's taken you long enough to –'

'Are your eyes still navy blue? Do they still go darker when you really want it? I can't wait to see you again, Zoe. God, why didn't I marry you? Why? What a bloody idiot I was back then. Too young, selfish and scared to go for it. I knew I was with the right woman, I just couldn't allow myself to *trust*. We always think there's something better out there when we're twenty-six, don't we?'

'Well, you certainly did.' My feet are now so cold from a combination of February, no socks and shock that they've gone mauve and lost all feeling below the ankles.

'Men always think they're going to get that lucky twice, don't they? How wrong I was. How bloody stupid. I've regretted it ever since.'

News to me. This, however, was more like it.

'You'd have made me happy, wouldn't you? You were definitely up there in my top five dirty, dirty women...'

'So who were the other four?' I blurt before I can stop myself. 'Was I, er, you know, one of the, ah –' *Say I was first.* Or at a pinch second. Please don't let me be third, and certainly not fourth or fifth –

'Sorry? Hey, look what you've done to me – just talking to you's given me a hard on,' announces Shaun, swiftly changing the subject, another special skill of his. 'Damn, got to go – urgent call incoming on another line... Yeah, yeah, put them through Nadine... no, not *now* Colin, can't you see I'm busy? Well, put the meeting back to two this afternoon. Martin, you pillock – I said, I *told* you, that I wanted to see a five-year projection, not a three-year one. These figures are as useless as tits on a bull... sorry, sorry sweetheart, signing out. There are five people waiting outside my office for a meeting. Call me, OK?'

And he is gone. Vanished off my radar screen.

Just like he did the morning after our riotous, house-trashing, moving-in together party. Even the police, summoned by the phenomenal noise, unplugged their walkie-talkies and stayed for the second half. Shaun staggered out for a well-earned pint next day after the clearing up and developed the very coldest of cold feet.

Bastard never came back.

A month later he sent a vast, guilt-and-rent check from Oman with a note saying stay on in the flat, and please to give him time. That was the last I heard of him for six years.

The phone shrills again. 'Mrs Harrington? Mr Lyon's *personal* assistant here,' says an Orpington librarian voice. 'He's asked me to let you know that after *due* consideration, he feels that the pilot project might benefit from an *informal* face-to-face brainstorming session, as a pre-merger prep. Now if this interfaces conveniently with your own schedule, Mr Lyon proposes Wednesday, at twelve *noon*. The address of the, ahem, pre-merger is forty-three, Old Compton Street.'

Heart gives a nervous thump. 'Right. Did he say anything else?' So already, the games are starting. This is the pre-emptive strike, the first move, the one that gives a player an immediate advantage. Well, we'll see about that. I'm not twenty-three and besotted any more.

'Ay'm sorry, but that's all he told me. Does that make any sense to you?'

'After a fashion. Thank you. Tell him I shall let him know in due course.'

She sniffs and rings off, clearly reckoning the boss has booked a cut-price tart for the afternoon.

A pre-merger huh? At least he's given up on his S&M evening, but all the same, Shaun's still not lost his habit of presuming a great deal. And what's number forty-three, anyway? A restaurant? An apartment rented by the hour? A comic emporium? It could be anything, for in Soho, addresses tell you little. But this is one of reasons women fell so hard for Shaun: you never quite knew what you were going to get from him, but you could bet it wasn't what you'd get from most men.

He's left me with a mixture of startled pride (hoo-*eee!!* Am fabulous sex goddess, undimmed by the years) and the sinking feeling that I am about to take an A level I'd not revised for. Oh, for God's sake, get a grip. This is lunch, right? A meal, and only a meal. If he really wants, I'll collect him from Old Compton Street. And if he must, he may regard a harmless if costly lunch as a pre-merger meeting. The fact that this is purely his own interpretation shall be made clear to him from the start.

In fact, just as a precaution I'll do a bit of pre-emptive striking myself. Ring back and change forty-three Old Compton Street at midday for one o' clock at, at – yes, San Marbella in Park Lane, which will cost him an arm and a leg. That'd teach him what was what. That'll show him that I am no easy blast from the past but a respectable woman with a career (sort of) a family (definitely) a husband (hum) and not to be taken for granted.

No indeed.

On my way up to the bedroom in pursuit of a few warm clothes, I catch sight of my face in the mirror shaped like a lightning strike which runs for eight feet along the bright blue stairwell wall. Can think of no good reason why the eyes should be those of a small nocturnal rodent frozen in the headlights of an oncoming Panzer tank.

The Man Himself

Shaun Michael Lyon. Blast from the past, unfinished business, the one that got away (and yes, he certainly *was* 'this big').

Half Irish, this stellar son of a Dagenham factory union boss and a Galway primary school teacher was only middling height but with heavily muscled shoulders, a promising trouser bulge, tight butt and a leonine head. Proud owner of a luscious dick – thick and curved like Pan's – a corrupting smile and knowing, evergreen eyes which stared straight into women's psyches and showed they liked (really liked) what they saw. A tongue so flexible it made cunnilingus an out-of-body experience, powers of persuasion sufficient to sell solar panels to the Finns in February, and a sexual repertoire that made *The Perfumed Garden* look like the parish allotment, at parties it used to be a case of walk in, watch the women surround him, then push off to find someone (anyone) to flirt with leaving Shaun radiating equal measures of charm and raw testosterone. It was either that, or hang about watching the chickpea dip go crusty.

In fact, the first time I ever clapped eyes on him was at a party in 1980 where he'd had a woman on each arm and another bringing up the rear. Lounging against the doorframe to the kitchen at a party given by three *City Limits* journalists living in a sprawling Clapham flat, Shaun had been the one man drinking straight from a bottle of decent red while everyone else was given poisonous punch afloat with wizened orange slices. Wandering over to see if the stuff tasted as bad as it looked, I felt his slow gaze slide over me then flicker away as a stacked brunette in white spandex leggings grabbed his bottle and wrapped her plump, squishy lips around it suggestively. As I squeezed back past them through the door, his right hand was slowly caressing her bottom while he pressed his lean left leg against an impassive Japanese girl with big hair and a tiny red plaid kilt. Tosser, I'd thought, trying to ignore both the look he was giving me and blast of heat coming off his body.

Having spent the rest of the evening dodging packs of drunken rugby players who bawled 'Get yer flaps out!' whenever they saw an unaccompanied female, listening to the *CL* film reviewer obsessed by Eastern Bloc cartoons, then dancing with some ex-Oxbridgers who said 'Yah' a lot, had the wrong sort of trousers and no sense of rhythm, I was thirsty and ready to go home alone.

Rifling the wrecked drinks table for a cup to fill under the tap, I felt a hand steal around my ankle. Kicking didn't dislodge it. Hissing expletives and bending down to wrench it off finger by finger, I found myself nose to nose with a tousled Shaun, reclining under the drinks table and hidden by its floor-length plastic tablecloth. He was swigging from yet another bottle of red and looked extremely comfortable. 'Is a big brunette still out there?' he demanded, offering me the small but lethal-smelling joint he was also smoking.

I took a deep pull and tasted the sickly tang of liquorice – flavoured rolling papers were big back then. 'Come out and see.' *Serves you right for groping two women at the same time.*

'Not bloody likely. The woman started tweaking my nipples while I was talking to my publisher out there. I mean, there are limits. Christ,' he added rubbing his wrist, 'are your nails always that sharp?'

'Perhaps she thought you liked it,' I suggested, taking another couple of deep tokes. Blimey, this stuff was strong. Better give it back. 'Just tell her you're not that sort of boy.'

'Don't want to upset her. She's his step-daughter.' He gave me an assessing look, then an indolent smile spread across his face: a tom cat clocking the clotted cream. I caught myself feeling a bit dizzy and wondering what it would feel like to trace that smile with my fingers. 'Tell you what. Look in that cupboard above the cooker.'

'You look in the cupboard.' I filled up a wilting polystyrene cup with metallic tap water, and downed it in one. Pleasingly, it seemed quite the wettest and most delicious stuff I'd ever tasted. 'I'm off home.'

'Only – I hid some champagne in there behind the tins when I arrived. Initially as a birthday present for our host, but since he's been well away for hours, I thought that the stuff should be saved instead,' he looked me straight in the eye this time, with no hint of a smile, 'for someone worth drinking it with.'

God, what had he put in that joint? I'd only had three big puffs yet already the floor was feeling a bit springy. And what was that aftershave he was wearing? Mmmm, cinnamon, sweat, androgens and a touch of bully boy Paco Rabanne... 'Well, don't look at me, sunshine. I don't go for men with wandering hands and the attention spans of gnats,' I snapped, cross that I found him so attractive, and was just heading for the door when shouts of: 'Fuck me, look at the flaps on that' announced the imminent arrival of a residual bunch of rugger buggers in search of continued refreshment.

'Oh God,' grinned Shaun, raising the tablecloth higher. 'In here, quick.' Without thinking, I scooted underneath, crouching next to his supine length as he hurriedly stubbed out the joint. Two trestle tables jammed together had made a space three and a half feet by seven, but it was still a squash. We kept conspiratorial silence as six pairs of big feet blundered in, felt the table lurch as someone steadied themselves; stifled laughter as, between belches, the boys described their evening as if they were shouting to each other across a crowded bar. 'That tart in black really rates me,' bawled one. 'Up for it? I tell you, I am *in* –' 'Yew wanker. She left after half an hour with some arrogant Trinity arsehole…' 'Fuck me, must have drunk ten pints of this piss'… 'crap party'… 'frigid bitch'…

There was a loud fart, then a farting competition, and more sloshing of punch into proffered cups. A terrible stench drifted under the table. Shaun buried his nose in my shoulder, then gallantly held my hooter for me.

My back started hurting so I hunkered closer to the floor, trying not to melt into his body as we squashed up against each other. Getting bored, he began to stroke the back of my neck absent-mindedly, the lightest of feather touches. I pushed his hand away, but the space was so enclosed, like a tiny tent, that it was getting increasingly difficult to screen out his pheromones. Strong enough to lubricate maiden aunts in Aberdeen, they were starting to give me ideas I'd never have entertained ten minutes ago. We listened as the lads moved onto the pleasures of the Back Door: 'Was up Fiona's chocolate speedway this time last night. Called me a closet poofter. *Me*. I ask you –'

Shaun grinned, and resumed his stroking in the gap between my purple Lycra top and black satin drainies, then began gently sliding his finger along the inside of their waistband. I sucked my stomach automatically, then reluctantly removed his hand. It was back in seconds, but somewhat lower. The sensation was such that this time, I couldn't move, especially when he began to apply his mouth to my neck.

Helplessly, I closed my eyes and arched my head back to give him better access, heat racing through my groin, nipples like bullets. As he bent his head and bit one gently, I gasped and he clapped his hand roughly over my mouth. I licked his salty palm and traced the big blue veins in his wrist up his arm to where they disappeared into dark, delicious twists of silken underarm hair, pushing against his other hand as it stoked the place where my legs joined, then curled over to lie facing him, one ear out the six raucous men only inches away. Slowly, Shaun ran the tip of his tongue along my closed eyelids and fiddled casually with the top button of the drainies. Then the next, and the next, flipping them open as he went, lazily circling the pads of his fingers around and around then to and fro along the top of my pubic bone, producing bolts of sexual electricity that shot straight to somewhere very personal indeed (He later told me he's had a Chinese girlfriend trained in sexual acupuncture who had taught him where, and how). Shaking now and wanting him more than I had ever wanted anyone, I still could *not* believe what we were doing. Stoned I may have been, but I'd always been the nervous, six-dates-before-it's-knicker-time sort – and here I was under the table with the hands of a man I didn't know ferreting in my trousers? It wasn't even private, it wasn't even safe, and with Them out there it was a really, really bad idea but God Almighty, whoever he was, I had never in my life met anyone who made me feel like this. And by now, nothing on earth would have persuaded me to stop for the sheer blazing lust we'd lit in each other was fast becoming too much to stand... I had to have him inside me right now, this minute, sod the men laughing and drinking out there, they can't see, they can't hear us, will never know... looking straight into my eyes, Shaun slid open his zip, and as I moved my hand down, it closed around the biggest, warmest and most lively penis it had ever been my good fortune to come across. Rock hard, it stirred and twitched plumply in my hand, developing a strong personality of its own as Shaun began working his jeans down over his hips, whispering divine obscenities into my hair, drowning out the drunken laughter, banter and chauvinist utterances taking place only a few of feet above our heads.

The scent and the heat of him, the touch of his body, even his open zip now cutting into the soft flesh my upper thigh felt like the best sex I'd ever had, long before he slid inside. When he finally did so I had to open up further than I'd ever had to before to allow his width the room it demanded and knew as he began to move, gently at first, rocking so lightly, that this one was the man I'd never thought I'd find but would give everything I had or ever would have, to keep. As he kissed me on the mouth for the first time – up until now, I'd not even noticed that he'd so far omitted this most primary of permission-to-play preliminaries – the warm, slippery cavern of his mouth become the entire world, the taste of it delicious with the tang of red wine and aromatic smoke, his lips waking a landscape of nerve endings I never knew I had, closing over me, making me feel both safer than I'd ever done in my life and like I wanted to fuck his brains for the next three days... When he pulled me round on top of him and moaned very softly in orgasm despite himself, I didn't bloody care, not if all the rugby players in all the world heard us. Let them, let them, for this is what sex was supposed to feel like yet never had until now, the real *gotta-have-it, do-it-now* thing. Past caring, we gave ourselves up to time turning itself inside out and a deluge of raw sensation breaking over our heads which drowned out everyone, and everything, but each other.

As we rested afterwards, breathing the air from each other's mouths, his hands twined in my hair and mine still gripping his shoulders, heart-rates hammering off the scale, bodies slick with sweat where bare skin touched, I guess we imaged we could stay blissfully in our table-sized bubble till the rugger boys went away. Unfortunately Shaun was getting cramp in his leg, and moved it convulsively, allowing part of his booted foot to emerge briefly from under the tablecloth. He whipped it straight back, but it was too late.

Conversation outside stopped. We both froze. A second later, a broad face with a broken nose thrust itself under the tablecloth and split into a chipped-toothed grin. 'Well, well, well. Look what we've got here lads. A couple actually *at it*, by Christ.'

'Bet she fucks like a rabbit. She fuck like a rabbit, mate?'

'Look at her – in a right state. Right little slapper.'

'Might clean up OK,' observed one with Brillo pad brown hair, hunkering down behind the first two and grinning lewdly. 'Mind you,' he added slowly, 'it's the end of an evening. Doesn't do to be too fussy –' I closed my eyes and buried my face in Shaun's neck, wishing I could dematerialize.

'Who gives a shit about cleaning her up? Me, I never say no to cunt,' said another with dreadful open pores, removing a wad of gum from his mouth, 'not even to sloppy seconds...'

'You know, you could be right, Chrissie-boy. Never look a gift horse in the snatch. What's a couple of blokes more or less amongst friends,' he added to me, 'now your boyfriend's keen kind enough to warm you up for us?' Shaun still hadn't said anything and nor had he moved a muscle, but his body was taught as wire. Oh Christ, I thought, it's going to happen. They're going to rape me one by one, beat him to a pulp and no one'll know, they can't hear, the music's too loud – they're all dancing or snogging anyway, I'll get some horrible disease from them, they'll hurt me...

Chipped Teeth suddenly reached in and grabbed my arm. 'Yes, I think we'll be having you out of there, love. Mike,' he added sharply over his shoulder, 'kick the door shut, and keep it shut. We don't want company.' He sniffed the air voluptuously. 'Smell that tuna, lads. Ripe or what? Right, then – who's first?'

Someone tried to come into the kitchen, pushing ineffectually against the door wedged closed by seventeen stone of solid muscle. 'Sod off!' yelled the players in unison. The pushing stopped 'And as for you, Romeo,' Chipped Teeth prodded Shaun in the buttocks while still trying to wrench me from under him, nearly dislocating my shoulder: 'we'll not take long, and you'd better stay there if you know what's –'

But he got no further, for Shaun had erupted away from me, ducking underneath the man's arm, rolling over like he'd just hit the ground running and springing to his feet. He didn't even bother doing up his flies but wheeled round, whipped his champagne bottle from its hiding place scattering tins in all directions while the other men, reflexes slowed by alcohol and taken by surprise, watched stupidly as he felled the nearest one with a single sickening thud of solid glass hitting living bone. Then without breaking stride, he smashed the bottle against the wall and stood in front of the table, shielding me and facing the five who were left, weaving his jagged glass club through the air in a figure of eight and rocking from side to side on the balls of his feet, incandescent with rage.

'OK, you bastard heaps of shit – listen to me, and listen carefully. One, this is my girlfriend, right, and I will not allow you to speak to her like that. Two, you scumbags are clearly a bunch of sad, voyeuristic wankers who've never had a decent fuck in their lives. And three –' he slashed at the nearest man who'd been unwise enough to try and edge closer, catching him across the ear which sprayed blood: 'if you don't clear this room immediately, I swear I'll carve up the bloody lot of you. One by fucking one.'

There was a dead silence for a few long seconds, broken only by the gentle drip of liquid onto lino and some heavy breathing, until Chipped Tooth lunged unsteadily for the bottle and got a wild cut across the chest for his pains. 'I mean it,' roared Shaun. 'Back off and fuck off, boys – or so help me, I'll shred your fucking faces for you.'

But it was no good. Shaun had hurt two of them and the rest, drunk and mean, were out for his guts. Looking murderous, the remaining men began to inch forwards in chilling unison, as if closing in on a rugger ball. It was looking very nasty for both of us when there was a hefty crash, then another – someone was shoulder-butting the kitchen door from the other side.

'This is your host, right?' bellowed a voice. 'Open up in there. Open up right now, or I'm calling the police. *Do you hear me?* Let us in or we'll smash our way in.' The two men who'd been holding the juddering door shut looked doubtfully at each other, but stood aside as one of the City Limits journalists, backed by two large friends, fell over the threshold. They too were drunk, but not that drunk. 'Fucking hell, wasss' going on here?' bawled the host, staying well back from Shaun but taking in the sight of seven angry men, blood all over on the floor and me under the table.

More curious guests were crowding in behind him as I scrabbled to do up my trousers, but Shaun merely hitched up his jeans and flipped his T-shirt over the exposed fly. 'Oh hi, Matt. These – animals –' he gestured with his bottle, 'were harassing my girlfriend. Get your bag, sweetheart,' he added, holding out his hand as if escorting me to Queen Charlotte's Ball. 'We're leaving.'

Early next morning I woke up in his bed, wracked by abdominal cramps, an ominous slippery feeling between my legs which had nothing to do with Shaun. Why's it always arrive early when you least want it? Sliding quietly put of bed and trying to keep my legs together, I nabbed my knickers off the clock radio and hobbled to the bathroom. This wasn't hard to find as the flat was minuscule and it was the only room apart from the bedroom that wasn't a tiny kitchen with dishes festering in the sink, grease spattered over the cooker and skid marks on the fake pine lino floor. The bathroom was cupboard-sized, with a mouldy white shower curtain, and scratchy budget bog paper which was difficult to fashion into a pad. Was just wondering how to tactfully evade the gorgeous man in bed – whose name I still didn't know – whilst encouraging him to ask for my phone number (should I just make a quick exit pleading lunch with parents/work deadline/a pre-arranged day in the country?) when he woke as I was inching back under the covers. Lazily pulling me close, he trailed a 'hi there' hand pube-wards. My nether regions rustled loudly. Bugger, I'd thought, skewered with embarrassment. That's torn it.

But hesitating for only the briefest of beats, he merely said, 'Thank God it's Sunday. Fancy a spot of breakfast?' I nodded eagerly. Perhaps there was a way out after all.

'There's a corner shop that sells bread, milk, eggs and bacon – you want some? But I don't think,' he added, kissing me on the nose, 'we're going to need the Sunday papers. I'll be back in ten minutes. Don't go.' Curled up in bed (a vast mattress on the floor amongst piles of discarded clothes, books and crockery) I listened to his feet going downstairs, heard the door slam, then sank back hugging a couple of musty pillows as Steven Harley's old *Come Up and See Me, Make Me Smile* started filtering faintly through the wall. Then the panic kicked in. Had he heard the noisy knickers? Want sex when he got back? Might an imaginatively-performed blow job be sufficient? Who was this man, anyway? Oh, bloody hell...

When he returned I was fully dressed and had pointedly made the bed. Had also looked round the flat – tiny, ferociously untidy except for a regimented writing desk bearing a battleship of an electric Golf-ball typewriter plus a set of bulging plastic in-trays full of press cuttings, legible shorthand notes and lists of media people I'd never heard of. The place smelt of stale dope, dust, his aftershave, cold baked beans and recent sex. He had a moulting black bearskin across one wall, a serious vinyl collection and a montage of black and white street-life photos stretching the brief length of the hall, ending in a framed copy of Rolling Stone's 1971 cover of *Fear & Loathing in Las Vegas*. A cursory look at his bookshelves had revealed *The Dice Man*, the *Illuminatus* trilogy, a book of extremely decadent Aubrey Beardsley drawings, *Ulysses* (which fell open at Norah's stream-of-consciousness masturbation bit), a stack of *Fat Freddy's Cat* comics, and a signed copy of *Hollywood*

Babylon. The view outside was of scrawny plane trees and cracked concrete. I had no idea where we were.

As Shaun bustled around his revolting kitchen, I washed up some plates for us using Head & Shoulders for Men. He then flung a clean green towel over the kitchen table, produced three purple plumes of buddleia ('they were growing out the front steps') putting them in beer glass in the middle, set a mug of tea with a big plate of bacon, eggs and mushrooms before me, and dropped a white paper bag on my lap. Inside were a pack of Tampax Super, Paracetamol, a slab of Bourneville chocolate, and a child's plastic tiara which he put gently on my head. 'The headgear's the crown I want to give you for being brave last night, and also for trusting me enough to come back here. The chocolate's for hormonal withdrawal, and the other bits and pieces are as a courtesy to my overnight guest.'

I fell in love on the spot. 'Brave? You're joking, I was petrified. But you were *phenomenal*. Both, er, under the table, and the way you stood up to those thugs. I've never seen anything like it. If anyone deserves a crown, it's – it's you.' He leaned over and gently blew my fringe out of my eyes. 'Rhinestones don't go with my complexion. Eat up, your eggs are getting cold.'

Later we shared a shower that lasted till the hot water failed and the pipes started clanking, then burrowed back to bed, me still wearing the tiara, free-falling into sleep wrapped round each other with the ripe-smelling black duvet pulled over our heads. 'Oh, by the way,' yawned Shaun, as his eyes started closing, 'what did you say your name was?'

Within a month I'd moved in, leaving my best friend Bel with eight weeks worth of rent and sole possession of our little flat by Kentish Town Tube over the Pearl of India, famous all over North London for curry in a bucket (two flavours only, one ninety-nine, all you could eat.)

She was very dubious until meeting Shaun for the first time in the pub, with me fluttering about hoping my Bestie would approve of my love, and praying he wouldn't go into flirt mode thus showing himself to be Shallow and Untrustworthy. He didn't. In between showing a remarkable grasp of modern Aboriginal art (hastily acquired, I later found, that afternoon from *Time Out*'s write-up of the new exhibition at SOAS) and insisting that Germaine Greer could never have shaken world sexism by its ears without the fearlessness induced by her fantastic Australian heritage, he brought Bel a pint of lager, browbeating the barman to get some really chilled stuff up from the cellar ('The lady's from Oz').

'A spunk rat *and* a gentleman,' she'd breathed, thoughtfully twiddling a long strand of her curly blonde hair, and eyeing his arse as he lounged by the cigarette machine extracting a packet of JPS. 'Yet back home they say you can't get cold beer or cunnilingus in London...' With a grin, she'd downed her freezing lager in one. 'Jeez girl, if you don't shack up with him, I bloody will.'

Brain fogged by love, I thought this man was practically a God (a sex god, but of the thinking, mentoring variety). He thought I was The One. When we were together we needed no one else and when we went out, we looked at no one else. If he so much as left my side to buy us a drink, I'd see women sidling up to him at the bar and buzzing around him like wasps on an apple Danish. But though he'd smile and flirt reflexively, for the first time in his life he wasn't that interested. Even the occasional handpicked playmates of both sexes he'd invite to join us for special games he would edge out afterwards in no uncertain manner, leaving us closer than ever.

When we weren't in bed, Shaun, concerned that I was bit of a pizza and mainstream movies girl, would take my hand and lead me off to poetry readings in sticky-carpeted Irish pubs, experimental plays by unknown writers in fringe theatres seating twenty, all-nighters at The Roundhouse, Truffaut double bills at the Scala, and fragrant 5 a.m. flower-markets followed by spicy Bengali breakfasts in the East End's Columbia Road. He also treated my mother and I to tea at Brown's Hotel when she ascended up to London (*Such a charming young man, and what beautiful manners*) never suspecting that he was feeling me up under the tablecloth.

Nor did she suspect the charming young man with beautiful manners habitually took her daughter to clubs whose strict membership policies and dress codes provided a home from home for those with specialised tastes. I built up quite a collection of leather and latex, happy to see Shaun enjoy himself even when the novelty had worn off for me. It did so rather quickly as I found I didn't much didn't care for people of either sex asking (albeit very nicely) if they might lick the black shiny thigh-highs Shaun had bought me, and whether, if they borrowed him, I might like to watch.

In return, Shaun came gamely along to the gigs my editor sent me off to cover four nights a week – *Peroxide Romance, The Flaming Groovies, the Burning Icons, Eddie & the Hot Rods, Big Geezer and the Dingo's Bollox* – he endured them all, then patiently made coffee and toned down the adrenalin-fuelled reviews I hammered out on his old typewriter immediately afterwards on a frenzied, post-gig high. 'A good review is punchy, originally observed, enthusiastic if you liked something but never hysterical. No, of course I'm not saying you're hysterical, but look at that string of adjectives. And para two needs work –'

Even Shaun's flat seemed romantically atmospheric, despite the fact it consisted of a bed-sit (studio flats came later and cost more) bog/bath and kitchenette on the second floor of a decaying five-storey block in the wrong part of Islington, thrown together in 1951 by an urgent new building company preaching urban regeneration, Frank Lloyd Wright and community planning. Once they'd secured the contract and landed a generous post-war government grant, they built fast and cheap where bombing had flattened entire neighbourhoods then disappeared when the places started falling apart ten years later. Chilly gusts blew in round the window casements, aluminium, unfriendly, and threatening to fall out. Children trekked miles to play elsewhere as pigeons shat and bred copiously in the tatty trees outside, balancing painfully on rotting feet.

We should at least have tackled the creeping black mould in the bathroom and put down some new carpet, but instead opted to stay out six nights a week. Hey, who cared? Not us. It felt like a penthouse we were so absorbed in each other, and anyway, Shaun always maintained that a flat was merely somewhere to keep one's clothes, and have lots of sex.

On his salary you'd have thought he could have had something better, for apart from fulfilling the then exacting post of my boyfriend, he was running an upstart new marketing magazine off Oxford Street, the youngest editor in the company's history. Good address, crap mag. Working for *Vinyl Graffiti* (a sulphate-fuelled underground rag about the London music scene) and a sexual health newsletter for students (VD clinics and contraceptive choice, punctuated by practical tips on how to deal with crabs) my own salary was a pittance which all went on clothes, taxi fares and presents for Shaun.

I never asked him why he had such a disgusting flat, because it didn't matter. He loved me, didn't he? The rest was just real estate. And anyway – look what happened when we did finally move somewhere 'nicer': a two bedroom maisonette in cherry tree-lined Cambridge Gardens, off Ladbroke Grove.

Initially full of enthusiasm for our improved living conditions, Shaun rapidly grew restive. Holiday brochures for the Far East began to appear, as did back issues National Geographic. He'd spend especially long looking at them after we came back from nesting trips bearing the rattan sideboard from John Lewis, the rug from Portobello Road, the orange sofa from Habitat. He began taking longer to read the Sunday papers' travel sections than their business pages. After spending a whole morning choosing cutlery from The Home Shop (brushed aluminium, bulbous handles, very now) we met one of his ex-girlfriends serving on the till. Blonde, with an open smile and generous bosom, she was really sweet to both of us – especially me – before covertly writing her phone number on Shaun's bill.

'But I thought she liked me!' I'd wailed as we drove home.

'She did. But you don't have a penis,' he explained, offering me the offending bit of paper with an odd sort of smile.

'Rather flattering really, wasn't it darling?' I'd laughed, reassured now we were back in our new home which revealed evidence of Shaun's devotion in every room (the set of shelves he'd put up for my rock biographies, the kitchen he'd painted in the colours of my choice). I handed him a beer where he sat on our tasteful new sofa with the fashionable Nepalese cushions, deep in a *Sunday Times* travel supplement about the Sahara. 'But I suppose you'll have to give up all that sort of thing now –'

'Yes,' he'd replied softly. 'I suppose I will.'

To affirm our newly legitimised coupledom and take his mind off foreign parts (of all types) I suggested a major housewarming party. He agreed cheerfully, throwing himself into hiring a DJ, buying a hundred bottles of cheap champagne, twenty of Tequila, me a new leopard skin dress from Swanky Modes, and scattering invitations right and left as we zigzagged through our favourite Soho pubs after work. The party was pronounced a complete success, ruining as it did most of the new furniture, all the carpets and generating complaints from those living two streets away.

Next morning, hung over to hell with a Hoover in one hand and scrubbing brush in the other, I looked round to find

Shaun had evaporated in the hot glare of encroaching respectability.

I later heard that he had also, during those twelve weeks of cohabiting in W11, managed to sleep with two other women and drunkenly proposition Bel, just to reassure himself he wasn't really settling down. Her response had been a study in sisterly solidarity: she'd smacked him in the nuts.

Mutual friends were only too happy to tell me of these indiscretions to try and cheer me up after he'd gone. They swore they hadn't before because they'd thought them, as his snide, middle-aged deputy editor put it, 'the final, convulsive struggles of a roped steer before it accepts its capture.'

When Shaun's work colleagues, with whom we often had a post-work drink before going home, heard he'd disappeared to the Middle East leaving me flat and breaking his contract, they thought he'd lost the plot. And in their hearts, those who'd been sore about his rapid rise and put out by 'just do it' approach, were thrilled. Like all good media workers, they lived for gossip and thrived on professional character assassination so spent many happy hours in the Dog & Duck on Frith Street imagining he had ended up a sad, hard drinking has-been, reduced to eking out a living running a lame tat-rag for disgruntled ex-pats. Better still, a roadside kebab stall.

And me? I was pathetic. I hung out with his ex-staff obsessively, hoping the fading scent of him clinging to their auras might help soothe the disabling withdrawal symptoms which, contrary to what everyone assured me, got worse as the weeks limped by. Every morning I'd wake feeling the emptiness of the known universe in the pit of my stomach. I slept with any man who asked me and several more who didn't, then took up smoking again and was soon racking up twenty a day.

I could never face going home without three double gin and tonics, preferably more. I fantasized all day that he'd be waiting for me back at our flat, or slumped repentantly in a hired car outside. I heard his voice across crowded pubs, saw his profile in tube carriages, recognised his back on the Up escalator as I went down; smelt his Paco Rabanne at parties. Every time I opened our front door I felt a flare of optimism that he might be waiting. Every time I answered the phone, I prayed it was going to be him.

It never was.

Gradually, crumbs of news filtered back. Shaun had indeed started working on an expat tat rag, the first job he could get after his abrupt arrival in Oman with only a toothbrush and the clothes he stood up in. But he didn't stop there.

First he'd tripled said rag's advertising revenue by introducing a large business section making it required reading for anyone wanting to invest or work in the country. On the proceeds, he persuaded his bosses to launch a sub-Tatler woman's title for the moneyed European and Arabic wives called *Boudoir,* which did a bomb and still does. Then came a glossy sports title, *Burn!* Again the advertising was monumental as there was little competition.

When friends who went to stay with him came home (since he was compulsively sociable, there were many) they reported his affairs in lively detail. Flayed by the barbed wire whip of jealousy, I heard all about the up-for-it American diplomat's daughter, the twin Emirates air hostesses, the fun-loving archaeologist, the Arabian oil sheik's wayward Westernised niece and the costly Omani call girl who let him have it for free. Up went my alcohol consumption and down came my knickers even faster than before. Because despite irrefutable evidence to the contrary, I still couldn't believe he'd do this to me.

Love isn't so much a bit blind as totally retinally detached, but others had better eyesight and used it. Shaun's ex-staff stopped buying me drinks and began to shake their heads when they saw me coming. Bel started calling me daily at work, intoning: 'Repeat after me: he's got a little dick and he's not coming back'; others kept producing Suitable Men, like pigeons from a conjurer's pockets. My mother booked me into an emotional empowerment workshop called *Women Who Love Men Who Leave (*promptly re-christened *Bastards Leave Suckers Who Love too Much* by the participants). None of it helped in the slightest.

It was also the time that London was Burning, with punk drowning the hairy stadium rockers in a deluge of scornful spitballs. So in an effort to distract me with popular culture, my other best friend Lucia showered me with backstage passes for The Clash, Richard Hell and the Voidoids and Stiff Little Fingers, arranging for my name to be on the guest-lists of every music venue in London from the Electric Ballroom to The 100 Club. The managers obliged for she was then kick-starting her own career as an edgy fashion editor by styling a succession of scowling punk bands for their mandatory one-off singles covers. I'd trail along as instructed, lacking the joie de vivre for even a teensy bit of a pogo down the front, and glue myself miserably to a barstool while the band's feedback made everyone's ears bleed. Then stumble off three-quarters gone with some unsuitable man or other, to have yet another go at obliterating the Shaun-shaped hole in my heart, leaving Lucia to escort herself to the backstage parties which, she assured me, were wonderfully diverting and simply heaving with platinum-blonde pretty boys in black string vests offering to blow free coke up one's nose.

It was very thoughtful of her, I'd reflected, after she'd chewed me out for disappearing yet again - but you had to be in the mood for that sort of thing. She herself was always in the mood, for Lucia Chalmers-Hulme was punk's posh tottie. She'd dropped acid with The Stranglers, her panties for the boys in Blondie and out of some of Britain's finest educational establishments including Wycombe Abbey and St Martin's College of Art. Dark-haired, skinny and sallow with a liking for rubber trench coats and torn lace tights worn with the family diamonds, Lucia could spot a trend blindfold at five hundred paces and was the first to feature Isabella Blow's hats, Body Map's stretchy skirts, John Galliano's frockcoats and Vivienne Westwood's bondage trousers on the experimental fashion spreads she was paid peanuts to fill. She was also quite kind-hearted for one so image-obsessed, and for some reason seemed to feel I was worth bothering with.

Meanwhile, between bouts of dedicated bed-hopping Shaun found time to launch a tourist guide called *Look,* a computer magazine about programming developments in the Middle East entitled *Hacker,* and his career seemed unstoppable. Six years later, he surfed back into London on a Wakikiki-sized wave of goodwill with a percentage of the company in his pocket.

He was also married.

Shaun used the cash to start up Ziggurat Publishing, his own media business, beginning with *Insider* – now a glossy must-read monthly media title – then spinning off a daily news-sheet and putting it on the net before anyone else really woke up to electronic publishing. Today, his stable includes two computer titles, a rugger magazine called *Ruck!* and a down-market car title. *Drive's* successful formula is a high tit-to-print ratio, lots of reader competitions and no article longer than four hundred words – sort of like *The Sun*, but with wheels. Extracts of each, updated daily, started appearing on sharply-designed websites; then recognising a new trend when he saw one, Shaun produced several straight e-titles in the late nineties.

There were also some other less salubrious – no, potentially explosive – business ventures which only appeared on his accounts sheets. They were never mentioned in the business profiles of him in *Publisher's Weekly* and *Campaign*. We'll get to those later.

I'm now basely hoping his new eagerness to meet means that his marriage to Ms Aluminium-Knickers from Auckland is a washout. It certainly deserves to be, seeing as he fell for her on the rebound from me in Oman, like a small boy careening off a bouncy castle.

At our first friendly 'what are you up to these days' lunch which went on to become annual occasions, Shaun had produced her photo. A low-rent Stevie Nicks, shaggy-blonde with a tip-tilted nose (like a pig's, I'd thought sourly) yearned out of the frame. Debbie was mid-seventies cute, regardless of the fact that it was now the mid-eighties. Professionally caring she might be (apparently she's a grief counsellor) but I couldn't help noticing a rosebud mouth that shut like a rat trap, a square little jaw, and that she'd dotted the 'i' of her signature on the back of the photo with a heart (Jesus, the woman was thirty-two). Those who knew said she carried a rod of iron in her little navy handbag that matched her little navy shoes, and referred to her as Sizewell D. Pretty, dainty Debbie – the last woman in London with a Farah flick and flesh-coloured tights.

Rumour also had it that she no longer slept with him unless he bought her a little present first (like a car). And he was reputedly scared to death of her, this working class internet entrepreneur, this dot.com adventurer who'd once held his sales director out of the fifth storey office window by the ankles because he'd seen the poor man talking to the competition in The Gaucho's gents. A hundred and twenty staff, a thickening pile of press cuttings, a premises off Soho Square and a silver company stretch yet the man still goes white at the thought of telling the wife he's going to be a bit late for supper.

Mind you, I had always harboured a sneaking suspicion that it would be very unwise for Shaun to marry anyone, ever. I had also feared that I was punching above my weight, swimming out of my depth because I never quite understood what he saw in me, not really. Never quite felt good enough, clever enough, pretty enough, sexy enough or interesting enough to have the monopoly of this carnivorously attractive, alpha male. Yet I couldn't help hoping, because for me, this had been the only real coup de foudre. The only time the power and the glory of the heart had spun me round and round like a dust devil, raising me up me to a place where I could scarcely breathe for excitement and desire and cared about nothing else.

It remains the only time it ever has.

Because Jim is very different – a slow-burner. More considered, more grown-up, whatever that means. When I looked at him I saw a Good Man, and an attractive, funny, sexy one at that. After Shaun, I needed nothing so much as one of those. Meeting Jim, I knew without a shadow of a doubt that here was a man I could live with, rather than simply play house with. Here was a man I could marry, when I had never considered marrying anyone before for more than a week at a time. This person would never throw me away like a piece of computer software that's ceased to be state of the art. He'd be in for the long haul.

Yet – I never could tell him about Shaun. I often wanted to, but I was too ashamed that someone I'd loved with all my heart had hated living with me so much, he'd actually done a runner. Even years afterwards, the hurt still ran so deep that it carried away the words I would have used to talk about it. And there was another reason too – the fact our time together had always felt, well, fiercely private: a universe of two isn't open to sightseers. So to Jim, I made light of it. Said I'd been seeing some journalist, but he'd taken a job abroad. Told to friends and family I'd prefer they kept quiet. And that was how we left it.

Now, cut off in our prime, the unfinished business between Shaun and myself had festered for two decades, for neither of us could quite let go of a shared past that had once been promise itself. Yet here was a God-given chance (well, maybe not Him, but Someone) to tie up what are still the very loosest of ends.

Last time I'd called him up, on the pretext of a piece in *The Guardian* about him launching yet another title and featuring a lot of ego-inflating twaffle about Lyon's Midas Touch, he'd asked how I was doing more meaningfully than usual. I'd mumbled that Jim and I were having a few problems, shamefully hoping for the sort of consoling noises only an Ex can make properly.

Something gallant along the lines of: 'I'd treat you right if you'd married *me*.'

Or perhaps: 'He doesn't deserve you, sweetheart.'

Even: 'Sounds like a right prat,' would have done.

He said none of the above, yet I could tell that he was Thinking Things, which was good since I was Thinking Things myself. Hey, if you can't rely on a violently attractive man who was once the love of your life for a stonking great flirt down memory lane, what is the world coming to?

However, I would also have done well to remember that ex-lovers who've a way with women, rampant commitment phobia and no visible scruples should be regarded all times as the radioactive pond slime they are.

The Trouble With Jim

The reason I'm in the market for lunch – and soon – with Shaun comes mainly in the shape of my husband. Lanky (formerly) sexy Jim, who's now so pathologically irritable and moody most of the time, he's barely recognisable.

It's difficult to say what's the matter with the man, but this much I do know. That it's difficult to work up any enthusiasm for someone who's pissed off ninety per cent of the time and the man you married for ten. Someone who, if you appeared at his office clad in nipple tassels and a leather thong brandishing a banner which said '*Take Me Now*', could these days be relied upon to observe that your cellulite was showing.

Jim used to be the dead spit of a red-haired Clint Eastwood: a slouching six foot two with a sexy squint, slow smile and an even slower swivel to his hips when he screwed. He also told great jokes, wore vintage Pucci shirts with verve, drank Tequila a bottle at a time, was a veritable coyote in the sack and invariably looked on the bright side. But these days, apart from those brief lighthouse flashes of humour and tenderness which remind me of how he used to be, he sulks and complains his way through life, Jim my-glass-is-half empty Harrington, the sort of bloke you don't want to sit next to at a dinner party.

Tequila now gives him wind. He bought a T-shirt last week which says 'Life's a bitch and then they tax it'. He will not see our GP for what could be clinical depression; take zinc supplements for his woefully shrunken sex drive, nor me for a weekend away. He won't discuss it either but the man who used to unwind with *Airplane II* because he liked the fart jokes now prefers the boxed set of Ingmar Bergman, saying that he finds 'their stark portraits of the black night of the human soul, comforting.'

Yes, somewhere along the line Clint has turned into Eeyore, and I can't seem to put my finger on how it happened.

But he hasn't always been like this. God, no. We fell for each other hard at a Glastonbury festival. Ian Dury, The Talking Heads, Elvis Costello, Spear of Destiny – seminal stuff and very exciting at the time, though it now reads like the first Woodstock line-up. Bel and self had gone along taking a real Mickey Mouse of a bright blue bubble tent which began to leak like a clapped-out colander as the rain came sluicing on the first night. I squelched out and rattled the nearest canvas shape, pleading for a groundsheet to put over the top, and came nose to nose with a beautiful man who owned the spacious four-person job next door. He gallantly offered it to us, while he and his friend Robert slept in the back of their car with the seats down. The next evening, friend Robert was once again relegated to the car in return for a shed-load of free drugs. Bel (*'I don't know why I bother with this country: the summer's wetter than dingo piss and the sky's the same bloody colour'*) got billeted on some hippies in a neighbouring yurt, leaving Jim and I exclusive use of his canvas palace. A week later I was so thoroughly in love with him, I'd have made sculptures from his dirty socks.

Yet in the last few years, this enthusiastic, hunky, funny man who minded about important things like the world's injustices and the whereabouts of the weekend's best party, has become a morose, self-absorbed stranger. And the worst of it is that this gloomy bloke, who's in imminent danger of disappearing without trace up his own rectum, is somebody I am supposed to love. Mornings like the one where he built the ramparts around us both in bed are now trebly precious because they are so poignantly rare. And I would give anything to find out why.

Because this is the same man who white water rafted down the river with me and two gay friends in a particularly homophobic part of Connecticut, wearing a purple taffeta opera cape, chewing magic mushrooms and singing *Tomorrow Belongs to Me*. The man who'd fornicated with me on the pinball table at that goth rock manager's party till all the pingers went off. The one who could banish colic, and do baby miracles. Who used to buy me La Perla underwear for no reason, liked to kiss the arches of my feet and told more *Beano* jokes than our children. The man who collected singing socks, had a wall of poetry books he's actually read, and used a mixture of maple syrup and double cream as a soixante-neuf enhancer.

Jim used to be – well, I thought he was terrific.

Now he chews his life over like gum that's lost its flavour, his once-perceptive comments have sharpened into barbed put-downs, and never makes any sexual overtures unless I fashion my hopeful hints into direct, nay urgent, requests. These are variously:

Oh darling, please, please, please.

But it's been weeks.

What's wrong with me? What?

If you don't fuck me tonight I shall make a postnuptial agreement with my vibrator and elope with it.

For after making enthusiastic love several times a week for years, it's now down to once a month, and what perfunctory occasions those are. I wake regularly at 4 a.m., fidgeting: not so much a case of ants in my pants as scorpions down my gusset. 'What am I doing wrong?' I'd beg him silently. 'Is it me? Are you fed up with us? Do you want a change, a break, a divorce, a holiday? Tell me. *Just talk to me.*'

Attempts to encourage the latter include setting light to his newspaper when he was brooding behind it for the fifth evening in a row; ending most sentences with 'Isn't it?' suggesting we take up a mutual pastime (variously salsa, sailing and SCUBA) and shouting at him. My mother, speaking from her magnolia Regency flat in Sussex Square overlooking Brighton seafront, suggested a frigid silence lasting several weeks ('Darling, it always worked on your father') but I couldn't keep that one up.

It has been several months since he has told any stupid jokes. Longer since he's worn any of his more eye-catching clothes. It's now faded, droopy-assed black Wranglers, splitting trainers, stretched black polo necks and the black leather donkey jacket with greasy marks on the collar. His favourite singing socks ('*What's New, Pussycat?*') sit silently in the drawer because the tune's begun to stutter. The last time he opened a poetry book was a year ago, and it was *The Wasteland*.

Once a five-nights-a-week-on-the-town man, Jim now won't come out at all and is always tired. Just once a week down the pub would do me – at least we could be together – but he's not interested. Yesterday when Bel showed him a flyer for the new Lindsay Kemp transvestite rap version of Swan Lake MC'd by Eddie Izzard (one night only) he'd said: 'But Horizon's on.' Last month, he turned down free C block tickets to see Moby at Wembley Arena ('I'm used to CD sound quality'). Formerly an avid filmie who'd watch anything, he has now read bad reviews of every movie you suggest. And with the exception of his best friend, a sardonic psychiatrist called Ade with two former wives, everyone who invites us out to dinner is either shallow, meritocratic, and/or has extravagant tastes in restaurants.

Ah, the front door's crashed open. He can never come into the house quietly. Wait for it.

'God, I'm tired.'

Yesssss!! In an uncertain world, there are some things we can all rely on. George Bush's stupidity, *Big Brother's* ratings, and Jim Harrington's opening words every evening.

Tim and Kasha leap upon him. Tim, clowning about and oblivious of Jim's mood, tries to climb on his back like an affectionate monkey. 'Get off, Tim, you're too big for that.' The disappointed twelve-year-old slides down looking crushed and tries to touch his Dad's hand instead, but Jim is too busy rummaging in his battered briefcase to notice. Our son looks even more crushed. I put my arm around him but he barely tolerates it. He wants his dad, and if his dad can't be bothered, he doesn't want anyone. This sort of thing happens a lot these days. Glare at Jim, but he doesn't notice.

Tim and Kasha do. Scenting disharmony, they potter out of the kitchen (Tim skilfully palming a packet of crisps from tomorrow's packed lunch) and switch on the TV in the sitting-room next door, hunkering down together on a pile of friendly, leaking chenille beanbags. On the TV screen, something sadistic happens to a grumpy hen in a baseball cap and the children burst into giggles. God bless Cartoon Network. It screens wall-to-wall *Cow & Chicken* cartoons late into the evening so parents can fight in peace.

'Jim, that wasn't very kind to Tim. He's getting older now and he really needs you to connect with him a bit more.'

(Ferreting in fridge and ignoring wife.) 'Bugger. Look at that.'

'What?'

'We're out of milk.'

'Jim –'

'Drop it, Zoe. I've had a long day.'

'You always have,' I mutter unwisely. 'What about mine?'

'What about yours?' he asks looking around at the comfortable disorder created by children, animals and our mutual aversion to housework. 'Any new contracts on the horizon?'

'Not yet.' Fourteen calls, resulting in four actual conversation and no work. Bad news travels fast, and writers who get their magazines sued enjoy the must-have rating of chlamydia in a whorehouse.

Selecting a dirty cup from the unwashed pile in the sink, he wrinkles his nose, a gesture that used to be endearing, and starts rubbing at a coffee ring with his forefinger under a trickle of cold water. 'Look, I do hate to be picky, but this house is a bit of a tip. I'm not surprised that my mother brings her own sheets when she comes to stay... and talking of which,' rub, rub, 'you could have been a bit more gracious when she did all that housework for us last week. She was rather hurt.'

Indeed, Ma Harrington had arrived last month clad in a Cacherel pleated skirt and silk blouse, her suitcase bursting with Pledge, freshly laundered bed linen and a large organic chicken wrapped in *The Daily Telegraph*. She promptly put the former on the guest bed I'd made up for her ('Too kind dear, when you're so busy – but I do prefer properly ironed sheets'), scrubbed our bath *before* she used it, and tidied Jim's and my bedroom without asking. We've not been able to find his *Stud Delay* cream since: not that there's been much call for it of late.

Eyeing our PG Tips with disfavour, she'd produced her own Jackson's of Piccadilly tea bags for breakfast ('I always feel it's a false economy to skimp on the essentials'). As we were all blearily eating breakfast on the second day, there was much snapping-on of Marigolds, frowning, and picking at invisible bits of dirt as she arose briskly from the table to re-wash all the pots I'd just done, then started boiling floor cloths which smelt disgusting and drove everyone from the kitchen. She also told me exactly how she wanted the chicken cooked for Tim and Kasha ('The effect of too much convenience food on The Young is such a worry, don't you think?') while ironing Jim's boxers, sliding the iron's tip into the crotches with a loving precision that would have made Freud sit up; and bleached our bog seats. I hope sitting on them gave her bum rash.

Jim, however, had merely looked fond. 'Mum, you're a wonder,' he'd beamed. Yes, a wonder her husband hasn't left her long ago. However, as a C of E vicar in Tunbridge Wells, I suppose he has to set an example. It's not as if he lets her push him around though, for the man's a bit of a bully himself, albeit of the prayer-reading and psalm-singing variety. Jim is always rather quiet after he's seen him.

'The house would be tidier if I wasn't so blasted tired all the time, or you agreed to help me pay for a cleaner for even a couple of hours a week. And I wouldn't be so tired if you did a bit more to help. But you're never back from work till gone eight. Come to think of it, why *is* that? Soho's only ten minutes away by bike.'

'I've got as lot on, OK? Perhaps if you earned more, you could pay for a cleaner yourself. Fifteen thousand, you did last year,' replies Jim, tugging off his motorcycle boots and scattering dried mud all over the floor. 'A receptionist in her first job gets more.'

'That's not fair, that is *way* out of order. You know that I only get seven months of the year to work that aren't eaten up with school holidays, half terms, children being ill, or inset days. And of that, when I've finished hanging out the washing and clearing up the cat sick, there's from ten in the morning to two fifty in the afternoon to actually work before leaving to collect the children, and that's if I don't stop for lunch, then if you add it up that's five hours work a day for seven month year –' dammit, can feel my voice rising '– so fifteen grand isn't half bad.' Must stop pacing up and down the kitchen. 'You try my hours sometime and see how much *you* get done.'

'OK, OK. I accept that every very little helps,' he amends swiftly, seeing my expression. 'But look at, say, Lucia. She's freelance, she has a son – but she did thirty-nine thousand last year. I know this for a fact because you made me help her with that tax return.'

'She's totally child-free in term time. That's an eight hour day – hell, even twelve hours or more if you want – seven days a week. And much as I love Lucia, most of her money goes on Harry's boarding school, then Harry's Christmas, Easter and Summer holiday camp fees which ensure her son's only with her three weeks of the year and even then they go to St Lucia with Crystal because the Kids Club takes him from 9 a.m. to 8 p.m. every day. Anyway, you wouldn't want to be married to her. The rest of her income is direct-debited to Jimmy Choo, her Wigmore Street BAPS man (retrospective instalments for the second lipo), the toe botox jabs –'

'*Toe* botox?'

'– so she can wear her teensy pointy stilettos sixteen hours a day, right (oh don't look like that Jim, all the fash-hags are doing it) and then there's her coke dealer, plus, because she doesn't cook, those weekly Selfridges' food hampers off which she has always lived.'

'Well, it's her money. Look, I'm not saying she's any more, you know, *talented* than you,' he offers, tiptoeing on conversational eggshells. 'In fact you could be, I mean you probably *are,* um, considerably more –' he stirs the coffee he's just made and looks into the middle distance, wondering how to get both feet out of his mouth.

'More what? Versatile? Marketable? Overdrawn?'

A bellow comes from next door. Kasha has kneed Tim in the groin.

'Yes. I mean, no! You're very marketable. Potentially. But if an overdressed fashion victim like Lucia can clear that sort of cash a year, I'm sure you could get a bit more. Why can't you raise your rates, like I keep suggesting?'

Because they'll just drop me for someone cheaper, and I can't afford to lose any more work. Start opening cupboards randomly and banging saucepans in a semblance of readiness for supper. Rebuffed, Jim adds: 'It might also help if you didn't dissipate your energies fostering so many stray animals. And what is that,' he points to a lurking, canine bulk, 'doing under the table?'

'Oh. Ah. Well, I was going to introduce you,' I explain as nicely as possible, shaking some ancient 'fresh' pasta into a saucepan. 'That's Wagner. Isn't he fabulous?'

'Adorable. And what's Wagner doing in my kitchen?'

'Our kitchen. Well, the Camden Dog Protection League called in a panic this afternoon. They had no more room. Darling, yummy onion and tomato sauce with capers do you?'

'You know I hate capers, and don't change the subject. Have you any idea how much half-grown starving Alsations eat?'

'Oh Jim, *please*, it's only for a few days. They said they'd have had to put him down if we didn't take him tonight – and nobody else would.' Wagner whines querulously in agreement. 'I'm not surprised,' mutters Jim, shooting the dog an uncharitable look.

'We can't let them, Jim, we just can't. Poor thing, he's *so* beautiful and he's done nothing except grow up.' Opening the fridge to get him another tactful Red Stripe, I catch sight of a bottle of very expensive Californian Wheatgrass Elixir (bought to boost his energy levels) festering on the milk shelf. Cross that one off the list too.

'Look, Dad, stupid people are always chucking big teenage dogs on the street when they realise they are not going to stay puppies and are too huge for their flats. It's not their fault, is it? Dogs don't ask to be bought by *morons,*' argues Tim, crawling under our battered old ten-seater pine table and feeding Wagner a Polo, whilst absently sculpting his over-gelled fringe between finger and thumb. The dog slobbers gratefully but seems disappointed to find it tastes of spearmint.

Jim snorts, slices the courgette directly into a pan, and cracks an egg.

Knowing what's good for him, Wagner slinks over and crouches at my husband's feet. Tim's spiky head pops out from under the table. 'Oh, you're making friends. Isn't he cool? Can he sleep in my room?'

'No.'

Wagner and Tim both look as soulful as they know how. Jim sighs. 'Jesus. All right then. Just for tonight.'

'Yay!' crows Tim, crawling out again and punching the air.

'But he's got to be out by tomorrow and he'd better not have ticks, like the last one.'

Dinner is an awkward affair, during which Jim eats behind the *Independant's* Media section and grunts in reply to all conversational overtures. As I clear the table afterwards, he rolls a joint of Rastafarian dimensions and starts opening his pile of today's post, which lies on the kitchen bench seat. 'Bill. Bill. N'other bill. Barclaycard statement: yours. Home insurance quote, dental hygienist reminder, double glazing circular –' His voice trails off, there's a long silence, then Jim pushes back his chair, goes over to the stove, lights a gas ring and deliberately holds the corner of one letter to the flame.

'Darling, what are you doing?' He doesn't answer for a moment, just watches the sheet of paper burn with deadly concentration. 'It's from that literary agents you suggested,' he mutters eventually. 'Chelmsford & Breene. Remember? I sent them my manuscript three months ago.'

'Ah. Not quite their sort of thing, then?' He's going to set the recipe books by the stove alight in a minute.

'It seems not. It says here they can't represent my novel because they 'couldn't persuade themselves to love it enough –'

'What?'

'– and this woman's also asking for five pounds ninety postage costs to send my manuscript back under separate cover. Second class.' He drops the flaming remains into the sink and turns on the cold tap hard sending charcoal and water droplets flying, and flumps down at the table.

The catty little tart. If I ever see that Carolyn Breene at another magazine Christmas party, I'll push those salmon morselettes she was hogging up her expensively re-modelled nose. But what if his manuscript really is bad? I wouldn't know, he won't let me see. Go over, put my arms around him and plant several small kisses on the top of his head. 'She's obviously a miserable cow. I'm so sorry sweetheart, she seemed all right at the party. Well, up hers. When your novel makes the Booker shortlist, she'll be pig sick. The woman's got no taste, right? Look, there are some forty literary agencies in London alone (plus a dozen likely publishing imprints) so fine, we'll try them all. Remember all those publishers who rejected the first *Harry Potter* book? Fact of life, Jim, most agents wouldn't know a good manuscript if it jumped up and bit them. But I promise you that one day your book will land on the right desk, I just know it will,' he pulls me onto his lap, 'where it will be turned into a film, a TV series and a T-shirt, then won't the myopic old trouts at Chelsmford and Breene be surprised?'

Jim kisses my cheek, draws heavily on his joint till it flares like a Roman candle, then develops a bronchial fit of coughing. 'Goddam London pollution,' he wheezes a few moments later, purple in the face. Silence falls.

I slide off his lap and start washing up, trying to remove the layer of grease from the frying pans but the water is barely warm (boiler timer has been acting up ever since the electricity went off the other day) and the surface thick with large yellow globules. Wouldn't mind a hand to get through this dirty crockery mountain, but Jim doesn't budge. And I don't want to make him any more negative than he already is by insisting because though he hasn't agreed to baby-sit yet, I am supposed to be going out tonight for the first time in three weeks – with Bel to the half-term show at The Hoxton Circus School where her toyboy Harvey teaches – lots of cute little circus lads to gaze at. When that's finished, Jim is still sitting at the table staring into space, so I try a bit of bracing wifely solicitude.

'So, darling! How was your day?'

'Bloody awful,' he replies, sloping off.

Ten minutes later I go upstairs for a pee to find him slumped in the bathroom's squashy armchair, head back and eyes closed. His desolation is more than I can bear. Shutting the door behind me and sliding the bolt across, I come and kneel at his feet to take his hand and rest my head in his lap. He sighs quietly and strokes my head a couple of half-hearted times.

'You know Mr Harrington, what you need is a good seeing-to.'

He is silent for a moment. 'I'd like more sex. Really I would. But just at the moment, I can't seem to get past the point of being too tired to do anything about it.'

His watch says 7.52. We have eight minutes before *EastEnders* finishes. Yet some kinds of love-making take less time than others, and perhaps a little unilateral pleasure might be in order. After all, sex columns (including mine) are always going on about the importance of spontaneity in marriage. Kiss his lap and snuzzle it gently. 'Zoe, I –'

'Sssh. It's all right. You don't have to do a thing – I'll do it all for you.'

By 7.58, he's stroking my head some more and smiling faintly for the first time in days. 'Thank you, that was really, er – oh God, I'm sorry love. Not much good to you at the moment, am I?'

Such rave reviews. 'Never mind. My turn next time, perhaps?'

The smile solidifies on his face. Get up abruptly feeling tacky, undignified and disinclined to pay him the compliment of swallowing, but try not to wipe my mouth while he's looking because that's supposed to be a sign of rejection, and tonight, thanks to Chelmsford & Breene, he's already had a crippling one of those. *EastEnder's* theme tune is blaring out as I stump into the downstairs toilet to attend to the original demands of my bladder. Feeling at a loss, humiliated and about as attractive as that quilted nylon housecoat his mother gave me last Christmas – a combination often associated with trying to get close to Jim these days – I slam the door shut far too hard, dislodging one of its pretty Edwardian glass panels and cracking two others. The glass shatters on the loo's tiled floor, all but severing two fingers when I scrabble to scoop the pieces up. Blood spatters briskly in all directions, for it is impossible to hold wads of bog paper in several places at once.

Keeping the hand up in the air, a delta of blood rivulets winding down my arm, I belt into the kitchen looking for someone to help staunch the bleeding. The children are now back in there, rifling through the cupboards for night snacks. Kasha looks up and screams when she sees the oozing scarlet mess.

'Its all right Kash, it looks far worse than it is. Can you help me get some plasters on? Hey, Tim, can you reach the first aid kit? It's on the top shelf of the biscuit cupboard.' The stuff's pouring out. Glass, like disenchantment, cuts deep.

'Oh, *yuck*.' Kasha examines my hand with fascinated revulsion, then backs away. 'Mummy, you're leaking.'

'Ji-iiim.'

After a long minute or so, Jim appears looking resentful, unfinished smouldering spliff in hand. Slowly, he takes in my face streaked with blood where I've pushed the hair out of my eyes, and the spreading scarlet splodges on the floor. He goes white, swaying gently. A confirmed vegetarian ('I will never eat anything that moves, not even jelly') he is also terrified of blood. Especially when stoned.

'Steady on, darling, it's just a teeny little bit. Look, please can you do something useful like take the children upstairs for a bath? Or help me with these plasters.'

Too late. Jim's knees buckle elegantly. And like a bad extra in a cowboy movie, he falls as if in stop-frame slow motion, cracking his head on the doorframe and hitting the floor with a wallop, sending Wagner's bowl of defrosted burgers flying.

No one moves for a second or so, until Tim backs away and runs for the phone to dial 999, but confronted by an operator, his emergency cool collapses. 'Hello, hi, um, yeah. My dad. It's my dad – where do we live? C-camden. He's, yeah, fallen over, his head's all – and my mum's hurt too. No, they weren't. At least, I don't think – oh, oh, I dunno. *Mum!* Muuu-uum…'

Kasha and I are on our knees in the blood, glass and burning bits of tobacco. She tries to lift one of Jim's eyelids. A brown eye stares back blankly. Search for his pulse. It's not there. Tim pushes the walkabout upside down into my non-leaking hand.

'My husband's hit his head. No, I did *not* do it. No, he's not moving. He's hasn't been sick either. He'd move if he'd been sick, wouldn't he?' Terrific. Ideal. They have put me through to an NHS assessor whose mission in life is to find out whether injured members of the public really deserve a valuable ambulance, or are quite capable of coming in by bus. 'No, he's not epileptic. No – oh please, I can't find his pulse. We're at ninety-seven Hartland Road. Please hurry, he's – yes. OK, right then. Thank you, thank you very much.

'They'll be here any minute. Let's get a blanket. Keep Daddy warm.' Sobbing, Kasha gets under it too and snuggles up to him. Tim divides his time between gluing his nose to the front-room window and running back to touch Jim nervously on the shoulder. The latter lies peacefully, an offended expression on his face. He would pull this now wouldn't he? I think irrationally, smoothing back his hair and holding a wet tea towel against his temple. This'll be the third time I've stood Bel up in succession, and she'll already have left. The bleeding's slowing but his pulse is still AWOL. Try the place in his neck like they do on *ER* but it's not there either, though he does seem to be breathing. 'Jim?

Sweetheart?' I put my lips close to his ear. Rewarded by a small involuntary fart, which seems as eloquent an answer as we are likely to get.

Suddenly, flashing blue light is streaming through our sitting room window, followed by a thunderous knocking. The ambulance has taken forty-one minutes to travel two miles from the Royal Free Hospital. Tim streaks to open the door. Two strapping paramedics sprint into the kitchen at the spanking pace of marines on a mission.

'Is he on medication?' asks the older paramedic, expertly rolling Jim onto a stretcher. 'Does he pass out much?' Tim and Kasha hover, their fingers in their mouths, eyes wide. Shake my head mutely, still stroking Jim's thinning hair. 'Hmmm – sorry to ask, but 'as the gentleman bin usin' drugs?' enquires the other, tucking the red blanket round my husband and looking at the remains of the joint kicked aside in the commotion. Stand on it swiftly, and shake my head again.

'And, beg pardon, but did he hurt you love?' he adds, seeing the dried blood on my face and trained to spot domestic violence, of which there is quite a bit in Camden and Kentish Town.

'Certainly not,' I reply with as much dignity as possible, following them out into the hallway.

Not physically anyway.

Only my feelings, for the past few years.

How Far Has My Bottom Dropped?

If you've ever been tempted to clip your pubes with a bloke's beard-trimmer – don't. One wrong move and you'll puncture your pudenda if your concentration falters for a single second. Or even if it doesn't.

Find this out the hard way as Jim bursts into the bathroom while I am doing a spot of routine muff-dressing. We haven't seen him since he was comfortably tucked up in an observation ward last night, awake but plaintive. Ejected early from hospital after an overnight stay and a single neat stitch in the temple, he's come home to change his fading black polo-neck for an identical one without the cranial bloodstains, and summon a taxi.

'Oww, bugger – *hi* darling,' I gasp, whisking up my knickers, humiliated at being caught doing what is possibly, along with masturbation, one of the things you least want your partner to walk in on. 'Just doing a little maintenance. Why didn't you ring? I'd have come to pick you up. How are you feeling?'

'Not good,' Jim closes his eyes briefly, putting his hand up to his stitch. 'Got a frightful headache.'

'You poor old thing,' I murmur, standing up and putting an arm around him. 'Come on, let's make you a hottie, find you some painkillers and a cup of tea, then put you to bed. I'll phone your office.'

He shrugs me off. 'I don't want a hot water bottle, and you know I don't like taking things. You do, of course, realise that this is largely your fault?'

'Look, I can't help it if you're haemophilic or whatever it is. And it's not like I cut myself on –'

'The word is haemophobic if you don't mind, as you should know by now, the amount of times I've told you. It's a recognised psychological syndrome and many famous people suffer from it. The point is that if you hadn't been quite so careless and cut yourself, this would never have – oh, forget it,' he breaks off sulkily, turning away. 'Some of us have worked to do today regardless of whether we feel up to it. And frankly, I don't have time to hang about here all day drinking tea. Just get me some Nurofen and a clean jumper, will you?'

'You can flaming well get it yourself,' I tell him furiously, frog-marching him out of the bathroom and locking the door. Work, my arse. He's off to commandeer his office's squashiest black leather sofa, tell the receptionist to field all calls, and enjoy a nice lie-down lasting till 6 p.m. What is the matter with him these days? When he's not being self-righteous he swings between gloom and pomposity, and I don't know which of the three is worse.

Doesn't take things, indeed. That man's got no problem with recreational drugs, yet he won't touch the St Johns Wort that I bought him after he cancelled three appointments in a row to see the doctor about his low moods. (And when I tried to accompany him that last time to make sure he actually made it to the surgery, he told me that having a nanny state was bad enough and he didn't need a nanny wife.) Nor will he consider the legendary herb yohimbine, tracked down via the net, for his disappearing sex drive. In fact, he won't even discuss that one.

Will someone please tell me why men wallow like this, inert but indifferent beneath the weight of their difficulties? And make everyone else suffer along with them? Huh?

In fact, I'm now so hacked off with him, what with the monthly two-minute sex, the endemic grumpiness, and the patronage of his last remarks that the minute he's out of the house, I'm ripping off every stitch of clothing to stand naked in front of a full-length mirror in a howling draught. For I did have an appointment – one that I'd thought over carefully and been intending to cancel this morning. But I'm now so fed up, I'm going to bloody well keep it after all.

The mirror is the cruellest I can find in the house. It's the one on the stairs by a big back window, and it catches the pitiless light filtering down through North London's pollution. For body defect spotting, it's as good as standing under those fluorescent strips in a Top Shop changing room. You know the ones. Where a bunch of underfed teenagers watch pityingly as you fail to haul a dress claiming it's size twelve up over your backside, having got the same one stuck over your head a moment ago.

And I bet I know what you're thinking but you're wrong. The reason why I am standing here goose-pimpled to the gills is not because Shaun's going to see anything beneath my dress, because he isn't. It's a personal confidence thing, like wearing your most fuck-off outfit for a radio interview – plus a matter of checking out any visible wear and tear so there's a fighting chance of camouflaging it. Look, who wants an ex-lover smiling into your eyes, only to watch him become distracted by the new crows' feet around the edges?

Having been on the verge of cancelling San Marbella several times over the last three days while dickering over whether to meet Shaun again, I'm now very much hoping he'll turn up. It took a lot of persuasion to get us a table there, too. Arguably the classiest Old Media joint in Mayfair (you can't get through the door without falling over Clive James with his arm round Terrence Stamp, schmoozing David Puttman) they initially said they were full for the next three months. Eventually got a table after whispering that my companion would be the Artist Disrespectfully Known as Madge, graciously giving last minute interview about the influence of Kabbalistic philosophy on the lyrics of her shocking new album, *Streetwalker Priestess* ('it's for *Vogue*, actually'). Though it's doubtful they believed this, even the tiniest possibility of having Mrs Guy Ritchie on the premises proved too much for the star-fucking Maitre d' to resist. When Shaun sauntered in, we would have to say he was her press officer, standing in for her at the last minute.

'Stop staring and go away,' I tell the Vicar, who is watching with a broad smirk hovering about the whiskers.

Right. Pretend that body in the mirror belongs to someone else. Analyse dispassionately, making brief mental notes as follows:

Face: fine lines running outside corners of mouth. Small smile lines round eyes (fine) and underneath (heavier). Vertical crease between eyebrows, fortunately hidden by fringe. Definite lines around neck. Last time he got up close, had none of the above. Shall wear high-necked dress.

Tummy and upper midriff: consistency: somewhat doughy. Breathe in and hold. Better but will show more when sitting down. Scrummage though dirty clothes basket for lacy vest top to camouflage squishy bits. Locate in Kasha's dressing-up box. Smells, unaccountably, of Maltesers. Spray liberally with Opium.

Breasts: 34B, reasonably free-standing, only lost one cup size during breastfeeding. Still best mid cycle and beyond. Currently day ten, so have not yet begun to show selves to best advantage. Unfortunately, during Top Tit Week my knees also swell up these days, so suppose one can't have everything. Don old purple Wonderbra, adding the lacy, midriff-subduing vest over top.

Bottom: all right, how far's it dropped? Has definitely progressed south. Abandon mirror to ferret out only pair of French knickers I possess. They cut me up the crotch, so must walk with care.

Inner thighs: have developed a detectable quiver. Not quite blancmange, more ill-set cheesecake. Will take months of Stairmaster hell to correct. Restrain with genius seven per cent Elastane M & S stockings.

Pubic hair: Jim's beard trimmer has done a nice job. Have lovely velvety muff. Not that Shaun will ever know, but still... oh dear God, is that a grey hair down there? Please let it be a blonde one catching the light... no, grey if I squint at it another way too, *and* it's got a friend. Pluck out immediately. Pain eye-watering.

Legs: shape OK, no varicose veins apart from *that* little one mid thigh (ah, and that one at the back of right knee) Apply fabulous Touch Eclat. Look like a damn sheep around the shins. Slather on thick layer of Immac.

Eyebrows: pluck artistically, but get carried away so one is now (bugger) fatter than the other. Telephone rings downstairs. Ignore it, tweezing away like grim death. Whoever it is I have no intention of talking to them now.

Voicemail kicks in prompt as a good PA but a cataract of clipped syllables is already splitting the air, the accent unmistakable. 'Zoe? Zoe, pick up if you're there, would you? Meredith here.'

Dammit to hell, it's Meredith Hungerford. One of the extra commissioning editors for whom I do regular freelance pieces, since *Yes!* was only part-time. She's the one I like least, and who's owed the most work. She effectively runs *FeelGood*, a posh 'proactive' health & beauty title read by women with large disposable incomes, children they seldom see, and collections of costly anti-wrinkle creams based on extract of virgin ewes' ovary in which I am developing a keen interest of late.

'Those feature ideas you promised me for last week? Don't seem to have come across them.' We both know that this is because I haven't done them. Crouch low on the stairs.

'You'll need to 'e' them again tonight if you want them to be considered at tomorrow morning's editorial meeting. We're doing a two-monther because the Editor's simply *got* to have her baby asap – she's re-scheduled her elective at The Portland twice already. Byeeee!'

That means if they're not in today, there's no work from her for two months. Got some scribbled notes in my shed that could (possibly) become feature ideas. Is there time? Better make time, we need that money. Maybe if I do Tim and Kasha's homework with them from a quarter to five till half past in the kitchen while simultaneously cooking supper, we could we eat bang on five thirty, finish by six; and then if they watch *The Simpsons*, plus (are the re-runs still on?) *The Fresh Prince of Bel Air,* that would give me an hour starting at six o'clock so long as we leave the clearing up. After which there's always *The Bill* between eight and nine if absolutely necessary (providing they're not running any more incest or urban cannibalism storylines) since it's doubtful Jim will be home, even then. His hours just seem to be getting longer and longer.

Really should get the leg cream off, and find some clothes. Noooo – telephone again. What's wrong with everyone this morning? It's not even a Monday. Leave it. Start going upstairs two at a time. 'Hi, Zoe. Veronica,' blares a Roedean-trained voice that would carry from one end of a grouse moor to the other. 'It's eleven twenty-one, no make that eleven twenty-two on Tuesday. Get back to me. Must, must chat.'

Hell. This one's *Chutzpah's* 'time is money' features editor at her crispest. I have been avoiding her for days but entertain vague hopes of a permanent freelance position to make up for the one cancelled by *Yes.* Crash downstairs clad in pink French knickers, and purple Wonderbra (so called because when I take it of these days, everyone wonders where my tits went).

'Hiiiiiii Karina, I mean Veronica. I'm here.' Must keep that guilty rasp out of my voice. 'Just on my way out to talk to a professor at King's who's doing some amazing research on in-utero learning. Apparently he's taught a thirty-five week unborn child the two times table. You know me, busy-busy, always on a tight schedule. Have you had a moment to look at my piece on crystallized urine therapy as an anti-ageing treatment?'

I'd be surprised if she has. Not done that one yet, either.

'Haven't seen it. You sent it when? It was due –' there's a businesslike shuffling of paper in background '– according to my flowchart, three days ago.'

'Bizarre. It was e'd last Friday.'

'Well, it hasn't shown up here yet.'

'Technology, ha! It's great when it works. Don't worry. I'll send it again today. When I get back.'

'Can't you send it now? Only take you a sec. By the way, when *are* you getting back?'

'When I've picked the children up from school. Four-ish.'

'You working mothers. All those little balls and whatnots to juggle.' Oh, the breeziness of those with no children carving cracks into the smooth plasterwork of their self-esteem. When she becomes pregnant, let it be with triplets, God.

'I don't suppose you have decent ideas for me?' Pleasantries over, she comes abruptly to the point.

Don't care for the way she said that. As if she very much doubts it. 'As a matter of fact, I do and it's an exclusive. Remember my Feng Shui man? He's that ex-Buddhist monk who came round last year to check out your toilet for you and said you had to take all the books out, because your creative potential was being flushed down it every time you pulled the chain? Well, he's told me about this extraordinary Franciscan monastery which has turned into a New Spiritualist health farm-cum-retreat, near Liechtenstein.'

'Dull.'

'Oh no, no, no – it's amazing. The place is the first ever *silent* designer retreat. Therapists and guests alike may only use sign language, note-pads or texting. Cosmically expensive, Shaker furniture, cuisine created by the River Café… and their cast of complementary practitioners makes the Hale Clinic look like a backwater GP's practice.'

'Sounds more *Harpers & Queen* than us.'

'All the Hollywood stars fresh out of rehab are being sent there by their studios to recover their spiritual equilibriums –'

'Ah. Better.'

'Or is it equilibria? Anyway, they say it's going to be the new Betty Ford.'

'Who does?'

The press release, actually. '*The Economist*.' I improvise wildly. 'In, er, that article last week about big banks like Morgan Grenfell introducing Quiet Hours during the working day for their staff because they have been told by their corporate spiritual advisors that –'

'Stop, we covered that *months* ago'

That would be remarkable, since I've just made it up '– purposeless verbal interaction is the new mind/body dichotomy pollutant.'

'Meaning?'

'Idle office chat and unfocussed interaction aren't just a waste of valuable energy, they have a measurable cumulative effect on the protective integrity of the individual's etheric shield which can in fact be a major health hazard in it's own right, and –'

When I risk drawing breath five minutes later, Karina says nothing. Perhaps she's fallen asleep? Is taking another call? There is an oppressive pause. Tuck phone under chin and start rubbing goose-pimpled arms. A thick layer of Immac is no protection against February temperatures.

'Got any Names?' she concedes, finally.

'Of what?'

'The Hollywood re-habbers. We'd need pictures, of course.'

'Well, not as such yet, but I'm sure we could get some.' Try and scrawl: 'Get pictures' on the pad by the phone table. Damn pen won't write. Shake it hard. Rewarded by drops of cold spittle flying out onto the wall. Feel despondent. Pretentious silent retreats and burnt-out celebs, huh? When I once wrote blistering pieces about NHS doctors bribed to test unlicensed drugs on sick patients, and uncovered scandals like suppressed research showing a new Pill doubling cases of cervical cancer when the manufacturers claimed the opposite... stuff that mattered, proper issues, stories that were actually worth something. But pay is poor when you're freelance: five hundred pounds for an investigative piece that blows the lid off a cover-up and takes a month to research. So now it's the Hollywood re-habbers and cosmetic surgery bungles – five hundred quid for couple of days' work. Yet the knowledge that I could (no, should) do better, gnaws at me still.

Karina however, doesn't care. Karina peddles trash, but trash pays and she likes her Notting Hill studio, her invitations to the openings of Barbadian spas, her freebies and her clout. She makes a small derogatory noise, somewhere between a throat-clearing and a sniff. 'Oh, do a synopsis and we'll take a look, two hundred words max. Ye-es. I see a cover-flash in silver: *The Sound of Silence: have you heard it?* Or something. Possibly. I'm not promising anything. But we'll need it today.'

'Today?' Oh, bollocks. 'OK I'll try. I'm up to my eyes –' Jesus, get off the phone, my legs are on fire... tuck the receiver under my chin, and start trying to remove the cream with a spatula improvised from a folded Post-It paper.

'You want the work? You get me the ideas on time. And don't forget to send that piece again. Five p.m., latest. Bye, now.' Scowl at the handset, hating her. Dear God, no wonder health journalists are all trying to write novels these days. However, I reckon *Chutzpah's* synopsis just got the *Simpsons'* slot.

Standing in the bath now, I hose my legs down thankfully for they are now the colour and pattern of Tesco raspberry ripple ice cream. Dab on hydrocortisone cream meant for eczema to kill the inflammation, sheath in camouflaging black stockings. Struggle for several minutes to anchor them to the suspender belt, which keeps releasing them with a mocking *ping*. Settle for black lace tights with a small hole in the toe. You only need suspenders if someone's going to see them, and he's not, so that's all right. It's now noon, and I'm starting to panic. If I'm late, he's quite capable of pushing off back to his office.

Frigging phone is squawking again. *Now* bloody what? The answer-phone cuts in again. Leave it. *Leave it,* that's what it's for. Now, where are those – oh Christ, it's Kasha's school. Has she had an accident? Please don't let her head be stuck through the banisters again. But it's only Ms Marblehead, the school secretary with the halitosis and the heart of gold, calling to thank us for making sixty-six Smartie cakes for the that fundraising tea for a new playground. Ah, and: 'Mrs Harrington, just a quickie to remind you that you said you'd give myself, our little head girl, her sister and the puppet theatre man – you know, who's doing a one-man show for us about the Snow Queen for your daughter's class? a lift back to Kentish Town today. I take it you do have an estate?'

Well, this'll represent a spatial challenge for Harriet, my trusty, rusty old Morris Traveller. 'No problem, Mrs Marblehead.'

I have no memory of this.

Spray mousse on my hair roots upside down to give it some body. Stands out wildly. Am trying to squash it down a bit, when my handbag starts ringing. Mobile's new hiding place proves to be in said bag, under a pile of coats on the end of the banisters. 'Hi, Zoe!' chirrups a little voice I've come to dread. 'Is this a good time?'

Shit, it's Bex, that terminally enthusiastic student from the London School of Journalism. Having agreed to mentor her last autumn in a fit of professional sharing, she has dogged my footsteps ever since.

'Not really –'

'Never mind. Just need to pick your brains for a sec.'

I have a distressing vision of Bex as a black crow, plunging her beak into my skull and sucking greedily on what she finds there. 'Again?'

'Ha ha! Look, it'll only take a *second*.'

That's what they say about smear tests. 'Bex, I am in a terrible rush.' Am trying to brush hair into shape – any shape – one-handed. Looks like a mutant privet hedge.

'Oh pul-ease, I'm *really* stuck Zoe. You are such a *great* mentor, you've been *so* lovely to me. I just need one *weeny* little contact more.'

More? She's had all my best ones already. Perhaps, if I give her just one last one, she'll go away for a while. In fact, if I give her a really duff one she may go away for good.

'For what?' The hairbrush is now stuck in my hair.

'I want to get some work experience. Preferably in a film company.' Her upbeat tones turn businesslike. 'But no one wants to know. No one's got anything. I'm getting desperate. As it's my final year, I'm supposed to be on work experience by the beginning of next week. Everyone else on my course is fixed up already, and if you don't help me, I... I don't know who will.'

This kid is the kind of pushy little cow who'll go far: ideally somewhere like Outer Mongolia, and preferably next week. Yet because I am in now in a panic, remember well how hard it can be trying to get started, and cannot think of anywhere else, I end up giving her Seventh Wave's address. Jim's company seldom says no to free staff who can act as receptionists or gofers, for their cash-flow problem is on-going and getting bigger by the day.

'You are *such* a star. Thank you, thank you, oh thank you...' Maybe she really is desperate. Must try and be nicer.

'I owe you a *big* drink.' She always says that. 'We *must* meet.'

'Absolutely.' Not if I can help it.

'Oh, I really mean it, you sound so-oo great. Isn't it *funny* we've never met yet?'

'Side-splitting.'

'Ciao!'

How can anyone still say that? Oh God. Am I ever going to get out of here?

Just The Once

I might have known.

I am just standing over the machine and switching it to silent to prevent any further interruptions, when it shrills yet again. And what do you know, it's Shaun's PA. Apparently, he's running frightfully late. There's no possibility of his making our lunch reservation, and everyone knows that if your *full* party doesn't turn up at San M within fifteen minutes of original booking time, you *have* to cede your table to the first people in the very long queue that's always waiting in their bar on the off-chance of a last minute no-show. So *would* I mind staying with the original venue? She really is frightfully sorry, hopes it doesn't inconvenience me too much, and helpfully offers to cancel the booking.

Yeah, right. The slippery bastard.

Oh, well. I shall just look round what is undoubtedly his private bonk-pad, admire, then whisk him off to the nearest do-lunch facility in Soho: anywhere except that new minimalist Tibetan with the yak meat and soured milk goulash. No way are we staying in some flat. Not if he produces a Fortnum's picnic, singing waiters and a crate of Crystal.

Wriggle into body-hugging red dress that buttons up front, thread feet into long flat black boots. Decant rest of the Opium down cleavage – the smell is asthma-inducing – grab the ankle-length black fake fur coat and leap into the street to look for a matching black cab because you can't possibly travel to have Lunch with an Ex on the Northern Line. By the time you got there, he'd have long since buggered off with someone else.

'Forty-three, Old Compton Street, please.'

'Off to work late, are we?'

'No, lunch.' I'm trying to open the window before the Opium fumes smother us both.

'All right for some. Wish I could stop for lunch.'

'Well, to be honest, I don't usually get the –'

'Yeah, and forty-three ain't a restaurant.'

'No?'

'Nah. That's The Café Columbia, number forty-two, if I'm not mistaken. Dropped a fare there yesterday. Packed out, it was.'

Well, well. 'Then they won't have a seat left for me will they? I'm going to a friend's flat.'

'Oh.' He winks at me in the driving mirror. 'Right.'

Ignore him all the way to Soho though he keeps trying to catch my eye. Start feeling sick half way down Frith Street where the traffic's so bad I jump out, hand over a tenner and start walking. This is better for I am caught up with the pull of people, all purposeful, all hurrying somewhere. Media clones in black wielding metal briefcases swarm over the pavements, and spill into the streets. It's too early for them to have reached the hanging out stage, so they're still in fashionably-stressed mode: off to close a deal, present a show-reel, do a meeting or nab a prime table in one of the hipper eateries of the month. But because it's almost lunchtime and it's the first sunny Friday of the year there is a powerful whiff air of urban holiday in the air, despite the February temperatures.

Ten different types of music – salsa, acid jazz, Brazilian funk and, unaccountably, Baccarach (so passé he's hip again in certain small, concentric circles) wafts out of the bars and restaurants mixing with the smell of Soho: a blend of fresh pasta, hot focaccia, vanilla coffee, Patisserie Valerie's chocolate and just the tiniest hint of dog shit, all underscored by diesel fumes and too much ozone. I inhale it happily, but have to hover near the doorway of number forty-three for a full minute before I have the courage to go up to it. When I do, there are five bells with no names, just flat numbers. He never mentioned a flat number. Do I stand in the street shouting up at the windows? Call his PA? Go home? It's perfectly clear what I should do, but I can't. I want to see him too badly. Try all the bells simultaneously using both palms, but no one appears. He's stood me up, hasn't he? He's not coming.

Retreat, embarrassed and deflated, to the little bookshop across the road. Its travel section is positioned so there's a clear view of the flat entrance. All right, I'm giving him ten minutes. Just ten minutes, and then I'm going. Going to eat a nice expensive lunch, all on my own, even if every mouthful of it sticks in my throat...

Hmm, well I've now been here for twelve (very long) minutes. This is clearly A Sign from the Universe. What's a married woman with children doing loitering in Soho anyway? Looking for a Life? Bah. Half crushed, half relieved, telling myself that this is definitely all for the best, am just leaving to buy Jim a guilt offering of a bumper box of Nurofen and a packet of his favourite rolling tobacco – when Shaun comes swinging down the street. Steering confidently through the press of pavement people, not a care in the world, his head's thrown back and he's squinting up at the sun, checking his watch, then eyeing up a pretty messenger spinning past on a red mountain bike. His hair really is thinning now and he is ever so slightly paunchy but I couldn't care less. My heart jack-knifes, and I want to touch his face very badly. Watch as he lets himself in, forcing myself to stay still for another few minutes. Let him wait for a change – doesn't do to appear too eager.

Eager? God help me, I'm a greyhound that's just spotted the fluffy mechanical rabbit of its dreams streaking round the track.

Find I'm flipping through books without reading a word, not even the titles, conscious only of palms sweating, skin prickling, boots pinching. I'm holding my breath. How long have I been doing that? No wonder I feel dizzy. Mindlessly buy a book I don't want to read about a place I don't want to go to (*Viva! Torremolinos*) to pacify the hovering Portuguese proprietor. He looks at it, which is more than I've done, and demands eight pounds ninety-nine. I'm shaking so badly I've dropped the open handbag. Portugal-man smirks – he knows – and taps a well-shod little foot while watching me on my knees scrabbling for the rolling coins, scrumpled notes, lidless Dior lipsticks and the battered Nokia. Retreat with unwanted purchase. It's time.

Cross the street slowly. It's fifteen minutes past one, fifteen minutes past one on a sun-dazzled February afternoon and I want to remember it all. The exact time when – when I totally lost my appetite. Maybe we could just have a quick drink somewhere. Kettners', The Dog & Duck, Monique's – anywhere, for every bar and pub will be packed so I'll be safe. Quite safe.

But London is shivering with energy all around me, its frayed nerve endings singing a very different song and I'm moving through syrup, slow, sticky, delicious. Someone's switched off the sound-track. I can't hear any traffic, voices, music, brakes screeching, engines idling or cabbies swearing, crowds shifting, surging, murmuring and squealing: 'Sweetness! We've saved you a seat-ette' as their friends arrive. I can hear nothing. Nothing at all. Except a summer sea roaring in my ears and my heart in percussive overdrive. It seems to have lodged itself halfway up my throat, which is going to be a problem if I have to say anything much to him.

It isn't lunch I'm here for, is it. Or a drink. Oh Jesus, am I really going to do this? What if it no longer works between us? What if I just don't like him touching me any more? Maybe he's turned into a sloppy kisser. Will he find me boring in bed because I've been with the same partner for so long? Or say: 'Well, this is a mistake, isn't it,' to me half way through. And what if I call him Jim when he's – oh, God.

There is no way to retain your dignity with your tights at half mast. *No. No, this is – no way. Think, brain, move it. There must be an elegant way to say: 'Actually, I've changed my mind.'*

I'm sure it'll come to me in a minute.

Better at least tell him his pre-merger's off. I can't just walk away, it'd look so rude. Stroke the top bell briefly with my forefinger (it's got to be the top one) take a huge breath and give it a single and hopefully businesslike, push.

Feet thunder on the stairs. Consider making a run for it, then plan several opening lines – cheeky, insouciant, laid back, dry, non-committal, apologetic – in the intervening four seconds, finally discarding the lot because I cannot get a word out. It turns out that I need none for the door is swinging back on its hinges and he's standing there smiling down at me quizzically, as if he's not quite sure why I'm here.

Though it is an entirely unremarkable looking door, it's as if he's revealed the entrance to a secret place reached only by powerful and spontaneous magic. The sort that sends you violently between worlds without warning whether you want to go or not, like those parallel universes you read about before you turned teenager – Narnia, Gormouth, The Land. I spent half my childhood in them, but I never thought I'd see them again.

Suddenly I'm inside, he's kicking the door shut and there's a fleeting impression of tired cream and olive paintwork, dark wooden banisters and a yellow mountain bike against a wall. The place smells of old carpet, damp, last week's takeaways and people in transit. No windows. The passageway timer light has clicked off. I can barely see, but who needs to see when he's holding me like he just pulled me from the path of a speeding car? His face is buried in my neck and he's pinning me to the wall, absorbing the imprint of my body. I reach up blindly and rip open the top four buttons of his shirt, wrenching his tie loose and sideways to lay my cheek against the silky hair and warm, Shaun-scented skin of his chest. Yes. It's still here. The velvet alchemy his touch always created curls around us, warming and hopelessly exciting. Like a lazy smile breaking across a shuttered face, the slow-dawning relief of returning to the only safe harbour either of us ever really had makes us sway, and shiver.

Just the once, pleads a soft voice deep in my skull, what harm can once do? You've waited such a long time to hold each other again and it feels right, completely right, so how can there be anything wrong in it? *Watch it,* whispers another voice, far quieter than the first. *Just watch it. Remember who this man is. You're not over him, you never were over him. And you've got a husband and family now. Don't you know you're putting them on the line...?*

I try to twist free but Shaun's warm, pliable mouth is closing over mine and it tastes wonderful. And suddenly it's all right. Everything's all right. The insistent whispers fade and my body's lighting up with starlight and neon. *Just the once.* Let me stay with him for an hour, just one hour to make up for all the years without the touch of him, then I swear I'll go home, cook tea, give Jim his Nurofen and forget this man for the rest of my unnatural life... Shaun's lifting me up now, my legs are coiling round his waist, we're leaning against the closed door for balance and he's tugging open the top buttons of my dress with his teeth, running his tongue along the hollows of my collarbone, saying my name over and over as if he cannot believe it. We feel and smell utterly dear and utterly familiar to each other. Too close to need to say each other's names again and too relieved to speak, we cling together in the tolerant dark.

Whatever took us both so long?

Truly, Madly, Weekly

This morning, I'm to interview a clairvoyant from Yorkshire who reads bottoms the way ordinary fortune tellers read palms.

Sitting in my drafty wooden work-shed at the bottom of the garden, I'm squinting at the relevant shorthand notes. Not a hundred per cent sure, but it appears that a Mrs Sue Armitage of Barnsley has developed an entirely new method of telling fortunes, in which the left buttock cheek reveals your past and the right indicates your future. She also says (I think it says here) that the spirits of departed loved ones communicate with her, for a small fee, via the same route. *Chutzpah* had particularly liked her quote that: 'the bottom is, you know, kind of like a channel. You'd be amazed what I can intuit from a little dimple or two.'

Unfortunately Psychic Sue refused to take our phone interview further last week, or give me any juicy case histories, unless I come up to Barnsley and have my arse eyeballed too. ('You could be here and back in a day, love.') She wants me to experience it in person so I won't misrepresent her or make tasteless puns in print. Pleaded distance, train stoppages, and the imperatives of the school run and transient bottom boils, but she remained adamant. No buttocks, no story.

No. No. *No chance.* Water all the window boxes instead. Catch fifteen minutes of the televised extreme winter sports. But afterwards, the notes about Sue still reproach me from the top of the huge pile of work. Panicking without any constructive results, my mind beetles from one unfinished piece to another, trying to assess which deadlines are the closest i.e. due last week. Closer inspection reveals that they all are.

This is Shaun's fault. We've been seeing each other for two months now and I'm getting worried. It's work, you see. Well, and the rest. That and my new habit sitting by Kasha's bedside in the middle of the night stroking her hair obsessively and knowing I've betrayed her – betrayed everyone in this little family. That and wanting to burst into tears yesterday when Jim spontaneously, for the first time in months, actually took my hand. That and surreptitiously hiding feng shui marriage-cures round the house – our wedding photo in a new wooden frame with a red flower next to it between a pair of tiny wooden ducks ('Where's the old silver frame?' Jim had demanded. 'Don't much care for this cheap Indonesian crap'); seven long pink ribbons in the Relationship Corner ('Going into Haberdashery, are we?')

And I'm not just a bit behind at the moment (normal) I can't seem to get anything done at all. Had a stab at being sensible last month, after clearing out the kitchen odds n' ends drawer and coming across an old holiday picture of Jim, the children and self sprawled in a sunny Labrador-puppy heap under my dad's old acacia in France. We all looked happy, relaxed, trusting of each other, whole. It was worse, far worse, than even looking at our wedding pictures.

So I told Shaun that we should stop seeing each other because the thought of him is taking over and I have a husband, children whom I love, responsibilities, and a proper life I can't find at the moment but should be putting first.

We managed ten days, during which Shaun called me several times to say how he understood completely, and entirely respected my decision. Unfortunately, Jim chose to work late every day that week bar one, never coming home in time for the let's-start-over suppers I'd made him. Then the night he laughed when I wore a new black semi-see-through number for him in bed saying he'd never realised that he was married to PornoBarbie, something inside gave up the ghost.

Puce with humiliation, I stuffed the wispy black garment back in a drawer, extracted the taupe velour pyjamas Ma Harrington had given me three Christmases ago, and began to long for Shaun all over again like the Class A drug he is.

Now I can't stop thinking about him, can't help wondering when he'll call, can't resist planning what we'll play next in our flat with the curtains drawn. And when I'm not doing that, I'm transfixed by our X-rated re-runs flickering through my head or marvelling at the sheer wonder of being back with someone who, though I'd never admitted it even to myself, I'd regretted for twenty years.

All right – I know I should have grown out of this sort of thing long ago. And I know I need a brain transplant since it's doubtful that Shaun feels the same. So much for being The One he's never got over. Perhaps, in his own way, he hasn't, but he looked far too cheerful and well-fleshed to have been pining all these years. Though in fairness, he'd been admirably forthright about what he wanted. A part-time playmate, regular lunchtime sex, some steamy fun between two special friends with a special history. But he'd made it sound like the opportunity of the century, and to me, it is because I'd forgotten it was possible to feel like this. It's… it's like soaking up the sexy Mediterranean sun after years of mildewing in Hebredian damp… it's feeling, well, bloody *gorgeous* even though you know perfectly well you've started to fray round the edges. It's knowing someone's ravenous for you that makes you ravenous back and to hell with your squishy backside and the odd grey pube… it's actually *believing* that Fortysomething's the new Thirtysomething, then behaving accordingly.

Then why am I sitting slumped at my desk with my head in my hands? Huh? Oh, come on. So it's got a little out of hand, but no one's holding a gun to your head, sweetie. And this certainly beats a terminally morose husband who doesn't want me, sex that if it were ice cream would be Mr Whippy (unsatisfying, droops rapidly at room temperature) and a self-esteem measured in millimetres.

For now, I feel like a veritable bedroom diva, wondrously appreciated – and, er, even strangely guilt free. Cannot for the life of me work out why the latter should be, so am settling for being grateful. Grateful that the polar worlds of Jim/home and Shaun seem to co-exist peaceably in parallel universes, which never cross and never will.

My Higher Self knows that this is either:

a) the height of sophistication

b) jaw-droppingly stupid

c) compartmentalization taken to a psychopathic degree, and is putting its money on the last two.

But you know what? Every time I come home from seeing Shaun, it gets harder to – well, feel as bad as I know I bloody well should. Feel bad? No, make that shrivel with guilt, curl up with self-loathing. For the truth is that though I know I deserve to be set alight by messianic, marriage-avenging mullahs, I hadn't felt this physically good in years, even if the mental bits are beginning to work loose from their moorings. And in one way, it seems to be a win/win situation with even Jim getting the benefit, since finally having some good (no, make that stupendous) sex again means I seem to be giving off come-and-get me vibes that even he can't ignore. Though he now gets home later than ever and is permanently rather than usually tired, he had been startled but compliant in an absent-minded, gentlemanly sort of way.

Try to see this as a hopeful sign, though I can't help remembering wistfully what it was like to have his full attention in bed *with the light on*. Five days ago (the last time he'd honoured me with his co-operation) he'd wiped his dick on the sheet seconds afterwards then shuffled straight off for a noisy pee while I lay in the dark, remembering that we used to want to see each other's eyes when we made love before falling asleep so close we were inhaling each others' CO_2. Shaun leaves the bedside lamp on. He looks into my eyes when he comes, holds me until I have to go and won't wash afterwards. Yet Jim prefers to erase me from his consciousness the way he washes me from his skin. Is this why people have affairs? Not because they hate each other, but because one of them simply can't be arsed any more?

Sigh gustily and inspect scribbled notes again, shorthand and short forms mixed in with indecipherable longhand. Give up. Try new batch, which are almost as bad. Never used to have this sort of trouble. Think this lot's about enemas, but there again – completely stumped, chew pre-pulped pencil and call Bel for encouragement. She's a senior counsellor at the Margaret Pyke family planning clinic in Soho these days, spends her weekends campaigning for the release of Tibetan nuns, and is not as pleased as I'd hoped to hear from me.

'Listen doll, I hate to be unfriendly but there's a woman outside my office with three children under the age of six, whose IUD hasn't worked and she's pregnant again. What can I do for you?'

'Oh, er, nothing really. I just can't seem to get down to any work today.'

'Yeah? You should try this place.'

I persist, needing a chat with an old friend too badly to take offence at something, which is probably quite true. 'Fancy a drink in The Ship later? Oh come on, Bel. Say yes. Angel's coming down before work too.' Bel likes Angel. She also likes The Ship, everybody does. It's our local, and a rare establishment in these days of pub-theming and gentrification. In a city where every other watering hole is part of a chain, the place remains a one-off original. It's opposite The Stables part of Camden Market, the tangle of old tunnels and sheds which once housed London's Edwardian horse-drawn buses and horse hospital. Damp but dazzling even on a chilly April weekend, the market's a browser's wet dream for it's where you find all those things you never knew you wanted till you saw them. From velvet chapel curtains stiff with embroidery, soiled and magnificent, to hot Chinese chicken feet; from cyber-club fetish gear to Fifites Hawaiian shirts, bargains or rip-offs all, depending on your point of view.

The Ship's sienna-coloured ceiling bears witness to air permanently blue with tobacco smoke. Its single bar has wooden benches where everyone squashes up together, Guinness on draft and spice-laden Thai food which when eaten by the sensitive, disagrees violently with the head-banging Irish stout for which the place is justly famous. And should a local woman want a quiet drink on her own, the girthsome Awesome Wells, twenty-two stone of legendary Forum bouncer turned barman, personally sees to it that no one bothers her.

'Oh, OK,' Bel's voice softens. I could just see her starting to smile a bit and twirling her curly fair hair around her forefinger like she used to do when we spent all those weeks revising together for our finals. I knew she had fond memories of the pub as it's where she met her toy-boy Harvey. 'I'm sorry. You and I just work on different wavebands, that's all, and I'm a bit stressed.'

I put my feet up on the desk and exhale comfortably. 'Oh dear, why?'

'Our barge is leaking again.'

'Aw *no*. But you got it fixed last month.'

'Fixed, ha! The thing's a condemned building in water.'

A pile of papers, nudged by my foot, starts wobbling. Make a grab for it and miss. A hundred sheets of paper fan themselves out on the floor with a soft phlatt.

'Bugger.'

'Fucking right. And there was us thinking a hundred and fifty a week for cosy living quarters right in Regents Park was a snip. Well, that's why it's so cheap. It's going to sink. Any day now.'

'What? Well, how *dare* they rip you off like that –' One of the things which fell on the floor is a nasty letter from an oncologist to *Chutzpah*, claiming that I had misquoted him.

The magazine has silently passed it on, and wishes to see my reply. Funny, there have been a few of those recently. 'Listen, we've got to find you somewhere else, sweetheart, preferably on dry land. Come over tonight with the *Standard's* property pages and we'll get straight on the phone. Then afterwards, if I can coax Jim into babysitting for an hour, I'll take you down the pub. Hera will be there too – we can see if she got her tongue forked for the good of publicity after all. *Cold Metal.* Some name for her new piercing studio, huh? She's put in this special Woman's Room for all the clitoral stud and labia-ring stuff called *Divine Agony.* Apparently it's already all the rage with the Muffia.'

'Who*?*'

'The literary lesbians who run the London media scene – God, where've you been? Apparently it's the equivalent of their local nail bar: the new girls-only networking joint.'

'Jeez. Well no needle-butcher's puncturing *my* pop tart in the name of contact-collection, I can tell you that for free. But help with flat hunting – babes, you're a diamond. Your place, about eight-ish?'

As Bel puts down the phone, the increasingly familiar mix of panic and apathy returns. Rubbing the back of my neck where the muscles are all bunched, I shuffle paper around on my desk to see what surfaces. That letter can wait. What comes up is a piece on miscarriage for *Woman* (need to contact two august but elusive professors of obstetrics) and, due tomorrow, my sex advice column. Its deadline has already been extended because I've told *Us* the children have a touch of scarlet fever – it will be the judgment on me if they do get it – and as their Ed. has a family too, she was gracious. Unfortunately, I have only answered two of the requisite five letters. Need to contact the Research Institute of Sexual Therapy & Human Behaviour for that one asking about the specialised pleasure of enemas.

Also outstanding: a pregnancy monthly called *Blooming Gorgeous* wanting a thousand words on whether it is possible to have good sex when you're the size of a Renault Espace, and the men's top-shelfer *Steam* wants eight hundred words on how to give a girl nipple orgasm, which is going to be like trying to explain needlepoint to construction workers. They want it, when? Day before yesterday. Shit, shit, shit.

How can I work when he hasn't rung for a week? A week. Is that acceptable? Did I do something wrong last time? The sex was terrific (backwards, standing up in his power shower with a vibrating massage attachment). Afterwards I'd listened contentedly, cradling his head on my breasts, as he described how Debbie has marginalised him sexually since the last child was born, and always has thrush. Residual common sense detected the mating call of the married man: *My Wife Doesn't Understand Me'*, but it had made my week. Especially when he mused, in a slightly muffled voice, for he had a nipple in his mouth at the time, that he really should have married me instead.

Throughout March and April, Shaun called every day. Yet to be brutally honest, things have gone much quieter since that rubber business, though wasn't my fault the outfit split. And talking of splits, I still haven't got over that condom ripping either. Shaun regarded this as a righteous testament to the dimensions of his dick: I shot into the shower and hosed vigorously up there for the rest of the visit. Better get him to wear an extra strong one next time (Bel says the Trojan ExtraTuffs they give out at Stopes are indestructible). I reach for the phone to have another shot at trying to locate a professor. It rings as my fingers touch it. Since the dropped calls stopped weeks ago I'm no longer afraid to pick it up without the filter of voicemail, and besides, I think I know just who it is. That man is a sexual psychic.

'Zoe, Zoe, Zoe... how are you, darlin'? I've missed you so-oo much,' he croons. 'Sorry I haven't been in touch, it's been madness here. Debbie's on my back again about always coming home late. The twins have chickenpox' - goodness, they do seem to get ill a lot '– and I'm trying to float the company. It comes off, there's fifty million in it. At least. Can you believe it? I could take you somewhere really special on that.'

'Humph. I'll book, you pay,' I reply in the tone of a bus-conductress demanding a fare from a drunk, while imagining, much against my better judgment, the Noel Coward Suite on Burgh Island.

'By the way,' he adds, dropping his voice, 'this lunchtime. You busy?'

Mmmm, that voice. Like whipping cream trickling, drop by drop, into a warm vat of Ballentine's. Sit up straighter. 'Certainly I'm busy. It's a Wednsday morning, and I'm self-employed with household bills to pay.' But just the sound of him makes my traitorous heart flip like a salmon. Cross legs and visualise cleaning out our dustbins, a time-honoured trick for decapitating the libido.

'Sweetheart, you're a little cross with me. I can tell. I'm sorry it's been so long. I've been drowning in work. But I truly have missed you so-oo much this week. And today – today I just can't stop thinking about you. I've got to have you. Got to. Right now. I'm sending a cab as we speak. There'll be a surprise package in it for you to open on the way over. Something special. I know how you love sexy surprises.'

Not half - no, no, *no.* Start imagining soggy rotting vegetables in the fridge veg drawer instead of dustbins. 'Can't today.'

But oh, how I wanted to. Just the memory of really good sex can drive you mad, in fact, I'm positively wriggling in my seat and remembering last time in detail. The howling hormones, the oestrogen-fattened anchovy cream lubricating the ripe pink pomegranate that is a welcoming, willing cunt; the wire silk hair meshing across the entrance veiling labia lips puffed up plumptious with wanting: yes, all that packed into one pair of pants… hey cut that out! I shout at my sex drive angrily. Stop it *at* once. *Hell, why doesn't Jim make me feel like this any more?*

'Aw – why not, babe? It'll be lunchtime, soon. Our time. So let's spend it at our place. I really, really want to see you. C'mon honey, how about it?'

And what about yesterday, the day before, or even last week? A phone-call wouldn't have killed you. 'Said I was busy.' *Go on then, talk me into it.*

'Never mind that now. Remember how it feels? We have to grab the time when we can darlin', we're both so horribly stretched. Tight schedules, tighter timeframes, endless deadlines. What about a little treat just for ourselves? Ah, c'mon darlin', let's duck out of school for a couple of hours.'

I stand up, hoping it will make me sound tougher. It's all right for him. He can stay in at his office and catch up afterwards till midnight if he wants to but I've only got five precious hours a day. 'Shaun I just *can't* today, really I can't. I'm so behind, it's frightening.'

'Behind? I know one little behind I'd like to have in my hands right now.' He exhales slowly. 'OK. Listen to me. I want you to imagine you're walking into our flat. Can you do that for me, Zoe?'

'Why?'

'Shut your eyes. Go on, close them, that's right. See yourself locking the door behind you,' he urges. 'The hall's in darkness. All the doors leading off it are closed, and there are no outside windows there, are there darlin'? There's a figure waiting for you, leaning against the opposite wall. A man. You knew he'd be there because I told you we were going to have a visitor. So you're not scared, not yet. You're curious.

'You have no idea who it is. It could be a male prostitute. Your husband. A friend of mine. One of my staff, young and ambitious and ready to do anything I tell them to. Or someone I just pulled off the street and paid. It could be anyone. You just don't know. And despite your better judgment, it is very exciting not to know.'

I'm annoyed to find that it is. Well, I guess there's no harm in just *listening*, just for a moment –

'He does not answer you when you speak to him. You can only see, very dimly, his silhouette and smell his skin and clothes as he moves across the hall to stand mere inches in front of you. You do not think he is black or oriental, probably a white guy as he is tall and broad and does not carry a black guy's skin scent about him. But that's all you can tell and anyway, you couldn't care less. You sense he is not smiling but can feel his mind focused on you. You can almost taste his anticipation. Feel the enjoyment this is giving him. You are a little afraid of him but also you want him to touch you. To see what he will do.' Shaun's voice drifts around me like smoke as his fantasy takes shape. I can see it clearly and I like what I see. Hurriedly, try to imagine unblocking a clogged drain, but by now I can almost smell the skin of the man in the dark.

'He's tall, your guest, and well built. And he says nothing, but pushes you back against the door. His confidence suggests he has been paid to do this, and so has every right to your body. Or perhaps it is he who has done the paying? Bought you from – whom? – for an hour. He's running both hands over you, feeling every inch. Now he's now holding your wrists behind your back hard with just one hand. His fingers feel rough on your skin. He doesn't spend all his time behind a desk, this one...'

Sit down suddenly. For God's sake. But surely it won't hurt to hear what happens next?

'He's sniffing you, and licking your throat... the back of your neck... the inside your wrists, your cleavage... breathing in the essence from your crotch where he bites at the curve of your mound like a dog that wants to rut. But he doesn't speak. He doesn't have to. For he knows you're going to let him do as he likes.'

We'll see about that. Dustbins, cat litter trays, blocked sinks...

'Now he's holding you gently but firmly round the throat with one hand, his other hand sliding up your inner thigh – he's ripping down your tights, hooking his thumbs into your panties, pulling them down to your knees... you're hobbled... aaah, Zoe. How wet are you? Feel yourself, just lightly... go on, touch yourself for me. Right now, at your desk, just slick one little index finger along there. Go on, now, darlin', do it. Good girl... I know you have your hand in your pants right now. You do, don't you?'

'Might have.'

I do, too. Hey, who wouldn't? The images of disagreeable domestic tasks flicker, and go out, one by one.

'The man, who still doesn't speak, is circling his thumb inside you. Now he's sliding his index finger into your arse. Don't pull away, Zoe. Let him – let him. Good. There, doesn't that feel good sweetheart? Doesn't that feel dirty? Excellent, it's meant to. He doesn't stop fingering you but is now breathing very gently on your neck as well, sucking in air and blowing it out, extra warm, onto your skin. Can you feel the hairs on the back of your neck rise? He's turning you around now so your cheek is against the wall, his groin slotting hard into your butt, and you're liking this Zoe, you're loving it because he's also slid his other hand inside your pants at the front... but you want more, don't you? A lot more – and you also want to see what he'll do next. And so you shall, because he's just feeling for the zip on his jeans –'

Christ Almighty, go on, go on, keep talking –

'All right, I think that's enough of that,' says Shaun suddenly in a completely different voice. 'I want to talk about me.'

'You want to do what?' My knickers are down around my knees.

'Your stranger has served his purpose. I have an erection the size of a horse's, for your own exclusive use. When I'm ready, of course. And when you are. But you're not quite ready yet, are you, Zoe? Nearly but not quite there, if I know you. Which I do, don't I? So very – very – well.'

True. But call me sweetheart. Call me babe. Stop using my name, you don't need it. 'Please... go on. Tell me some more.'

'That's it for now.'

'Huh?'

'Do you want the rest?'

'Well –'

'Be at the flat. One o'clock. If you're late, even five minutes, I'll assume you won't be joining me, and I shall leave.' The phone goes dead.

Bastard!!!

1 p.m., and it's 11.50 already. It would take half an hour to get to him, a couple of hours there what with a shower afterwards and everything, half an hour to get home, then off to collect Tim and Kasha from school. Oh God, the children... whatever would they think of their appalling mother if they knew about this? No, no, cancel that thought at once, don't even *go* there, Zoe. Realise in a blinding flash of late-coming insight that I do not physically have time to have an affair, work, run a home (albeit erratically) and be a mum, even if not a very good one right now – am far too butter-fingered for all the expert juggling required. *No. Just forget it. Let him sweat, I've work to do.*

Strangers in the flat, indeed.

Now, that professor's phone number –

Ten minutes later, I'm back in the house.

A small pair of fur-covered handcuffs from which the red velvet padding has been removed, are in my big black shoulder bag. So is a six foot leather plaited bullwhip that used to belong to my colonial great-uncle from Kenya. It is old, but supple and as the handle's eight inches long, it also fits diagonally into my big black shoulder bag.

This has really got to stop. But perhaps not quite yet, for Shaun Lyon needs teaching a few manners.

Pity he'll enjoy his lesson so much.

Losing My Bus Fare Home

I am kicking myself. I cannot believe I've done this, but I left that bullwhip on the bus, together with the black, furry beg-for-it-baby handcuffs which were clipped to its handle.

Shaun was very disappointed. And the driver of the number twenty-four red double-decker who I seem to remember was a dour-looking Indian gentleman in his late fifties, must now be the proud owner of his very own six foot correctional toy with accessories. I do hope he is making the most of them.

But since then, life has been unravelling like knitting wrenched off its needles. The chaos, which has now seeped into every corner of it, began stealthily many weeks ago with me simply forgetting stuff. First, it was little stuff. A dentist's appointment, a PTA meeting, the exact word for 'bucket'. But the errors are getting bigger: failing to collect a friend's child from school (aaagh) or missing Lucia's birthday meal when I'd booked the restaurant myself.

I am also thoroughly muddled about whether I'm supposed to take those revolting Valerian and Tryptophan capsules Bel's made me try (she means well, and I guess this anxiety stuff is getting ridiculous) with food, without food, two hours before a full meal or two hours after a snack, and whether they mix with all the evening primrose oil I've been shovelling down to deal with the PMS which lasts all month, or go with the flower essence remedies. A nice naturopath prescribed Bach's Mimulus for 'fear of known things' (avenging editors pursuing copy), White Chestnut for 'worrying recurrent thoughts' (Jim finding out) and Pine for Guilt (yes). Since I keep missing different bits of this complex medication schedule, eating and working routines having gone to hell, our overworked GP has also put me on 'a short focus course' of Prozac. He said that I only need to take it once a day, implied that not even I could screw that one up and insisted that it has transformed the lives of millions.

Personally, I am not so sure. Maybe I should be proud to be a member of Prozac Nation, but the list of side effects, which even the manufacturer now admits to, is not encouraging: mental and physical agitation, depression, suicidal thoughts, violent behaviour and *dissociative reactions, making those who take the drugs insensitive to the consequences of their behaviour.*

Well, not the latter. Obviously not. But I'd certainly tick the boxes next to the agitation and mood swings. Bloody hell, do people really take this stuff?

Those promised improvements had better start kicking in soon. The doc said four weeks, it's already been six, but if anything I feel odder than ever. When I tentatively returned to ask him about time-scale, he rattled off a sixty second lecture about the variability of the individual's response to drugs and bustled me out with a repeat prescription. Went straight home, logged onto the net, and found a slew of websites set up by ex-Prozac users that didn't make me feel any happier.

Oh God, I wish I could just *talk to someone.* My head's splitting like an over-stuffed carrier bag, bursting with all the things it now contains. Guilt strobes like a wrecker's light in my guts. Brushing my teeth in the bathroom mirror, I can see the shifting shadows of secrets and lies in my eyes – which must stay lowered tucking Kasha in at night, or having an evening chat with Tim perched on the end of his bed. And Jim? I seldom dare look him in the face either, for if he catches sight of those sliding, tricksy phantoms, *he will know.*

'How's the tryptophan going, doll?' asks Bel, as she perches on our kitchen table. We have a brief and uncharacteristic cup-of-tea window since Kasha's with her second-best friend, and Tim at Karma Studios' Nei Kwando class, hopefully developing his co-ordination (or ability to thump school bullies like Lardarse, whose name have been coming up rather too often these last few weeks). 'Sleeping better? Sends me and Harv off like babies on their mothers' tit.'

She's brought over yet another plant remedy, this time from the rocky red outback of her homeland. 'Waratah,' she pronounces, thrusting a little brown dropper bottle at me. 'Says in my book it's the Australian Bush Flower remedy for *'courage, tenacity, and an ability to respond to crisis'*. Not that you're in crises or anything but you're looking kind of tired these days, and I, er... well if you don't need it, I sure could use it instead.'

The longing to tell her is almost overwhelming, like the deathly, dreamy urge I once had to jump when Jim and I stood on the edge of the mighty Grand Canyon at nightfall. But fear of the condemnation I'd see in my friend's eyes suffocates all confessions at source. 'And you thought of me. Thanks, sweetheart.'

Bel refuses my offer of chocolate Hobnobs with trucker tea, producing instead her own rice crackers dipper in carob and a biodynamic chamomile sachet. 'I need Calm,' she breathes, raking her hands through her blonde curls so they stand up in front like an angry parakeet's crest. 'Today was total roo-shit at Stopes. There was this young girl I had to see, aged eighteen and on her third termination. Same bloody bloke each time. The bugger sits there during the counselling session, knees apart and arms folded over by the door. Say he doesn't do condoms, the Pill isn't natural and that an IUD tail once spiked his knob so she's not having one of them again. This time I lost it – told him he wanted a knot tied in his bloody widger. He called the Clinic Director. Oh Zoe, these bloody men. What chance has that girl got? Why do I *bother?*' Bel has the first tears in her eyes I've seen there since her mother died six years ago, but this time they are tears of sheer frustration. I take her hand and tug her gently off the table. 'Come on, you. I know we've got no time, but let's go do something nice.'

'No, no I can't. I've got a stack of client reports to write up, and I need to talk to Harv before he leaves for the circus school's evening stint. We rowed again last night about him going AWOL whenever he feels like it. I know he's a free spirit and all, and that's one of the things I always liked about him... but he's taking off so often now. It's just not –'

'– not on. It certainly isn't. Come with me, sweetheart. You need the Marine Ices Cure.'

Twenty minutes later we are sitting on the arched bridge over Camden market canal, swinging our legs over the edge, giggling, and eating the best ice creams in North London. Or rather, Bel is stealing my Double Coconut Cream with Belgian Chocolate and I'm sneaking bits of her Mango and Blackcurrant sorbet. Ducks dip and bob below our feet, an exhausted-looking mother mallard with a teenage family of five; while a yellow and green barge with a ginger cat on the roof approaches unhurriedly from the left, intent on negotiating the lock, oh, sometime before supper. A summer-city breeze riffles our hair, blowing Bel's curls across her face and tugging at her green Nepalese skirt. She smells of her habitual Tiger Balm mixed with Jo Malone. To our left, two darting, diminutive Cuban waiters are opening up the Lock Brasserie, flinging the big windows open and wiping down tables. From the open door of a cushion-and-throw shop opposite the zoo barge's berthing place, David Bowie's old *Heroes* floats across the water. I take Bel's sorbet-sticky hand and give it a small squeeze. She grins, and punches me gently on the arm. We swing our legs some more.

'Oh, Bel. Why don't I get to spend much time with my friends any more?'

'2K-MAH.'

'That some new type of chronic fatigue syndrome affecting freelance working mothers?'

'Nah: Two Kids, Mostly Absent Husband.'

Later this evening, I'm frantic. We can't find the enchanting *Saffy's Angel* that Kasha and I have been curling up with every bedtime to encourage her to read, something she sees no point in bothering with when she can hear stories on tape. Tearing the house apart ('It's all right, Mummy, we can read *The Worst Witch* instead. Mummy?') determined that we must, must have continuity in this, if nothing else, I'm almost in tears and throwing things out of the old toy box in Kasha's room right and left when I hear Jim's voice in the hall.

Sibilant whispering breaks out from both children at once, snatches of which float back up the stairs.

'– only a dumb book –'

'But nowadays, she gets so –'

'Yeah, *whisper, whisper:* stressy, or what?'

'Sssh, I'll find it. What did you say it was called?'

'– *whisper, whisper* – yesterday, yeah, when we haden't even done anything'

'– not feeling very well recently –'

'Will she be better soon?' I creep further downstairs, eaves-dropping miserably.

'I expect so. Our nice doctor, you know, the one who gave you the banana drink for your tonsillitis? has got her some terrific *whisper, whisper.*' Shamed, I peer round the banisters and down into the sitting room. Jim is methodically shutting drawers I've left gaping, and closing cupboards swinging on their hinges. 'Got it. Come here, I'll read it to you.'

'But Mummy always –'

'Leave Mummy be for the moment.'

'Can I listen too?' pipes up Tim, unable to bear the thought of Kasha getting anything all to herself from his father, even some girlie tale aimed at eleven-year-olds. Increasingly wired when he comes back from school, he seems to find stories for younger children soothing, and these days often asks to listen in. Jim thinks this is evidence of his son's appreciation of all forms of literature. I think he's being got at again.

'If you've cleaned your teeth. Show me. Revolting, go and do it.'

'Dad?'

'Now what?'

'I'm old enough to know, right. What's really the matter with Mum?'

Sleep deprivation, that's what. Unable to do so for more than a couple of hours at a time, I am permanently tired. Important items are getting mislaid (now there's a word): keys, handbag, credit cards, the car – could have sworn I'd left it in that street – library books, Tim and Kasha's homework sheets and their dinner money.

And we keep running out of food. Today's was the sixth trip to Safeway this week because I keep forgetting to buy vital items. Last time it was the bog rolls and bread, next it was butter and milk. Yesterday the list got lost altogether, and I stood shaking in Safeway's booze aisle for many minutes before failing to remember what we needed apart from Frosties and cabbage. Jim ostentatiously put a little of both on his plate and ate them, very slowly, for his supper.

Tampax are turning up in the fridge, biscuits in the freezer, clean clothes in the dirty linen basket and cat food in the Hoover cupboard. This morning I put dishwasher powder in the washing machine (it foamed like a rabid dog) and reduced the children to helpless sniggers by trying to start the car with our front door key. Constant sell-by date confusion means food's rotting in the fridge. We're getting regular threats to terminate our gas, electricity, water and sewage because the bills keep disappearing and I have no idea whether they've been paid. Our plastic money's racking up interest charges because I can't find the statements. Assuming this is simply shag-vacancy, I've been hoping it will pass. But it hasn't.

Then there's the Gratuitous Crying. I cried when Bel's smelly old cat died: a hostile and unlovely beast, all claws and naked resentment. When the irritating Wagner was re-homed, I shed buckets. I cried when I dropped a bowl of Shreddies yesterday, cried when my computer hung, cried because I can't read my shorthand notes any more, and I'm crying now because I am so blasted tired. Mornings are the worst, for a millrace of anxiety washes over me the second the alarm goes off. When I prise sticky lids apart, I'm already panicking that today, this morning, something truly bad is going to happen. Yet five minutes later, I'm skipping about the bathroom because I just know this is going to be the best day of my life. What the fuck is this? Hormones? Psychosis? My imagination?

The worst of it is that it's come to feel usual.

The last few amps of nervous energy I've got left are all being spent on Shaun. It's possible to put up an excellent front for him for the couple of hours it takes, then return home convinced, despite mounting evidence to the contrary, that this is all wonderfully rejuvenating. During the hours I don't see him, I can just about handle dressing, getting the children to school then wobbling back to the shed at the bottom of the garden to stare at the computer. Yet even there, it's increasingly hard to concentrate. I still have ideas for articles. Lots of them. I just can't seem to finish any these days, then when I do, they're late.

And people are starting to notice. Last week, *Yes* (who had graciously started re-commissioning) dumped me again and all Karina would say was 'I think, sweetness, that we're getting a little too used to each other.' *Chutzpah* has stopped giving me work since I failed to get them those additional features ideas on time and calls to suggest more are met by Meredith's voicemail. Only *Steam* remains. And unfortunately they want a piece called *Lucious Lads – the Lure of the Ladyboy* based on explicit interviews with a second division football team who'd partied with three transvestites in the Grantham hotel, only noticing that the objects of their admiration had penises rather than pussies when they were too drunk to care. They've got the picture captions already: 'Surgically tightened is sexy', 'Better tits than a Page 3'.

Writing has always been my refuge. The one place in the gridlock of a life ruled by children, debt-juggling, a depressive husband and an ill-advised affair which had clear purpose, definition round the edges and a smooth momentum all of its own. Now that last bastion of ordered mental space had been colonised, its neat white picket fences trampled, the locks that kept the craziness out, picked and shattered.

I am so behind that if my copy was as good as my excuses for not writing it, I'd be raking it in. As it is, the remaining few assignments sit like dead albatrosses around my neck, smelling worse by the day. If this is – whisper it – losing it, it isn't just the plot that's gone AWOL. It's the script, the theme tune, the credits, the exact location of my numbered seat in the great cinema of life, my ice cream cone and the bus fare home.

Agh, the phone. What now? *What??*

'Mrs Harrrington? Marjorie Hobson here, the Headmaster's secretary at Primrose Hill,' announces a not-too-friendly voice.

'Oh! Hello. I mean, good morning –' *Tim... please don't let anything have –*

'It's concerning the appointment you'd requested with Mr Westchester. The one at 9 a.m. this morning.'

'Oh no, I'm so terribly sorry –' *hell-fire and damnation –* 'I, er – I've been rushed off my feet and, and I'm afraid I just totally forgot. No excuse, which is awful when I know how busy Mr Westchester must be. And after you were so terribly kind as to squeeze me in at short notice like that too,' I grovel, kicking myself hard.

But Mrs Hobson isn't having any. 'We cancelled another Parent who had a long-standing appointment to discuss the running of our Summer Fayre to fit *you* in, Mrs Harrington,' she elaborates, a quiver of reproach creeping into her Tooting Bec twang. 'You were, if you recall, most insistent. But perhaps it wasn't so very urgent after all?'

'It was, actually. It still is, though I really am sorry to have missed this morning, and inconvenienced you so.' Do I crawl some more? No. The Mrs Hobsons of this world aren't placated by mere apologies: they want blood, substantial donations to the gym fund, and for petitioning parents to go away quietly. 'But could you *please* fit us in again sometime this week? I think, in fact I'm sure, that Tim's still being bullied, and –'

She bridles down the phone, as if the school's entire pastoral care reputation is being called into question. 'We're keeping an eye on the situation as you know, and frankly Mrs Harrington, our staff never see any indications that –'

I feel my claws growing long, and the big black leathery bat-wings of maternal protectiveness beating the air above my head. '*Excuse* me, but last week, our son came back with a cut above his eye, having allegedly walked into a door. Next day his new trainers went missing, reportedly lent to a friend who doesn't have a name. His history project book has been defaced. He's been getting some nasty text messages – from whom, he won't say. Does that not suggest, even to *you,* you that, that –'

'We have read all your letters Mrs Harrington, and the headmaster has noted their contents. So in consideration of your on-going concerns, we can offer you a window a week from today. For as I am sure you can appreciate, the headmaster is a very busy man.'

Last week, I forgot three days on the trot to go and water some plants for our friends Rufus and Annie Cottingham-Smith. They live off Hampstead High Street, go away at enviable six week intervals and won't trust a) their cleaner b) anyone else they know, with care of their banks of delicate

Malaysian orchids. Because I once did a stint in a Kew Gardens coffee shop they have got it into their heads that I know about temperamental greenery, and being enviably rich, have offered me a tenner a day plus return taxi fare to see to theirs whenever they're away. And I'm afraid that if someone is stupid enough to pay me seventy pounds a week plus travel expenses for watering a few ferns, I am certainly not (yet) stupid enough to turn them down. However, it would help if I could remember to do it.

Last night, three pink, eager faces had appeared at the sitting room window around eight thirty at night when I was on my way up to bed, and Jim was down The Ship – something about my having invited them to dinner.

This can't go on.

The Thin Pink Line

Strung out, broke and hate each other's guts?

It's either what Lucia calls a Spousal Exchange Opportunity – time to legally separate and ensure you get all the decent furniture – or the ideal moment to go on your annual holiday. We choose the latter.

There is much to put behind us. The boiler's packed up, Shaun wants to do golden showers. I'm down to a third of my usual salary, and so worried about money (not to mention The Rest) that my periods have ground to a hesitant, knicker-spotting halt. Then yesterday morning, Seventh Wave heard they'd been turned down for a lucrative Pringles ad starring an animated crisp called Melvyn, which was to have kept them afloat for the rest of the year. Without it, they are likely to sink without trace by October.

Then a week ago, there'd been the Awkward Encounter. My mum had ascended up the Brighton line and swept us all out for early dinner at the place of the children's choice for her birthday. Seated in Smollensky's Balloon in Covent Garden watching a clown do conjuring tricks, blowing up the balloons provided by the management, trying to turn them into farting sausage dogs as per instructions on our napkins and giggling, I glanced casually across the room and saw none other than Shaun doing the same. He was at the best corner table with three boys (the smallest having just climbed onto his lap) and a woman with frothy blonde curls who was roguishly cutting up his pizza and feeding it to him. Alerted by the force of my appalled gaze, he had glanced over for a second, stiffened, raised his glass minutely then shifted his chair so he had his back to us.

'Now come along, darling,' my mother kept saying. 'Stop poking good food round your plate, and eat something.'

And Jim had some more bad news in the post this morning. I found him sitting on the stairs in the hall, his nose in a letter, rubbing his face tiredly.

'What's up? Not another big bill?'

'No, it's from Inkpress. You know, that little radical publishers in Ireland.'

'Oooh, the ones who say they like to nurture new talent? They run that first novel thingie, don't they? What's it called, the Axeblade Award? No, First Folio, that's it. *Brilliant*! Anything doing?'

'They say here,' Jim starts folding the letter into smaller and smaller sections, 'that my novel isn't a novel as such but strikes them more as therapy; assure me that it's no less worthwhile as a first try for all that; suggest I remember that there's a great deal to be said for writing for its own sake, and wish me luck.'

'Oh.' Sit on the stairs above him and begin to knead his rigid shoulders gently.

'They also say, in the interests of constructive criticism, that most of my dialogue has, what was it now? oh yes, 'all the clarity and pace of a conversation between two illiterate drunks –'

'Bastards,' I mutter inadequately, kneading harder.

'– and suggest that I might like to try again once I've got all the autobiographical stuff out of my system.'

'Darling, I didn't know the novel was about you.'

He removes my hands. 'It wasn't.'

Our vacation destination is The Farm. A sunny sprawl of ramshackle buildings basking in the green and gold Dordogne, owned by my ex-Marine father who battles daily with the rheumatism, that slowly twists his powerful frame and saps his formidable energies. The place boasts an alga'd swimming pool; a cavernous dust-choked hay barn for droppers-in with sleeping bags, and a warped wooden veranda built by Dad and Jim eight years ago that's now smothered in purple passion flowers. In July, the house is surrounded by acres of sunflowers and fields of indolent, creamy cows peacefully chewing their days away, hock deep in the richest grass in the country. When the burn of the day makes the dishevelled great garden uninhabitable and temperature glides into the nineties, everyone drifts into the shelter of the farmhouse's ground-floor rooms, with their icy stone floors and fireplaces you can sit in. Here at last is space we can only dream of in our cramped little house in Camden. Which would nevertheless have bought two such establishments, with money left to eradicate the scum from the pool and re-surface the pock-marked tennis court.

As inept but enthusiastic players, everyone loves that court. It democratises the game, the uneven surface producing such random twists to the ball's bounce that it levels out good players with bad. The umpire can hop up into the crook of one of the old fig trees around the edge, eat the pudenda-like purple fruit in season, and shelter from the sun under broad green leaves while they adjudicate vicious disagreements over the score. The cries of the middle classes at play frequently drift across the garden to the house: 'Forty Love? That was fucking well out! Are you fucking well blind?'

The place is always full as my Dad had been married three times and has five children (including me) from his three brief and unlikely marriages, the first of which was an eighteen-monther to my own gentle, ladylike and rather eccentric mother, Isobel. Despite the fact that she threw him out when I was six months old, she is the only one he can now stand.

Though thankful not to have to live with him full time, my half brother and sisters all adore our father and come as often as they can bringing along their friends, school projects, and detailed complaints about their mothers to which Dad is more than happy to listen. As a former commando, ex-criminal barrister and once-keen rider to hounds, he misses bloodsports dreadfully – at least, in the army, he had been able to shoot at the enemy and in court he'd been allowed to savage witnesses. These days, in the absence of any dissident guerrilla fighters, guilty defendants or fleeing wildlife he has to be content with sniping at his exes.

They include wife number two, a stunning but humourless blonde with eyes as cold as her native Norway's ice floes, whose cheekbones once graced *Vogue*. Lavinia is now fifty-three, and big on animal rights. Having ditched the Yves freebies for army surplus, she has also, to my father's horror, cropped her river of platinum blonde hair because it got in the way when lay photogenically in front of Dover-bound cattle trucks. She and Dad lasted a record five years during which she produced two nervous but beautiful children, sixteen-year-old Ralph and fifteen-year-old Giselle.

Wife number three was Edwina. Small, with a head of red-blonde curls, the build of a whippet and the disposition of a ferret with PMT, my father had fallen for her scalpel tongue and teenage-boy backside. Her children by Dad include the equally sharp-tongued Jemima (fourteen), a pale, clever girl with skin freckled like the inside of a foxglove who regards the world as being populated by fools unworthy of her notice. The result is that she seldom speaks to anyone, and reads constantly to avoid having to do so. Missy, her sister aged twelve, is Jemima's polar opposite, liking nothing so much as other people's business, noticing everything and gossiping incessantly. Anywhere you see small groups of children with their heads together, and hear shrieks of 'She never!' and 'You didn't!' you'll be sure to see her head of mad strawberry curls shaking with forbidden laughter.

Time flows like slow honey here, while the motley visitors come and go. However, you have to enjoy communal living and ignore the stupendous mess for like all barristers, politicians and actors, Dad needs an audience even more than he ever needed a salary so there are never less than ten people staying. Yet The Farm generously absorbs then all, provided they help with the food bills, don't all hit the pool at once, and do a few odd jobs about the place.

His technique for facilitating the latter is lethal.

'Morning,' booms a voice as you lie catatonic in the noonday sun. And there will be our father, Panama over his nose, stumping along with his six-foot shepherd crook of polished beech, a lengthily hand-written list in his battle-scarred hands. 'Got a couple of little things here that need doing.'

Family, liggers and hangers-on sit up guiltily as one, shaking the sweat from their eyes. We pass round today's list, which reads, in the neat writing beloved of military management:

'Weed driveway (ass. children)
Repair tree-house lower plank.
Whitewash kennels. Front only.
Fix ballcock – outhouse loo.
Dead-head clematis on south side of porch.
Linseed oil veranda roof timbers.
Trim lavender patch.
Cook/shop for basic supper for 14: guests coming (Zoe)
Tidy linen cupboard. Is disgrace.
Return cow to Farmer. In washing line area again.
Remove dogshit from front lawn. Explain to Mme Vaubarnier she must keep Matilde *away* (someone with decent French – Jim?).
Do moles.
Many thanks.'

'No hurry,' he assures us genially, as we scan it, aghast. 'Take your time, take your time.'

'Um – I'd be happy to do the plank,' suggests the gentle curly-haired scriptwriter, a younger brother of one of Dad's barrister mates, here to recover from a ferocious divorce. Wincing, he peels pale, sticky limbs off the plastic lounger.

'Oh, I'll take the cow back, I've done it before,' offers silver-blond Ralph grandly, picking the easiest job on the list for the dairy farm is only half a kilometre away. Returning stray animals always earns a reward of an alcoholic nature from the farmer's wife, who is fond of young men.

'I have to write to Mum.' Such is her agitation that Jemima actually speaks as she hotfoots it towards the house.

'I promised I'd finish my French project this week,' puts in Missy swiftly. 'It's Bridges of France and I've only done Pont Neuf and The Bridge of Avignon –'

'Blimey, I'm burning,' observes their friend, thirteen-year-old Sam, as he struggles to his feet. 'Gotta get some sun-block.' Sam has never used sun-block in his life.

'I'll just go and see if Daddy wants me to trim his hair first,' murmurs Giselle sweetly. 'He *did* say it was bothering him.' 'I'll help,' squeaks Missy. 'Ooh, bags me too,' adds her friend Ana, a half Italian eleven-year-old of such advanced physical development that everyone takes her for fifteen until she opens her mouth.

'That wasn't on the bloody list,' mutters Jim.

The girls form a pretty group fluttering around Dad and manage to make the titivating last for the next hour and a half by also attending to his toenails, neck, blackheads, ear whiskers and nasal hair, clustering around him in the dappled shade of the apricot orchard like something out of Chekov. He is very happy.

Jim, whose sunny disposition has been returning steadily since we arrived, watches them and grins. 'No such thing as a free holiday I suppose,' he says planting a kiss on the top of my head. 'OK, I'll do the cooking, if you do the moles. Tim, Kasha: get weeding for an hour. Find your sunhats and T-shirts, then take a bin-liner each. I want to see them full.'

'Why *us?*'

'I *hate* weeding.'

'– and then this afternoon you may watch *Matrix 3* on my laptop.'

When the temperature hits thirty-eight centigrade, I give up sticking sonar thumpers down the molehills which have sprung up all over the lawn like fleabites on a forearm to stagger back into the house, stepping over the damp swimwear, stinking single trainers, Adidas shorts and Cacolac cans which lie scattered across the veranda and along the hall. Ashtrays pyramidal with fag ends brim on every surface, soggy towels and bikinis (Giselle brought six) drip on the banisters and over the back of every door. A tittering Tim and Kasha have opted for *Goldmember*, having filled half a bin-liner of weeds between them.

The smell of tomatoes, garlic, and fresh oregano from the patch by the tumbledown stables wafts in from the kitchen as the sounds of people following their own pursuits in peace drifts through the house. Muffled giggles come from the tree-hide round the back, and there is the dry shuffle of yesterday's *Observer* as Jemima sprawls in the striped veranda hammock, wrestling with the sheer acreage of her first broadsheet read. A quivering haze distorts the green and gold of Dad's rioting garden under a heat-bleached sky. A cow lows lazily to the left, and a small scarlet lizard scuttles across my foot, seeking shelter in one of the many cracks splitting the farmhouse's two-foot thick walls. This is more like it.

After months of constant anxiety, months of waking up worrying before even opening my eyes, we can simply sit and stare at sunflowers. And I haven't thought of Shaun in days: in fact, I haven't thought of him at all. That hopeless addiction to his touch, physical presence and lewd suggestions, the constant craving to hear his voice and feel the attentions of his probing fingers have dried up in the hammering heat of sun. In fact, it's a relief not having to find the energy to come up with the goods any more, since his tastes have been getting very specific of late. Or could it be that, when he's being not being morose and dismissive, I really prefer my husband? Who maybe, just maybe, is starting to like me back again a little bit? Shaun is beginning to feel more like an exam I've finally passed, albeit one in something pulse-stopping like nude sky-diving.

No one tells you what it's really like to have an affair when you're married, do they? They are too mindful of being rumbled themselves to discuss the practicalities, though feelings ('Frank has made me feel like a woman again') and sexual attributes ('Nine inches, terrific buns') are legitimate topics between female friends. Films gloss over the problematic logistics, presumably because you'd never get a bum on a cinema seat again. So do books. For the truth is that it's exhausting, expensive and best left to those who are both childfree and independently wealthy, for you are leading two lives. Sometimes even three.

They don't tell you how it feels to swing between lust and panic daily. How the strings of excuses and cover stories told to your legitimate partner and your children begin to stick in your throat. About all the different kinds of lies there can be: the lies about where you've been, the lies about what you've been doing, the lies by omission for information withheld, nor about the sheer scale of the necessary ongoing economy with the truth. They never suggest that the constant battle to stay with the logic of the fiction and the dogged focus required to keep your stories straight, will drain you of every last ounce of energy (and serve you right). They don't say: 'How would you like it if someone did that to you?' because you wouldn't. And you won't want to think about that.

But these last few days, since starting to feel back in my body again rather than floating a permanent three feet above it (perhaps the Prozac's kicking in at last?) I have been thinking a good deal about how I'd feel if someone did this to me – and the late-coming guilt is booting me so hard up my cheating backside that it finally occurs to me that Shaun isn't worth it. What the hell do I think we've been doing these last few months? Trip down Memory Lane, my arse. I've been living in LaLa Land.

Standing barefoot, soaking up the cool of the hallway's stone floor and watching dust dance an aerial ballet in the sunshine that's streaming in through a half open shutter, it finally sinks in. That man has been using me as a freebie park n' ride for months but I've been too besotted with our shared Past to notice. It also strikes me that there is something important which I'd overlooked about the past that had better be taken on board immediately – that it is, by definition, over.

Is it too late to repair Jim's and my marriage, too late make things up to him without telling him exactly why? Logically speaking it shouldn't be, for he doesn't know anything (er, does he?). *Maybe not. But didn't you read The Rules? You play, you pay* hisses the scarlet lizard, who's now inching up the wall.

'Hello,' says Jim snuggling up behind me, his hands automatically going to my breasts and my bottom slotting easily into his groin. I jump guiltily, but force myself to relax as he rotates against me lightly, experimentally. *Life is definitely looking up.* It's been so long since he asked, rather than acquiesced. I co-operate, but cautiously, lest he become nervous and flee.

This seems to be the right level of response, since he presses against me some more, a once-familiar hardness materializing in his shorts. 'Gorgeous tits,' he whispers, slipping his left hand inside my T-shirt and rolling a nipple between slim, practised fingers. He gives the other breast a gentle but appreciative squeeze. 'I've done the food. Why don't we go upstairs and, ah, put some after-sun on you while they're still glued to Fat Bastard and Austin Powers?'

When we wake up in a contented sprawl of limbs and sheets, the sun has shifted and the burn is off the day. Screeches and splashes are coming from the pool, and the silence of the house suggests everyone else is down there. 'Want a proper coffee to help wake up?' yawns Jim, sliding long legs out of bed. The light from the window turns his muscular back warm gold, and seen sideways, his recently-acquired gut is definitely shrinking. His dark red hair is tastily tousled from bed and there is a fantastic smell of warm musk and man in the room. In fact, this is one lovely bloke but it's much easier to see it on holiday when neither of us is working, and he's not permanently pissed off. 'Oh, yes please –'

'For tits that cute, anything.' He leans over to kiss the nearest one before wrapping my faded green sarong round his lower half and going off in search of caffeine (must get that wrap off him when he returns – it's proved essential this summer for hiding the cellulite that's been creeping onto my thighs these last two years.) Lapping up his physical appreciation like a thirsty cat, I'm also knocked sideways by something which for the first time in years, feels hearteningly like the love that used to wash through me every time I held him, absent now for too long. I want to pull him back down on the bed again when he returns so we can fall asleep, nose to nose, tangled in each other's arms like we used to every night till disillusionment, tiredness and small children got the better of us. Might it be possible to get some of that closeness back after all? Can we find our way back to the time when we were us?

I squint down underneath the sheet at my breasts. They are indeed looking fuller than usual, and it's no good pretending they're not – which means – oh hell – that there is something which can't be put off any longer. Removing a small oblong package from its hiding place in my canvas handbag, I pad off to the loo, squat, and pee inaccurately over a plastic wand bought yesterday from the local pharmacy.

Five minutes later, the wand has developed two pink lines. Two. Which means, and since my period did indeed fail to arrive properly last week for the second month running, that I am now anything between seven and nine weeks' pregnant. Sit down heavily on the bathroom floor, both hands protecting my stomach. So it wasn't the financial worries, the guilt and the stress after all. One ruptured condom, just one and this is what happens. Oh bloody hell, of all the absurd, *unfair* – I mean, what are the odds of that, at my age? Huh? *Pregnant.* Accidentally pregnant by a lover in my forties – how undignified, how inappropriate, how bloody *unlikely* can you get? A baby. A… a miraculous, against-all-odds little baby the size of your fingertip, who in three weeks will be able to suck her own. Oh dear God, Christ and Mother Mary, what happens now? *What have I done?*

Jim had a vasectomy two years ago.

Will he demand a DNA test? Ever speak to me again? Be present at the birth? Shaun certainly wouldn't.

Something else is badly wrong too. I am trying to panic and nothing's happening. I'm not down in the nettles behind the pig-pens, trying to phone the British Pregnancy Advisory Service on the mobile. I'm not swigging Dad's Bombay gin by the bottle. The alarm switch is Off.

It's off because already, there is no question that anyone, or anything, will be allowed to hurt this baby. But also because – years ago – I used to dream secretly, guiltily (and because he'd disappeared by then, pointlessly) of one day, maybe one day, having Shaun's child. But not like this. Never like this. Not now I'm married to someone else whom I have loved with all my heart. Not now there seems to be a chance for our marriage after all. And certainly not now there's a whole family to keep together… but God Almighty, what am I thinking of? *What if there's something the matter with it?* yelps what's left of my common sense. My eggs must be past their use-by date, or at least their best-by date… what about Down's syndrome then, and spina bifida? Ante natal tests aren't infallible; what if they miss something? And what about me hitting (agh) *sixty* when the kid's still in their mid teens – how about that, then?

Then there's Tim and Kasha: whatever are they going to think? Seeing as they got there first, they might never forgive me even if they thought the baby was fathered by their dad.

You can't foist another sibling into older children's lives without checking how they feel about it first. If they had to handle both a new baby they never asked for, and separated parents (both of which would be my fault) would they hate me, turn delinquent, become depressed? Perhaps run away from home, ask to go live with Ma Harrington *(no)*. What?

You cheated!' an angry squawk floats through the open window. It is Kasha.

'I did not. *You* cheated, you always bloody do,' bawls Tim.

'That ball hit your legs.'

'Didn't, did *not* –'

Jim returns, bearing coffee. 'Think I'm going to have to do a bit of umpiring,' he grins, chucking my sarong onto the bed and shucking on fraying denim shorts. 'Here'. He holds out a chipped but steaming old mug with Darth Maul's face on it and disappears out of the door, cracking his head on the lintel as usual.

'Bloody did cheat!' shrieks Kasha.

'Well, stress-*eeee*.'

'Bloody did, did, did –'

'Sore loser, yeah – ow! Shit! Dad, you saw that, right? You saw what she –'

No, I don't think Jim is going to want another one.

What the hell am I going to say to him? Which words can you possibly use to tell your husband you're pregnant by another man?

Supper is a protracted French affair that night, at which everybody except me and Kasha get pissed, including the twelve-year-olds because Ralph has spiked a jug of Orangina with the duty-free Absolut vodka he keeps hidden in his rucksack. Tarzan howls and sounds of growing bodies belly-flopping into the pool continue far into the night. Jim sits up till two in the morning with my father and the scriptwriter while I slide off to bed early taking a reluctant Kasha with me, lest she be drowned by drunken teenagers bombing the shallow end in the pitch black of the rural night.

My daughter snuggles down in the wide parental bed, a light sheet lying soft and cool over us both. We can no longer make out what the men are saying, but the talk beneath our window is flowing, companionable and punctuated by a good deal of laughter: a comforting soundtrack to fall asleep to. The light from the verandah dims as the oil lamps hanging from its rafters go out one by one; the citronella flares die down and only the red glows of the men's cigarettes remain, floating in the dark. Kasha's comatose in minutes but it takes me a long, long time to fall asleep, one hand on her shoulder. The other aches to cradle the tentative new life inside me – and I think I can feel that it's another little girl – yet with my here-and-now daughter snuggling up, it feels flagrantly disloyal to do so. Next morning she and I wake hand in hand to blinding sunshine, with my free arm wrapped protectively round my abdomen, and Jim on the other side sprawled half out of bed.

It's only nine o'clock but the heat, sticky and searing, is already rising and I must be up and doing for today we go home. Finish cramming our belongings into Harriet to the sound of terse exchanges about personal packing-space quotas (*Take those Steve Earle CDs out of my suitcase, Dad*). I'm just filling Leclerc carriers full of crisps, biscuits, apples and Evian to stash under seats and on laps, when Giselle, Jemima, Ana and Missy arise from their beds to collapse at the kitchen table, yawning, scratching and staring into space. Ralph and Sam are nowhere to be seen. When no food is forthcoming, the girls condescend to pick irritably at a packet of Frosties bars offered reverently by Kasha, who, thrilled to be of service, is now casting about for something further to press upon them.

The car's metalwork creaks alarmingly in the heat as we each hug my father in turn, wishing we could stay forever. I am not looking forward to a fourteen-hour journey, for I have woken up feeling sick and out of sorts. Not to mention dreading going home, dreading telling Shaun it's over, dreading choosing between coming clean with Jim or getting a secret abortion (*not that, OK? Never that,* I tell the small life deep in my belly*)* and very afraid indeed of seeing our fragile new armistice blown to hell.

'Everything all right, darling?' asks Dad kindly, relinquishing me last. Briefly I consider the facts: a late-coming illegitimate pregnancy, an affair which I cannot handle and never could, a failing career – and how right now, more than anything the world, I should like to stay here and be Dad's housekeeper. He is getting so absentminded, it's doubtful he'd even notice someone going into labour right in front of him. I also want to stay because we love him and can see he is beginning to need someone to look after him, though he'd sooner eat slug pellets than admit it. His bad days come more often now, and he is looking tired today in the strong morning light.

'Of course. We've had a brilliant holiday.' I kiss him on each cheek and adjust his battered canvas bush hat. 'Thank you. Thank you so much. It's been – it's been lovely. We just don't want to go back to our debts and stuff. That's all.' He bear-hugs us all over again and waves till we can't see him any more, already relishing the next lot of visitors and the diversions they will provide: 'Three old Marine pals. Bringing a raft-load of drink, plus some political female from LSE who wants some peace to finish her book. Well, she won't get much of that here.'

Thirty kilometres from The Farm and back on the featureless autoroute, we've already given up playing *I Spy* and the kids are fighting over what to watch on the laptop, when it starts. Gently at first. So gently. By Anglouleme I can't seem to get comfortable. By Poitiers, a pain like a belly stitch has taken hold. When we stop for lunch at the next autoroute complex, there's a sly scarlet trickle sliding down the inside of one thigh.

I pack my pants with STs from the travel shop, and pray.

But by Tours, I'm starting to feel icy cold, and by Rouen, to shake. Jim's sigh suggests this is making a rather a fuss over what I've assured him is just a heavy period. On the boat, I stagger for the hot, airless loos while Jim takes an enthusiastic Tim and Kasha to have their first burger and chips in three weeks. Hiding in a shiny aluminium cubicle, head between my knees, pulses of blood flowing into the toilet, I can't stop the tears because I know I'll never see her now: it's just a case of how long this is going to take. The smell of metal, vomit, piss and pine will stay with me forever.

Newhaven, everybody off. Tie my cardigan round my waist to hide the scarlet stains on the crumpled sundress. With a wad of stiff paper towels stuffed inside a new pair of knickers purchased from a Freshen Up machine in the Ladies, I weave down to B Deck to find the rest of the family already in the car. 'Where've you been? I was about to come and look for you,' snaps Jim fretfully. He is beginning to get very tired, since he had been doing all the driving and child-minding for twelve hours now. 'Hi Mum, how's your tum?' chirps Tim, before turning back to *Mission Impossible III*. Kasha is mercifully asleep. I give my son's head a pat, slide back into the front, shut my eyes and pull my knees up by jamming my heels into the edge of the seat 'Rough one, huh?' inquires Jim.

I can't speak.

After two more toilet stops on the road to London and a slow crawl through the suburbs, we are five minutes from home and just passing the sparkling new facade of University College Hospital on Euston Road when I find myself tugging Jim's sleeve. 'Let me out.'

'What?'

'Please.'

To his credit, he pulls over. I lurch out of the car thinking 'It's three hundred yards. Go.' Then fall flat on my face on the pavement.

Next thing I know, I'm lying on a hospital trolley, flying down interrogation-bright corridors, one pair of double swing doors after another whipping open. Someone crying. A circle of four faces with green hats bends over me, the light flaring off the glasses one of them wears like a morse code signal for help at sea. A stab in the arm, blessed sleep racing in like a flash tide. Then waking up in a hard bed, arm in a drip which itches, tucked away in a quiet corner of the ward, hearing the hum of other people keeping their voices low, the squeak of rubber soled shoes on the floor and seeing Jim's anxious face wavering into view. 'Where's Tim and Kash?'

He touches my hand, and smiles down at me. 'With Angel, at home.'

'Sorry about all that –'

'They won't tell me what's wrong with you.' His familiar face is chalk white and sweating. 'What's going on?'

'Um –' What was left of my brain rolls up its sleeves and digs down into the sludge. This is where being a health journalist might come in really useful for once. 'Well, from where the pain was, and all that bleeding, er – it could possibly have been a burst uterine blood vessel –' Squint nervously up at him to gauge his reaction.

'Jesus, you could have bled to death.' Jim grabs my hand and holds it against his face, looking stricken. 'There, Zoe, hush. It's all right darling, there's no need to cry like that –'

Oh yes, there is. If only you knew. I don't deserve an atom of your love and sympathy. I feel deeply, bitterly ashamed and want to bang my face against the wall. OK God. You've made your point. I get it. I'll do the right thing. Tomorrow. Tomorrow, when I've had some sleep. And I'm very, very, sorry. Tell *her* I'm sorry too. Tell her that it wasn't her fault, that it was mine. Tell her – that she didn't do anything wrong, she just had the wrong mother. And please God, please, please will you look after her for me, now you've got her?

Unfortunately, God doesn't think this is good enough.

The next morning after runny porridge, leather toast and stewed tea, Jim drops in on his way to work with a small pot of pink roses and a concerned expression. Seconds later a young Korean doctor makes a beeline for us, smiling kindly. 'Ah, good, you're awake Mrs Harrington.' She perches on the bed and lays a warm hand over mine for a second. 'And you are Mr Harrington, yes?' she inquires, taking in 6ft 2in of dishevelled, red-haired Jim.

'Yes. Look, is she OK? She will be OK, won't she? What happened to her?'

'She'll be fine now. But I am so sorry Mr Harrington –' she begins.

Oh no. NO. Shut up, shut *up*. 'Erm, hey, hang on –' I croak before being silenced by a fit of coughing as the residue of the anaesthetic leaves my lungs.

'– so very sorry about the baby.'

The word lands between us like an unexploded landmine.

'Which baby?' asks Jim, reasonably enough.

'That is, the miscarriage,' she corrects herself gently. 'I'm afraid there was nothing we could do. It's commoner than people think. One in eight confirmed pregnancies ends like this before the tenth week. You must both be –'

'Just a minute,' interrupts Jim, levering himself slowly to his feet to tower over us. 'Would you mind saying that again?'

'It was probably never viable, you see,' she continues soothingly. 'It's likely there was something wrong with it, and that the body recognised this and let it go. Women's bodies are wonderful things you know. They have such instinctive wisdom.'

Watching outrage battle with incomprehension on Jim's face, it looks like someone else round here is about to be let go too.

'I'm afraid we also had to remove a damaged Fallopian tube, possibly the result of an old sub-clinical infection. To leave it in place might have put your wife at risk of ectopic pregnancy in the future. Though really,' she added delicately, 'from a purely obstetric point of view we don't *especially* advise pregnancy at all after the er, early forties watershed, unless the circumstances are –'

'Am I hearing right?' Jim leans over me, his voice dangerously level.

I slide down the bed, wishing I could vanish underneath it. 'We do understand,' empathises the doctor. What a nice man, I can see her thinking, good-looking too and so worried about his wife. 'Even when the foetus is just a few weeks, it's still a baby to the parents, isn't it? But believe me, it will have been for the best.'

'I'll say. *Zoe?*'

'We have a wonderful counsellor,' she adds, laying a hand on his rigid shoulder. 'He's very good with male partners. Perhaps, when you've both had time to adjust?'

Jim sends me a look of such blazing contempt it nearly takes my eyelashes off. Then he wheels round and stamps out of the ward.

'Mr Harrington, your pain is most understandable,' bleats the doctor, scuttling after him, stethoscope trailing, 'but really, you must also consider your wife at a time like this –'

I pull the sheets over my head.

Oh Bondage, Up Yours

It's raining, it's four weeks later and I'm locked in the shed, sobbing my guts out. Books and papers carpet the seven foot desk, the floor, my lap. Cannot make sense of any of them.

Though all the files have logical labels, I can't even decide where to put each bit of paper. I mean, does this behavioural research survey: 'The Truth About Italian Stallions' from the University of Milan about how eighty-two per cent of Italian men orgasm in under ninety seconds, belong in the Sexual Dysfunction, Foreign News, the *Why Sex Aids* folder or the bin?

I am also very tired, and look like shit. Since the miscarriage, wake-up time's around four every morning and I lie there, riddled with guilt and misery, while Jim sprawls on his back snoring peaceably like a badger with asthma. Perhaps I should have taken the four weeks off like the doctor said rather than start trying to work again after ten days, but we need the cash. And with little to do, I find myself staring into the parched hollow where a baby used to be, knowing I'll never have another, knowing how badly I've let her down. How badly I've let everybody down.

Voicemail carries several messages along the lines of 'Where's the copy?' Four, at last count, for today alone, and I daren't even open my Inbox. Have kept Shaun at bay by sending a few: 'things to sort at this end' holding messages, but apart from two phone calls (friendly but not over-eager) and a couple of suggestive e's, I've heard nothing more. Clearly he has other distractions, which is fortunate though not flattering.

A vicious headache's battering at my temples. Am obviously coming down with something. Stumble back to house in search of industrial strength painkillers and chocolate. Locate a half eaten block of Galaxy under the sink, next to two tins of Whiskers, and the Always STs – so that's where they went – a welcome find because the bleeding still hasn't quite stopped. Wrench open the fridge door in search of milk for more coffee to see the Flash in there, next to the chocolate chip cookies. What half-wit put those in there? Why, me. Does this mean the mince is in the biscuit tin? Unfortunately, a quick check reveals that this is so.

Take now milky coffee, painkillers and biscuits into office and pick up another file half-heartedly. The little shed feels like a rubbish cupboard whose walls are sliding towards each other – shades of Edgar Allen Poe – not the cosy retreat I've always loved. It also seems smaller than it was yesterday, and I could swear there's something in here that smells. Perhaps it's me.

Oh God. It's twenty past twelve and I have done nothing, today, nothing. The house is a tip as usual, the children – God, the children. I've got to go and get them in three hours, and must be a) cheerful and b) punctual, because since the hospital, both become anxious if I am so much as two minutes late.

Do something. Write something. Why can't I bloody work? The phone's screeching again. 'Yes?'

Silence thrums along the wires. I wait, sensing someone on the other end. They don't speak, but as I put it down again, I am *positive* I hear someone – laugh. Shiver, and look at the machine with dislike. Who in their right mind wants to ring someone up, breathe, snicker, then hang up? Oh God, what if it's someone we know? There's been a spate of these over the last few days, and I'm now starting to get nervous of picking the thing up at all. Yet how dare someone do this? How bloody dare they...

Peer cautiously at my Inbox – a hundred and sixty-six unopened messages, mostly press releases but at least six looking suspiciously like the sort of thing I should reply to. Yesterday there were a hundred and twenty. Cannot face opening them. Instead, lay my head on the desk for a little nap. Technically I know my cranium's resting on about a week's work: that it's only tying up the loose ends, getting the last few little quotes, facts and figures in for each of the pieces then e-mailing them off. Yet I cannot seem to do it. For these days if I make a call and the person isn't available I simply cannot find the energy to try again in half an hour. There is potentially two thousand pounds' worth of features here but I seem, as Ade would put it, to have lost the knack of closure.

It's not so much fear, lack of motivation (one look at our bank statements is enough) or a mental block. It's just that all I really want to do – the one thing I'd really like – is to get into bed with several packets of Jaffa Cakes and that battered old copy of Jilly Cooper's *Riders,* draw the curtains and never get up again. Ever, ever, ever.

Oh please, no. There's another call coming through.

I used to leap on the phone within a single ring, thinking, yippee, another commission, a contact calling back, a friend on the line, Shaun fancying a quickie. Now it is more, as Dorothy Parker put it: 'What fresh hell is this?' Dimly, I recognise that I am at my wit's end. I just can't believe how quickly I got there.

Jim's voice. Him, I'd better speak to. So far, he has not even asked who got me pregnant. Nor has he discussed the likelihood of his tubes rejoining spontaneously and it having been him, though I showed him a *New Scientist* cutting saying it's as high as one in five hundred during the first two years and have denied all extra-marital activity. He is now careful that we never touch, but taken to calling every day, ostensibly to see how I am. He also watches me all the time. Watches me, instead of talking to me.

'Hi, sweetheart.'

'Ah. You're there.'

'Of course I'm here, where else would I be?'

'Yes. Well, I'm doing our monthly cash-flow here. How much did you say you're projected to earn this month? I need a figure,' he continues in the slightly bullying tone he's adopted recently whenever my earnings, or lack of them, are mentioned. 'We're quite tight at the moment. As you know.'

I did know. Seventh Wave has had no juicy ads for six months now. The show-reels go out, but the jobs don't come in. They cannot work out why.

'Well, I've got around two grand's worth nearly ready to send out. They just need a few tweaks – honestly, I'm on it, really I am – then I'll invoice and it usually takes six weeks from there. Um, hopefully…'

'Good. But I seem to remember that you said this last month too. Forgive me, but is it the same two thousand – or a different lot?'

There is a bit of a pause. 'The same,' I whisper eventually, covered in the shame of financial inadequacy. There is a bit more silence while Jim suppresses his natural response to this. Finally, he restricts himself to: 'I see.'

'You don't. You can't. I'm not even sure that I do.' Am major failure. A pathetic has-been.

He sighs. 'I think we'd better sort this out tonight, after the kids are in bed. Find your invoice book,' *what book? I send polite letters*, '– your last two months bank statements, your work schedule sheets –' *which?* – 'and your business cheque-book stubs. Then when we've got that out of the way, I'm inviting my mother up for a few days. She – she can help you sort out the house, or perhaps do the school runs and a bit of shopping so you can get yourself straight.'

Accounts Panic begins to spiral, followed by a blast of the defensiveness which Ma Harrington's presence invariably triggers. 'No way.'

'Why not? I'm fed up living in bloody chaos, even if you're not.'

The shed fills with a blinding vision of Ma Harrington brandishing her tartan suitcase and a party-sized can of Shake n' Vac. Cornered, I give the phone a savage yank in an instinctive attempt to keep the woman at bay. It flies out. Scrabble for it on the floor, but holding it my sweaty palm I can see the double plastic prong is twisted out of shape. My God, the business line. What the hell am I going to do, no one can call me –

Hey. No one can call me. Feel a shaky smile spreading across my face. Well – *good*. Perhaps I can finally do some work without being interrupted. The phone can be fixed later. And maybe if I look at some new stuff rather than the fag ends of all the pieces yet to be finished I'll feel inspired, actually finish something and get paid for it. Then Jim may even address a neutral remark to me, bordering on civility. ('Mumm-eee, why's Daddy so cross with you all the time?' 'He's not cross, darling –' *no, more like livid, repulsed and rejecting* '– he's just been rather worried recently, and he's working very hard.' 'Not cross with you because the baby didn't work?' 'No, sweetheart.' Short pause. 'Is that why he's never back before I go to bed any more – he's working hard?' 'Yes. Yes, that's it.' Kasha's expression suggested this was, even as adult excuses went, pretty unsatisfactory, but she let it go.)

Let's see now: my first piece for *Mine!* An 'investigative' article exposing the carrion underbelly of the billion-dollar cosmetic surgery industry i.e. how fat and collagen from corpses is being used to create luscious lips, fuller breasts and bigger dicks ('a single body is worth around eighty-five thousand pounds to the industry, twice as much if its bones are also harvested'). The editor says to be sure to cover what happens if the costly transplanted fat blackens and becomes necrotic, an occupational hazard. Perhaps we'll just try something else for the moment.

Bitchin' wants – oh. A piece about the scandal of a certain French family car manufacturer doing crash tests involving child cadavers rather than plastic dummies. With pictures. *Chutzpah* has relented, and commissioned twelve hundred words on why phone sex is the new safe sex (no icky body contact). *Steam* requires a devil's advocate job on why the age of consent should be lowered to fourteen for girls (*'And keep it short, right? This is a five or six stop mag')*. Surely I didn't agree to do that?

Shut the Pending file with a snap. Jesus, they've all gone sex and death mad. Why not combine the two with a piece about how necrophilia is the new natural Viagra, and have done with it? No point leaving anything to the reader's imagination any more, they haven't got one. They lost it somewhere between the media force feeding them details of Jordan's new boob job (rumoured to be dropping a cup size in a bid to be taken more seriously) and what Brad cooks Angelina for brunch.

Dah – celeb voyeurism, gore, and sex, sex, bloody sex. Who *cares*? Only the magazine editors who've got to hit their circulation targets. *Nothing's* new anymore, nothing's shocking, and we're tiring of the Next Big Thing so fast it barely has time to appear on Oprah because our attention spans aren't just short these days, they're Lilliputian. Saving It's the new sex, random's the new order, wheat's the new Coca-Cola, nylon's the new linen, bum cracks are the new cleavage, analogue's the new digital, underwear's the new jewellery, the North's the new South, and, if the BBC is to be believed, slander's the new libel. Say what? *What?*

And anyway, says who?

Why the TV, magazines and newspapers, that's who. And I've become one of the cybourgs who are supposed to tart this crap up with a few well chosen statistics or doctors' quotes to kid the public something kinky is really happening, that this truly is the latest bit of schlock to crawl out of the slimy pit of reality – readers, would we lie to you? not the last convulsions of yet another brain-dead journalist on a deadline with nothing to say. I don't understand what went wrong. This isn't how it was supposed to be; this is not what I meant at all. I wanted to work on stories that mattered, pieces that shook people up, articles that showed the truth behind the million pound ad campaigns; I wanted to tell readers the stuff they weren't meant to hear about, to warn them when they were being conned. But Jesus Christ, *this is all such useless bollocks...*

Suddenly I'm on my feet, my feet, kicking open the door and hurling the heavy files one after the other into the muddy patch of briar, balding Astroturf and ironic plastic tulips we call a garden. I'm wrenching out the answerphone and throwing it into the raspberry canes growing along the fence, hearing the crunch of plastic hitting wood and plastic coming off worst. Now I'm running into the house. When I come out again I've got Jim's Zippo lighter and am looking down at my three fat phone books of precious, hard-won contacts. Dog eared and solid, it's taken twenty years to compile this lot. They bulge with names and numbers written in black ink, pencil, red biro and purple felt pen, watermarked with the ancient coffee and tea spillages. Some of the older contacts are surely retired, disgraced or dead by now but without these books I am nothing, for editors don't pay for what you know, they pay for who you know. Yet I am pulling out the pages one by one, setting light to handful after handful, watching them burn, whirling round and around on the soggy grass, flinging them in the air and screaming '*Yessss!*'

'Fuck the lot of you! Yee-ha!' I'm laughing my head off. My God, this is better than Prozac any day. We're already up the Fs when it hits me this is a celebration and we could do with a bit of party music. Race back into the house and drag Jim's big speakers as near the back kitchen door as possible for this moment calls for vinyl, music with heart and history, the big black platters that set your feet on fire before the advent of the soul-less silver CD. Scrabble through our racks of beloved but neglected old LPs, but the only music that flicks a sufficiently large V-sign is vintage punk, not heard in this house these fifteen years. Ha! Perfect – X-Ray Spex's immortal anthem *Oh Bondage, Up Yours!* floods the garden, and am just returning to the flames with more fistfuls of pages when our right-hand neighbour pops her head over the fence.

She looks like Betty Boop (wait till you get a few sleep loss lines on your forehead sweetie, then you'll have your fringe down over your eyebrows like the rest of us) and we've not seen her face to face in months. However, urban osmosis being what it is, we knew that she's in her late twenties, has four-month twins, a mother who comes to help each day, and no horrible job. 'Everything OK?' she asks cautiously, which is dialect in our street for: 'You're making a great deal of noise.'

'Having a little clear out...' Set light to a handful of M pages and throw them up in the air too. 'Bombs away! Off you go my pretties.' *Oh Bondage* is ending and the next track's crap so I scamper back inside and stick on an ancient party tape. It kicks off with The Jam's *A Town Like Malice* so I dance about a bit, amusing myself by crumpling the next the next few sheets of S's and Ts into balls and throwing them into the fire from different vantage points, like a ball-in-the-bucket village fete game.

'Oh. Good one,' she ventures warily, which round here translates as 'Would you like my psychiatrist's emergency mobile number right this minute?'

I lob in the Qs and Rs in a single big ball, push back my sweating fringe and beam at her. Betty Boop stares, then remembers her manners. This is Camden Lock. One does not peer over garden walls nor express curiosity over next-door's behaviour unless there is irrefutable evidence of someone being butchered next door, like entrails all over the decking.

'Well. So long as everything's all right.' She ducks back down behind her fence again. I am touched, for I can tell she really means 'I feel your pain, sister, let me help you.'

126

'Never better,' I screech happily, above The Who's *Won't Get Fooled Again,* whose raucous disillusionment seems just the ticket. There go the U's to Ws, blazing into infinity, and bloody good riddance. I'm just adding my precious cuttings file to the flames (which up until then I had been quite proud of) when a little voice in my cerebellum pipes up: *But that's the last four years of your best stuff. You'll have nothing to show future employers.*

Well, ain't that the truth? hoots another voice from the depths of my brainstem, and calls for a large joint. Dropping the remains of my last contacts book on the fire and skipping back to the shed, I scoop the piles of work off the desk – which I'd been agonizing over only half an hour ago – together with the big red business diary. It contains all the deadline dates, interview times and press conference details for the next few weeks.

No, no, no – you won't know what you're supposed to be doing or where you're meant to be, wails my Superego. My Id agrees cheerfully, and suggests some serious alcohol intake. Out comes Jim's treasured Glenfiddich. Chugalug it straight from the bottle, have a coughing fit, pour a slug of it on top of the diary, add a pile of my precious reference books including *Gray's Anatomy* and *Roget's Thesaurus,* then stand back to watch the whole lot go up like a torpedoed oil tanker. The heat is remarkable but only lasts for a few minutes. Warming my hands over it, I watch contentedly as my professional life turn to ashes.

There is now so much smoke that Betty Boop's mum is whisking the babies' designer washing off next door's line, looking very disapproving. Leaving the fire to its own devices I trot into the kitchen, and from the pine dresser drawer, remove five postcards bought when we last went on a day trip with Mum from Brighton to Eastbourne. They featured the suicide's favourite, Beachy Head. Address one to each of the editors to whom I owe work making a guess at the postcodes, write: 'Why don't you go and jump off it?' on the back and sign my name neatly below. Then skip, heart as light as helium, off to post them at the end of the road.

There. Almost finished. Just one small thing left to do.

A little further down from the post-box is the red and black curve of Camden Market bridge. Run down to it and peer over the edge, watching the willow trees' leaves quiver in the light breeze and the slow swirl of opaque green water. Four homeless men from Arlington House are sunning themselves below against the towpath wall. Leaning over as far as possible, I throw the silver shed key into the very centre of the canal, watching the shining streak it makes before vanishing forever. As it does so, the manic momentum that's been powering this morning's orgy of destruction shudders to a halt leaving me feeling like I've been up all night for a week. Then the glorious elation fades too, leaving in its place – absolutely nothing.

It makes a very pleasant change.

I wander home, kick off my boots and fall into a dead sleep on the sagging sofa amongst the cats, cushions and this morning's cereal bowls until it is time to collect the children from school.

'You're in a good mood,' says Tim cautiously, as I hug him fiercely and hand over the latest copy of the violently coloured Nintendo magazine he loves, plus a bumper bag of Minstrels. He's right. The thudding angst that's stalked me since the operation has gone: in its place, a soaring heart and the desire to hug total strangers. I feel great liking for everyone I see, and begin to wonder if someone's slipped me half an E.

'Look,' says Kasha, pointing skywards, as high above us, a sliver zeppelin sails across London, its progress slow, stately and free as a cloud.

The only worry now is money. Consider this as I potter about the kitchen, my heart at peace, grilling chops and boiling sweet-corn for the children's supper. Better not tell

Jim till I've got another job though, preferably something that requires neither thought nor responsibility. And I can now deal with his reaction when it comes (fury and incomprehension registering, oh, say a ten on the Richter scale of marital discord) because finally, at last – *I don't give a shit.*

We drop into Morrison's after the children's supper to buy Jim's dinner and cat food for our current three strays. I'm afraid they'll have to go too, and the idea of saying No to the animal charity for once feels pretty good as well. The supermarket is only two minutes down the road making it the biggest corner-shop in town, a shimmering cathedral of food, an aircraft hanger stuffed with every conceivable edible perched on the old tram-shed site, dwarfing the market, Victorian rail sheds and new Legoland townhouses huddling around its skirts.

Swinging effortlessly through the great building's revolving doors, we step into a different world: one where the lights are always bright, the temperature forever constant and, thanks to some smart air-ducting, the scent of new baked baguette permanently wafting past the entrance. Calm looking people in green and white striped uniform are pulling loaded carts around the aisles, stopping and filling up where necessary. All the time in the world. We watch them for a few moments. One is even smiling.

The deputy duty manager, a tall skinny man apparently half my age with a pustule on his neck, an assessing eye and engaging smile, tells me the basic wage is four pounds twenty an hour rising to four pounds sixty-five when you were experienced. He also says that mature ladies are welcome (thanks a bunch, Junior) uniforms provided, and mums preferred as he's found staff more reliable if they have kiddies. Hours are flexible, there is a ten per cent staff discount and I can start next Monday because they're a bit short at present. I am to bring references with me on the day: two, preferably hand-written, no relations. Induction training lasts a week, but we get paid for that too. Fill in the sheaf of forms he offers me on the spot, shake his pale, damp hand and leave swiftly before he can change his mind.

'Do not, whatever you do, tell Daddy.'

'Why do you want to work *there*?' asks Kasha, eyeing me narrowly and taking stern possession of my left hand as she marches along. 'Can we get free food? Aren't you going to do writing any more?'

'I just need to do something different for a bit. That's all.'

'I feel like that too,' says Tim kindly, touching for my other hand, 'towards the end of term. And sometimes,' he adds quietly, as if to himself, 'near the beginning, and the middle too.'

Maternal antennae go ballistic. Why should he have to put up with this day after day? Vow we will get him into a gentler school *now* even if we have to triple mortgage the cats and hock every single thing we own (not that there is much worth popping). As if in answer to an unspoken question, Kasha starts absently rubbing my little engagement ring with her forefinger, her hand still in mine as we pass the brightly lit windows of the Chalk Farm pawn shop. Gunter & Parr's window display is crammed with watches, silver picture frames, Edwardian hip flasks, ugly gold jewellery, and the place is considered by those who live around here to be a truly retro chic way to raise some instant readies.

We stop as we always do to see if there's anything good in there, noses up against the glass, breath eventually fogging the view. That ring will join the others in there tomorrow. And we'll use whatever money I can possibly persuade them to give us as an immediate part-deposit on a new school's fees. Perhaps if we tell them why, and take Tim along as Exhibit A, they'd be generous? Probably not. In forty-two years of trading they've heard every hard luck story going, and the violet-rinsed Frau Gunter who runs both the shop and her husband with a well-manicured iron first is tougher than old Doc Martins.

'Hey,' I whisper in Tim's ear, 'how about you and me taking the day off tomorrow? And, hmm, possibly the one after that?' His slow, revelationary beam says it all. Try to drop a kiss on his head. He dodges it, but if anything, his beam gets bigger. Some things you don't need to say to your children out loud.

Kasha takes my other hand again and we walk home past the old Theatre Bookshop and Bridge the World in companionable silence. It is now past seven o'clock but still light and the first soft speckles of summer city rain are beginning to fall, giving the pavements a satiny sheen as home-going cars and taxis form an endless, muttering chain all the way down Chalk Farm Road. As we turn into our street, we can see Jim's acid-green Kawasaki swinging to a halt outside the house and hear the familiar reproachful roar the bike always made as he guns its engine into silence.

'Dad-eee!' squeals Kasha, dropping my hand and pounding down the road, bunches flapping. 'I'll show him my new magazine,' says Tim, accelerating. 'It's got a review of *Karnivore: Wrath of Cortex II* in it this month. He was asking about that yesterday.'

Follow them sedately, inhaling the heady scent of a ready-roasted chicken that I haven't had to cook myself. Mmm-hmm.

As I draw level with our house, my eye falls upon Harriet, rusting bravely on the other side of the road, and I feel a tug of great affection, mixed with sadness. Because, dear old lady, the time has come to let you go too: your gallant wheels represent a good half term's fees...

Briefly visualise Jim's reaction to having no car. Not pretty.

Stunted Emotional Growth

The cold blue light from Jim's laptop draws me like a magnet. It squats on the sagging velveteen Chesterfield in the sitting room amidst a welter of papers spilling from his briefcase, and the be-noodled remains of a Wagamama takeaway for one. Jim is nowhere in sight. I can't resist a casual peek en route through from hall to kitchen, arms full of overpriced emergency rations from the corner shop on Kentish Town Road.

He's halfway through a message flagged: 'Anne Widdicombe on e'. That's good, he's having ideas for his humorous animated shorts again. In the continued absence of any ads to film, Jed wants Seventh Wave to put a couple of wacky three-minuters together. He reckons that, spliced through the company's show reel, these may catch the attention of some of the agency creative teams – frequently twenty-two-year-old wonder duos raking in a hundred thousand a year and so zeitgeisty, they talk only in the present tense. Lean over the back of the sofa for a closer look.

– or possibly in the last couple of weeks, Anne Widdicombe on e: won't listen to reason, scary turns but spookily cheerful. Well, you said it would be a useful psychological focus exercise to describe my feelings for her five words or less. Hasn't helped. So come on psycho-boy, if this was a private case and you were charging me £80 a session, do I stay or do I go? Answers on a postcard please, to this address while I'm still at it. Also... There's no time to read the rest as a hand snakes over my shoulder and flicks the e from the screen with a shake of the mouse. 'You said you were going up to Morrison's to do the week's big shop,'

132

mutters Jim, looking flustered. 'We're out of practically everything –' He's round the sofa in seconds, shutting his laptop with a snap, gathering his papers, fussing with the sofa cushions, looking everywhere but at me standing there with the sliced wholemeal, Frosted Shreddies and four pints of semi-skimmed.

'I – couldn't face an hour slogging round there. Went to Pete the Greek's instead. Got some thing to tide us over for breakfast.' *Anne Widdicombe is my least favourite woman in the whole world.*

'Didn't hear you come in.'

'Evidently. Jim –'

But he's already scooped up all his things and appears to be almost squeezing past me as he heads for the door, despite there being plenty of room. 'I'll just say goodnight to Tim and Kasha, OK? Then I have to go out.'

'Where? It's supper time.'

'For a run. Feeling stale –'

'But it's raining.'

'Well, a swim.'

'Kentish Town Pool shuts at eight.'

'Then I'll take Ade out for a drink. He's a bit down.'

'That's nice. You'll be able to deliver your email in person.'

It's gone midnight before he returns. And he doesn't smell of drink.

In the interests of maintaining his distance, Jim has also taken to sleeping on Tim's floor, ostensibly to give me some 'peace and quiet' at night. And having adopted the traditional English Public School method of dealing with feelings – yes, you too can stunt your children's emotional growth for twenty grand a year – he's still not discussed the matter of who had the privilege of getting me pregnant. Though I'd give anything to be able to have a proper talk with him, being the sort of man who'd sooner walk naked down Regent Street than have any sort of confrontation, he is out by eight in the morning, back at nine, even ten, at night. Wonder which new after-work pub he's discovered because no one's mentioned seeing him in The Ship or the Dog & Duck for weeks. When he does get back it's a shower, sandwich, and a newspaper read stubbornly in the kitchen if I'm in the sitting room, or vice versa. The last few times I've tried to talk to him, he has walked out leaving me in mid sentence. Weekends, he takes the children out (never me) to the places we've always gone as a family – Hampstead Heath, Primrose Hill, Marine Ices, the old Parkway Odeon. In fact, it's remarkable how little you can manage to see of someone when they're married to you.

Perhaps our last exchange, the one in the kitchen where he asked if Harriet was languishing down the garage again, and I admitted to selling both her – well, she was mine, not his – and my engagement ring, has put him off conversation for good. When we got to the bit about us having Oyster travel smartcards instead, and me going part-time at Morrison's ('You mean you're going to earn even *less?*') so Tim could stay home before starting at – gentle, private – Cavendish House School the second we raised the rest of the fees, he finally lost his temper.

'And do you mind telling me where you think we're going to get those from? Or the next few year's worth, come to that, now you've lost Tim his free place in the state system by defecting to the private sector?' he bellowed with all the conviction of a NewLabour-voting state school supporter who'd attended one of the top public schools in the country from the ages of five to eighteen.

'Perhaps we could, um, second mortgage the house, or something?' I faltered. 'I know other parents who have, and for the same reason. *Please* Jim. This is really, really important –'

'Jesus Zoe, you want to do *what?*' Jim mastered himself with visible effort.

134

'Look, OK, I do realise Tim's not especially happy at school. And of course I'm concerned, who wouldn't be? But it's also true that you are, if I may say so, over-reacting. I understand that you're worried (you're his mother so that's perfectly natural) but I'm not convinced that it's as bad as you think: I mean, Tim's never said anything to me about bullying. And I'm sorry, but the bottom line is that he'll just have to hang on till things pick up at work, which I hope to Christ they do, so I can get some proper money in.'

'You just don't get it, do you? Fine! I'll just – find the cash from somewhere myself. Perhaps my mum – or maybe your dad since he's so hot on education – could lend us a bit, just for a little while?'

'I'm not asking my father for a penny, we'd never hear the last of it. Anyway, he's a vicar, he doesn't have any money. That nice Georgian vicarage they live in belongs to the Church and they give him what amounts to pocket money on top. But why,' he demands, banging his fist on the old kitchen table, 'do you ask if you can do something, get told 'No', then say you'll do it anyway? Or throw yourself headlong into situations that affect both of us without consulting me? And that ring was special, I *gave* it to you. It was a token of my commitment to you, Zoe, a mark of our love. Yet you, you just cash it in like some bloody savings coupon without a second thought –'

'Jim, it wasn't like that, OK? Not a bit. It's more – oh please try and understand – it's more that I had nothing else to sell, and it's a question of what's necessary at the moment. Your ring *was* precious to me, really it was, but Tim is even more precious. Doesn't his happiness – and safety, godammit – mean more to you than a piece of jewellery, *a thing?* Don't you care about your son?'

'Of course I do, but I also care that we are heading for real financial trouble at work, and that you've not thought this through. Say you do scrape together enough for this term – what about next term? Or the one after that?'

'Like I said, we'll second mortgage the house,' I shot back at him, quaking. 'Or second mortgage my half, since you can't bring yourself to touch yours. Who cares? It's only *money*, for Christ's sake. Right now I would be happy to sell every single thing we own if it meant Tim could be happy. And as his father, so should you.'

'Mortgages don't work like that Zoe, they –'

'Stop trying to confuse me with economics, you pompous git. It's you who doesn't understand, because you've never been bullied in your life. Well, *have* you? Big Jim Harrington, captain of Highgate's second eleven, Head of House, one of the boys… you were *popular* at school Jim, you were *ordinary,* right? You weren't a bit eccentric and dyspraxic to boot. So of course you've no idea what it's like to be picked on day after day and have your self-esteem hacked to shreds. But surely even *you* couldn't have missed the expression on your son's face every school-day morning?' Which provoked a major rant about how broke we are, and how there's no point in being married to someone who insists on acting unilaterally.

'Well, how am supposed to I act, when Tim's in trouble and you just won't listen?' But Jim had already flung out of the room, and the last we saw of him that night, he'd got the Ballentine's open and the TV on loud.

'That discussion didn't work so well for either of us, did it?' I venture an hour later, raising my voice to compete with the soundtrack to Jeremy Clarkson driving a new all-terrain off-roader in *Top Gear*. 'Could we try again?'

He keeps his eyes on the screen. 'Shut the door when you go out, would you? There's a draft.'

Late Again

That was the last thing Jim said to me. He now communicates with me via Tim, voicemail and yellow Post-It notes on the fridge.

But I don't need that, his absences or his late night returns to tell me that Shaun was a big mistake. Huge. Because I've learnt something in these last few months, something that should be written in large red letters on the wall of every home that houses a restless heart. *Re-starting a relationship with a special ex is like standing on the doorstep of a once-beloved house, trying to slide your old key into the door – only to find some kiljoy's changed the locks.*

Whatever gave me the idea it was all right to do such a thing, or that there was a hailstone's chance in hell of handling it? Boy, was I stupid. The state I was in, I couldn't have managed a new stick insect, much less the ex-love of my life. Now, thanks to a few months' supreme idiocy, it looks very much as if I'm losing my husband along with my marbles, my work and my sense of proportion. And it probably serves me right that Jim is now the one man in the world I want. Well, he would be, wouldn't he? seeing as he hates my guts.

Yet he is the same man who's been on my side, and me on his, for so many long years and that is where we should be still, not at opposite ends of some emotional wrestling ring. Now his shuttered face accuses me daily, and he grinds each questing tendril of communication I send out underfoot. ('Sweetheart, would you like a glass of wine?' 'Yes, I think I will just pop out for a swift one.')

Jim used to be one person who didn't mind me eating baked bean sandwiches in his bed, who knew all the words to

Dancing Queen but wasn't gay, and the only man I could ever truly sleep with rather than stay awake next to. He used to say I was the only one who believed in his novel without even having seen it, didn't object to his singing socks and made him laugh before breakfast. Now he can't bear us to be in the same room. Yet thinking about him, I cannot help sensing the tidal pull of a marriage, which might, even yet, be salvaged. There's good stuff in there too, fighting for breath beneath all the toxic silt; stuff I don't reckon we should give up on without trying just one more time.

Jim's fund of *Beano* jokes, the smell of his hair when it needs a wash (red earth and sweet sweat) his obsession with the films of the appalling Ingmar Bergman, and the fact that when sent out to get a nice comfort curry he will return with chilled sushi on the grounds it's high in protein – I like them all. I like them because they are part of the package that makes up the man I've been too dumb to realise I love. The subsidiary matters of his gloom, sexual disinterest and coming back too late to be helpful of an evening can surely be worked upon. If, that is, he ever speaks to me again.

What was it he shouted that night over a year ago, when I accused him of never saying he loved me any more? *Why do I have to say it? Why don't you just try looking at what I do?*

I'm looking now. And I see someone who had spent the last two years trudging through our marital wasteland, doggedly hoping it would get better. Someone who, while he was at it, has continued to bring home the bacon, take out the rubbish and defrost mince for stray dogs he didn't want as he battled daily with the diverse disappointments of a failing film company.

Yet if he also did some looking, he might see someone as well. Someone who's been trying to keep things cheerful at home while he's been terminally morose; who managed to earn a bit of extra money while they were at it and ensure our children were warm, loved and fed. Someone who kept trying to talk to him, offer sex and suggest help for his black moods despite the fact these things were consistently turned down. Someone he's made feel about as attractive as an old slipper, but who couldn't help loving him anyway despite the fact they often didn't even like him.

Unfortunately, this person would be on far stronger ground if she hadn't – oh Christ, the very thought of losing this man without a fight is unbearable, this man who suddenly seems so necessary and important. So what am I going to do about it then?

'Mumm-eee, what's that funny smell?'

Shit, the children's Irish stew's burning – that's what you get if you try a bit of emotional introspection round suppertime. Scraping layers of incinerated pearl barley off the bottom of the saucepan (stuff Ma Harrington and her shaming us into making home-made food every night: this never happens with chicken nuggets) I scald my hand because I'm so busy remembering what it's like trying to share a bed with Jim these days. His warm, solid nakedness used to be the ultimate haven of comfort and safety: now the curve of his back is about as welcoming as Arctic tundra and there's a quasar force field separating us.

We can't go on like this, like the walking marital wounded. It's time to try and start over if I can find the strength to make him hear me without insults or outrage, and the courage to listen to what he might have to say. For tonight, though he'll never remember (and probably wouldn't care these days, even if he did) is the anniversary of the day we moved into this house with nothing but boundless optimism, a second-hand mattress and a bottle of Rebel Yell whisky. Yes, I am going to make him a nice dinner tonight and we are going to Talk.

'Mum –'

'What?' Tim's in the bath, a flannel draped modestly over his lap, and I'm combing his hair through for the nits which are endemic at Primrose Hill, where he remains in waiting – punctuated by many days off – till I raise another six hundred quid. Ha, there's one, 'Look sweetheart: a big fat momma, with legs and everything. This is why we have to –'

'Yeah, cool'. He scoops the louse off my finger, pinching it flat between finger and thumb. 'Did you know armadillos always have four babies of the same sex?' he asks, apropos of absolutely nothing.

'Really?'

'And with seahorses, it's the males who have the babies.'

'Smashing idea.'

'How do they manage that? Have they got fannies as well as dongers?'

'Well, I'm not quite sure about –'

'And by the way, what's a hermaphrodite?'

'That's a jolly interesting question. I'm very glad you asked it. Can we talk about it later?' He slides under the water's surface and farts theatrically.

'Come here, Kasha, your turn.' She retreats to the loo seat. I advance, comb in hand. 'Gah, Tim, you *reek,*' she squawks. 'Noo-ooo… my hair's *fine* – ow, leave *off*, Mummy –'

Eventually we all flop onto Tim's bed to re-read the bit in *The Order of the Phoenix* where Harry has to face a Ministry of Magic tribunal for producing a Patronus off Hogwarts' premises. Once they're in bed and settled ('Can I have another drink… the Vicar's being sick on my trainers… but if I don't have a cardboard starfish head-dress for drama tomorrow, I'm *dead*') I can sidle off to do something about looking a bit better than I do.

Dinner, and candles (half burnt down, but grown-up white ones not the children's old coloured birthday ones) are miraculously on the table by eight thirty. Have had a shower, knocked back the last Red Bull, wriggled into a tight T-shirt, reasonably bum-flattering jeans and flipped on some lipstick. Better put a bit of sexy but civilized something on the CD in case of awkward silences: that new Norah Jones would do, though when last seen, Kasha had been using it as a frisbee. All set, I wait expectantly.

No Jim.

By nine twenty I've rung his mobile three times ('Sorry, the person you are calling is *not* available') drunk two glasses of wine through sheer nerves, and swallowed four Pro-Plus because the Red Bull is wearing off.

At a quarter to ten it's three glasses, and have started picking at the supper. It is the best that Chalk Farm Road's mini Sainsbury (gourmet microwave meals for the cash-rich, time-poor) could provide and looks positively home-made now it's been decanted it into earthenware serving dishes, with shredded parsley on top.

Now it's ten fifteen and I'm contacting local hospitals – UCH, The Royal Free, The Whittington – even phoning Jed and Ade, but they've not seen him either. Please God, don't let him be hurt. Not now. I'm sorry about everything I did, God, really sorry, but it won't happen again ever, ever, ever so please won't you send Jim home? Make him talk to me. And while you're at it, God, don't let the food congeal.

The celestial hotline must be oversubscribed this evening, because that was forty minutes ago and Jim's still not here.

Pouring another glass, and wondering which female friend would, at this time of night, be good for a little advice on the subject of Unaccountably Absent Men when Lucia springs to mind. Her pragmatic cynicism on the vagaries of the opposite sex has been a source of illumination for many years. Light up a Silk Cut (since the miscarriage I'm back on a dozen a day) and call the Chalmers-Hulme Advice Line.

'Probably out on the razz, duckie,' she suggests, raising her voice the sound of breaking glass and squeals of laughter. 'From what you've been telling me over the last two years, it sounds like he needs to reconnect with his inner party animal.'

'Not something *you* ever need worry about. Blimey, what's that racket?'

'Oh, just having a little drinkie in Cassandra Mapplethorpe's office after work. Take your hand *out of there*, Miles.'

'Oh Lucia, bad time, I'm sorry. But do you think I should –'

'Well if you want my advice, you'll invite some night owl over to supper pronto, and be discovered having a nice time with them when your husband does finally deign to roll up.'

'Oh sure, like who? It's nearly eleven o' clock.'

'Go through your old address book. No, call LateDate. You've have seen their ads, I presume: Instant Escorts for Independent Women? My dear, it's London's fourth emergency service for girls. They can always find one some lovely man who's a mere tenner's taxi-ride away, so long as you call before midnight. Use my account number. *Sandro!* Take that dress off immediately. It's a Gucci original and your year's salary wouldn't buy it –'

'I can't order up a man like he's a *pizza,* just because my husband's a bit late.'

'Nonsense, it'll teach him to be on time in future.' The background volume at her end rises to a crescendo. 'Brace up now, sweetie,' she shrieks above it. 'Show a little backbone. Men do so loathe needy girlies – I said *stop that* Sandro, put that poor little bike messenger down. Really must go now, darling. Call me tomorrow, and tell all – but not before noon. Byeeee!'

By eleven thirty I'm squatting by the front window, vaguely contemplating the smart dark car opposite (possibly a Merc or an Audi), which is there till late most nights but never in the mornings. Wouldn't mind one like that, but fat chance, that's a good thirty thousand on wheels. Must be some high-earner who works nights (an on-call specialist at the Royal Free? A well-heeled sex worker?). Peering closer, I can see someone in it, sitting in the dark, doubtless enjoying the state of the art stereo and the seat warmers. I'm still looking idly at the car, when the figure inside slowly turns their head and stares right at me.

I can't see their face. Can't see their eyes either but by God, I can feel them, and they're boring straight through me. Yet I cannot look away, cannot move, not even to drop the curtain back in place. Hairs start to rise on the back of my arms, and I'm hardly breathing. Christ, who is that out there – a neighbourhood psycho, a prospective burglar, who? And what in hell can they possibly want from me?

Suddenly, the unwholesome spell is broken by the slam of the front door. Shake myself, and try to focus.

This had better be good.

Guess Who's At It Now

'Darling, your dinner is in the dog,' I joke, rearranging my scowl and hoping to make him smile. He doesn't. There is a short pause, but no: 'That looks nice' or 'Sorry, got held up.'

'You're rather late. Pity, I made some nice supper. Where'd you get to then? Your mobile was off.'

'I know. I turned it off.'

'Why?' I ask, politely, sloshing some wine into a fresh glass and holding it out to him. He doesn't notice as he's started peering through the kitchen window into the darkened garden like it's the most fascinating thing he's ever seen.

'I was having a drink.' Jim still hasn't looked at me properly.

'With whom?'

'Rebecca. Rebecca from work.'

'And what does Rebecca do?' Be nice, keep it friendly. She'll be the new model-maker, the transient freelance producer, the new production PA, Jed's latest trophy secretary. It turns out I could have phrased the question better.

He continues to look intently out of the window. 'She's this girl I've been seeing a bit of recently.'

'Seeing?'

It was as if he'd told me our house is being repossessed by bailiffs tomorrow. *'Recently?'*

So that's what she does. She does Jim.

He comes no closer, but as I boggle at him, he goes over to lean against the wall next to the fridge and starts playing with the little word magnet kits we collect, making a sentence which reads 'Oh! hot bottom yes'.

'You really are extraordinary, Zoe. You haven't noticed, have you?'

'I've – I've noticed you've been coming back too late to ever give me a hand or say goodnight to your children,' I stutter, trying to absorb the enormity of what he's just said.

Seeing. Recently?

'Oh, please. You've noticed neither my absences, nor how unhappy I've been these last few months. Correction, how unhappy *we've* been. And that means you haven't noticed I've been more cheerful recently. Well, have you?'

Feel like he's coshed me with a sack of wet fish. 'Oh, right, the absences. Yes. I mean, no! That is, you never said...'
My God, this bit of her he's been seeing. Which bit is it?

'Every time I've said I'm coming back late, you just say 'Oh, OK'. Did you never once think to ask me why?'

'I was trying not to be a nagging wife. You kept saying you had a lot on at work,' I mutter, struggling to gather thoughts which have scattered like glass dropped on concrete. 'Look, if this is about what I did, please, please won't you let me –'

'Oh, it's not about what you did. Though these days, I can't help looking at friends, or the guys at work, and thinking – Was it you? Or you? Or maybe it was you who's been *up my wife while my back was turned* –' he stops himself with a visible effort, dashing his knuckles briefly across his eyes before then opens the fridge and clumsily extracts a Beck's. 'The fact is, Zoe, you've also made me feel invisible in my own house,' he continues in a voice that's not quite steady. 'You barely notice whether I'm home or not, and give the distinct impression that you don't care much either way.'

'No! No, I do care, of course I care, and I do want you here. It's not my choice you're around so little. It would be really nice if – that is, I'm always asking you to come home earlier, but –' *Rebecca. He's seeing some tart called Rebecca...*

'Presumably so I can do my stint at childcare, not because you want my company. Do you think that I can't tell the difference?'

'That's not true!' *Why aren't I breaking chairs over his head?*

'And what's the point of me coming back anyway? I can't talk to you these days. You never seem interested in anything I have to say. We have little in common these days, except the kids. We don't sleep together any more –'

'That is incredibly unfair. How can I talk to you if you're never here? How can we sleep together if you won't come near me?' He hunches his shoulders and starts fiddling with the ring pull on his beer can. 'The only reason we're not having sex together these days is because *you* don't want to... hardly surprising really, from what you've just told me. And as for talking to you, it would help if you didn't bugger off every time I tried.' *I can't breathe properly. Why can't I breathe?* Have a sudden vision of his hand cupping some unknown female's breast and want to vomit, kill, scratch and bite my way through the fog of incomprehension that's descended upon my stuttering brain. 'Oh Jesus, Jim... why are you doing this?

There is a bit of a silence, during which he plays with the words on the fridge some more. 'If you must know, I got lonely,' he mumbles eventually. 'In fact, I have never felt so lonely in my life as I have these past few months. And you can feel just as isolated in a crap marriage as you can in some bed-sit on your own.'

'Lonely? *Lonely?* Me and the children are always hanging about at home hoping that, oooh, perhaps it'll be this evening that Daddy actually comes home early enough to exchange a few words – and you say *you* felt *lonely?* Christ, you'll be saying I don't understand you next, you self-absorbed bastard. Isn't that what men always say when they having a, a –' *Hell, I can't say it. An affair. Jim of all people, is having an affair.* 'Anyway, our marriage isn't that bad –' Is it? Well, even if it is, perhaps now we've both got our backs up against opposite walls of our domestic cage, we'll finally be forced to talk to each other. And maybe, just maybe, something positive might come out of all this.

'I'm afraid it is. But then, I suppose it would be, being married to a dishonest, duplicitous little bitch like yourself.' *Or there again, maybe not.* 'You've been shagging someone else so often that you got yourself pregnant, and not even you could talk your way out of that one.' *Here we go.* 'Naturally, I no longer trust you as far as I can throw you. And you know something else? You're right. You don't understand me. And it's a long time since you bothered to try.'

This is not going well. 'And I suppose – Rebecca – does?'

He bends over the kitchen worktop and starts rolling a cigarette, scattering tobacco strands and dropping his naked lady lighter. Good. He isn't as calm as he appears. 'For a young temp, she understands a hell of a lot.' He's puffing hard on his roll-up in an attempt to get it properly alight.

'The temp?' I screech, some spirit returning at the thought of some office Junior being understanding to Jim in the office night after night. 'She's just after a permanent position. Underneath you, with her legs apart –'

'That's enough! I like her a lot, Zoe, and she really likes me. Which is more than you seem to do, so it's something of a novelty. And, let me tell you, that's pretty damn sexy in itself.' The effect is somewhat spoilt by the fag sticking to his bottom lip while he talked, waggling up and down with each word. 'When I make jokes, she laughs at them,' he elaborates, keen to offer some working examples. 'She asks me how I'm feeling like she's interested, and, guess what? She listens when I tell her.'

'She must have a lot of time on her hands.' *Ooooh, shouldn't have said that. Shouldn't.*

'Now, that is exactly –'

'All right, so she's a good listener. Well, I – I could be too.' The temp. He's screwing the temp.

Jim shrugs, starts pulling dead leaves off the huge spider plant that hangs from the ceiling.

'What else?'

'I don't like your tone, Zoe.'

'I said *what else is so bloody great about her*?' persists my four glasses of red.

'Well, she's jolly bright,' he enthuses, suddenly looking more animated than he has all evening. 'She's only just out of media college but her father's the editorial director at Dibmarsh & Day, you know, that coffee-table academic publishers? so she's also remarkably –'

'What? Useful?' Perhaps Daddy can get Jim into print after all. 'Shaggable? Solvent?'

'Well-read, actually. And very mature for her age. Anyway, I really enjoy her company –'

'Is that so?'

'– but frankly,' he adds, folding his arms, 'over the past two years, I have not, at any point, enjoyed yours.'

I reel like he's rabbit punched me in the throat. What about France? And he doesn't even sound angry. Or triumphant ('*Ha! See what you made me do*'). Just matter of fact, as if explaining the laws of gravity to a twelve-year-old.

'Jim,' I rasp miserably, 'I can see this means we're in trouble, but please can't we –'

'I don't think we're in trouble, Zoe,' interrupts Jim, but in a gentler voice than he's used so far. 'I think we're finished.'

I can't think of a single thing to say. Well, maybe just the one. 'How – how old is she?'

'Twenty-three.'

She's twenty-three. And I – I am not.

'Do you –' I'm tugging at my hair, trying to extinguish lurid images of them snogging and worse, 'L-love her? Or what?'

'I don't know,' he admits after a few seconds, and has the grace to look uncomfortable.

My brain's darting everywhere at once, a minnow pursued by a pike. It can't be this bad, it just can't be. And the office *temp*. I don't believe this, it isn't happening: I mean, how naff can you get... yet Jim's face confirms that he has indeed been making out with some concave-bellied media-brat for months while I've been trying to repair our tattered marriage. No wonder he wasn't interested.

'So. Have you slept with her?' This seems very important.

'For God's sake, weren't you listening? This isn't about sex, it's about –'

'I *said*, have you slept with her?' Gripping the back of the nearest kitchen chair I'm starting to rock it to and fro, feeling a thunderhead of distress and rage gathering like an Atlantic storm. For it has just hit me that while Jim's almost certainly reported my infidelity in detail to anyone who'd listen, it's unlikely that he will have risked tarnishing his reputation as Wronged Husband and Father of the Year by breathing a single word about his own.

He stands a little straighter. 'Once or twice, yes.'

'Which?' Rock, rock.

'What?'

'Was it once? Or twice? Or have you been at it so often, you've simply lost count?'

'Oh, this is good. This is really rich coming from you.'

'My, my *thing* was a mistake, OK? A big mistake, which should never have happened and never would have if I'd been thinking straight. It was also over some time ago. Apparently, yours isn't. Come on Jim, how many times? And where did you do it anyway? Up against the wall in your boardroom, rattling all those pretty golden industry awards? Quickies in the company kitchen?' Look around wildly for something to hurl at his head. Perhaps the coconut rice? 'Or did you manage to contain yourselves till everyone went home so you could fuck her on your nice, big, black shiny *desk*?' The small, reasonable part of me that has tiptoed away into the wings to watch us screaming at each other hopes Tim and Kasha are too deeply asleep by now to hear.

'It is clearly pointless discussing this any further in your present state.'

'Well at least I'm showing an interest in your life,' I howl, banging my fist against the wall and hurting it. 'Isn't that what you wanted? Me, to take an interest? How long has this been going on?'

'That's beside the point, and let's be quite clear about one thing at least. This isn't revenge. If you must know, my relationship with Rebecca had already begun way before you pulled your pregnancy stunt, though in France I was having second thoughts about her because it really did seem that you and I –' he shrugs. 'Well, I was way off beam there, wasn't I?'

'You weren't, *you weren't*. Oh Jim, please, it's not too late. Oh do listen –' I've grabbed a napkin off the table (it was to have been that sort of supper) and am shredding it convulsively.

'I've listened to you for far too long, and you have told me lies. You want the truth? It is this. I've been seeing Rebecca because I wanted to, not because I needed to pay you back. I didn't do it to get at you. I did it because I wanted her.'

Slide slowly down the wall, and end up sitting on the floor, eyes still on his face. He continues to fix me with a dead straight gaze, his face tough and unfamiliar. Then says the three small words that are the death rattle of any relationship: 'Look – I'm sorry.'

He doesn't look sorry at all. Merely intent upon escape.

Graphic images are gate-crashing my brain, jostling for centre stage. A tiny dead baby, the way Jim's back looks as he walks off leaving me in mid sentence, his evasive eyes as he turns down sex at home before going straight out to shag his twenty-three-year-old, him with his tongue down another woman's throat – when suddenly a switch trips and there's a cleansing rush of pure, blessed rage lifting me up, clearing my mind and setting me squarely back on my feet.

'You are an arrogant, oversexed arsehole,' I pant, cheeks on fire, scrambling upright and stalking across the kitchen to pin him again the cooker. 'A sneaking, creeping, dick-directed maggot with the staying power of paraplegic gerbil –'

We were now nose to nose. 'How clever you are, how *original*, to have an affair with some minging little temp who's half your age. Yes, you are really *out there*. I'm quite sure that has never happened before in the entire history of, of –' fuck, I can't think of a name bad enough to call it after all that booze –

'Age is not an issue between Rebecca and myself,' he pronounces. 'And you can rage all you like, it makes no difference. Because for your information (not that it's any of your business any longer) we're moving in together. She has a little place just off Charlotte Street. Well, actually, it belongs to her parents but they said that we –' he stops, clearly feeling he's said too much.

I laugh bitterly, God knows how. So he's even met the parents. Fast work. 'I just bet she does. Charlotte Street. Parents with money, huh? Dream on, asshole, you can't afford her. Girlfriends like her are expensive, so are families, and we got here first.' Find I'm pulping the remains of that napkin convulsively. 'Planning to live out, are we? Not going to bother with our children either, except at weekends? Well that's nothing new, so at least you won't be confusing them.'

He shrugs. 'Take look in the mirror, Zoe. You got yourself pregnant by another man while I was subsidising you to sit at home on your backside, pretending to write. And don't think I don't know that you were planning to fob that bastard baby off as mine. With, I have no doubt, a lot of convincing figures from your medical files about vasectomy failure.' *How did he know?* 'Rebecca says you'd still be seeing that bloke if he hadn't come to his senses and dropped you.'

151

'Oh – she does, does she?' Thrashing around for a truly incinerating put-down but too livid think of one, I snatch up both glasses from the table and hurl them to the floor at his feet. 'Get out! Just get out, you two timing heap of – of slug-shit. Go back to that predatory little tart who's young enough to be your daughter, see if I care. I hope your wizened little dick drops off. Preferably tonight, *inside her.*'

He pushes the broken shards aside with his foot. 'I take it you'd like me to leave?'

Ha, Psychology 101. First: Make your adversary hopelessly irrational with fury. Second: Push them into such a humiliating a corner that they have no option but to tell you to sod off. Third: exit briskly, with a clear conscience.

Works every time.

Though it's obvious what he's up to, I'm so disorientated by rage, distress and jealousy that I fall right into it and am appalled to hear self bawl: 'Right, *you do that*! Shed your responsibilities, your kids, your marriage, why don't you? Start over with a brand new model and no baggage. Exactly what every man needs for his midlife crisis: permission to leave home. Well, you've got it, you lying, selfish, sexually incontinent creep. And I hope you fucking well enjoy it. *To the full.*' Not entirely sure how the dishes of chopped egg, chicken and bean sprouts made it from the table to his head, but Jim looked considerably less attractive backing away with shredded poultry in his hair.

Five minutes later, still flicking bits of soggy bean sprout off his collar, he came back as far as the kitchen door carrying a large black canvas bag stuffed to bursting, looking wary but as if he'd like to say something further. One of the earthenware dishes seems to have given him the beginnings of a black eye.

I am still sitting at the table, but now working my way through a second bottle of wine, which under the circumstances, seems the only thing to do. 'What?' I mutter, aware that I am now extremely pissed but nevertheless feeling a bubble of hope. Maybe he was going to –

'I'll be round on Saturday afternoon, OK? To see the children.'

And with that, he is gone.

Dead Vicar

Five weeks later Tim, Kasha and I are sitting around the dining table doing homework, when a suspicion that has been niggling away like sand in a sock worms its way to the surface of my brain.

Rebecca. Rebecca. Now who –

'I don't see why Jesus had to make do with two loaves and seven fishes. Why couldn't he just magic them all to McDonalds instead?' Kasha gives her RE book an irritable shove.

'Listen, dumbo, they've only had McDonalds for the last twenty-five years,' sneers Tim. 'This was two thousand years ago. Don't you know *anything?* Du-*urr*, brain-dead or *what?*' Kasha winces and gives me a wronged-puppy stare. I waggle one of her fingers and try to soften Tim's words with a wink. He never talked like this before Jim went away. But his dad's absence, compounded by his own inability to put things right are eating away at my usually kind-hearted, funny son, his perceived impotence souring him the way Jim's used to sour him. Try to put a retraining but friendly hand over his, but he snatches it away.

'Well sor-*eee*,' sniffs Kasha, recovering fast. 'Anyway, *I* wouldn't have eaten any. Poor little fish. God's supposed to love animals, so how come he lets people eat them?'

I give her a hug, and think some more, absentmindedly sharpening the coloured pencils that she pushes towards me. That post-grad journalism student who'd cannibalized most of my best contacts. Last time she'd called, ooh, five months ago, hadn't she been desperate for a job? I'd given her a list of names to try, even put her in touch with Jed. Haven't heard from her since –

'Mum. How many shields on a Viking long-ship?' demands Tim.

'However many you want to draw, darling.'

'Oh, *bii-ig* help. Thanks a million –'

Don't snap back at him, just don't. Now, Seventh Wave have a new PA on work experience. I seem to recall a glimpse of her when I'd dropped in one evening as a nice surprise, babysitter all arranged, to try and tempt Jim out to see that new Almodovar. He'd declined, but nicely, claiming he had urgent work to finish and asked me to give him some notice next time.

Yes, she'd been slim, milky complexioned, long dark hair, a black T-shirt with *urbanfox* in lower case letters above the left tit. In fact, I remember her rather well considering I'd only clapped eyes on her the once. Eye colour? Don't know, she'd kept them on her work. At the time I'd thought she was either a bit graceless, or merely shy of the boss's wife...

My God. The bloody cow. It was *her*, it had to be. And I'd got her the job. So having acquired all my best contacts, she's now got my husband as well. It had taken me long enough to work it out, too. Twenty-three, huh? The little *slut*. She'll be after the house next. And she'd not been nervous when I'd seen her, had she? Not a bit of it. The reason she'd avoided looking me in the eye was that *they were already fucking like ferrets.*

A shrilling starts up next door. 'I'll get it!'

'No-ooo, I wanna get it –'

These days, the children compete viciously for the telephone whenever it rings. 'It's Daddy, I know it's my Daddy –'

'He's mine too so piss off, and it's *my* turn to pick up –'

'No, mine!'

'*Mine* – agh! Shit! You little *bitch*, get your teeth out of my arm...'

'Tim, language! Kasha, stop that *immediately*. It's not going to be Daddy, but you know he always comes on

Saturday, right? That's in two days. So sit down *both* of you and finish your homework,' I bark, sprinting into the next room. 'If you're quick you'll catch the last half of *EastEnders*. Tim, concentrate. You have to at least write a page about an imaginary journey by long-ship from Sweden to Kent. OK, OK, I'll come and help you *in a minute*. Jesus. Yes? Hello?'

On the other end, there is a moist gulping noise.

'Sorry?'

Some gasping.

Oh, *lovely*. A funny call. And now he's making noises. Take a deep breath and say with as much authority as I can muster: 'Piss off, you nasty little man. Go wank down someone else's phone.'

'No, no, sorry Zoe. It's, it's, er, me.'

'Who?'

A new sound, a cross between a gasp and a hiccup. 'Jim.'

Doesn't sound like him. 'Are you drunk?'

'No, no, of course not –'

'Well, what do you want? If it's sympathy or company, you can just sod off back to your little office slapper.'

'Never mind her, *please*. Can I come over? I've got to see you.'

'Gone off you already, has she? Serves you bloody well right. And guess what, I've just realised who she is. The talentless little tart.'

'Zoe, please –'

'No.' Oooh, that does feel good. 'So you're as bit low, and you suddenly remember you have a family. Well, it's not your day for it, Buster, and I don't want Tim and Kasha disrupted. You promised you'd stick to Saturday and Sunday afternoons, so bloody do so.' Kasha is shaking my arm and whispering loud as a shout: 'Mum-eee. What colour was Jesus' hair?'

'Probably dark brown, darling. He was Jewish.' I twiddle the old-fashioned curly phone cable round my fingers, and toy happily with the thought of replacing the receiver. It's been ages since I've had anything he wants.

'Zoe, are you listening?'

'What's Jewish?'

'It's – can we talk about this later, sweetheart?'

'Yes. Oh, yes please. That would be wonderful. If I can come over now, say in about half an hour?'

'I was talking to Kasha.'

Another few gulps. Sounds of a man in travail pulling himself together.

'I'm sorry. I'm sorry. I'll wait till they're in bed, or come over now and help you. Anything. Whatever you say.'

'I don't think so, Jim.' I'm starting to feel more curious than vengeful now. 'And why so accommodating all of a sudden?'

'I need to talk to you.'

Definitely been dumped by the London School of Journalism's answer to Morticia Adams. Chew a thumb hangnail, taking my time. 'And what if I don't want to see you? You've barely said hello to me the last few times. Just taken the kids and pushed off to Burger King.'

There's sniff like a drain being unblocked, then the unattractive trumpet voluntary of a snotty nose being blown at close range. The words emerge clotted with mucus:

'But Ag's' dead.'

'Sorry?'

'I *said* my *Ag's* dead. '

'Ag who?' I ask, carefully.

'*Dad*. My Dad. My fucking *father*. Yesterday…'

What? But he can't have, he just can't – that man had been the healthiest sixty-nine-year-old I'd ever met. Vegetarian, worked out three times a week, cholesterol reading lower than mine… 'Oh *no*, Jim, that's – oh God, I don't know what to say. That's *appalling*. You poor, poor thing – but what on earth happened?'

'He was working out down at Dave's Gym. You remember what a fanatic he was about his training? They used to call him the Fit Vicar –' Jim's voice is wobbling up and down the scale '– anyway, he, he had this massive heart attack. No warning. Dead before the ambulance even got there. I saw his body in – in the mortuary. They'd put him in a *drawer* for God's sake, a bloody great cold steel drawer. He looked –' it's a moment before Jim can go on, 'I mean *it* looked... no, never mind. Anyway, there's going to be a post-mortem, all sorts of nasty stuff... oh God, Zoe, I can't take it in. Nor can mum. She hasn't even cried, she's so shocked. I've been with her all day receiving a succession of parishioners turning up with covered dishes, wanting to hear the details. And I don't think I can hack it (or her) any longer.'

'Steady on. She really loved your dad you know, even if he wasn't always – I mean, they'd been married for forty-three years, hadn't they? Don't you think she has every right to be –'

'No, no, no, you don't understand,' he interrupts, sounding like he's looking over his shoulder. 'I've never seen her like this. She's gone all needy, but horribly determined. She's already made up her mind she's going to live with me. Keeps saying she's going to buy *us* a flat in West Hampstead with an extra bedroom for when the kids visit.' Jim blows his nose again vigorously. 'She's been on the phone to London estate agents all afternoon, even though dad only died yesterday. And every time I turn round she's there, because she's taken to following me from room to room. I know she's my mother and all that – but I'm telling you, I barely recognise this person. *I've got to get away from her –*' his voice rises hysterically.

'Stop shouting, Jim, and calm down. Breathe. Are you breathing? Good. Now, where are you now? Is she with you?'

'Christ, no. I'm at Waterloo station – by W.H. Smiths. I've just got off the train.'

'Jim, I'm so, so sorry to hear about your father. Terribly sorry. It must have been the most appalling shock.' Part of me wants very badly to be a nice person and sympathize, listen, support. The other part is fighting exasperation because he's wrong-footed me yet again. I try and give my cheating, lying (absent) husband the justified brush off, and he tells me his dad's just dropped dead. Further, much as I dislike the elder Mrs Harrington, she must be in pieces and it sounds like she needs a good hug from her son lasting several days. 'Listen, I know this won't be what you want to hear – but I really do think you ought to stay with your mum tonight.'

'Mum?' Tim is standing in front of me, bobbing up and down, eyes bright. 'Is that Dad?'

I nod, then put my finger to my lips and shake my head. His face falls and the light goes out of his eyes. He sits down on the floor at my feet and starts tugging the phone cable. I put my hand on his head, and rub it gently. He shrugs me off, and tugs harder.

'Aunt Julia is with her tonight. Please, Zoe, please can't I come over? Just for a bit?'

The hurt flares up again like eczema dipped in lemon juice. 'What, and upset Rebecca? She's your significant other now, not me. Go to her. Stop that, Tim.' A large part of me would give a great deal to bury my pride and comfort him, but I can't do it. For a start, I keep seeing that love bite he'd had on his neck last week.

'Please, Zoe, I need someone who knew him. Someone who knows me. I'm all messed up –'

'I hear you, but mightn't you be better talking to someone like Ade? He's a good friend, having been at school together you go back a long way, and he knew your dad quite well. Better still, he's a psychiatrist.' *And seeing as it wasn't him you left for another women, he's likely to be nicer to you than me*. The tugging begins again. 'I want to talk to him too,' hisses Tim, kicking at my foot. Shake my head, mouthing back: 'Not now.' Tim drops the phone cord and stumps off upstairs, banging the sitting room door with unnecessary violence.

'Ade doesn't do listening without analysis, preferably over a five-year period. And if he tries to do that to me now, I'm telling you, I'll come apart. Oh Jesus,' Jim babbles miserably, 'I'd always wanted to talk to Dad, you know? Really talk to him, even if it was just the once. Each time I went down to see them, I'd think: This'll be the weekend. The one when Dad opens up, the one where we have a proper conversation, the one when I can make him see who I am. Never bloody happened, did it? Polite roast dinner, most subjects of conversation off limits expect how well my Cambridge contemporaries were doing in various branches of industry; walking that overweight Labrador, then back to London. Now I'll never have the chance. I'll never get to tell him…' his voice tails off.

'Go on. I'm here.' This is very peculiar. Though I feel pity and sympathy for Jim and his mother, his father's death has shocked me but no more than that. Perhaps because I never liked the subtle bullying and needling the man dished out to his wife (also to his son, whom I loved) nor his own particular brand of resentful discontent, all of which sat oddly on a man of God. Mind you, he never liked me, either.

Kasha comes and lays her head on my chest. '*What sort of fish were they, you know, for that supper –*' I mouth 'Shhh, not when I'm on the…'

'… you know,' sniff, blow '– how much I, er, admired him. I did, you know,' he adds, almost defensively. 'Even wanted to be a vicar like him, until I was nine. But nothing I ever did pleased him. Not ever. Not getting a two-one, not setting up my own small company, having a home, children – nothing. It was why hadn't I got a first, or did I really find filming 'advertisements' a sufficient intellectual challenge…'

160

More sounds of mucus being evacuated from large nasal passages. 'And he was a bit of a shit to my mother too over these last years because he was losing his own faith, and took it out on her –'

Kasha thrusts the pencil into my hand and smoothes a scrap of paper onto a book she is holding. 'Which *fish?*' Scribble 'Haddock' and she goes away, satisfied.

'Zoe, I can't handle this. I don't know what to feel.'

Suddenly I feel terribly sorry for him. 'Jim – look, maybe it is a good idea if you do come over. Come now, and – and you can talk to me all you want. If you feel it'll help.' Not knowing what else to say, I take refuge in practicality. 'Have you eaten? You need to eat. I can rustle something up, and listen while I'm doing it. You can stay the night if you like, in Tim's room. I mean, that is you could if you, er, needed to,' I add hastily, remembering Rebecca crouching expectantly in her Charlotte Street web.

There is a beep, and Tim's on the upstairs extension. 'Dad? Sounds like you're a bit down, I've got a joke to cheer you up. What do you give a dinosaur with diarrhoea?'

'Nine o'clock,' gabbles Jim, 'Right. I'll see you then. Thank you, Zoe, thank you –'

'Lots of room!'

The line hums quietly.

'He's gone, sweetheart.'

Stalking Infidelity

Jim's washing is lying on the floor at the end of my bed. So's Jim.

To be more accurate, he's sleeping on a single mattress behind our Edwardian screen (the one covered in a collage of black and white family photos) with his stuff piled up around him.

It started seven nights after he came over to talk about his father. I stayed awake with him till around four in the morning while he got drunk, cried, then ranted on about his father's emotional inflexibility and his mother's new eagerness to share her son's life more fully, before finally crashing out on the sofa with his head in my lap. Unwilling to risk waking him, I stayed put, crawling off to Morrison's next day baggy-faced after three hours' broken sleep. Then he dropped in again, wild-eyed after the funeral (to which, thanks to both our estrangement and his parents' reservations about me, I'd not been invited) asking for a coffee, and whether he might read his children an unscheduled bedtime story. As I fiddled with filter papers and dithered, Kasha appeared on the stairs in her nightie and threw herself into Jim's arms, so that settled that.

Next, he returned to do another unexpected mid-week story, a bag of dirty clothes strapped to his motorbike. Feeling that was pushing it, I allowed him in but not his laundry.

Two days later, he appeared at nine o'clock at night with an Indian takeaway and a meek expression, wanting to know if I was hungry and whether he might leave the rucksack he had with him under the stairs for a day or two, since he was a bit short of space where he was staying. I'd sooner have sawn off my own tongue and eaten it than ask where that was, but he was looking a little ill-kempt for a man shacked up with a doting young girlfriend.

More washing, his own little packet of Persil, my favourite Vietnamese takeaway, a tub of Celebrations for the children and a bottle of Chablis arrived yesterday.

I gave up.

However, 'Oh, all right then,' remains the nearest we've got to a reconciliation speech. And instead of feeling jubilant, awash with love or any of those other things couples are meant to feel when one of them returns from straying, it was more: 'Well, whatever.' So I've bought a pair of green and white striped old men's pyjamas from Mind in Camden High Street to discourage nocturnal familiarity, Jim's sleeping in a tracksuit despite the summer temperatures, and we have left it at that for we are both too punch-drunk to do otherwise.

'See how it pans, girl,' advised Bel who'd been a tower of tough-talking strength for weeks, when I told her the news. 'A bit of experimental co-hab never hurt anyone. Mind you, if you ask me, a woman needs a man like a seagull needs a fucking laxative.'

'Harvey AWOL again?'

'He is. And you know what?' her soft Melbourne accent voice became harder, 'I don't think stud muffin's been going walkabout entirely on his own.'

At least Jim's taken to coming home at seven in the evening, no longer races straight upstairs to have a shower, and reads his newspaper in the same room as I'm in. Am reluctant to ask whether this means he's been ditched by the Pussy-Powered PA, but and at least it's progress. As for the atmosphere in the house, it's closest to that which exists between reasonably compatible work-colleagues, which certainly beats the brooding disaffection we had before.

Our children are monitoring their parents' antics closely. Tim has taken to haunting the upstairs windows every night to spy out for Jim's returning bike. He will not settle until his dad's back then demands, most uncharacteristically, prolonged academic assistance every single night ('Dad, I just don't get this bit –' 'Aw, but I've got to do this for *tomorrow* –') the second Jim steps through the door. Kasha's approach to dad-nabbing is to save up invisible school-related injuries for him to inspect ('My knee, Daddy, look, it's all scrapey. No, there…' 'Can you rub my hand better where Azaria got me with her lunchbox?' 'My ear: it so hurts when I pull it –') However, we reckon we're lucky it's not the full blown, absent-parent induced behavioural dysfunction evident in a good third of their schoolmates.

Jim and self are also making every effort to re-occupy the world of coupledom by doing Normal Family Stuff, like taking everyone out for Saturday picnics on Primrose Hill whether they want to come or not ('But I *hate* eggy sandwiches, and we're missing *Ant n' Dec…*') or enduring the latest packaged Disney ('Oi, wake up Dad, this bit's dead funny…'). To re-grout our own relationship, we are being sure to cook supper a deux – you chop, I'll peel – and go out occasionally in the evening. The latter feels like a blind date that we're both too polite to cancel, the former like getting to know a new flat-mate. So far we've seen a blues band at the Parkway Dublin Castle (good), the new longer version Bergman's *Persona* in Swedish (bad) and spent two reasonable evenings at The Ship, perched at the bar and chatting cautiously to each other under the benevolent eye of Awesome Welles.

Last time, we even had the Reassuringly Normal New Car Conversation. 'If we can ever afford it, it's time we had something grown-up, yeah, like that new Audi that's usually parked right opposite us. The guy often sits in it for hours, you know –' *I did know. And that's not all he does.*

'In fact, he was there again last night –' Jim took a wry slug of beer. I stiffened, then tried and dismiss it. *It's nothing, nothing, nothing…* 'Poor sod –' he added. *Darling, did he stare at you, too?* '– he seemed to be set for the duration. Probably not, er, getting on with his wife.'

But tonight, we're off to something better than the local pub. It's the preview of a play by Jim's friend Rob, for whom success has been a long time coming, but it looks like he's finally cracked the West End after twenty years of writing plays that no directors ever wanted to read, and which only the odd community drama group ever bothered to stage.

Thoroughly looking forward to an evening together for once, we leave the pub and whiz into town by motorbike to save time, leaving it in Soho Square bike park. Letting go of Jim's waist, I slide off the big Kawasaki and am just trying to tug off the helmet without removing both my ears and my make-up, when I see him.

There, emerging from the side road leading onto the little square looking prosperous, inviolate and rotten to the core is Shaun.

Killer smile firmly in place, wearing a crumpled petrol blue linen suit and open necked bottle-green shirt, shades and a light tan, he has two younger lieutenants respectfully bringing up the rear and his arm lightly on the shoulder of some piece in a dusky pink suit who is flicking whiskery fronds of hair out of her eyes, and laughing up at him prettily. I'm kicked in the guts by a gust of startled distress so strong it nearly winds me.

OK, so I've been avoiding him for weeks and want out. Fine, so I don't have the energy to cope with him any more, have gone off sex for good anyway, and at some point, am going to have to stop sending holding pattern e's and get around to formal closure. But – well, just look at him. Viciously attractive. Not a care in the bloody world, in his element, the picture of corporate satisfaction, and he used to be mine. *Hi I'm Shaun. You can tell from the way I walk that I have a big dick, am dead successful and rather rich.*

As I watch, he says something in Pink Whiskers' ear, then throws back his head and laughs at her reply. Dah – it's like watching him grope her. I wonder how long it's been since I even crossed his mind. How fast the happy forget.

Jim tugs at my arm for we have slowed to the pace of a racing snail. 'Come on, we'll be too late for a drink at the bar at this rate.'

We follow the happy party down Dean Street at as discreet a distance as I can manage. Once, when Shaun flicks a swift glance over his shoulder at one of the suits, I have to duck behind Jim's six foot bulk. Dear God, this is undignified. I'm turning into some sort of stalker. Stalking infidelity.

Hang on. The two men and the girl are going into Hiroshima, the fashionable watering hole for those who feel that overpriced Japanese beers, adult Japanese cartoon books on the tables, and huge video screens showing Tokyo girls mud wrestling are just the thing to help you wind down from a hard day in the editing suite. Shaun gives them a lordly wave and keeps going, turning sharp left into Old Compton Street. Seconds later, so do Jim and I because this is the way to the theatre off Charing Cross Road. We round the corner just in time to see him disappear into number forty-three.

I feel myself go hot in the face. He's having a shiny new affair, isn't he? He's nipped in there to meet her. She's his new bit after work; I'd been his occasional lunch timer. We probably crossed over for weeks, if not, months, I think feverishly feeling small, worthless and grubby.

'Darling –' dammit, my voice is coming out as a sand-blasted croak. 'Jim, I'm just nippling – I mean nipping – into the paper shop here. We need some chocolate for the play, and it's three times the price at theatres.' Jim looks put out at the prospect of missing sixty seconds of perfectly good drinking time. 'You go on. Get me, er, a tomato juice and vodka? Please. I'll catch you up.'

'Oh all right then. But for God's sake don't be late, not for this, it would look so rude. Hey, have you got some grit in your eyes? They're a bit watery…' He gives my eyes a vague dab with a piece of rather suspect loo paper from his jeans pocket. Hovering over the magazine section and glancing over my shoulder, I buy a slab of Green & Black's and a copy of *New Scientist* for Jim, then go and lean against the wall opposite the flat, face hidden behind *NS* like a spy in a forties war movie, struggling through an impenetrable feature on the future of the hydrogen economy.

Ten minutes later I am about to give up, when someone appears. But it's not Pink Suit. It's some woman in a black jacket and a glossy black bob, Louise Brookes style. She has by the arm a kid of about fourteen or fifteen, skinny, pretty, long fair hair, scruffy-hip, carrying a pink hold-all. Black Bob buzzes one of the bells outside Shaun's but since her back's to me, it's impossible to see which.

While I continue to keep an eye out for Pinky on her way to visit Perky, the woman waits for a minute or so, then looks up in exasperation. Obviously mother and daughter, up in London from Surrey to see The Phantom of the Opera, wanting to get changed at a parental colleague's flat. Hell, it's time to go. I have no business whatsoever here, and a dog in the manger is a very unattractive creature. Just starting to walk away when the young girl slumps down on her big squashy bag and lights a fag, shielding it expertly against the eddying grit of the street. The woman takes no notice. Funny, you'd think a mum might object to a young daughter smoking in front of her. Perhaps she is more liberal than she looks.

Antennae twitching, I decide to stay put after all.

Rewarded seconds later by the sight of Shaun, minus his jacket and tie, opening the door with a flourish. The woman shakes hands with him briefly, but the girl continues to smoke and ignore the pair of them. He smiles, cups his hand under her chin forcing her to look up, nods, and beckons the pair forward. The woman prods the girl to her feet. At the last moment, the kid half-heartedly pulls away but Black Bob makes a practised grab for her, and catching the hair on the side of her head, yanks her sharply inside. A transvestite wheeling a tartan shopping trolley on the same side of the road looks a bit startled, but no one else seems to notice.

Feeling ill, I lean more heavily against the wall and stare over the top of the magazine at Shaun's bedroom window on the fourth floor. Sure enough, after only a couple of minutes, someone starts letting down the blinds.

He never did like wasting time.

Very late indeed, still wanting to throw up, and treading on every available toe in our row, I sidle in during one of the play's many poignant bits, 'Sssssh' hisses a vast Valkyrie of a woman with a mass of blonde plaits. 'For Goddess's sake, *be quiet.*'

Jim shoots me an accusing look, but accepts his bar of chocolate and the magazine. My seat has a broken spring, so spend the rest of the last two acts taking most of my weight up on my hands, too chicken to ask to sit on the other side of Valkyrie Bottom where, as luck would have it, there is a perfectly good vacant place.

The celebratory reception in the downstairs bar of the Assembly Theatre is hell. Jim, exasperated at my lateness, deserts me pointedly on arrival and since the bar's in a windowless basement, the fug and noise levels, even after twenty minutes, are stupendous. Assorted guests and liggers are throwing drink down their throats at a rate suggesting that they are all going into rehab tomorrow. The rest of the social interaction involves congratulating Rob, or asking what *you* do, then vanishing briskly if you don't sound interesting enough. I keep thinking about Shaun, and what he must now be doing with that young girl.

Jim now has an arm round Rob's woolly-jumpered shoulders: not even for this august occasion will the latter abandon his treasured Afghans. The playwright's round face is shining with pleasure as he accepts drinks, hugs, congratulations and requests for media interviews with an endearing mixture of bafflement and delight. His play, an affectionate, funny but pitiless look at the lives of those in an old people's care home, the greedy indifference of their younger relatives and the coarse patronage of the all-powerful staff has the theatre critic of the *Sunday Times* in ecstasies. Ideally, these will last long enough to find their way into print this weekend.

Tired with being the spectre at the feast, I plead period pains and take the bus home. At this time in the evening there is a plentiful supply of number twenty-fours for people too pissed to drive and too broke for a cab fare.

Lying in bed waiting for the sound of the front door and the stumble of an inebriated pair of feet coming upstairs, I review the options. So far as there seem to be any, especially with the prompt hangover produced by cheap booze, it seems best to wait till Shaun calls again then nail him to the confessional wall, though now he has Pink Whiskers on board he may not bother.

But if he does, how the hell to tackle this one? I know what I saw, but my brain slithers to a halt every time it's confronted with the facts, like a horse refusing a fence. His skill at convincing you that black is just another form of white depending upon your point of view and the amount of available light, cannot be discounted either. Well he isn't going to get away with it this time. I'm going to light Shaun Lyon's fuse for him, all right.

Yet if I'd been able to foresee the explosion it would cause, I'd have stamped out the match instead.

No One Walks Out On Me

Two days later, there are eight vibrators lined up on our kitchen table. They seem to be watching me cynically.

I am sitting here (rather than in my derelict office) with Jim's portable, wrestling with a highly technical piece about dildos for *Steam*. Apparently the magazine's psychotic voyeur of a publisher has decreed the piece must appear in the October issue to justify his claim to potential advertisers that the magazine doesn't just fob readers off with a high nipple count – they've got cutting-edge consumer journalism in there as well.

My husband's been happy to lend the machine because, since he found out about Morrison's last week (and yes, it did take him several days to return from orbit) he's been nagging me to go back to writing. No chance; head's still a brain-free zone.

However, this piece is an exception since the article's virtually been done in-house, the journalist concerned has walked out, and having no time to polish it up the features editor has offered me a very handy two hundred quid to do so. This will only take a day, which is now available as I've told the supermarket I've got the runs.

The brief is to jazz up an overly-earnest *Which?* style report about why all best selling vibrators for women came in brightly coloured, whimsical, gel-filled shapes (like the ultra-popular lime-green Jessica Rabbit) rather than the big phallic bombers that buzz like bluebottles on heat. In search of the 'why?' aspect, I've got some quotes from a humourless sex therapist who's clearly never used a dildo in her life. Unravelling the politically correct semantics, her thesis is that all women are subconsciously and latently lesbian because of their ongoing oppression by men, and therefore prefer sex toys that bear as little resemblance to actual penises as possible. Regrettably this isn't the sort of thing that the bike-seat sniffers who read *Steam* wish to hear. They want to be told what they already think they know: that women are only driven to use appliances when they can't get a man. Start typing, three fingers for a very inaccurate sixty words a minute, and am just beginning to remember why this used to be fun, when the walkabout bleats.

He sounds on top of the world. 'Sweetheart, sweetheart. I've missed you, I've missed you. Where've you *been*? It's time you stopped hiding from me. Has everything sorted itself out now at your end?'

Startled, I delete most of what I've written by pressing the wrong mouse button. Aaagh, dammit, oh *sod it to hell* – 'My God,' is the best I can manage, floored by hearing his voice again after so many weeks. Furious, try hitting Undo Edit several times. Screen remains blank.

He powers along as if we only met up last week rather than two and a half months ago: 'It's a perfect day, it's Friday, I've made half a million this morning, and you are everything I need to make it complete.' Hammer different keys in a frenzy. What about Pink Whiskers, then? Bet she's away and he's at a loose end. Still, I want to talk to him, don't I? Sort him out? Though the shock of the other night is still fresh, I might not have the guts to corner him later on so this is going to have to be it. Oh, Christ –

'I have champagne, some new toys, and the afternoon off. Come on over, darlin', let's make up for all that lost time,' he urges, oblivious to my silent swearing and key-stabbing on the other end. 'I've been respecting your requests for space, but it's been way too long and I'm not going to wait any longer.'

Am as non-committal as it is possible to be when you are ripped apart by longing – bugger, he always could do this to me – extreme suspicion, and your Undo Edit button won't work.

Wrestle with my own cowardice and the recalcitrant laptop for the next hour before packing it in and arriving at his flat dressed as if for a job interview, and buttoned up to the neck.

He buzzes me in, and as I cross the threshold, swings me round and round, clearly in tearing spirits. Then muttering loving filth and pornographic promises, carries me into the bedroom and dumps me on the bed, producing a bottle of champagne and two glasses from underneath it. Shoot off the other side as if electrocuted, clutching the headboard and sniffing the air for traces of the other two women.

'OK, princess, we'll do it standing up,' he smiles, expertly sliding the cork out of the bottle and filling both glasses with the minimum of foam and fuss.

'What's all this in aid of?' *Hell, he looks fantastic.*

'It's in aid of me having missed you – a lot. It's in aid of the last few weeks showing me, without a shadow of a doubt, that I may have lost you once but that I'm not doing it again. I've been feeling you slip away from me, Zoe, but I've finally realised (and Christ knows it's taken me long enough) that I really do need you in my life. And I had to tell you this before we lost yet more of the precious time that should be ours. That's all.' He smiles as if he's just presented me with a fifty karat diamond, takes my limp hand and wraps it around the champagne glass stem. 'I never thought we'd be together again – but nor did I forgot what it was like to be us, and secretly, I suppose I never stopped hoping. That's how come the yearly lunches. It was all my stupid fault for running off the way I did. I just didn't know what I had.'

All the breath seems to leave my body. I have been waiting years to hear this. Years. *So why is he telling you now?* hisses my inner policewoman. *Remember you want to get free of him, remember you can't keep up with him, think about all the others he's surely got.* Yet I can feel myself leaning imperceptibly towards him, reeled in by the magnetic pull of words I'd been secretly, disgracefully, longing to hear for the last twenty years.

He takes my other hand and places it against his sandpapery cheek. Despite myself, I find I'm rubbing it gently to and fro. 'Listen. At twenty-six I saw all my options dwindling to a single person, when I was more used to hitting a bar any night of the week just to see what happened, and I was – scared, I suppose – to give all that up,' he says quietly, looking me straight in the eye. 'The excitement, the possibility that maybe, just maybe tonight, the perfect woman was going to be there. Don't look at me like that, that's just what men think. All men. The promise of something even better shimmers out there in front of you every time the sun goes down, the neon lights up and the girls come swarming out of the offices all perfumed and up for it –'

I take my hand back sharply. Shaun sighs softly with what, had it been anyone else, I'd swear is nostalgia, scratching his well-muscled arse thoughtfully and ducking his leonine head in an irresistibly self-deprecating arc. 'Those weeks we lived together in Ladbroke Grove – I was scared shitless.'

He what? And there was me thinking they'd been the best weeks of our lives.

'Classic male met-the-right-one-too-soon funk,' he adds hastily. 'But I've regretted running off ever since. Well,' he amends, uncharacteristically truthfully, 'the last couple of years anyway. Debbie's changed out of all recognition. You've no idea what it's been like.' Why do men always say that? My bullshit detector starts wobbling, but I cannot help staring at him dumbly, scuffing my foot on the white fluffy rug under my feet. 'You've turned my life around, Zoe,' he says softly. 'Again. You did it once before – when we first met – and you're doing it now. Everything feels better to me now because of you. I didn't realise how much I needed you till you disappeared a second time. Other women – well, they're just not the same.'

This is everything I've ever wanted to hear from him. Everything. I just don't want to hear it today.

'Honey, you seem a bit uptight. What's wrong?' he holds out his arms. 'Come here. It's OK, you know you can tell me anything. Anything. And while you're at it I think you'd better tell me what's been going on recently because you had me really worried. Did something happen? Did Jim start to suspect? Did you get the guilts? What?'

If he does know something, he's an excellent actor. Even though this all seems a little too timely, there is nothing I want so much as to run into his arms, tell him everything – the baby, Jim, the Prozac, Tim being bullied, my career down the pan – and be hugged better. He could always make everything better.

'No thanks, Shaun,' I hear myself say, as if from a very long way off. My voice sounds thin and high, like a nervous eight-year-old's. 'We're not going to play today. And you'd better stay exactly where you are.'

He raises an eyebrow.

'I, er, look here –'

'Yes? Come on, sweetheart. Talk to me.' His voice is a loving caress. 'I think I know what it is. You were feeling neglected back in June weren't you? Was that why you backed off from me? Were you feeling all taken for granted? I'm sorry darlin', I was up to my eyes in work and there were problems at home, and – well, there was so much going on, I wasn't sure then of what I wanted. I promise you it'll be very different from now on. But you understand what it's like, don't you? We've both got so many other commitments, you and I, it's a miracle we've been able to snatch as much pleasure from each other as we have.' He moves towards me and places a warm hand on my collarbone. 'Did you think I didn't love you any more?' He kisses me on the very edge of my quivering mouth. 'Just goes to show how wrong you can be.'

He's right, as usual. I couldn't handle him any more (not that I ever could) but I *had* thought he was going off me, and it had hurt. Conviction drains away, like water poured onto sand. Just shut up, it's not too late; don't ask about last night, didn't you hear what he just said? No. *No. You want to end it, remember? Properly? You have for months. And don't forget that girl being pulled through the doorway –*

'I want to talk to you. And I want some straight answers out of you for once.'

'Fire away, sweetheart,' he drawls, going over to stretch out luxuriously on the bed with his hands laced behind his head, the champagne at his side. 'I do love it when you get strict –'

'This isn't a game.'

He still smiles, but changes his expression from loving to benign, which is easier to maintain under pressure.

I take a deep breath as if for a shout, and jump. 'Like young girls, do you, Shaun?'

He looks a bit puzzled, then smiles agreeably. 'Not especially. Mind you, these days it's difficult to tell how old some of them really are. I've even been confused by some of the larger twelve-year-olds.'

'Confused to what extent?'

'Darlin, we don't have long, and we should be making up for lost time. Come and lie down beside me. Let me hold you.'

No, you don't have long. It's later than you think.

Seeing me immobile and making no answer, he tries again. 'Just what is all this about? Jim *has* sussed something hasn't he? You're mad at me for not coming to fetch you back sooner, yes? Or – ah – I know. You've got your period. Is that it?'

I look away in exasperation. He interprets this as irritable assent.

'You know it doesn't bother me if you have. For lovers like us, that's just a minor laundry problem, right?' He smiles encouragingly, thinking he's got to the bottom of it, and licks his lower lip slowly. 'Come on over here, you luscious –'

I shrink away. 'Don't touch me.'

He sighs patiently. 'Zoe, what is all this about?'

'It's about the other night.'

'Ye-es?' he drawls, a tolerant smirk on his face. 'Which other night?'

'Forty eight hours ago. How long have you been shagging underage teenagers, Shaun?' There. It was out.

He confounds me by throwing back his handsome, leonine head and roaring with laughter. 'Darlin', you're priceless. What are you on about now?'

'You. You and your, your extra-curricular activities.'

He raises another polite eyebrow. I would give every single thing I own for this not to be happening.

'I saw them. I *saw* them. Don't even think about denying it,' I rasp, waving my glass for emphasis and spilling some drink on the tasteful flowered duvet, clearly a Debbie cast-off. The stain looks like semen. 'A woman in black and a young girl with long hair. Here. Two nights ago.'

He looks at me impassively. 'Have you been spying on me, little darlin'?'

'I was on my way to the theatre. With Jim.'

'And just what is it that you think you saw?'

'Them at your door. And then someone – let down the blinds in your flat.'

'Probably getting changed for the evening. Look, Zoe, forty per cent of my workforce is female. Some have kids. And I always say my more responsible senior staff can borrow the flat for family purposes as long as I don't need it. Perk of the job. They sort it with my PA.'

I move away slightly. The scent of him, even this far away, is making my head light, though its not so much a scent as an all-encompassing pheronomal signal...

concentrate. 'How come you don't know who was here that evening?'

'I told you, my PA –'

'Shaun, I saw you let them in yourself.'

'Did you, now.' He shrugs, then turns away to pour himself some more champagne. 'And what else did you see?'

'That woman pull the girl in by the hair.'

He couldn't look less interested if he was standing in the slow queue at Argos. 'Perhaps they'd had a mother and daughter fight,' he suggests casually, turning back, and offering me the bottle. 'And who says she was underage?'

I take a deep breath. 'You're a lying shit.'

There is a long pause. Then he smiles broadly and holds up his hands in surrender. 'You're right.'

'What?'

'You've got me.'

For a second I can only stare at him. 'You admit it?'

He yawns as if I'm drawing his attention to a parking fine he can well afford to pay. 'So? Half of them are sexually active at that age anyway, these days. Happy now?'

'You, you – pervert.' I am livid to find I'm crying. 'You *pig.*'

'Pervert? Oh, please.' *The little woman's making a fuss because she's seen her man chatting up the barmaid.*

He gets up and comes towards me, but I back away in revulsion.

'You total creep. You slimy… '

'Steady on, don't overdo it.' Since I'm now flattened against the wall, he changes tack and returns to the bed, sitting down on the edge. 'It's no big deal. What's a year or two between friends? You know I've always liked a little variety.'

'Is that what you call it? What are you?'

'Someone whose life runs the way they want it to. Just like yours would if you weren't so disorganised.' He places his hands on his knees the way they tell you to at counsellor training courses, to look open and unthreatening.

'You know what that kid probably thinks you are? A dirty old man. A balding punter –' Shaun automatically puts his hand up to touch his hairline and shows the first flicker of real concern I've seen all afternoon '– who pays underage girls because there's no way they'd let you have them for free. For God's sake, if they're fourteen or fifteen and you're fortysomething, don't you understand that you're just too goddam *old* for them? You, you… must be sick. '

'You don't know much about men if you think I'm sick to like young girls. Get this into your head – men like sex with young girls because they're not supposed to have them. There. How normal is that? The age of consent's pretty arbitrary anyway. I mean, there are respectable Muslim families in Britain, India and Pakistan marrying their daughters off at fourteen or fifteen; many rural and indigenous cultures do the same the world over. Don't worry. I don't pick any who haven't done it before, so it's not as if I'm doing them any harm.'

'No harm? *No harm?* Is that what you honestly think?'

'No harm in the world.' He sits up to plump the pillows on the bed and lies back against them even more comfortably than before. 'Sweetheart, you're really overreacting. Stop hugging the wall like that, come over here and I'll explain.'

I clench my fists. 'For God's sake, don't you realise what you are? What this makes you?'

'I told you, it's not like that. These girls aren't professionals or anything, they're very part-time. Just ordinary teenagers who want a bit more money to spend. And since you make such a point of it, most of them *are* over the age of consent, but they like to shop.' He risks a collusive smile in my direction. 'My friends and I merely look upon ourselves as – ah, income supplement.'

'Your *friends*? Pass them round from hand to hand at directors' tea parties, do you?' I grab my bag off the floor.

'You're disgusting, deluded and I'm leaving.' He's on his feet so fast I barely see him move, and standing right in front of me. Try to push past him but he moves back fluidly to block the bedroom doorway. 'I never, ever want to see you, hear you or speak to you again. You make me want to throw up.'

He looks down at me thoughtfully, but doesn't move.

'Get out of my fucking way, Shaun. *Now.*'

'No need to storm off in such a hurry,' he tells me, taking a belt of champagne straight from the bottle.

A feather of ice floats down my spine. For no one knows we are here, no one knows we know each other, and this man has just admitted something which, should it come to the ears of the wrong people – his shareholders, his wife – would cause an explosion to make Chernobyl look like an GCSE chemistry experiment.

'We've also got another little matter to attend to, haven't we?' he continues, putting the bottle gently back on the floor. 'I didn't ask you over here for nothing. I said I'd missed you, Zoe, and I have. Come here.'

I look at him carefully, measuring the distance between us, and shift back a fraction. For I feel something new for him now, something which I have never felt for him before.

It is fear.

This appears to please him. 'There, there, it's all right, little love,' he whispers, stepping closer and sliding his arms around me. 'Everything's all right. You need never be afraid of me, I promise. Unless, of course, you try to interfere with things that are none of your business again.' He smoothes a strand of too-long fringe back out of my eyes and gently strokes my hair. 'Unless you persist in talking about matters of which you know nothing –' one of his hands begins moving downwards. 'Unless I have to teach you a lesson about the wisdom of minding your own business.' The hand gently caressing my head suddenly seizes a chunk of my hair at the roots, jerking my head back sharply and forcing me to look up at him. '– or unless, of course, you continue to push your luck.' He lowers his mouth slowly onto mine, probing insolently with his tongue, stopping abruptly many long moments later to add: 'And believe me, you *have* been rather lucky so far. Or didn't you know?'

'And what is that supposed to mean?' *Let go of me, just let go –*

'Small world, Soho. You wouldn't want your husband to know that you've been back here again. He knows you had an affair, didn't he? That's partly why he left. But now he's back in the marital nest, and you won't be wanting to screw that one up. Well, will you?'

Flinch as if he's about to hit me – *he really has been keeping up with the family news.* 'Way off target. You clearly don't have the slightest idea of what goes on in our lives.'

He releases his grip abruptly and holds me at arm's length. 'Don't I? What do you think that Audi was doing parked outside your house night after night? I know you've been a bit distracted recently, but don't tell me you didn't see it, Zoe. It's gone now, hasn't it? My decision to leave you alone for a couple of months was soundly based on – information received. Did you really think I'd forgotten about you, all those weeks we didn't see each other?

'No! No, of course not.' The grown-up green car. Had it been him sitting in it? Someone on his payroll? *Night after night.* 'I just thought you must be, er, busy, that's all.' Sod it, my knees are shaking. Suddenly I cannot bear his hands touching me nor being this close to him, and try to squirm free. Shaun tightens his grip.

'Well, believe me, I'd not forgotten. You're important to me, like I said. So I've been keeping tabs on you, sweetheart. Looking out for you.' He lets go one shoulder to cup my chin gently, then forces it up so I have no option but to look at him properly. 'Ringing to check you're there, that sort of thing.'

Suddenly, my whole body feels as if it's stepped into cold water. Up to the neck.

'Nice little house you have. Cosy-looking. Mind you, it was seldom practical to keep as personal an eye on you as I'd have liked. I usually sent someone else along, and he'd report back.'

'Report what?'

Shaun's not smiling any more and he's still holding me by the shoulder, his fingers like iron. 'Oh, this and that.'

'You – you *utter shit*. What with the silent calls and all, I did begin to wonder whether someone – but then I thought it was just me being paranoid, because I've been going a bit strange. But you, you of all people. What ever did you get out of it? And what in God's name did you ever think you were going to see?'

'Maybe nothing. But it's the attraction of the hidden that gets me. Everyone's got a Watcher inside them, everyone. It was amusing, that's all. I've been amusing myself with you, Zoe, but perhaps not the way you'd imagined. I'd never have told you if you hadn't made all this silly fuss. If you hadn't spied on me, hadn't presumed to judge me. Yes, I've been amusing myself with you all right. Now, what do you think of that?'

Shocked to the core, I can find no answer apart from snatching at his eyes with dagger fingers but he's primed for assault and deflects them easily, laughing and kicking my legs from under me with one swift, vicious movement. Then he's on top of me in an instant, ripping the crotch of my tights, tearing at my clothes, forcing his tongue back into my mouth. Revolted, I bite down on it hard and as he recoils, knee him in the groin. There isn't room to do it nearly as hard as I'd like, but the two shocks of unexpected pain stop him short. He appears to be thinking things over for a second or two while continuing to hold me down, but then sighs, and pushes me away dismissively.

'I think,' he murmurs, wiping the blood from his bitten tongue as he stands up, 'that I would prefer to wait until you ask me for it. But you'll have to ask very nicely indeed next time because you've disappointed me, darlin'. Really disappointed me.' He turns away, dabbing his mouth on the back of his hand, taking no notice as I scramble clumsily away from him on all fours and pull upright on the chair by the door. My pants, hanging limply round one ankle, get thrust into the pocket of the sweaty jacket I am still wearing, my shoes jammed back onto bare feet, rubbing painfully without tights. Where are those tights? I think vaguely, snatching my bag off the bed and stumbling for the door, wiping his saliva off my face with a sleeve and risking one last look at him.

He's reclining on the bed now. Propped up on one elbow, shirt undone, bottle in hand, the picture of unconcern, looking at me with an ironic, possessive affection and the quiet confidence of someone who's about to get their own way again. 'You'll be back, sweetheart,' he tells me calmly, taking another belt of champagne. 'Didn't I tell you? No one walks out on *me*.'

I grab the door lintel for support. 'You are never, ever going to see me again. I don't care what you do or what you say. Don't bother putting the word out that I came here today in the hope that Jim will hear, because I shall fix up an alibi the second I get home. And I'm warning you, Shaun: come near me again and I'm calling the police. I know more than enough to put you inside, do you hear?' Hell, I can feel my throat seizing up, my eyes stinging with unshed tears. 'How could you? How could you do all that stuff? You can have almost any woman you want, so why those youngsters? And you didn't need to spy on me, because I loved you and would gladly have told you anything you needed to know. You're ill, that's it, you must be... and, and the worst of it is, because you look and sound so bloody normal, who would ever *know*?'

Fuck it, I'm starting to cry. Clattering downstairs, catching my toe in the hole in the carpet on the second landing, in my mind's eye I see the young girl move from the shadows to take my place. As she kneels obediently between Shaun's knees, I see her burying her face in the lap of the man I had adored. As the front door slams, his big hands are already on either side of her head.

His eyes are closing.

Tim's New Idea

Falling out into Old Compton Street, the sun hits me like a stage light shone directly into the eyes. I check my watch. Either it's stopped as it often does or I was only in there an hour. It feels more like a week. Christ, is that man psychotic – or just pathologically accustomed to doing as he pleases? And how do I make him stay away from me? The thought of him continuing to keep tabs on us is like the first chills of a nasty virus.

There is no place to slip my pants back on so I have to wait at the bus stop on Charing Cross Road feeling drafty, exposed and unpleasantly aware of the gritty exhaust billowing up my skirt. For the first time ever after being with Shaun I feel dirty, contaminated by the things he's done. My breasts crawl, my fanny itches. I don't just want to wash my body, I want to disinfect it, to step out of my skin and leave it behind in the street.

Trailing down our road opposite The Stables part of the market thinking of hot showers, scrubbing brushes and new knickers, something comes into focus. There is a figure hunched on our doorstep, half-hidden by the dustbins. It is small figure, and it is wearing a dark-blue school uniform. Tim barely looks up as I run the remaining few yards to kneel down beside him and fling a protective arm around his shoulders. 'What's wrong? How long have you been here?'

He looks at me tiredly.

'Tim, did something happen?' *Stupid, stupid, stupid – I should never have listened to Jim. Never.* I shouldn't have let him go back to that place, even for a few weeks while we tried to find the rest of that money…

'I've been waiting here for an hour. I looked through the window but it didn't seem like there was anyone in, so I sat here. I knew you'd come.' Berating myself savagely for not keeping him at home I find I'm patting his back in distress, a gesture more appropriate for a toddler than a twelve-year-old. He seems to think so too, and leans away. 'There, it's OK, sweetheart, you just –'

'It's not OK. Don't say that. Parents always say that. It doesn't mean anything.'

'I'm sorry, sorry; you're right.' Backing off respectfully, I kneel further away from him, knees together, mindful of my corrupted and knicker-less state. Can he sense the pollution clinging to me? Is that why he doesn't want me to hug him? 'Why are you here, darling?' I ask as evenly as I can. 'Was it an Inset Day today and I forgot? God, I am so sorry –'

'I walked out of the playground at lunch break.' He speaks in a flat, loud voice, totally unlike his own. He won't look at me and seems to be finding our overflowing dustbins rivetting. It is a minute or two before he can speak again. 'I can't go back there any more. It's like going into hell every day.' His face is the colour of paper but his voice, perfectly steady.

'Did those boys have a go at you again? They did, didn't they? What did they do to you?'

'The usual.' He swipes at his reddened eyes angrily with dirty knuckles, rubbing hard in the corners. 'The other boys don't ever let me play football with them even when I ask, even when I take my *own*. No one will sit next to me in class. They keep calling me gay – wanker – trannie – and, and stuff. Well, Lardarse starts it then they all do it –' He finally looks at me, his face pale and pinched from anger, incomprehension and misery. 'All I wanted was to be friends. I hate them now. I hate – bloody all of them.' He kicks a bit of decomposing satsuma peel.

'I hate them too. Little scumbags. You're worth a hundred of any one of them. No, a *million*. A hundred million. Look, Tim, how about –'

'I've got no one to talk to in break times now Luke's left,' he continues, his voice getting louder. Luke had recently been sent to Highgate School by parents who second-mortgaged their flat to do so. They were distraught. Not because he was being bullied senseless like Tim, but because he picked up such a marked Norf London accent so fast.

'And we're not allowed in the library at lunch play any more so, so –' he turns his face from me, creased with the humiliation and the distress of not understanding, of not belonging. 'What did I do wrong? Tell me, Mum, what did I do? I never did anything to them, so why –' His whole body is rigid with the effort of not breaking into tears.

'Oh, darling – look, I'm coming in with you tomorrow. We'll see the headmaster again.' I touch his arm gently, but he flinches as if he's been burnt. 'This time we'll make him listen even if we have to tie him to his own desk with those stupid yellow braces of his. We'll take Daddy, too. And I'll get hold of that boy's mother –' I quail a bit. She is a large woman with beefy forearms and a chip on her shoulder, for whom Lardarse (now what is his proper name?) an aggressive, overweight only child with the eyes of an assassin, can do no wrong. 'Well, on the phone first, perhaps.'

'It won't do any good. Pritchard just says stay out of their way. How am I supposed to do that, then? If they won't leave me alone?' He scuffs his shoes to and fro on the pavement.

My bare knees on the pavement are starting to hurt. I get up to lean against the railings that Jim half-painted bright green a year ago and never got round to finishing. Like most things in our house. 'Come on, sweetheart, let's go inside. We'll have something to eat, then we'll phone the school.'

'Don't bother, Mum. Just don't bother. I'm not going back there any more, so forget it, right? You can't do anything, and the teachers can't do anything. They say they can help if we come and tell them but they can't. Just *leave* it.'

'Tim, your school has an anti-bullying policy and we're going to make sure they enforce it.' I am shaking now from anger, distress and a sinking feeling that nothing I say to the school is going to make enough difference. I've tried to get this stopped before, many times. After each maternal rant at the headmaster (Jim's approach is to write polite middle-class letters) the results last less than a week.

'No! You're not listening to me! No one ever listens to me! You go to Pritchard, it'll just make it worse. They call anyone who tells a dobber, a grass – and then no one speaks to you – not that – not that they speak to me anyway, any more. I mean it, Mum. I've had it.' His set face, streaked with grubby tear tracks, brooks no argument.

'OK, OK. Fair enough. There's other schools...' Yes, all far rougher than Primrose Hill Primary, which parents fought to get their children into. There's no other possible option – unless you have money. Unless you can pay. Oh God, where can we get the rest of the cash?

'No.' he said firmly, though his voice is now barely above a whisper. 'I've thought about it.'

'Uh, huh,' I say encouragingly.

'I'm going to stay at home with you. I've, I've brought all my school books and stuff,' he stammers, scrabbling at the rucksack by his side. 'Well, I couldn't find the geography one, but – I can do schoolwork while you're out and you and Dad could help me with the hard bits when you get home. I've got the term's text books for Maths and English right here. I could help you too, you know. Do the washing up and stuff when you go to work. And I could stay in my room the rest of the time,' he adds humbly. He raises his head to look me properly for the first time. 'I can, can't I? ' he grabs my hand in his dank, chilly one for emphasis. 'Stay here, with you?'

Take a deep breath. 'You most certainly can.' *Jim can get stuffed.* 'We'll do our work in the mornings, then bunk off swimming every afternoon. You're a hero, Tim. You are special, and brave, in every way a complete star and I am immensely proud of you, sweetheart. *Immensely.* And since heroes have nothing further to prove to anyone, they deserve breaks, right?' I give him a hug, which this time he not only accepts, but returns convulsively. 'It'll be excellent. You'll see.'

As we go inside hand in hand, we are brought up short by a businesslike clatter from the kitchen. And who should be there but my mother-in-law, scrubbing behind the taps with a Brillo pad.

'Oh, there you are, Zoe,' she greets me. 'Hope you don't mind, but Jim did give me a key. Well – I can see it's a good while since this was last done.'

Out Of Our Depth

Life has just leapt several degrees higher in the good luck charts. For months, Jim has been punting a business plan for a new film industry service around potential backers. Now an independent media company has finally bitten, and its boss wants to take us all out to dinner. Not next week, not tomorrow but right now. Tonight.

The first I had heard of this was half an hour ago, when Jim blew in at 6 p.m. in an unprecedented good mood. 'Zoe! Zoe? Where are you? Listen to this,' he'd shouted excitedly, shedding bike jacket, gloves, helmet and briefcase in all directions.

Tim was in his room glued to the normally forbidden Gameboy, having scorned to join Kasha, Bel and self under the zebra-print blanket on the sitting room sofa. You couldn't blame him as we were all wearing dark glasses and fake pearls, drinking lemon barley out of champagne glasses, watching *Breakfast at Tiffany's* and taking it in turns to do Holly Golightly. 'Oh, Mummy,' breathes Kasha, who has developed a slight tummy of late. 'She's so *thin.*'

Washing was dripping from every radiator in the house because the Lazy Susan had fallen out of the kitchen ceiling earlier on, bringing down chunks of plaster which still lay all over the floor, and supper wasn't ready. Expecting him to complain, I braced myself. Instead, he hauled me to my feet and demanded: 'Am I or am I not an innovative genius whose talents have at last been recognised? Evening, Bel.'

Tricky question. 'Er –'

'I think I've got a backer for *FirstPencil*. A backer, Zoe! This company is actually considering giving me money for an idea that *I* thought up. We're to have a dinner with them

189

this evening.' He was so ecstatic he seemed to have shelved the Pregnancy Question, at least for the evening. Perhaps he needed a wife to put in a respectable appearance.

'We?'

'I've even arranged a free child-sitter since Angel's not back from Ibiza yet,' he added virtuously. This is just as well. Since plucking Tim from Primrose Hill Primary last month and enrolling him mid-term at Cavendish School down by Inverness Street market, we are even more cash-strapped than before. For though I've flogged my office furniture, computer, Harriet, the Edwardian amethyst pendant Mum gave me for my 21st, and my beloved vinyl collection is for sale in Rich's Retro Records meaning Tim's fees are sorted till the middle of next term, I hadn't counted on the three hundred and eighty-five pounds' worth of private school uniform and games kits.

'*Who?*' demands our son, appearing behind Jim, Gameboy in one hand and a can of Fanta in the other. He is getting very picky these days about who supervises his evening TV and checks his teeth. I look at him happily. Two weeks at a gentler new school and he's already losing his strained pallor and feeling safe enough to get stroppy.

'Hey, I could do it for you,' volunteers my friend.

'Thanks, Bel, but it's OK. Zoe, it was Maggie who offered. She's been here before, remember – to drop over those storyboards? Ended up staying for an hour to play Risk with the kids. She's now our new production assistant. We had to get another one since Rebecca – well, anyway,' he hurries on, aware that he had just dropped not just a brick, but an entire lorry load of the things, 'I told her how important this is for the company so she's doing it for nothing. So come on, Zoe, get dressed. We leave at seven fifteen.'

I fling myself at Jim and plant a huge kiss on his cheek before breaking away, embarrassed. We haven't hugged since that business in the hospital. And he's still on the single mattress, though the screen has been put to one side.

'Darling, that is brilliant, just brilliant. I knew someone would bite, it's a bloody great idea.' He grins, and pushes me out of the sitting room. 'Go on. Get all dolled up. Ah, and not the ball-dress and black leather stuff. We're going to The Grenadier House.'

Bel lifts her champagne glass and toasts the pair of us. 'To gratuitously expensive meals bought by other people…' and starts to gather up her bags.

Whoopee. This must be serious. The Grenadier House is so exclusive it doesn't even have a sign outside, though occupies the whole of a four-storey Queen Anne town house in Mayfair. It is so posh it hasn't got a dining room, just several intimate little suites furnished like the sets on *A Month in the Country*. The guest: waiter ration is roughly 1:1; the Maitre d', a famously disgraced Housemaster from Eton. Your bill is handed over in a pale mauve envelope, and there are no prices on the wine list. If you need to ask, you can't afford them.

I start emptying cupboards like an Interpol agent who's got sixty seconds to search a room, throwing piles of rejected garments onto the bed and upending drawers. Nothing that's even *clean*, let alone suitable. Who can lend me something to wear? Perhaps darling Bel who is a) nearby b) a prop and a stay, albeit one with an hourglass figure and a blunt manner? Unfortunately, her evening wear leans towards Balinese prints and Birkenstocks, both of which do much to conceal her many and varied attractions. No, there is only one person who can help me now.

'Lucia? Thank God,' I squawk into my mobile. In the background there's the predatory hum of a room-full of mediacrats on the pull. 'Burn rubber. Bring clothes.'

'Zoe, I am just having a drink with the sweetest little attorney who practically owns half of Nevada. He's just *exactly* what I have been looking for all these years.'

'Please. *Please.* This is – rather urgent.'

There is a brief silence, punctuated by blasts of unidentifiable music. 'Like that, is it?' When Lucia makes up her mind, she is magnificent, and she understands the power of proper clothes in a civilized world. 'Oh, very well. Colour?'

'Er, black.'

'Too draining over thirty – better be dark-green. Length?'

'Cocktail.'

'Shoes? Accessories?' she snaps, her professional instincts asserting themselves.

'Oh, yes please –'

'Occasion?'

I tell her.

'Well, hurr*ah*,' she drawls in a blasé manner perfected over years of incarceration in overpriced single-sex schools. 'You'll have your first decent meal in months. Sit tight, sweetie, I'll be right over.'

She arrives in a black cab thirty-five minutes later, which must be a record from Notting Hill via her Great Titchfield Street flat, and flings a vast black canvas bag down on the bed with a flourish. You can see why she's a top stylist. A dark-green Betty Jackson jersey dress, fitted to kill goes on first (*'A fraction snug, sweetness – I thought you were still size 10?'*) Vicious black moc-croc Blahnik heels, the right size. Donna Karen black lace stockings, ninety-five pounds the pair. Butler & Wilson earrings in dark-green and red glass the size of satellite dishes. ('Big ears are back'). A knuckleduster of a green onyx ring which looks incongruous next to my little circle of engagement diamonds. Yep, the ring's back home. Jim's mother, appalled to hear I'd popped such a token of her son's former esteem, had endowed it with the importance of a family heirloom and bought it back for us (well, for him really) having first offered to put it in her bank for safekeeping – before reluctantly letting me wear it.

Best of all, Lucia's produced a billowing black fifties-style evening coat of parachute silk with a mandarin collar and a huge red Firebird embroidered on the back, which I am sure I've seen in *Elle's* catwalk predictions for the coming season. *'ool*ian 'uck*onald*,' she tells me, her mouth full of hair grips, cutting across my tearful thanks, from which I understand her to mean that she has nicked me a Julian MacDonald original for the evening. She lays some of the grips on the bed in a row. 'Thought you needed something fuck-off fashionable for this very exciting occasion.'

'Oh, thank you, you're –'

'Don't gush, darling, it's too demeaning. Now come here. We must do something – anything – with your *hair.'* She rolls up her elegant sleeves and spits daintily on the brush. 'Do not, what ever you do, drop food on the coat.' I nod mechanically. 'Nor are you to perspire in that dress. It's for a *Marie Claire* shoot tomorrow, and I've not had a session from them for an absolute age. We're doing Chinese Imperial Decadence.' She proffers a canister of *StopSwet,* the pore-clogging deodorant catwalk models use, prescription only. 'Might cause a rash but you'll stay dryer than Death Valley.'

Which was exactly where it felt like we were going as our cab pulled up outside The Grenadier House, for despite becoming an obedient member of the Prozac Club, I'm still finding unexpected developments difficult to cope with.

Jim however, is six foot plus of lanky elegance and radiating enthusiasm in his one Boss suit (dark-blue, fluid, fits a treat) which sets off his dark-red hair and turns his eyes tawny. On the way here, he'd confided he was also wearing his lucky singing football socks but fortunately, his fashionably long trousers and Cuban boots hide them well, so no one should notice providing he doesn't rub his ankles together, which always sets them off.

'Don't be nervous,' he whispers ringing the bell. 'If it's dinner here, they must be keen. And you look great.' He gives my arm an encouraging pat as the cobalt-blue door opens just wide enough to allow us to squeeze inside. A be-suited arm attached to the most supercilious Greeter we have ever seen extends itself for our coats. I hang firmly onto mine.

He inclines his head graciously: 'This way,' and leads us to a mahogany door just below an elegant wooden staircase polished within an inch of its life. There are two stone pots of pale mauve hydrangeas positioned on either side and a vast expanse of dark brown polished boards sweeping away from it down the hall as far as the eye can envy.

The place is very quiet, with none of the bustle and purposeful pzazz you normally associate with a Mayfair restaurant that charges a week's salary for supper. In fact, there seems to be no one else here. A Gregorian chant is playing almost inaudibly; and there's the faintest, mouth-watering whiff of rosemary, garlic and roasting lamb. Greeter-man stands to attention outside the door in the gleaming corridor and turns the crystal knob with all the reverence of a state archaeologist opening up a tomb. Jim gallantly thrusts me over the doorway in front of him into the cosiest sitting room you ever saw. It has a cheerful little open fire, pale-lavender watered silk walls, tasteful originals of aristocratic Georgians in tarnished gilt frames, two overstuffed purple velvet sofas and the sort of chairs that usually have ropes across the seats in stately homes.

It also has five people in it, their eyes on the door. There is one in particular leaning against the pretty Adam mantelpiece, while another lights his cigarette.

It is Shaun.

I take a reflexive step backwards, crashing into Jim who is immediately behind me. Two of the suits spring forward; Shaun stays put. Picking me up off the floor and retrieving my left shoe from underneath a spindly side table takes a few moments. When the fuss subsides, Shaun looks straight past me at my husband, whom he favours with an assessing stare. Now he's holding out his glass to one sidekick and his cigarette to another without looking at either of them, and moving forwards to greet us.

'Jim.' It isn't a question, even though Jed isn't yet here. 'A real pleasure.'

His thrusts a manly hand forward for my husband to shake while his dark green gaze flickers across me, agate hard. 'And you have brought your charming wife, Zoe. Welcome, welcome.'

'Evening,' I gurgle, as well as you can when it feels like someone's just whipped a strand of razor wire round your throat. Directing a shaky smile at his tie knot merely achieves an expression normally associated with myxamatosed rabbits. Shaun smirks slightly. 'Damned polished floors. So sorry.'

What the bloody hell are you doing here? This is like waking up in the middle of the night and finding Hannibal Lecter sitting on the end of your bed with a kitchen knife in one hand and a chopping board in the other. *It can't be your firm, it just can't be,* screeches my brain, which has now shot from reverse to fifth gear without passing Go.

'Hi Jim, Hiya Joey,' rumbles one of the suits in a glorious Texan drawl, breaking into my hysteria as he bounds forwards. A dead ringer for General Schwarzkopf in a pale pink Harvey Hudson shirt and lightweight grey suit, he's grasping our hands with both his as if he'd never been so pleased to meet any two people in his whole life.

'It's Zoe, actually,' I mutter gracelessly, trying not to hyperventilate. That deodorant is already letting me down.

'Our trusted lawyer, Forrest McLean,' explains Shaun jovially. Lawyer? I thought this was supposed to be a friendly, getting-to-know-you supper.

Shaun's mouth seems to be moving but I cannot hear what he is saying because of a huge skin drum beating in my head

– the sound of a heart trying to cope with having a bucketful of adrenaline thrown over it. *How do you tell when a man's lying? His mouth moves.* Christ, he's doing it again –

'Uh, sorry?'

'I asked what you would like to drink,' repeats Shaun silkily.

Oh, I dunno: brake fluid, petrol, prussic acid? I'd swallow all three if only we could get out of here right now, this minute. Jim slips a steadying hand under my elbow, concerned that the wife's finding an evening with Mr Big unsettling. Try to concentrate on not falling over a second time, but Shaun's mouth is moving again.

'I'm glad you could both make it at such short notice, ah – Joey,' he says with a malicious undercurrent heard only by me, implying we are sorry cases to jump so fast when the corporate whip cracks. 'I'm afraid mine couldn't make it,' he tells Jim matily, beckoning the hovering wine waiter over. 'The children, you know. Chickenpox. Ghastly, even when you're small.'

Strange, they'd caught it a few months back too, when he rang up to excuse his lack of communication for a week. 'What, again?' I blurt before I can stop myself, shock having demolished all command of the social graces. Shaun ignores me.

'Allow me to introduce every else. Maxwell Fordyce, my right-hand man and second sight.' A swarthy bloke with big shoulders and a perfect pinstriper smiles like a hammerhead shark. The backs of his hands, when he shakes ours, are unpleasantly hirsute. He smells powerfully and unsuitably of Davidoff's *Cool Water*.

'Martyn Sharp, our chief accountant. A genius, nay a visionary with numbers.' Sandy-haired with innocent eyes like pale-blue marbles and an air of public school entitlement, Martyn's smile does not reach his eyes and his hand is soft. What did Shaun need to bring *him* for? He's massing his troops isn't he? At 5:2 we're outnumbered and outclassed since Seventh Wave has brought neither lawyers, accountants, nor what looks suspiciously like –

'Alicia Wallace-Browne, our director of marketing,' says Shaun, introducing the last of his posse with a flourish. 'Our favourite import from America, via the London School of Business. Muffy, to her friends.'

Muffy? They must be fucking.

A woman in her late twenties with perfectly streaked chestnut hair and a violet silk cocktail dress arises gracefully from the nearest sofa, holding out a languid hand. With her supercilious grey eyes and calibrating stare, she looks more like the head of a cut-throat modelling agency than a marketing director. I look at her more closely. It's Pink Whiskers.

'Good evening, Jim. Fabulous to meet you. I'm just so intrigued by the idea you sent us,' she purrs, in looking my husband up and down and totally by-passing me. What am I this evening – chopped liver? Her gaze then flickers briefly over me like a CAT scanner, and I just know she can tell that my clothes are on loan. What little bravado I arrived with, shrivels. I'm cocktail dress roadkill.

'Well, jolly good,' says Jim, slightly stunned but still enthusiastic, particularly having clapped eyes on Alicia. 'Marvellous to meet you all, I must say –'

Under cover of the flurry of introductions produced by the arrival of a timid-looking Jed and Maeve, I can watch Shaun more openly. He astonishes me. Seeing him chaff Jed whom he has never met before, be gallant to Jed's wife Maeve, have a sharp aside with Maxwell, fling a quiet word to Martyn who hurries off looking purposeful, then reel Jim in like a trout all in the space of five minutes, is dazzling. What an operator he has become. The perfect companies director, affable and in complete control – another persona, fully formed and functioning. Just how many can this man pack into his head? Professional opportunist, media pirate, venture capital chancer, achingly tender lover, stalker and pervert, professional bastard, Husband and Father of the year. The billion-dollar barrow-boy with the heart of a market trader and the soul of a gambler's whore, my digerati aristo from the Dagenham council estates made very good indeed. I watch him some more.

He's resting his hand lightly on Alicia's shoulder and she is almost arching towards him, a glossy little cat rubbing scent on its owner. Yet he barely glances at her, occupied instead by talking numbers with Martyn, and feeding a monosyllabic Jed, who this evening is displaying all the charisma of an out of order parking meter, the perfect pickup line to bring him into the conversation. This man dances with so many of his own shadows, he practically has his own chorus line. And I don't know who he is this evening or what he's after, but it certainly isn't dinner.

'Darling, could I just have a boring domestic word in your ear?'

Jim recognises something in my voice, the way you do when you've been together for years. Thank God, he's stopped talking to Maxwell and is turning towards me. Unfortunately Shaun hears it too, and cuts in swiftly: 'Jim tells me you're in journalism, Zoe.' I don't know whether to laugh, admire his sangfroid or punch him on the nose.

'Oh, *fun*. I thought about doing journalism,' breathes Alicia. Is this my passport to personhood in her eyes? Perhaps she's going to talk to me like an equal instead of not at all. But the cold grey eyes suggests differently. Hell, has Shaun told her about us? 'But, well, it's gotten so superficial, hasn't it? I mean, take health journalism.' *Yes, he has.* 'Ten years ago one could rely on the quality media for the inside track on medical scandals and cover-ups like BSE and the MMR. Now Britain's so celebrity obsessed, people only want to read about them or look like them so it's all bottom-sculpting and the botox backlash. I ask you.' She reaches daintily for a weensy won-ton snack but unfortunately hasn't quite finished with me yet. 'Yes, I do feel the *edge* has gone from popular media coverage. Newspapers are all bowing to the sound byte, even the broadsheets. And as for magazines, well frankly I feel the ads tell me more about mainstream cultural preoccupations and readership profile. Don't you?'

'Well that's certainly one way of –'

'– but I can just *tell* from looking at you that you're a current affairs journalist,' she simpers artlessly, 'so I know I'm preaching to the converted.'

Grounded on the sandbanks of professional one-upmanship, I wonder whether to admit I've given up sound bytes for cereal stacking. 'Well, I wouldn't exactly say –'

'Oh. So what *are* you working on at the moment?'

'Maintaining my equilibrium, mostly.' I see a smile flicker in the corner of Shaun's mouth. 'Excuse me. This coat's a bit –' I start shrugging it off to illustrate. 'I think I'll just –'

A silent waiter who looks like Johnny Depp materialises from the designer gloom under the stairwell. I slip off the billowing silk and hold it out to him. He bears it away as if carrying the papal investiture robes.

The Ladies loo is a delightful harlot's boudoir with shaded pink lights, a thick creamy carpet, a gauze canopy bellying down from the ceiling and a scented apple-wood fire. It looks like the best place to spend the rest of the evening. There is even, in case you needed to check up on your fellow guests' credentials, a thoughtfully placed copy of *Debrett* amidst the *Vogues* and *Tatlers*. Best of all there is a small dish of rose cream chocolates on the dressing table. Mindlessly eat three, but still too demoralised to go back. So, though I know I certainly shouldn't, I dig out a little something which Lucia pressed upon me earlier to stiffen my resolve if required. It's a small silver heart container attached to a tiny silver tube with a stopper. The stamp on the back says Tiffany's NY.

Inhaling hard, the coke hits my nasal septums like powdered bleach on a fresh graze. It feels like the top of my head is coming off, but who cares because my guts are already catching fire with pharmaceutically induced bravado. I'm going straight back in there to fix Shaun good. Ha! I know things about that man that would make his minions' hair curl. And as for Muffy the Vampire Slayer, what's so special about *her?* Marketing, bah. Bet she knows sod all about it and spends her days fiddling bar charts and assembling mythical consumer profiles.

Regrettably, I know that this happy state is going to last about forty minutes at most, and put me right off my food.

Sniffing delicately, I march out of the boudoir brimming over with misplaced confidence, only to run slap into Shaun who's leading everyone upstairs for supper like the Pied Piper. Muffy has a firm grasp on Jim's arm, with Martyn and Forrest close behind like a pair of FBI agents.

'Ah, welcome back,' smiles my ex lover, taking my wrist in a grip like a python's. 'I think we shall have you sitting next to *me.*'

Being Had For Dinner

Our private dining room is a beautifully proportioned little circular space whose crimson silk wall hangings remind one of a womb, or perhaps a large vagina. The atmosphere is heady with the scent of the sort of white lilies usually associated with the state funerals of Eastern Block dictators; the dark wood floor gleams, reflecting the light from fat white candles in silver candelabra, and the temperature's Kew Gardens' hothouse.

As we approach the table, Shaun ushers everyone charmingly to their places, manoeuvring me firmly into the chair on his immediate right.

Waiters stand against the walls in tight black and white livery. We seem to have one each. They move smoothly into action behind us, whisking out chairs and spreading starched damask napkins reverently over each guest's knees. Half expect them to give us an Indian head massage each and cut up the food for us later as well. Perhaps I can ask mine to eat my dinner for me too when the time comes, since my appetite's gone where the dead crabs go.

Everyone starts talking at once now the social wheels have been oiled with some decent drink. But it's like being in a video on jerky fast forward for I'm zoning rapidly in and out of conversations, and can only concentrate on snatches of talk here and there. I also seem to be drinking a lot, but it's not helping. Fortunately Shaun is leaving me alone apart from offering sun-dried tomato bread sticks, tiny Corsican olives and seeing that the waiters keep my glass full.

On my other side, Martyn Sharpe is making an Effort and telling me all about the effect the Euro had has on Britain's economy: 'It's dissolved so many borders for commerce, but then of course e-business has already done that a hundred-fold. We are witnessing the global democratisation of capitalism,' he enthuses, pale eyes aglow.

As the starters arrive, I steal a sidelong glance at Shaun's tough profile as he chats to Muffy and Jim about hyperdrives. Simply cannot credit any of this. He's behaving like the last few months – no the last *twenty years* – never happened, and acting like he's never met me before. How can he? And why can't I?

Oh God, what does this social animal with the office-do manners want? I cannot believe he's only asked us for a friendly chat about a business proposal, and if he has, that hardly justifies him having the rest of the management team here as well. Because he's so close I can feel the warm air move between us as he stirs, sense his relish of the situation, his amusement, and his control freakery in full flood. He's watching Jim too closely and smiling at him just a bit too much, drinking little himself yet seeing that Jim and I are permanently topped up. Indeed, in the combined warmth of Muffy's skilful flirtatiousness and Maxwell's fascination with every single thing he says, Jim is becoming expansive and coming across like a Labrador let loose in the long grass.

But my confidence is fading. Coke-induced ballsiness only lasts about half an hour and if you're not off the conversational runway by then, you've missed the flight. Check out the plate of chanterelle mushrooms in front of me, which looks like a pile of sea slugs. A cautious mouthful confirms that it tastes like them too. Am unpleasantly aware of the heat coming off Shaun's thigh, next to mine. *Don't speak to me, please.*

He doesn't, being far too busy giving the assembled company the benefit of his entrepreneurial analysis '– though of course the re-evaluation of the world's stock markets was probably the first collective unconscious movement in the history of mankind –' and smiling so his eye teeth catch the light. What's he on about? Jed nods enthusiastically but contrary to his usual florid ranting, still has little to say. Me neither. I can only register fragments of talk flickering across the table and none of it's making any sense for the words are rattling, bouncing and spinning like silver balls shooting round a pinball machine.

'Cash burn –'

'B 2 B –'

'Internet speed –'

'– crash n' burn –'

'– ninety per cent club –'

'What's that?' I ask the room in general in an attempt to get in on the conversation.

'A historical term describing those members of the private investment sector who saw the value of their e-investments fall tenfold,' explains Shaun.

'Gosh.' So much for coke-induced fluency.

'Why do you think we're so into venture capital now?' he demands, not smiling any more, addressing the table at large.

'Not that we don't still want to keep our traditional business base,' puts in Martyn quickly. 'Our magazines, web sites and information lines are still doing incredibly well.'

'Oh, most certainly,' amends Shaun. 'But we're concentrating more on print and niche phone-services now, not new sites. There are far too many of the latter, even after the millennium cull.'

But – Jim's idea is net based. So why've they asked us to dinner? Try to scribble: 'Be v. careful of S' on my napkin underneath the tablecloth using Lucia's Lancôme eye pencil, then deliberately knock a pudding spoon to the ground, intending to scrabble after it and shove the napkin onto Jim's lap when I'm down there because he's sitting opposite. Foiled by two waiters throwing themselves forward and competing for the honour of providing a clean bit of cutlery.

'Which is where you come in Jim, Jed,' continues Shaun. 'You've put forward what is potentially one of the best new proposals I've seen in years. And no matter how crowded the market, there's always room for an A-list idea.' Jim and Jed beam in unison, but my stomach drops. Is this it? No. First, apparently, we have to have pudding. Hell, where'd the main course go? Don't remember eating anything. As if sensing my panic, Shaun smiles at me and squeezes my thigh in a friendly, reassuring manner.

Though startled (just the smile would have done, thanks) I feel happier than I have all evening. Perhaps he's trying to say he knows how this must look, but he's on the level? Begin to feel like maybe I could eat something after all, then freeze. A warm hand is working its way under my dress, seeking the soft space at the top of my thigh where the stocking-top ends. Though I've grabbed a dessert fork and am now stabbing it under the tablecloth, it begins sliding its way under my right leg's knicker elastic. Skewer it viciously. It merely burrows harder.

'More wine, Jim?' asks Shaun a few moments later, casually sucking the index finger of his right hand.

'No? Then it's coffee time, I think.' He places both hands flat on the table, catches the eye of everyone around it, and gets to his feet. 'Ladies, gentlemen: time to adjourn downstairs.'

As I start to slide away from the table to try and walk downstairs next to Jim – a quick whisper in the corridor might do it – Shaun takes my arm once more, and escorts me himself. Our party mills around as we enter the sitting room, everyone seeking a strategic place to sit.

Disengage myself and sidle over to Jim, who's corralled on the sofa between Martyn and Forrest. 'Darling, can I have a very quick word?'

The three men look up. Jim seems a little annoyed. 'What about? You look a bit pale, love. Aren't you feeling well?'

'Yes. I mean no,' I do wish Forrest wouldn't stare like that, 'I'm fine. Terrific. I just –'

'Darling, not now. Sorry Maxwell, I missed that.'

'Jim?'

'Later, Zoe. I'm talking.' *Yes, in fact you are talking far too much.*

'May I get you a coffee, my dear?' offers Maxwell, not waiting for my reply but steering me gallantly back to Shaun who is standing with Alicia in his favourite spot by the mantelpiece, and motioning to a waiter fussing with little cups. Muffy undulates away with a sly smile to chat up Jed and Maeve, who are looking a little lonely again in adjoining armchairs. Perching on the arm of Jed's, she's revealing several inches of taught, shiny thigh. His wife looks put out. A Steiner eurhythmy pianist so ideologically sound she makes Arundatti Roy look like a media whore, Maeve regards shin hair as a woman's birthright and consequently has legs like Mrs Tiggywinkle.

'So. How are you?' asks Shaun quietly, standing two feet closer than socially necessary.

The coke speaks. 'Fine, considering I had a miscarriage recently.' I have the tiny satisfaction of seeing him flinch, tempered by the urge to clap my hands over my mouth. This has to be Number One on the list of: Things you don't say to your husband's backer in public when he's the one who impregnated you in the first place. No one else can see Shaun's expression as he is three quarters turned to me, with his back to the room at large. They can't hear either as we were talking softly and they are all at the gassing and backslapping stage. Jim is hemmed in again by Martyn, Forrest and Maxwell, a large brandy in his hand.

'You *what?* Christ, when? Why didn't you say anything that day at the flat? I'd never have –'

'We had other things to discuss. If you remember.'

He fingers the knot of his tie. 'Yeah, well, so we did.' Then lets out a long breath and pulls himself together. 'I suppose that now you're going to try and tell me it was mine?'

'Yes, because it bloody well was. And it wasn't an it, I think it was a *she* –'

'A little girl.' To my astonishment he looks momentarily gutted. 'No, come on,' he rallies harshly, 'you had an abortion, didn't you?'

'I did *not*. I had a fallopian tube out too, it was blown to hell. I was in hospital for a week. Ask Jim. He's barely spoken to me since.'

A funny expression skitters briefly across his face. 'You poor sweetheart. You must have been – hang on a minute. You didn't tell him it wasn't his, did you?' I grasp my tiny coffee cup tightly in both hands to prevent myself from boxing his ears.

'Well, what did you say to him? Whose did you say it was? I hope you presented it as a little accident, as any normal woman would have –?'

I can feel steam coming out of my ears. Enough is enough. 'Jim had a vasectomy. Two years ago.'

'Ah.'

'Oh, don't worry,' I reassure him sardonically. 'He has no idea it was you.'

'Well, thank – I mean, I suppose that's something.' Shaun runs his hands though his hair. 'Look, I'm sorry. I'm sorry. I –' he looks at me properly, without calculation or false bonhomie, for the first time this evening. 'I wasn't expecting this. Do you – did you really think it was a little girl?'

Nod briefly, not trusting my voice.

'Zoe, listen to me,' he says quietly, urgently, lowering his voice even further. 'I accept that it's over for us. You made that plain enough recently. But this changes things, doesn't it? We need to talk. And I think we also need to –'

'Shaun! Hey, boss. I believe that Jim has something to say to us,' calls Maxwell from the sofa next to my husband. Ziggurat's staff arrange themselves as if for a team photo, leaving Jim, Jed and Maeve a few feet in front. Shaun's people are now looking alert, slightly malicious and ready to be amused, an audience at the beginning of an illegal blood sport event. And Jim is the sport.

Shaun shoots a last glance at me, then the shutters come down as he realigns his loyalties. Holding my elbow lightly he makes his way back to his posse, dropping me off as if at a bus stop next to my husband. The atmosphere has changed from holding pattern to landfall. It's deal time.

Shaun looks like a Mafiosi capo surrounded by his lieutenants. He's got the power all right tonight – over all of us. For what is power, if not someone holding the thing you long for in the palm of their hand and showing it to you? Jim had been a gonner ever since Shaun had opened his fingers that first fraction and let him see what lay inside: solid backing, real money, a last chance.

'Over to you,' announces Shaun, making himself comfortable next to Muffy, his charming mask back in place. 'Make it come alive.'

Just as I'm wondering whether to stage an epileptic fit (they'd surely let us go then) Jim fills his lungs. At first he stands with his legs apart, arms folded defensively, but he's talking, he's enthusing. Moments later, he's unknotting his arms and gesturing elegantly, spinning them a scenario for Ziggurat out of pure atmosphere, intuition, and substantial knowledge of his industry and very attractive he's making it sound.

His confidence grows as he speaks. He makes eye contact, walks to and fro excitedly, draws each person in one after the other, milks responses from them, small comments, questions, and then finally approval. He's good. Really good. They're beginning to smile. First Forrest, then Maxwell, then remarkably, Martyn. Jed is nodding furiously over by the fireplace, a silent Greek chorus. Muffy has whipped out a tiny gold notebook and is scribbling notes as if her life depends upon it.

'...we get every one of the creative film and ad production staff on line within the year. We target ads, five and ten minute film shorts, commercials and pop promos first. If that works, we widen out into features staff, but many do both. Producers, directors, line producers, directors of photography, clapper loaders, PAs, assistant directors, props specialists, make-up artists, hairdressers, location finders, gaffers, best boys, production accountants, electricians, model makers, animators, editors and post production people –' he risks drawing breath.

'We'll keep on-line availability calendars updated by the artists themselves,' quavers Jed, finding his voice for the first and only time that evening, 'correct to within twenty-four hours. It'll save producers and their assistants days – *weeks* – of useless phoning around. If it's not kept up, they're automatically dropped.'

'Good thinking,' concedes Maxwell.

'*FirstPencil* will also encourage directors and producers to work with *new* crew members,' explains Jim, now really on a roll. 'They get stuck in their comfort zones, which is bad for creativity and bad for new talent trying to break in. Since mistakes can be disastrous when a new face doesn't work out, directors will often only work with the same small circle of people time after time.'

'So?' challenges Shaun, by now puffing on a small black Havana, which wreathes his face in smoke and makes him look both inscrutable and arrogant.

'So their work goes stale faster than it should, their crew options become very limited and the talent pool ultimately stagnates,' explains Jim with a warm smile, barely breaking stride. '*FirstPencil* provides full information and tasters of what other crew and artists really offer because a Client-Only click through (to which the members themselves don't have access) will give comments and ratings on the artists from other producers and creative directors who've used them. They tell companies the things they really want to know – not just who's won which awards, but: did this producer bring his last ad in on budget? Does that director habitually rub crew up the wrong way? How is this line producer at managing location crises, how does that chief cameraman react to input or criticism from advertising clients? We call that the Fuck Up Rating facility. Mistakes are expensive in film. An up-to-date FUR for each creative will help companies avoid them.'

'Oh, neat idea,' drawls Muffy.

'Our site would knock competitors like Call Up sideways. It gives the creatives the exposure they need to potential new clients, speeds up availability checks a hundredfold, and gives the hirers the inside track in seconds.'

'I like it,' allows Shaun.

'And the same pattern can be used in LA, Sydney, Bollywood, France – it'd spread out like a franchise, country by country –'

'Excellent,' pronounces Forrest.

'– within eighteen months. Profits thirty/seventy with our backers.'

'Remind me of why we should do this with you and not with a bigger film company?' asks Martyn coolly.

'Because we thought of it, have the contacts and expertise to run it and the idea's patent pending,' says Jim in a level voice, taking a big swallow of wine.

A silence falls, broken after about fifteen very long seconds by Shaun.

'OK. I'll give you what your business plan said you needed for start up.'

'Half a million?' checks Jed swiftly, remembering, rather late, that he used to be a (decent but bored) accountant before becoming a (below average) video producer who doubles as the company's financial director.

'Yes. But we'll need collateral.'

'Of course –' choruses Seventh Wave.

'Well, that's it then,' announces Shaun. 'Forrest?' He needn't have asked. The Texan has already commissioned the opening of three bottles of Bollinger and the waiters are filling up glasses. 'To *FirstPencil*,' smiles my ex-lover. 'To *FirstPencil*!' agrees everyone else.

Suddenly they're all shaking hands (even Alicia air-kisses me twice) and slapping each other on the back. Forrest is doing his double knuckle-cruncher. Maeve is positively teary, Jed's behaving as if he's responsible for the whole thing and Maxwell looks like a benevolent uncle tipping the waiters at his nephew's bar mitzvah. No discussion, no 'we'll get back to you after we've thought about it.' Wham, bam, in the can. What is wrong with this picture?

Jim flashes a look at me and I wonder if I've spoken aloud. I squeeze his hand and whisper: 'You were absolutely terrific. I'm so proud,' while continuing to wonder what the catch is but am distracted by the first proper smile he's given me since University College Hospital: the wide-open wonder of a schoolboy who's just won the scratch-card jackpot. I don't want to spoil this, but I must. 'Jim,' I whisper in his ear, 'I've got to tell you something. You see, I've heard of Shaun before. And apparently, he isn't very –'

'I don't give a monkey's whether our backers are nice people or not,' he hisses back. 'I just want their support.'

'It's not that he's not *nice,* he's –'

We are interrupted by Jed, looking smug. 'We did good there,' he tells Jim. 'Very nice.' We? Jim is used to him by now so he doesn't thump him, but I'd like to.

'Zoe, don't get worked up,' Jim mutters out of the corner of his mouth. 'I can see you've had something on your mind all evening, but it's going to have to wait. We'll talk on the way home. OK?'

'OK,' I reply dully. I suppose they've done nothing Jim can't get out of if necessary. But get out of it he must. Even if he has to hear (a heavily edited version) of the past few months' events. Even if he starts sleeping in Tim's room again and gives his mother another key. Even if he (please, no) moves out again. Because I cannot, will not stand by and watch Shaun Lyon play him like a xylophone.

The sudden release of tension in the room makes me want to pee. Since the business of the evening has clearly been concluded, it seems like a reasonable time to go. Scamper to the Ladies, collapse into the roundest and pinkest of the armchairs and whip out my Nokia. 'Lucia?'

'Sweetie! How's the dress?'

Sticking to my back as we speak. 'Perfect. Listen, Jim's idea, Lucia. I can't believe it. The backer is Shaun, yes *that* Shaun – and he's said yes. Sorry? Well, God knows. Yes I suppose it is wonderful, but I'm a bit... no, but I just am. Oh, Jim was *amazing*, he did a superb number on them. Look, I *have* been trying to have a word with him but he keeps waving me away, and now they're all stuck into the drink –'

'Hmm. And how *is* That Man conducting himself this evening?' she demands beadily, being the one person I'd told.

'Shaun's been – OK, I guess. I don't actually think he's that interested any more.' The burrowing finger had, I suspect, essentially been mischief-making. Just to show he still could.

'Well, we'll see. Have you signed anything yet?'

'Of course not. It's a bit early for that.'

Her voice rises several decibels. 'Do you mean to tell me you've left Jim and that bellicose airhead he calls a partner, with That Man and his henchmen all on their own?'

'I needed a wee.'

'Get back in there this instant.'

'Oh honestly, Lucia, you are so –' I'm trying to squirt some of the restroom's free Aperge down my cleavage with my spare hand '– suspicious.'

'I said *now*.'

'Why?'

'Do it. I have a hunch.'

When Lucia says she has a hunch, people listen: her sense of survival is second to none. And sure enough, sprinting back to the party, the first thing I see is Shaun and Forrest positioned either side of Jim on the sofa. The second is that Jim is writing something, using Forest's briefcase as a

211

desktop. I watch incredulously as Martyn brings Jed over and hands him a pen too. 'What's that you're doing, darling?' It sounds like I've been sniffing helium.

Jim looks up and smiles happily. 'Signing the contract, of course.'

'What, already?' Lucia would never have fallen for this one. She'd not have left him for a second, not even if her bladder had exploded.

'Oh, they had it with them.' *I just bet they did.* He relinquishes his place on the sofa and comes over to draw me into the room, handing me the glass that I'd left on the little Sheraton table. I take a medicinal swig. The champagne goes down like a barium meal.

'It's all above board. Quite usual to offer up a private residence as collateral in an unsecured business deal,' mutters Jed defensively, seeing my murderous expression. He's even talking like Forrest now. 'Ah, terrific. Marvellous,' he tells Martyn Sharpe loudly, as the accountant appears by our side for his turn at contractual handshaking, then turns back to me cheerfully. 'We have a few loose ends to tie up but apart from that it's all perfectly –'

'Jim, what did you just do?'

'What do you mean?'

'Whose private residence is being used as collateral? Not ours, surely. Tell me it's not ours.'

'Well –'

'My God, it *is* ours. Unsecured business deal? We're the ones who are unsecured,' I whisper, glaring into his drink-rouged face. 'And that house is half mine, even if it's yours on paper. You have no right, *no right* to put that on the line without asking me too.'

'Look, be reasonable. You can't expect them to hand over half a million quid for nothing,' Jim tells me quietly. 'Anyway, it's perfectly OK. Jed's already checked it all out, since Ziggurat intimated this morning that this is the sort of guarantee they'd need. It all works out fine, because these days that little house, because of where it is, is worth nearly six hundred thousand.' Alicia and Forrest are approaching, but sensing friction, veer aside talk to Maeve and Forrest instead. 'And do keep your voice down.'

'It's not *that* little house, it's *our* little house.' This is not an easy conversation to have in a whisper with your mouth fixed in a smile, it's a five star shouting match that needs its space. 'Could you not have suggested something else? And your idea's not Nothing. It's so good, they're prepared to pay half a million for it. You don't know that man, Jim. But I do – I mean,' I correct myself hastily, 'I've certainly heard of him, and if you hadn't been giving me the brush off all evening I would have told you all about –' Shut up abruptly as Shaun sharks over to stand in front of us, Muffy in one hand, cigar smoking like Vesuvius in the other.

'Everything all right?'

'Oh, absolutely,' says Jim a bit too quickly. 'A technicality. The collateral aspect, you know. My wife –'

'Collateral is just a tedious legality, and par for the course in business start-ups,' Shaun assures me, correctly assessing why I am going puce in the face.

'Right, so's bankruptcy.'

'Zoe,' murmurs Jim, placing a restraining hand on my arm.

'Ha ha,' laughs Shaun, the business magnate taking a joke in good part. 'More champagne?' Then he starts explaining what 'joint and severally liable' means.

The Harringtons taxi home in silence. 'Well, I showed the bastards, didn't I?' says Jim brightly as we pass Euston station. 'Pity Jed didn't talk much. He's really good when he gets going.'

For the life of me I cannot say a word.

'And what was wrong with you tonight?' he bursts out suddenly. 'You were really rude to Shaun. And what was it you needed to tell me about him? That he's not very *what*?'

It's a bit late to put my marriage on the line to prevent something which has already happened. 'Oh – a friend of mine came up against him a few years ago. Apparently he's a ruthless shit.'

'He's a successful businessman. He has to be,' says my husband, with all the certainty of one who's just met his new role model. I mutter something, then look out of the window, for I have a bad feeling. Very bad indeed.

'Why can't you just be happy for me? Just for once? Why do you automatically assume I'm going to fail?'

'I don't. I think *FirstPencil* is a great idea.' And it is. But how come no one else has bitten? There've been twitches of interest upon Seventh Wave's fishing line, but nothing more. No one wants to invest in dot.com sites any more. No one except – someone who, by his own admission, is also getting out of that area.

The cab disgorges us at our front door and as always, we go straight upstairs to see Tim and Kasha. Maggie is fast asleep on the sofa, and the only sign of life is the fish tank flickering in the darkened hall. The children lie sprawled on their backs, limbs splayed, covers trailing, blameless and beautiful in sleep, their floors treacherous tips of clothes, Lego, and in Tim's case, robotic spare parts. Kasha has eleven Beanie Babies in bed with her and the Vicar asleep on her pillow, one paw against her face.

I lie wide-eyed and wakeful in our bed: a mixture of coke, alcohol and paranoia will keep you up every time. Jim is breathing deeply, dreaming perhaps, of millions to be made, of bastards who'd been shown and of a big mill house in Devon, just like he's always wanted.

Roll over in the bed, feet seeking the edges to cool them down. I had been cherishing the very small hope, nurtured as one would a sick begonia, that Shaun would – what? Be genuinely interested? Let us off, for old times' sake? He has, in a way, done both.

But that isn't all he's done. And I think I know why. *Sweetheart, didn't I tell you? No one walks out on me.*

The Summons

Three days later, the object I've been dreading arrives. Just looking at it gives me heartburn.

An envelope, my name on it, scrawled in that familiar spiky black writing from way back squats on the doormat amidst an avalanche of bills we cannot pay. In contrast, there is also a cheerful postcard from Dad featuring a picture of Johnny Halliday, saying would we like to come out to France for October half term and if so, that the clematis needed subduing and the piggeries, repainting.

Jim picks it up both postcard and letter and politely gives them to me on his way out as I scuttle round the kitchen. He has crammed the bills into his briefcase unopened. I look up from making Kasha's packed lunch (she's on a salad cream and Marmite sandwiches kick) and scanning *Loot* for second-hand sofas. Ours is now collapsing so completely that even Jim can't stand it, broke as we are. 'Just find us something under two hundred quid,' he'd said, a budget more suitable for a single designer cushion from Liberty's. 'Or – hell, go splurge out if you like. Ziggurat's cheque'll be here any day now.' He leaves, shoulders back, head up, whistling '*The best things in life are free.*' Since the dinner party he's been far more friendly, though he still won't lay a finger on me in bed nor discuss anything that is not of a strictly practical nature. However, friendly is progress.

I pick up the letter cautiously between finger and thumb, toy with the idea of belting after the postman and asking him to take it away again, then prop it up against the kettle where it sits, sinister as the envelopes which brought anthrax to the Pentagon. Two bickering but cheerful children are taken to school. In the playground of hers, Kasha rummages in her bright pink Pussy Galore bag to extract a hand-made calendar covered in sparkles and scraps of bright material ('Oh Mummy, they said to do a picture of our mum the way we see her to use as a kitchen thingie, but you've got to mount it on card for me first, so here –'). Look at it mistily, only to see a figure in green and white stripes with mad dark hair juggling – and dropping – a bucket and mop, a mobile, two cats, a plate of chips and a large brain. She's flying through the air, apparently powered by a nervous fart. 'I did the brain big, cos you used to be quite clever.'

'Thank you, darling.' *My daughter thinks I'm crazed and thick.* 'Oh, it's Wednesday isn't it? Is Azaria coming back to tea with us after tap, as usual?'

'Um – well, she likes her mum's food better than ours but she did say I could go back to hers. Can I? Her mum does proper cakes and real shepherds pie, even though she's a high-up doctor.'

By ten to nine I'm home again, putting on my green and white striped uniform, ready to leg it up the road for the nine till three Mothers' Shift. Unable to leave without looking, I tug the letter open very slowly to find a single typed slip:

'Business partners should be friends. Call me.'

So – the summons has arrived. He's demanding his dues after all, not because he specially wants them, but because he knows that he can. The brief whispered conversation that night at The Grenadier House was just more of his usual bullshit. *Someone just make him go away.*

But tell him to sod off now and he'll pull the plug on *FirstPencil*, when they are so nearly there. How long will it take before they are up and running, with all the legal stuff signed and sealed: two weeks? Three, at most. All (all) I need to do to safeguard Jim's new company launch is play nice for three weeks. Just three weeks, after which, it should be possible to pull out safely, since he's too good a businessman to axe a successful project that's up and running. I can do that. I think. Oh Christ –

Ring his office using my maiden name, the one I had when we were together, and make an appointment to meet him at the Holly Bush in Hampstead at seven tonight. Shaun's PA says she'll let him know. Will think of something to tell Jim. Perhaps an unsuccessful second-hand Chesterfield hunt. He did say to get a sofa.

Run upstairs two at a time to bang on Angel's door. A muffled voice asks what sort of time I call this, but it also agrees to baby-sit from six o'clock, providing I'm back by ten thirty because she's doing a lucrative late at Cottonfella's.

Pounding up to Morrison's through the flying grit of Chalk Farm Road, I calculate this should give me enough time to get ready. For what, depends on Shaun. Still at least if we meet at that particular pub, I can always kill two birds with one drink and drop by Rufus and Annie's afterwards to water their blasted plants. They'd flown off last week for another of their power-breaks – Rajistahn again, they (like the rest of London's design freaks,) can't seem to keep away from the place. And these days, I am really grateful for that extra tenner a day.

The day passes in a panic-stricken blur which six hours of patrolling the stone-ground pitta-bread shelves fails to soothe, though it's restful to know that the worst case professional scenario here is not being harangued and discarded for failing to meet your deadlines, but a shelf briefly empty of organic breadsticks.

Three twenty-five, and have just made it to the gates of Cavendish School in time. The playground is aswarm with children in grey and blue uniform shoulder-punching their friends, tripping over school bags, hugging their mothers and clustering round the ice cream van that's parked by the gates in all weathers.

Tim detaches himself from a group and approaches with a bouncing new stride he never had at Primrose Hill. Collecting him from school these days is a pleasure. No longer do I have to scan the playground for a pale, shrinking figure hanging back from the others, or try to gauge from the way he walks just how bad a day he's had. Cheerful, garrulous and flushed with recent laughter, he falls into step with me as we turn right down Inverness Street. Tie askew and shoelaces trailing, Tim's now telling me a stream of jokes which would disgrace a Woolworth's cracker. ('What did the vampire doctor say to his patients? *Necks*, please')

The market's had a slow one as it's been drizzling on and off all day, so the pungent cheeses stall is already packing up, putting its huge Bries, runny Camemberts and rancid Stiltons into wooden boxes packed with pale straw. Battered vans clog the street, doors flapping as the stall-holders re-load their unsold wares. You have to watch your step at this time of day as the road is slick with squashed grapes and splodges of beef tomato. Mikey the flower man is flogging off wilting red roses cheap ('Ere girlie, they'll go wiv yer eyes').

'We listened to Peter and the Wolf today in music. Can I do oboe lessons?'

'Sure. I mean, maybe. How much does it –'

'I got three out in cricket too. One was a golden duck, one for a single run. It was right good.' I wince, sad middle class to the core. He'll be saying 'them trees' next. And Cavendish School with such a high proportion of academics and media parents too.

'*And* I got a Phage The Untouchable. Swapped it for a Trained Armadon, and two Shocks,' he finishes with satisfaction, nudging me to make sure I am listening.

What? 'A good day, then –'

He picks his nose and eats it voluptuously, savouring both the cricket memory and the succulence of the bogey. I avert my eyes, and wonder if or when he is going to grow out of either Magic cards or nose-picking. 'Can Bradley come back for tea tomorrow?'

'Why not,' I answer absently, tugging at a ragged cuticle with my teeth. Those nails used to look nice. 'Who's Bradley?'

'The new boy, even newer than me. I'm *hungry*. When's supper?'

At home, we are using a screwdriver to prise a block of mince free of the freezer drawer when an argumentative Kasha is dropped off by Azaria Winston's dad. A session bassist, he's just come off an all-nighter that ran on a bit at Chalk Farm Studios and is looking wondrously dissipated. It is one of the great inequalities of life that if men have been up all night they look like sexy buggers, but when women are exhausted they merely appear haggard.

Flick on the TV to keep the children quiet (*Art Attack* – educational, twenty-five minutes). Five minutes later, I am also clamping the walkabout under my chin, listening to a tirade from Bel whose circus boy sounds like he's been juggling more than wooden clubs. 'He's been seeing two other women, *two,* while he's been living with *me,*' she screeches. 'The triple-timing reptile, the snivelling little lizard... I'll castrate him with a pair of bricks, I'll drive his fucking van over his testicles, I'll ram his buggering juggling balls down his lying throat – Jeez, Zoe, what did I do to deserve this? And where's the little piss-ant get the energy?'

He's twenty-six, that's where.

Trying to break up that mince into cookable lumps with one eye on the clock and an earful of Bel isn't easy, with just half an hour to feed the children and get ready. 'Bel, listen to me. No, *listen.* He's a lowly insect, a pile of slime, a randy, overgrown schoolboy and you are a Goddess, OK? A *Goddess*, whose dirty trainers he is not fit to lick. Men fight to get into your pants, I've seen them. Small boys barely past voting age are a waste of space, and you're better off without him. Sweetheart, you're worth a thousand of –'

'All right if I have a chocolate chip cookie, Mum? Ta.' Tim sidles past, cramming three into his mouth.

'If you must. Pick those crumbs up. *Tim!* You just trod them into the carpet again.' I break off to stare abstractedly at the sitting room with its sagging sofas, grubby cushions, drifts of newsprint, toys underfoot and dirty windows. My head feels like it's floating off my shoulders again, nerve-endings crackling, spine spitting static as I gaze at the once cosy little room. Its carpet needs Hoovering, the wooden sideboard is smeary, the mirror dull with dust. Has it always looked like this?

'Mu-umm...' blares Kasha. 'Tim's pushing me off the sofa and I got here first.'

'*So sit in the bloody armchair*. Sorry, Bel, sorry. Look, something's come up and I have to go. But I'll call you tomorrow. Without fail. Promise. Yes, double-promise.' The mince is now sticking to the bottom of the pan, still half-raw and needing immediate attention if it is to be remotely edible. 'Just remember. You: Glorious Sex Goddess archetype, him: unworthy pile of rancid cockroach droppings.'

Ten minutes later as the children are eating their tea, Angel floats down from her first floor boudoir, skinny but big-boobed under her scarlet satin dressing gown, to join us for some indifferent spag bol, then sweeps the children off to her room to play cards.

I shower, dress with care in something Shaun will like if he sees it, and put four small items into a squashy black shoulder bag along with Rufus and Annie's keys. God, I'm knackered. Locate Jim's old bottle of Guarana capsules. The label says take two at a time. Swallow four. Finally, from the depths of the cupboard below-stairs, I pull out a battered Ravel shoebox swathed in Sellotape. It takes a bread knife to get it open, but inside there's an old black T-shirt wrapped round a metal object Dad gave me many years ago – concerned father to feckless daughter – when I told him I was moving into a Brixton squat after uni ended. The fake Beretta (which he'd used in the army for demo purposes) had convinced everyone I'd ever shown it to, including a flat-mate who was neurotic about intruders, an ex boyfriend who'd become threatening, and a half-hearted mugger outside the Little Bit Ritzy cinema. Hopefully, Shaun would be no exception.

Throwing on iridescent khaki trench coat (a relic from the days when we could still afford proper clothes) and belting it tightly, I step out into the street and flag down a cab. An hour's wages at least, but what the hell.

For it's time to ask that control freak in trousers exactly what his intentions are. Towards me, but especially towards Jim's company. And should he be unable to convince me he's on the level, if I get so much as a flicker of a suspicion that he's planning to stitch Jim up, he's in for the shock of his charmed life.

At the thought of what I might have to do, my heart starts trying to batter it's way out through my ribcage and my mouth goes dry. *It's all right. You can do that if you have to*, whispers my self-confidence, a shy creature whose voice is rarely heard these days. *You can, you know. It's a piece of cake.*

Oh, God help me…

My handbag clinks ominously. I grit my teeth.

Anything I've Not Thought Of?

The Holly Bush is on a quiet, dimly lit corner in the Hampstead backstreets. The nearest street lamps (Art Deco) glow at the far ends of the two little roads leading down to it, the cobbled pavements are high off the road and the streets just wide enough to admit one car at a time; causing polite, rock-jawed stand-offs as the wealthy residents crawl cautiously down the narrow lanes in their Lexus convertibles and Mercedes, to meet head on round every narrow turn of this exclusive corner of NW3.

Stepping into the pub's welcoming wood-panelled crush, I'm scanning the tables when he comes up behind me, announcing his presence with a proprietal hand on the small of my back, before steering me to the most private booth of all in the darkest corner, already staked out with a pricy Italian overcoat, bulging black leather briefcase and two glasses of driest white. Perch nervously on the threadbare velvet banquette opposite him, carefully arranging my face into my best 'polite drink with new work colleague' expression.

'It's good to see you again,' he offers warmly, looking me straight in the eye.

'Oh yes, right, jolly nice to see you too. Rather unexpected actually. Not that I – um – well, cheers, then,' I witter, totally unnerved, taking a desperate slug of wine and spilling most of it down my chin.

Well, that told him.

'May I take your coat?' he asks, sounding like the butler in *Gosford Park*. 'It's a bit warm in here.'

'Certainly not. I mean, not at the moment.' I'm still flustered by him creeping up on me like that, but he bursts out laughing, reaches over and pats my hand.

Take your hands off me. 'What's so funny?'

'You are. Calm down. I'm not going to eat you.' He continues to smile at me, as if I was an old school friend he is fond of, but knows is a bit of a dipstick.

'I didn't imagine that you were. What is it you want from me, Shaun?' Bracing myself for blackmail, bullying or innuendo, I dive right in because I'm now so worried there seems to be no other way. 'Just what do you think you're playing at, manipulating Jim like that? Do you usually bond with new business partners by shoving a finger up their wives' knickers during dinner? Or – or make a habit of grabbing the deeds to their houses over coffee? Is this is your way of getting back at me just because I object to you having young girls delivered to your door like *Chinese take-aways*?' Bugger, my voice is starting to wobble. 'If you're playing power games again, you can just forget it, right? I'm perfectly prepared to tell Jim the lot if I have to, just so he knows what he's dealing with. And I don't care what he thinks, do you hear? I don't give a flying fuck any more, because I'm not going to stand by and watch you screwing up our lives on some spiteful whim –'

'Woah! Stop. Stop right there.' He's holding up his hand like a traffic cop. 'Slow down, will you? I only wanted to tell you, in person, that I am very sorry about the other evening at dinner.'

Oh sure. If you'll believe that, you'll believe –

He raises his hands slightly off the table, palms up in a continental 'What can I tell you?' gesture. 'Listen, it was a bit of a bizarre situation to be in, wasn't it? And rightly or wrongly, I felt it was best if we were seen to have no previous history together. You know.'

I remember the way he'd stacked the odds against little Seventh Wave, his bully boys massing behind him, Alicia's

224

strychnine condescension. 'Oh, don't worry about that. We had a lovely time. Such a bonus to meet all your heavies too, when you'd asked us to a purely social meal. And I simply *adored* Muffy. Where did you pick her up? I'll bet it wasn't the London Business School...' dammit, I can hear my voice rising and feel my cheeks flushing. 'And I got such a charge from coming back from the loo to find our house had been signed away. You bastard, how *dare* you? That was a shitty trick to pull. Well, I'll have you know that the place is also half mine so you can't have it without my consent, and I'm not giving it so you can just –'

'Calm down *please*.' He is still smiling. Perhaps it's sewn on for the evening? It has also gone rather quiet at our end of the pub. A young couple, seated not seven feet away, are listening in shamelessly. Shaun sends them such a filthy look that they resume their own conversation immediately. We lower our voices.

'We don't need to get into all that. I'll sort the house angle out if you're so upset about it. And I wasn't manipulating Jim. I would genuinely like to do business with him. His idea's very good.'

'I know it is, but, but what do you mean, *we don't need to get into all that*? That house is where we *live* for God's sake.'

Unexpectedly, he reaches over the narrow oblong wood table and cups my chin in his hand, tilting my face upwards till he could see the frightened tears gleaming in the corners. Then he fishes out a handkerchief (Shaun, with a handkerchief?) and wipes as if he is mopping up a six-year-old who's fallen off her space-hopper. 'I said, I'll sort it. Perhaps we can take Seventh Wave's premises as surety instead, as I understand they own the lease on it for the next twenty-seven years. That's got to be worth a few quid in Soho.'

'Oh.' I take a deep breath and attempt another slug of wine (forgetting I've already drunk it all) trying to return from orbit. 'OK. Yes. I mean, thank you. That – that would be much better.' I chance another direct look at him. 'So, er, what do you need to talk to me about then?'

'Us.'

Ah, ha.

'No, not in that way,' he adds swiftly, correctly interpreting my expression. 'I guess that part of it's over. Isn't it?'

It is? Just like that. Then why isn't he looking a bit sorrier? This doesn't sound right. Shaun never relinquished anything he regarded as his in his life.

He lays a warm hand over my damp, chilly one, which is still clutching the empty glass. 'Zoe, things were coming apart. It was all starting to go wrong for us, wasn't it? What with the miscarriage, your er, work changes – and, from what you told me when you had to cut that afternoon at our flat short to get back to see his teacher, your son's difficulties at school. It's not playtime any longer, is it?'

He turns my hand palm upward, and slowly traces the sticky curve of its lifeline. 'You were right, you know – that last day you came over. At first I thought you were simply being over-sensitive, but it showed me how differently we think about so many things these days.' *Over-sensitive to girls being dragged into your place by the hair?* 'It was a bit much, I suppose. I can see that now.'

'You can, can you? Remarkable how the emotional eyesight improves when convenient.'

He chooses to let that one float past, and cranks up the throb of sincerity in his voice: 'Darlin', I mean it. Trying to carry on now would be giving the lie to everything we've ever shared, to everything we've ever been to each other both first *and* second time around. And I think you know as well as I do that, as my Dad used to say, after the best comes – well, the rest.'

Boy, he's good. Anyone would think that he means it, instead of being yet another two-faced adulterer who's encountered the P-situation and run for the hills.

226

'But hey,' his voice deepens, cream dripping on velvet again, 'you and me – our times together – they will always be immensely precious. Not many lovers get a second chance. We were special that way. But I guess we always have been special haven't we? We're not like everyone else. Never have been.' He lifts up my hand and gives it a sweet, most un-Shaun-like squeeze. 'You know, for years after we first split I always measured every woman I had against you. There was never anyone like you.'

Oh absolutely. In fact, you were so besotted with me that you married the next female who wouldn't get out of your bed.

'Look – I, ah, did hear a little bit about your breakdown,' he adds, a specialist telling a patient that beauty spot she is so fond of is actually a melanoma.

What breakdown?

'It's OK,' he soothes, feeling my hand grow rigid under his. 'You don't need to say anything I can understand that it's private. But I had lunch with Jim last Thursday, and he –'

'You did? Why?' The idea they might be socialising regularly over a pint of Best is stomach-churning.

'We've got the pilot of *FirstPencil* up and running. The clients are falling over themselves to sign up, both creatives and companies. We have some really big ones interested. Jed's meeting with Channel Five tomorrow. Working Title's on board, Planet 24, Wall to Wall, RSA, Moving Pictures – all the quality independents are knocking on the door drawn by word of mouth as much as anything, and all in the last couple of weeks. Seems that all you've got to do to put the word out in this business is sit in the right bar, buy a large round and start talking.'

'But that's *brilliant*. I didn't realise it was going so well.' I should have, though. Doesn't Jim tell me anything these days?

'Total target marketing,' says Shaun with satisfaction, looking more comfortable now he is on neutral territory.

'Seventh Wave said it often worked like this. At first, I thought that was merely sales talk, but now I do believe,' he gives a contented, cat-like stretch, 'that the proposition is really going to work.' He takes a deep breath and lays his hands flat on the table. 'But Jim, ah, did mention that you'd been rather unwell, and were, you know, taking a bit of a career break for the moment...' he trails off uncharacteristically. 'Nice bloke, your husband,' adds Shaun thoughtfully, as if this had come as a considerable surprise. 'And I think he's been rather worried about you.'

'Well, he's got a funny way of showing it.'

'Things not going so good, huh? I'm sorry. Look,' he drops the soothing tone he's been using up till now and grabs both my hands, pulling me across the table until our faces are inches apart. 'I am also really sorry about the baby. It sounds like you were pretty ill. I guess that must have had a certain amount to do with, um, you not being working in the usual way at the moment.'

'Oh for God's sake, Shaun, I haven't had a *breakdown*. I merely burnt all my contacts books whilst dancing round a bonfire to vintage punk; told my editors to sod off, and got a job shelf-stacking at Morrison's. Don't make it into something it isn't.'

Shaun looks appalled. 'You did what?'

'I downsized.'

'Right, right. You simplified your life. Dumped your ballast. Cut loose. Great idea,' he empathises wildly, 'but Christ Almighty, Zoe, your *contacts* books?' As an ex journalist, Shaun knows we are talking Destruction of the Sacred here. 'Wasn't that a little drastic?' He blows out his cheeks. 'I mean, your choice, of course – and obviously we all need a break sometimes –' He relinquishes my hands and rubs his chin, eyeing me as if I'd just admitted to hearing voices telling me to assassinate Tony Blair.

'Anyway, this, um, baby business,' he ploughs on, with all the finesse of a flamenco artist trying to dance in

Wellingtons. 'Try, please, to look at it from my point of view. I thought you were on the Pill and the condoms were just insurance, a health thing... The possibility of pregnancy never even entered my head.' *It never does enter men's heads, does it? They're not the ones who get up the duff.* 'You just sprang it on me that evening, sweetheart. Then I had no time to say anything because Maxwell barged in.' Shaun takes a large slug of his drink, leans even closer and runs his forefinger slowly down my cheek. The noise level in the pub drops to a distant rumble, and we are enclosed in a capsule with just two people in it. *Blast and hell, he's always been able to do this...*

'I won't lie to you,' he assures me, shifting in his seat. 'There is no way I could have officially recognised the baby as mine if she'd been born. You understand? But I could have helped you out quietly, with money perhaps, if you'd wanted me to. And I'd liked to have, you know, met her one day. Seen if she looked like me. Said hello, that sort of thing.' He actually looks sheepish. 'There. I've said it.'

'So you have. I'd like another drink.'

'Of course.' He shoots to his feet and casts about for something further to offer. 'Would you like some salted pistachios? Pork Scratchings? Kettle crisps? Anything I've not thought of?'

'Yes, our house back.'

'Right.' He muscles over to the bar and despite the press of people around it, gets served immediately. I watch his broad back in its now trademark Armani crumpled linen. Dark olive-green, today. He is being so nice, give or take a bit of bare-faced arrogance, that I barely recognise him. I have to remind myself that this man can talk you into believing that hot is actually cold: that it is just a matter of degree. That his motivating force is self-interest. And that he has only been able to sustain one long-term emotional relationship in his life, and that's his long-running affair with himself.

'So.' He bows gallantly from the waist to set my new drink and a packet of cashews on the table. Having got That out of the way, he appears to have recovered his bullet-proof self-confidence.

'So?'

'So, like I told you, I will take care of everything. In fact, I'll settle the house issue tomorrow if it's bothering you so much. Look, you and I need to be able to get along, we're in each other's legitimate orbits now. We'll have to meet socially from time to time if *FirstPencil* takes off and as I said, it looks like it will. You can believe me when I tell you,' he insists, looking the very picture of sincerity, 'that I reckon your husband's idea is sufficiently good for me to have been interested anyway, regardless of your involvement.'

Yes, and the Pope's a woman.

Shaun again reads my thoughts. 'I would, you know,' he says, crinkling his avocado eyes at me. 'All right, I admit that the sting of the situation appealed and that it was the reason I didn't immediately bin Seventh Wave's proposal without reading it. I get a dozen such letters a week. But when I did go through it, I saw it had potential, real potential. Even though the dot.com boom's over, there's still room for a service that fills a really strong market niche. And no matter how piquant this scenario is, I can promise you that I wouldn't be throwing half a million at it purely for my own entertainment.'

I stare at him, trying to screen out how dangerously attractive he still is and work out how much of what he is telling me is plausible bullshit. 'I'm sorry, but I still find it extraordinary that out of all the backers in all the world, it turns out to be you. And only two weeks after – you know.'

Shaun shrugs. 'With new business proposals it's a matter of an idea landing on the right desk at the right time, and Jim's happened to land on mine. You know darlin', I think I can help your husband make a lot of money. From what I hear, it's time his ship came in.'

Siren words. And it is clear that I've only really got one option: to take the role he's offering: the feel-sorry-for ex with the nervous breakdown, married to the talented but failing creative whom Shaun is going to turn into a late-blooming success.

For a substantial cut, of course.

A small altercation breaks the silence that had now settled on our table. An older man with a red face and an immaculate dark suit has fallen over a fellow drinker who is booted, dreadlocked, nursing a pint, and had been reading *Road Protest Today* on a stool by the door. Picking himself up with cross-eyed, swaying dignity from the resulting mess of arms, legs and beer the older man belches once then lurches through the door. A stocky barman is over in seconds, picking up the startled drinker, offering him another pint and whisking about with a J-cloth. 'Very eminent QC, Sir William. Lives at the end of the road. Gets a bit tired some evenings,' he explains to the room at large in a tone that invites no argument, installing himself back at behind the bar. 'Next, please.'

'I think I'd rather my sons grew up to be road protesters than QCs if that's the way they turn out,' Shaun confides, switching effortlessly back into Old School-Chum mode.

'Do they show any signs of either yet?' I ask, playing along politely.

'No. The only thing the eldest is showing signs of is an awakening awareness of the female form.' He grins proudly. 'Of course, he's fifteen now.'

Consider remarking that this was a lovely age, but settle for: 'I hope that's manifesting itself in a socially acceptable form.'

'It is. You know, the other night I heard a Britney Spears song seeping under his door. He's frequently said what crap she is so I couldn't resist going in, and there she was on

MTV, rotating her splendid little spandexed groin inches from the camera. 'But I thought you hated Britney?' I teased him. 'Dad,' he said. 'Look at her.' And I thought: *I have a son!'*

We both laugh merrily.

'So how's your boy?' Shaun asks casually. 'Still happy at his new school?'

'Oh, yes. I can't tell you the difference it's –'

'It must have been great relief,' observes Shaun, even more casually than before. 'Yes, some of those inner city comprehensives are real zoos. Still, it's all money isn't it? And what's money – but protection from the harsh realities of life?'

Suddenly, I don't want any more cashews.

'Mate of mine had to take his kids out of Stowe last year because the backer pulled out of his design business. They had one a hell of a time getting his boy settled at the local comprehensive,' he confides cosily. 'Pretty rough, by all accounts. Well, here's hoping *FirstPencil* makes it, then…' He clinks glasses with me, and smiles. I smile tightly back, skin several sizes too small for my face.

'Of course, my people will have to monitor Jim's turnover and profits carefully month on month to keep the rest of our backer's money coming through. But he knows that, and it's perfectly usual. *FirstPencil* gets two hundred grand for the initial start up costs, then probably fifty thousand a month for the next five months. Theoretically,' Shaun pauses to take a thoughtful sip of wine, 'our venture friends can pull the plug at any time, any time at all during this first year should they feel Jim's not making the grade. Sounds harsh, I know, but this lot cut their losses sharpish if something's not working.' He upends my packet of cashews, to take the last, highly-seasoned handful. 'Yes, it's all about steady performance. But obviously – well now, I trust that Jim *can* perform?' His slow smile is that of the wolf wondering which little pig to eat first.

So. The lousy shit really is going to hold this over our heads for the rest of our lives. Am I going to let him get away with that? Over my dead body. Well, over someone's. We stare at each other for a few long moments. *Now. Tonight. Do it now. Go, go, go –*

Take a deep breath and stand up slowly, brushing one lapel back accidentally-on-purpose so Shaun can catch a flash of what I'm wearing underneath.

Nothing whatsoever.

It is fortunate that my back's to the rest of the pub. His eyes darken in a way I know well. 'I have something to do at an adorable little house just round the corner. The owners are away. I go in each day to water their plants.' I have his undivided attention, but he is looking a bit startled. 'Perhaps you might like to come along and give me a hand?' *Don't make me spell it out.* 'You see –' *oh pick up Shaun, pick up*: '– there are rather a lot of them.'

His primal instincts reassert themselves. 'Put like that, what can I say?' he exclaims gallantly, leaping to his feet and grabbing his coat, the rounded outline of a burgeoning erection evident beneath his trousers.

'Number ten, Star Street. I'll leave the front door open. Come up the stairs, first on the right, as by then I may be, ah, watering the ones in their bedroom. However, I shall need a ten minute start.' I will too. Rufus and Annie have a bank of temperamental tropical plants spread across an entire wall up there. It costs them a fortune in replacement fees because the things keep dying, but they simply won't have weeping figs like everyone else.

I push Shaun gently back into his seat and suggest he buys another drink while he is waiting. Weaving my way through the good-natured crowd and praying that I haven't bitten off more than I can chew, I can feel his eyes burning into my arse.

Tie Me Up, Tie Me Down

The house is in darkness. Apparently the Cottingham-Smith's automated light system (linked to their state of the art burglar alarm) has packed up again, so I grope my way inside, scrabbling at the Chubb box on the wall. For a few heart-stopping seconds the night air is torn by mechanical screeching, but punching all the numbers simultaneously shuts it up so the door can be left on the latch.

Feeling for the light by the door, I flick it on and look warily about.

They've gutted the inside of the Victorian house, recreating the interior from scratch under the design-fascist influence of one of the brightest young architectural stars in the city, who is famously indifferent to the fact that clients actually have to live in the inhospitable spaces he dreams up. Beautiful, but the entire place has a shadowy expectant feel that puts you on your guard. It needs parties, people, music and light to work. I've only been up here in the afternoons before. Uninhabited at night, it is distinctly sinister.

In the bedroom I switch on the dim bedside lamp, setting it on the floor to make it even dimmer. Ferreting in my bag, my fingers close over metal and withdraw the steel handcuffs we used to play with when we wanted a change from the more comfortable padded variety, clipping them to the top of the curved wrought iron bed frame, checking the wearer can move them all the way along and down the side.

The next items brought along in case they were needed for Shaun-sorting purposes include some inch-wide black masking tape and nail scissors. They go in the bedside cabinet, a tastefully distressed sixteenth-century Captain's Locker. In the bag's zip pocket are a lighter and a dozen little

234

wax nightlights, which are lit and positioned at strategic points around the room. The fake Beretta goes under the nearside foot of the bed for later, the heavy grey-gold folds of their fake wolf skin counterpane arranged casually around it.

Breaking out in goose pimples, I switch on the wall recessed fan heater and for the sake of both warmth and privacy, pull the rippling old gold silk curtains closed. They trail across the floor, a sumptuous six inches longer than necessary. The opposite wall is covered in a collage of antique gold framed mirrors, some no bigger than an orange, others five feet across, which reflect the gold from the curtains and soft nightlight glow. Annie's tiny enamelled clock on the dressing table says nine o'clock. Having said I'd be home by about ten thirty (how long can you look at a Chesterfield for?) we'd better keep an eye on the time.

Hell, where is he? What if he doesn't come? I'm stroking the wolf skin compulsively when there is the unmistakable sound of the front door opening – and shutting quietly.

Footsteps advance across the mosaic hall and start up the stairs. It's him. At least, I certainly hope it is. But what if it isn't? Christ, I just left the front door open in a wealthy area of Hampstead at night. It could be anyone. What if it's a burglar? Or some sociopath of a serial killer the police haven't yet managed to catch? Whoever it is, they aren't turning on the hall light, and they're getting closer. This has some nasty echoes of Shaun's favourite phone sex fantasies and those never end the same way twice.

My God, it isn't him down there at all, is it? He's sent along someone else in his place, I know he has, set up the scenario of the unknown sexual predator in the empty house so he can watch. Is it his chauffeur summoned by mobile, someone in the pub he's paid, some head case off the street? Having talked about it for so long, he has finally decided to do it for real, and who better to try it on than me – no, no, *no*, please go away. I don't want to play this, really I don't. Dangerous sex with total strangers isn't my thing Shaun...

just because I'll listen to it doesn't mean I want to try it. Now the footsteps are stopping outside the door. Yet though it's ajar, nothing further happens for a moment. Whoever it is, they're out there and they're waiting, taking their own good time. Crouch down slowly by the foot of the bed, feeling underneath the counterpane, eyes fixed on that door. It swings open slowly with a soft creak. But no one comes in. The doorway remains empty.

Beginning to whimper from sheer terror, at first I can only see a rectangle of darker dark. Then fingers, fingers curling around the doorframe. God in heaven, whose are they?

Suddenly, Shaun's head appears round the edge too.

'Cosy little place,' he observes. I open my mouth but nothing comes out.

'It's OK, I locked the front door,' he adds coming in quietly as if there are other people about, and he's slipping into my bedroom in the dead of night. 'One can't be too careful.'

For a second or two I am so relieved I can't think what to do next, so try standing up and letting the coat slide slowly to the floor. 'No wonder you're shivering, you must be freezing,' he says quietly, his voice thickening. 'Leave the little boots on.' His gaze drops to my tits, which are heaving up and down in true bodice ripping fashion due to extreme fright. 'The garter belt, waspie – mmm, velvet – and black lace stockings may stay too,' he smiles, doubtless imagining tits' furious blancmange-like action reflects well upon his sex appeal, and makes a grab for them. Whip back out of reach. *Now.*

Drawing him over to the bed and slipping off his coat and jacket on the way, I push him sharply back, sitting astride to remove his tie and undo his first few shirt buttons in a businesslike Nurse Knows Best sort of way. He makes another grab for a breast but I slap his hand away sharply. He smiles appreciatively and, hooray, lies back with one arm crooked behind his head as I lean across to unzip his trousers.

When he tries to reach down and finger my right nipple which is almost brushing his leg as I'm bending over him, I find I've gone rigid with distaste and am swatting him away again, this time using my nails.

He winces. 'I'm sorry – Mistress.'

Ah good, he's joining in the spirit of the game. He always did like this one.

Swivelling round to work his trousers down to his ankles, I nearly hit the ceiling as he pinches my thigh lingeringly, lasciviously. '*Stop that!* Did I give permission to participate? You may not touch me till I say so. Do it again – and you will be punished.'

'Forgive me, Mistress,' he says again but so low I can barely hear. He's not smiling any more, and his eyes have gone feral. *Gotcha.*

'In fact,' I add, raising my voice, 'I think we'll just have to find another way of stopping your grubby little hands wandering, as you seem quite unable to keep them to yourself this evening.'

Slipping off the bed and whipping round, I reach up and guide his hands into the cuffs, Shaun almost helping since he always did love a little S & M. As the cuffs click shut he closes his eyes and moves his pelvis languidly, drawing attention to the straining bulge in his black designer pants.

'Keep still,' I snap, averting my eyes. 'I said *still*. Later, perhaps, if you're good. If I'm feeling generous.' A brisk fingertip smack on his balls from underneath as I'm sliding his pants down makes him groan softly, half in pleasure, half in pain, but he at least he stops writhing. 'That's better. You just need a good, firm hand, don't you?' Shaun says nothing, but if anything, his erection grows slightly larger as he throws back his head, eyes closed, arching one knee and twisting his body sideways – the picture of languorous, sensual submission. For heaven's sake, does he have to look so blasted sexy?

As I back away hurriedly, Shaun opens his eyes a fraction. 'You may watch, but only if you behave yourself. However, you *may* be permitted to speak (to show your appreciation and respect) later.' Why does my voice suddenly sound like Minnie Mouse's? And – sexy, ha! What in hell am I thinking of? You shouldn't have sex with people like him. From what I'd found out about the bastard recently, you wouldn't need a condom, you'd need a wetsuit though doubtless he'd enjoy that as well. Returning swiftly to Plan A, I feel inside the Captain's chest, remove the tape and scissors then with a shaking hand, cut off an eight-inch strip, placing it quickly across his mouth before he can react. 'Mmmmmf?' he exclaims, eyes wide. In answer, another strip goes on slightly above the first.

It's narcotically atmospheric in here now: dim, candle-lit, smelling powerfully of sex. But we are not here to enjoy the ambience. He may look like the prince of all sex slaves lying on the bed naked, expectant and one hundred per cent up for it but frankly, in view of to his recent behaviour, there's not a man in this world whom I'd like to shag less than Shaun.

Dropping the scissors, I fish my mobile out of my bag, a flash freebie upgrade pressed upon me by Nokia last month. How'd you work this bloody thing? It seems to be on camcorder mode – no, no, it's connecting me to the net – now it seems to be running some stupid music video thing... ah, got it. Oh. Shit, these are no good, the image definition's pathetic and I can't get a printout anyway unless they can be sent to another phone (*whose,* eh?)... gah, this is *hopeless.* Good job I brought the old Polaroid Instamatic too, the one used for taking shots of bands when I'd worked on *Vinyl Graffiti*. Their shaky execution (pogo-ing and photography didn't mix) had been in keeping with their place of publication, but this time perhaps we can get something clearer... providing he keeps *still*... and if I can get some more light in here...

Five minutes later, an initial glance through the peeled and drying Polaroids laid out on the floor confirms that a spot of photo exhibitionism has revived Shaun's erection like a shot of rhino horn. The angle makes it look twice its natural size but a couple have also caught his features in detail. I hold up one in particular, blowing on it to dry it faster. 'Look – what do you think, sweetheart? A good likeness?'

But Shaun is frowning slightly now, and gesturing at his handcuffs with jerks of his head. Oh dear. I think we've come to the difficult bit. What am I going do with you now?

Retreat to the bathroom to have a drink of water, a pee and a think. After several minutes of splashing cold water on my face and doing some deep breathing, I feel like I can face him again but back in the bedroom, it's clear that it was a mistake to leave him so long. He's getting annoyed. Well, more than annoyed, he's throwing himself from side to side and heaving at the cuffs, his powerful shoulders bunching…

Bugger. It's going to be impossible to get out of here in one piece with the photos if he's on the loose. But if he's not untied, he'll go ballistic and then what? He's pretty strong. He could wreck the room, even beat me up. At the very least, he might take away the pictures. Since the day he wouldn't let me out of his flat I have learnt to be a bit afraid of him. Perhaps if I leave him for a while to cool off? Not enough time, Jim will expect me home soon. Maybe – maybe if he's left overnight, he'll burn himself out?

Trouble is, I hadn't really thought about what was going to happen to him after the photography session, since it only became apparent that this would be necessary an hour ago and I'd sort of envisaged that I could slip out leaving him naked on the bed, with instructions to shut the front door properly when he left. Shaun draws my attention to his on-going displeasure by kicking me sharply on the thigh as I sidle closer to the bed, half fascinated, and half appalled by what I've done. It is definitely time to go.

'Sorry, but this is where you and I say goodbye.'
Watching me put on my coat he lies completely still for a
moment, frozen with what is possibly the first real shock he's
had in years.

Scoop up everything I'd brought along apart from the
little Beretta under the bed, and check at my watch: half an
hour to get back home and talk to Jim about imaginary sofas.
But seeing me actually walking towards the door electrifies
the man on the bed. He gives an almighty heave at his
manacles, though only succeeds in falling off the mattress
(ouch) as the cuffs slip easily down the curved side of the
Deco bed frame but continue to hold him fast. And while it's
reassuring to see he isn't going to go anywhere anytime soon,
it also occurs to me that there are times when it is imperative
to do so, biologically speaking.

I turn back to remove an expensive Indonesian tree fern
from its bronze outer pot (checking it has no hole in the
bottom) and put it on the opposite side of the bed from where
he is now thrashing about on the floor. 'This is your little,
um, pissoir. You can reach it by sliding the cuffs along the
bed frame in the other direction.' Shaun stops struggling and
radiates furious disbelief.

'Look – I really am sorry about these,' I mutter
awkwardly, backing away but holding up the other Polaroids
for a moment, 'If there'd been some other way... but you
gave me no alternative. You didn't. Can't you *see* that?'

He's now staring at me hard, an outraged question in his
eyes. 'You want to know why I needed these?' he nods,
brusquely. 'All right, I'll tell you. I'm going to pick out the
ones that'll reproduce best and be suitable for the
newspapers, that's what I'm going to do. And believe me,'
swallow hard and try to sound tough for my blasted voice has
risen to a squeak again, 'that is precisely where I shall send
them if you mess with Jim's company. Do you hear me?
Well perhaps not the quality broadsheets, but *the News of the
World* will just adore them. And perhaps *The Daily Star*.

They've never been that keen on you have they? Too successful, too keen to leave your working class roots behind and worse, not willing to give them any chatty quotes.'

Shaun struggles harder, wrenching at his manacles like an escapologist on LSD and aims another wild, lashing kick in my direction. He would clearly like to beat me to a pulp, but I am past caring, for the adrenalin high of successful crime-commitment is starting to kick in like the rush of a class A narcotic.

'Can't you just see the headlines? Not exactly heavyweight news, but wasn't it you who once told me that the one thing which finishes both politicians and businessmen isn't scandal, but ridicule? And even if no paper will use them, do you really think that they'll be able to resist a look? Then they'll show them around the office, have them scanned, email them to their friends and before you know it, the entire journalistic staff of every major newspaper in the country will be laughing themselves sick. You – you just try talking to them about Ziggurat's expansion plans after that. After all, it's not the sin is it, sweetheart? It's the indignity.'

There is a frantic metallic scraping noise as he saws the cuffs up and down on the wrought iron headboard, tugging savagely. Really hope they are not going to break. After all, they are only sex toys, cheap ones at that, and rather badly made. Shaun twists his body furiously, but only succeeds in banging his back on the side of the mattress frame.

'*Please* stop that, you'll only hurt yourself. And I really do have to go now. I promise that I'll be back – quite soon – with something for you to eat and drink.' He becomes still, eyes narrowed like a cornered lynx's.

'If I call your office for you tomorrow, I could say I'm someone's PA. From BuzzData perhaps? Maxwell did mention them at dinner last week. I can tell them that you have an all day meeting with my boss and don't want to be interrupted. I give great secretary. In fact,' kneeling, I rummage through his supple black leather briefcase, 'best look after your mobile too, just in case.' Shaun makes a stifled sound partway between a bellow and a growl.

'We'll say – that my boss's company has just invited you up North for a day or so to check out a new business proposition. Very hush-hush, rather urgent. It being Wednesday tonight, it'll be Monday at least before your office starts looking for you. And Debbie's quite used to you going AWOL at weekends, isn't she?' Step carefully over his fallen jacket, abandoned coat and gaping briefcase towards the door, and lean against the frame, clutching it for support. 'If you get bored, you could always amuse yourself by thinking up a few snappy captions: you were always good at those. *Venture capital king's got it taped,* that sort of thing, though I'm sure you'll be able to come up with something better.' Shaun stops hauling at his handcuffs, but he's breathing raggedly, his eyes boring into me like twin dentist drills.

'Oh, and by the way – this house is unoccupied until a week on Friday.'

With that, I blow him a kiss and hit the street with a banging heart. But by the time the brief walk to Hampstead tube's over, the disbelieving elation at a job apparently well done has faded, leaving the more rational response of blind terror, with the words *really, done it,* and *now* ricocheting around my frontal lobes. Can't get my breathing back under control, and have no idea how I'll find time tomorrow (between Morrison's, children and husband-nurturing) to return to Star Street and set Shaun free. There is also the horrid but very real possibility that he'll have escaped by then anyway, and ample time to imagine this in detail while waiting on the tube platform, watching the travel board inform passengers of the cancellation of a succession of trains.

'See anything good?' asks Jim idly, looking up from the end of the *Ten O'Clock News,* as I sidle in and try to edge upstairs before he notices that I'm a bit underdressed and my knees are going like castanets.

'Absolutely nothing you'd want me to bring home.'

Independence Day

Slept like a baby last night – the one hour asleep, one hour awake and whimpering routine. By six in the morning, Jim's off his mattress and shaking me awake, complaining that I'm punching pillows and shouting unintelligible things about Polaroids.

It is one of those mornings. I feel like death, the milk is off, Jim has no socks again ('There's a black hole in this house and all my socks are in it. Is it so hard to pair up a few? It's not as if you have a very challenging life these days.'). Worse, sometime last night, Psycho the golden hamster whom Tim is babysitting for a friend, had houdini'd his way out of his cage and been butchered by the cats, who've laid out all the bits they hadn't eaten with sinister precision on the loo mat. Tim had trod on Psycho's tiny liver lined up next to half his head and both back paws as he went for his wake-up pee, and is now in floods of heaving, guilty tears under the bed.

Kasha is also deeply offended this morning, not by the rodent giblets but by me. 'Mummy Mummy, do look, I did a drawing specially for you last night,' she'd called, pattering into the kitchen half dressed. She found me darting about making milk from stale Marvel, wrapping hamster remains in Clingfilm and trying not to think about last night

'Oh, darling, thank you. It's terrific,' I admired dutifully, pausing in my labours to bag up Psycho's now plasticated fragments in kitchen towel for good measure. 'A sausage sizzling in a pan. How yummy.'

There was a short, stony silence. 'Actually,' snapped my daughter, snatching back her artwork, 'it's a trout in a hula skirt doing the high jump.' She stamped out of the kitchen, clutching her painting to her training bra. 'Oh belt *up,* Tim, he wasn't even yours.'

Somehow, I get kitted out in my uniform, retrieve Tim from underneath his bed, and deliver both children to their respective places of education. 'Keep your coat done *up,* Mummy,' hisses Kasha, dodging my goodbye kiss at her school gates and savagely pulling my coat flaps closed where the green and white Morrison's stripes are peeking through. Arrive at the supermarket, breathless and wrung out already with a minute to spare. After seventeen self-employed years, I'd forgotten the watched-clock fascism of company working hours.

Paul tells me I am standing in for Trudy on Cereals so the next two hours are spent hauling shrink-packed towers of Frosties and Weetos up and down the aisles, replacing a packet here, another there, and trying not to run the lumbering beast of a trolley over customers' feet.

First break, I shoot off to the staff loos which lurk at the end of an ill-lit, labyrinthine corridor beneath the supermarket. Newcomers can get lost down here for days. Huddled in the far end cubicle, I tap out Shaun's office number in such a panic that my fingertip misses a button and I get Boots in Piccadilly. The second time, it's some holistic vet in Islington. After the third attempt however, Ziggurat's new receptionist answers, and claiming to be the BuzzData MD's secretary, I can explain that Shaun's been invited up to Manchester to see my MD on important business, that they would prefer not to be disturbed, and are currently in an all-day off-site meeting.

'My, that *did* sound official,' drawls a patronising voice from the next cubicle. Bugger, it's Sara Dukakis, the glossy Greek management trainee on the post-grad fast-track programme. She's only been here a week, but already notorious for her powers of observation, keenness to report all infringements of duty, and ability to eavesdrop for England. I emerge looking as casual as possible. 'Had to pass a message onto my husband's work.' I mutter, heading for the washbasins. 'Realised I'd forgotten. You know how it is: mornings, huh? Total chaos in our house today. Heaven knows how I managed to get in this morning – on time – at all.' As I speak I remember that I left the gas cooker on and my happy pill on the kitchen worktop. Reckon the stuff is doing sweet FA but the GP assures us that without it, I'd be even further off the planet than I already am.

'I can imagine.' She flashes me the loathly smirk of a child-free female with a pristine flat. 'Who's Mr *Lyon,* then?' She's making a mouth like a jam doughnut at the mirror and applying fuchsia lipstick which, I am pleased to see, looks atrocious with her olive skin. 'Kept your maiden name for work, have you?'

Back in the kitchen at home, in between making Tim Nutella and peanut butter sandwiches to tide him over till supper (now happier, he has a roaring appetite and comes home ravenous) and Kasha her usual ration of post-school banana-with-jam butties, I'm also trying to do some for Shaun because he must be starving by now. Might he like Marmite and cheese in wholemeal, which is good and filling? Want a MiniBabyBel to go with, plus a carton of juice?

For God's Zoe sake, never mind the bloody sandwich fillings... there's a man tied up naked in a house that's not yours, and he needs to be got out of there. Quietly, and without him either ripping your head off or frog-marching you to the nearest police station.

I really could do with an accomplice but even Lucia might balk at this one, Bel would be horrified, and Hera's, despite her appearance, is only into bondage for stylistic purposes. Yet if I can only get the drop-off logistics for Shaun's Independence Day sorted out the rest should fall in to place for the Polaroids are good enough to use if necessary, and I think I've made my point.

Tonight. It'll have to be tonight, but very late so no one sees. And where to leave him, that's the question. That all night fry-up joint on the North Circular? The middle of Regents Park? What to transport him in now we don't have Harriet, that's a problem too – one quickly solved by calling VanTastic van hire (*'Transits to Troop-carriers'*) off the top of Kentish Town road fifteen minutes' walk away, whose Yellow Pages entry promises wheels for forty quid a day.

'Wotjewant it wiv rollbars for? Rollbars is for bigger vehicles, innit,' protests VanMan in response to my second query, adding peevishly that he's shutting, right, in five minutes but for an extra tenner maybe he could stop in. Can hardly tell him they're for clipping the handcuffs to so Shaun doesn't strangle me while I'm driving.

Leaving Tim and Kasha safely absorbed in Nintendo's *MarioKart* with Angel in the bath upstairs, I beetle through the traffic fumes of crush-hour Kentish Town Road, still in Morrison's drag, a Barclaycard (not used for many months) stuffed down my bra. Come juddering back half an hour later in a large rusting white thing which was quite the worst of a bad bunch. However, it has the advantage of blacked out windows at the back and the required safety feature, but it feels like you're driving a No. 47 bus: 'erratic' would have been too kind a description of our progress home, since being in command of strange vehicles always illustrates why it took five attempts to pass my driving test.

And forty pounds a day, my fanny. VanMan claimed he had nothing for less than sixty, then it was another fifteen for petrol, a tenner for the stay-open bribe and a hundred and fifty for deposit. Park, after many attempts, in the parallel road to ours under the streetlight that hasn't worked in months, scraping the pavement and having terrible trouble fighting the reverse gear, which is stiff as buggery and keeps slipping out so the thing buckets forwards.

However, it goes.

And there is room – even for even the most unwilling of guests – in the back.

Va Va Voooom

So tonight's the night. Please Lord, let him come quietly.

A few hours later, it will become clear that I should have asked the Almighty to take care of one or two other things as well.

Yet plans for the first part of the evening progress beautifully. Having refused supper hinting at digestive disturbance, I've taken off all my makeup, shadowed my eye-bags (no need to fake those, they look like suitcases) with Clinique's Graphite Grey and, if I say it myself, am giving a passable imitation of feeling like ten types of shit.

Hunched on the sofa with a hottie pressed to my abdomen, I selflessly offer to sleep separately from Jim, on Kasha's floor. The family's reactions are both varied and characteristic.

Tim: 'You'll feel better when you've had a good squit, Mum.'

Jim: 'Well, just don't give it to *me*.'

Kasha: 'Poor Mummy, I'll look after you.'

According to LBC, inner London's streets are at their most deserted between one and three in the morning so I borrow Tim's old X-Men watch while he sleeps, setting it for 1 a.m., safe timing as Angel won't be back from Cottonfella's till two. Kasha, enchanted to have parental company, chatters interminably until she crashes out in mid-anecdote at a quarter to eleven.

Padding quietly downstairs to get a nice Horlicks to calm my nerves, I stop dead in the hall. Jim talking to someone on the phone. And since the door is slightly open, I can hear every word.

'– no improvement whatsoever. Well if you say so, but I thought all SSRI inhibitors were the same. No, I doubt she'd agree to talk to you. You've never seen eye to eye and she's so defensive these days that she flies off the handle at the – what? Not violent, no. God, do you think so? Oh, Mum, you are terrific, but no, not for the moment. Look, might this still be hormonal? Uh-huh. Well, frankly the effect on the kids has been...' Stump back upstairs, resenting Ma Harrington with all my heart. Hormonal, huh? Just because I had a miscarriage, am a bit stressed and got a different job; just because *he* won't see the danger that's in front of his face. I'm trying to save his company here, and all he can do is gang up with his mother –

Kasha is thrashing and muttering as I enter the room, her duvet half off. Bundle her back up again and blow softly on her forehead, which always used to calm her when she was a tiny baby, and still does. She begins to smile in her sleep. Kiss her eyebrows and tuck her up.

Too cross and edgy to drop off, I lie on her floor in the sleeping bag watching the shadows play on the walls of her purple boudoir, counting the Beanie babies lined up on her bed and trying to get my heart rate down below a hundred and sixty. Jim wanders off to bed at eleven thirty having fallen asleep in front of *Newsnight* again, and the house settles into stillness. Having exhausted the therapeutic potential of beanie counting, I can now amuse myself with:

* What Jim would say if he knew I'd got his white knight tied up in an empty house two miles down the road.

* The cataclysmic revenge Shaun might take if he decides that all publicity is good publicity and he doesn't care who sees those photos.

* The scenario of getting stopped by a keen young policeman, bored and beady on the late shift, with Shaun trussed up like a turkey in the back.

At half past midnight, I can stand it no longer and inch out of the sleeping bag, doubled over like an arthritic caterpillar because the zip's got stuck. Kasha sits bolt upright.

'Mum-eee, is that you?'

Bother. 'Yes. Just going to the loo. Now you lie back and –'

'Oh please, can you get into bed with me? I'm all cold, and I had a horrible dream about –'

'All right, all right. Shove over, darling.' I am now so tired that, wrapped around my snuggling daughter in the warren-like warmth of her bed, I fall asleep and don't wake up till a quarter to three when she accidentally knees me in the groin. Dammit to hell. Inch out of her bed with infinite slowness and this time she doesn't wake. Start groping through the dark towards the bathroom on the next floor.

Suddenly a nasty thought strikes me, the first of many that night. I have no clothes. Jim will hear for sure if I started opening drawers in our room – oh bugger, bugger, bugger, you can't drive a getaway van in a pair of old men's striped pyjamas with gaping flies. A scan across the bathroom reveals the rich detritus of last night's bath and bed preparations. There's a pair of Tim's muddy grey school trousers flung over the threadbare red velvet armchair, one of Jim's black jumpers hangs on the back of the door smelling powerfully of rolling tobacco, Kasha's size three navy socks are balled up beside the loo, and there's a festering red T-shirt (possibly Angel's) in the Chinese lacquered laundry basket in the corner. These will just have to do.

Creeping downstairs and wincing at every creak, I discover a pink ballet slipper, Tim's trainers (white, one size too big for me, noxious) and a single pink sparkly Wellington caked in mud amidst the tangle of coats, scarves, backpacks and biker gear in the darkness of the stairwell. Choose the trainers, hoping they won't fall off at a crucial moment. Lovely. I look like a bag lady who's forgotten her bags, a real case of 'Darling, remember me this way'. Feel very let down by self. Lucia would be dressed head to toe in D & G black leather and full makeup for such an occasion.

And she'd have been on time.

Sneaking out of the front door and into the darkened street is, momentarily, pretty exciting. This is It. To my addled sensibilities it feels like eloping, fleeing the country, a midnight dash to escape the Mafia, a proper adventure at last. Another plus is that because the streetlight nearest the van still isn't working, it's sitting in a pool of comparative darkness. Then things begin to get difficult.

First, the door won't open. Next, the van won't start, and when it does, emits a roar like a mastodon in labour and leaps several feet backwards. Finally, with a grinding of gears and a triumphant, wheezing bellow we are lumbering down Ferdinand Street, across Prince of Wales Road and up towards Hampstead Heath, encountering not one single car en route. All lights seem to be green as we positively *va va voooom* past the Royal Free hospital, then up the hill beside the Heath to hang an unsteady left at Whitestone Pond, bleached bone pale in the moonlight. But screeching into Star Street awash with excitement, we encounter an unforeseen difficulty, one that all Londoners are familiar with – there is nowhere to park.

With both sides of the narrow street stacked solid with sleeping cars, we have to lurch to a halt outside the a small but perfect Georgian manor house on the road which forms a right angle with Star Street, leaving the van in front of gates bearing a tasteful copperplate sign that says: *Don't Even Think About Parking Here.*

Number ten's hall is pitch dark and as I swat frantically around for the light switch, I'm positive Shaun's cat-footing up behind me to clap his hand across my mouth. Opening the door to Annie's bedroom, again I have to fight off the terrified certainty that he is crouching behind the door. In fact, having opened the curtains to let in a bit of light, he needs to be prodded awake. 'Come on. Hey. Hey, *Shaun.*

Time to go home.' Switching on the little bedside lamp to help him come to reveals the extent of the disorder in the room. Imperative to get back here tomorrow and give it a really good clean, *and* I've forgotten to water their wretched plants these last two days.

He shakes me off with a twist of his big shoulders and mutters 'nk'. Bend over him once more to peel the tapes back as carefully as possible, but the upper one still catches on the skin the top of his lip, leaving a small red pulpy area. Wincing, I fetch Annie's soft black John Rocha flannel from her Moroccan en suite, dipping it in water and dabbing carefully at the sore patch, before holding a glass up gently to his mouth. He gulps greedily, then sighs. 'I suppose a shower is out of the question?'

'Sorry. Tight schedule.'

'What's the rush? I've been festering in here for *twenty-four hours,* Zoe. A whole day and a night. Now suddenly, it's Everybody out?' He runs his tongue across his lower lip, cautiously feeling the damage. 'What time is it, anyway?'

'Three in the morning, and I'm illegally parked.'

He smiles the very ghost of his old sardonic smirk. 'I'd say that was the least of your worries. Just untie me, will you?' I comply, first feeling around under the bed.

'Jesus Christ, where'd you get that?'

'Never you mind. But you'll have noticed this is not a mascara wand,' I snap, pointing the fake Beretta in his approximate direction with a shaking hand, 'so no funny stuff. OK?'

'And how do I know it's loaded?' he demands, locking eyes with me over the gun barrel. 'Or even real?'

'You don't.' I'm holding the thing in two hands now, levelling it right at him. Shaun drops his eyes first and contents himself with sitting on the bed, keeping his genitals covered and easing his sore shoulders.

Thank God he's calmed down. I was terrified that he'd start shouting again but he must be totally played out. The

253

tying up had, I still feel, been regrettably necessary, but leaving him here? Yet he'd turned homicidal after the photos, so what can you do?

Picking up his scattered clothes one-handed, throwing them onto the bed while standing well back and trying to keep my stage prop pointing at him is a clumsy process, but Shaun doesn't seem to be looking out for an opportunity to grab the little gun. He dresses himself slowly with fumbling fingers, staggers to his feet, then makes several attempts to pick up his briefcase ('Shit, my arms have gone totally numb') only to have it slide each time from his grasp. Finally he's standing in the middle of the room clutching the bag to his chest, looking like a jet-lagged businessman awaiting instructions from a dodgy tour guide.

'We'll just put one side of the cuffs back on now.'

He tenses. 'Haven't you had enough?'

'Only for the journey. They'll come off for good when we get where we're going.'

'And where's that?' Shaun is beginning to look anxious, an emotion probably not seen on his face since he wore shorts and long socks, but holds out his wrists.

'Somewhere quiet.'

'I trust that I'll still be in one piece when we get there?'

'Of course you will.' Snapping the cuffs shut, I begin pushing him nervously out of the room in front of me, keeping the Beretta hovering over the back of his neck in the time-honoured fashion. Holding the other circle of the cuffs in my left hand, we move unevenly down the stairs like a mistress taking a Doberman out for a night widdle it doesn't want. As the damp night air wraps itself around us, he stops for a moment by the garden gate filling his lungs gratefully, tilting his face up and back.

'Turn left up the street. It's the big white van.'

'*This* is your getaway vehicle?' he enquires a few seconds later, checking out VanTastic's finest in urbane amazement.

'Drive something this size, can you? I do hope you know what you're doing.'

It takes me a while to unlock the back, one eye on him, the other on the recalcitrant key. I can feel his smirk growing but he still makes no attempt to grab the gun, and I wonder why. Perhaps, at this stage, he just needs a lift.

'In you get.'

He sighs and we clamber up into the back, me still keeping a tight hold on both the gun and the other manacle ring. 'Now what?'

Good question. 'Hands.' The empty cuff ring gets clipped to the roll bar. Goodness, these little things are bearing up well. 'Open wide.' Carefully tuck Annie's flannel back into his protesting mouth.

He spits it back out. 'That's not necessary.'

'Sorry, but it is. It's only for a few more minutes.' Eyeing the fake firearm I'm waving about again, Shaun opens his mouth again sullenly. Back goes the scrap of John Rocha, but gently, in deference to his sore lip. 'Now, I'd recommend you sit down. She rolls a bit.' He does so with great dignity on the ridged and rusting floor then braces his feet, doubtless in anticipation of some sub-standard driving.

The van starts beautifully without any undue noise or sudden movements backwards, and chugs past Whitestone Pond then along Hampstead Lane. Ah, there it is. A dark, yawning gap opening out at the side of the road, the small car park on Heathside that's rarely locked. I hope there are no other vehicles already in there sheltering fornicating couples or minor drug deals. In the past, I've used it for both. But my luck is in. The place is deserted and the barrier unsecured, its red and white bar swinging in a light wind.

We drive in carefully, bouncing over the potholes and mud ruts, pulling up on the far side where the tall grass of Hampstead Heath begins and the amber glow generated by thousands of orange street lamps fires up the skyline.

I let Shaun out, undoing his cuffs and motioning him away from the van. He moves stiffly, stumbling as his feet hit the ground. When he turns to face me six feet away looking exhausted, I know I'll have no more need of the gun.

The cold breeze of the last hour before dawn makes it surprisingly chilly up here, even in summer. No birds sing yet but the trees are rustling insistently, their leaves shivering the way they do when rain's coming. I wish we were up here for a night picnic, an illicit quickie, an argument. Anything really. Anything but this.

'Off you go then.'

'Where are we?' He's rubbing his head and looking around as if waking from sleep.

'Hampstead Heath.'

He shrugs resignedly. 'At least it's not the Watford Gap. Which bit?'

'The deserted bit. Goodbye, Shaun.' I answer sadly, and turn to go, feeling the need of a bath, a whole handful of Prozac and a fresh start, though not necessarily in that order.

Unexpectedly, he grins. 'I suppose it's sort of flattering in a way.'

I have one foot on the van step and am just about to swing myself up. 'What is?'

'Well,' he waves his arms vaguely, 'all this. Missing me so much you had to have one last slice. Turning up for a drink in your underwear. Punishing me like that.' He smoothes his hair down across his balding patch and smiles faintly, tugging at his earlobe as he always does when he's acting flattered but modest.

'You must be so furious at me ending it. I never imagined you would still feel so strongly for me and it's – it's pretty incredible, I suppose. In it's way. But calling a halt really was the best thing for both of us, you can see that now can't you? Oh, and Zoe, those photos,' he smiles confidently. 'I presume that was your kinky little revenge for me ditching you, but that you never really intended to use them. Am I right?'

Him ending it? The man's ego is not only intact, it's alive, well and re-inflating as we speak. He's conveniently forgotten his recent fear and humiliation. And if I was so desperate for his dick one last time, has it completely escaped his notice that I haven't actually fucked him?

As usual he takes my dumfounded silence for complete agreement. 'Look, I do understand that you've not been yourself. If you were in your right mind, I know that you'd never have done anything like this.'

'I certainly w –'

'– which is why I can't really bring myself to be angry with you. Amazing,' he sticks his thumbs in the belt loops of his crumpled but expensive trousers and flexes his knees. 'I've never driven a woman clinically insane before. I guess that's a first, even for me.'

It gradually dawns on me that he is serious, because that this is the only explanation that his monumental arrogance can entertain. 'Listen *Warren Beatty*. I took you to that house not because I wanted your body one last time (frankly, I wouldn't care if I never saw it again) but because I needed those pictures. And I don't want them for a keepsake, since the sooner I forget about you the better. They're my – our – insurance that you leave Jim's business alone, and that Tim can stay at his school. Because if you pull out from *FirstPencil* on a whim, Jim will be bankrupt, the best idea he's ever had in his life will be dead in the water, we won't be able to afford Tim's fees and he'll be back in that dreadful –'

'Hold it. Who says I was going to pull out?'

'You did. You as good as told me you might, all couched in hints and threats. '*Business partners should be friends.*' What was that all about, then?' I poke him in the chest with the gun for emphasis. 'And all those remarks about the friend who had to take his sons away from their school when his backer pulled out, and 'here's hoping *FirstPencil* makes it then.' I'm not stupid, Shaun, those were barely veiled *threats*. Well, I'll tell you something for nothing: you're not holding that over our family for the rest of our lives.'

He puts his hands on his hips and laughs. A hollow laugh, with a humourless ring. 'Not stupid? Zoe, you have been quite astoundingly stupid.'

'I beg your pardon?' He seems to be forgetting he's the one with the manacle marks who's been pissing into a plant pot for the past twenty-four hours. 'If you're trying to tell me those weren't threats, I think you'd better explain just what you *were* talking about.' The wind is whistling through the loose stitches in Jim's old jumper. Brrr... it's all right for him, he's got his wop designer coat –

Shaun passes his hand over his face, giving an excellent impression of a wronged man barely hanging onto his patience and sanity. 'Schools. We were talking about schools. It was parent chat, Zoe. The sort of ordinary conversation you have *with someone who is an old friend.*'

There is a short silence while I digest this, feeling my stomach disappear in the process. 'Uh – let me get this quite clear. Are you honestly telling me you weren't threatening to shaft Jim's company?'

'Why should I want to do that? I'm *backing* it. I'm about to give it at least six months' start up clearance, minimum, probably nine. And if it hadn't been for your ludicrous kidnap attempt, Jim would have had my cheque on his desk by this morning.'

'And you wouldn't – take our house away?'

'Of course not!' Shaun shouts, totally exasperated. 'I wouldn't have anyway. I don't need to. If *FirstPrint* goes belly up I can simply have become your landlords and Jim, worst scenario, could pay me rent instead of your mortgage company. Or something.' The wind is really getting up now, and Shaun begins to button up his coat with still-clumsy fingers. 'Your husband's new company has a perfectly reasonable chance of making it. Why are you so pessimistic?

You seem think he's programmed for failure. And did you seriously think,' he barks, turning up his collar up against the cold, 'that I'd have turned you all out on the street?'

'Well, yes, actually,' I mumble in a very small voice.

'God almighty, I don't believe this.' He speaks with deadly calm to a point several feet above my head. 'I was going to see about using Seventh Wave's offices for collateral instead. I told you in the pub, remember? You just weren't listening properly, were you?' He grabs my arm and shakes me like a fox shaking a rabbit: 'I said, *were you,* you silly little bitch?'

There's a rumble of thunder in the distance, a God with indigestion. Rain starts to whisper down in soft, penetrating needles. 'I'm sorry. I'm so sorry,' I mutter, utterly mortified. 'I thought, well, I was afraid that –'

'I know what you fucking well thought!' he bellows, really angry now. 'Thanks a bloody bunch. Go home and take your mothers little helpers Zoe, it's all you're fit for. And be very thankful that I like both Jim, and his big idea – though this is hardly the way you should treat your majority shareholder.' With that he pushes me away from him, picks up his briefcase and starts marching across the car park in totally the wrong direction.

Utterly humiliated, I climb back into the van and attempt to start it as the rain begins bucketing down in earnest. It responds by leaping backwards, but this time continues rapidly in the same direction because I seem to have left her in reverse. There's a flat little *wumph* noise as the back bumper catches something a glancing blow. Oh, brilliant: have I damaged what's left of the chrome-work still further? Swivel round to check what that was. But even leaning out of the window I still can't see properly what with the dark, the rain and all, and a driver's mirror is no help in a van with blocked-out back windows. What a bloody silly place to stick a rubbish bin.

That *was* a rubbish bin. Wasn't it?

Unfortunately, it wasn't. And Shaun is now hanging onto the driver's door handle shouting at the top of his lungs, for the soft thump had been the sound of meat hitting metal.

'My fucking shin! Christ, it feels like it fucking broken! What are you trying to do, kill me? Get down out of there. I knew you couldn't drive it. *I said,* get down now before I break your stupid little neck –' he howls, trying to wrench the driver's door open. You mean get down *and* I'll break your neck, I think, locking it hastily, and the passenger one too.

But the unexpected pain on top of his past indignities has sent Shaun over the edge. He's heaved himself up and is pressing his screaming face against the windscreen, mouth distorted with rage, body halfway across the bonnet, hanging on for dear life and battering at the windscreen. I try to swing the van around towards the exit but he's clinging on, now pulling himself round to my side and smashing his fist against the side window.

'Do you know what you are, Zoe?' he yells, his face inches from mine. 'Shall I tell you? Some washed up little schlocker of journalist with *mental health problems* – yes I'll say it if I want to, it's time somebody fucking did – with a sad git loser of a husband. *You're totally delusional, you know that?*' Hell, he's still across the bonnet, but is managing to reach round and wrench at the driver's door. 'A paranoid schizophrenic! A pathetic little head case –' Dear God, now he's tearing at the windscreen wipers… *I've got to get him off.* Haul the wheel down sharp right, then with all my strength, slew the van to the left but it fails to dislodge him.

'Do you think I'm going to let you get away with this?' he bawls. 'I'll bury the lot of you – you, him, and your whole family! You're sick in the head and your kids are better off without you –' Still hanging on, he manages to rip off a wiper and fling it away, pounding his fist on the glass, his mouth a shapeless, howling hole. 'Lose your house?' I'll see you lose more than that when I'm through. You'd both better get down the DHSS and get a place in that queue –'

I stamp my foot on the brake but he's grabbed the driver's door again, screaming: 'I'll teach you to try and hurt me! I'll make you sorry you ever, ever –' Sobbing, I grind into reverse and floor the accelerator. The van ricochets backwards and Shaun's finally flung off the bonnet by the momentum.

I swing round hard to the left so as not to run over him and turn the wheel again sharply to the right to go to the exit, jolting over what feels like a speed bump. Get me out of here, just get me *out*... completely panicked, try wrenching the wheel the other way but my shaking foot slips and she kangaroos forwards, her back left wheel running over something which lets out a crack like a rifle shot as it gives slightly beneath us. *Jesus, what now*?

Hanging out of the window again to get a closer look at this new obstruction, I find I can now see rather better. In fact, I have a very good view of Shaun.

Only he isn't shouting any more. He isn't doing anything.

Utterly appalled, I leap out and hurtle back to him through the puddles and the rain. He is lying like a bundle of old clothes in a bin liner, rasping rather than breathing, his face torn and welling blood from an open cheek, his left leg bent back at an impossible angle. Splinters of bone protrude half way up his thigh through a huge rip in his trousers. So that's what a snapped femur sounds like I think wildly, trying not to throw up. Shaun's right arm is arm crumpled under him in a way I've never seen an arm fold before, and even I know I can't move it without making it bleed even harder than it already is.

I back away slowly, not daring to touch him, terrified that he might open an eye and look at me.

What if I've killed him?

What, after all he's been saying, if I haven't?

Birthday Girl

I'm dragged out of foggy, fitful sleep by the tweeting of Jim's watch alarm, which has gone off early at about 5.30 a.m. Thrashing a clenched fist about on the sticky bedside table to hammer it into submission, my eyes remain screwed shut against a lowering dawn shot through with piss-yellow streaks.

The damp inertia of a muggy urban morning wreaths our little house. While blindly locating the watch, a glass of stale water gets knocked over Jim's head (yes he's sleeping – but only sleeping – in our bed again). Wake up properly with a tightening chest, his curses in my ears and a list of twenty three things to do.

This was normal enough while I was writing, yet since Morrison's I've been relatively free of the wave of panic, which used to wash over me the second I opened my eyes, if still a bit muddled. Now it's back again big time, fuelled by many surreptitious calls to the Royal Free's IT Unit.

I haven't seen Shaun since I phoned an ambulance from his mobile, waiting with him cradled in my arms till I saw its blue lights blazing up the road, then running to hide in the long grass at the edge of the car park to watch them ease him onto a stretcher and take him away, sirens blaring, tires squealing. The feel of his broken body on my lap will stay with me to the end of my days.

I've had to throw away those pale grey school trousers of Tim's because of the blood, and though Jim's jumper's been washed a dozen times, I still can't look at it. It's hidden at the back of his wardrobe where he cannot find it so I won't have to see him wear it.

I need to go and see Shaun – I must – but haven't yet dared, probably for fear of being confronted with the awful reality of what I have done. So I speak to the same kind nurse every day on the phone, sometimes twice or three times. She thinks I am an old friend of the family, and once helpfully offered to put me through to Debbie who was standing by the reception desk at the time. At first he was critical; then it was stable, then comfortable. The past two days, he's been The Same, which means he is still in a coma but doesn't look like dying just yet. Oh, Christ. I have completely and utterly misconstrued that man's intentions in almost every possible way. And despite his underage preferences, I would now willingly give twenty years of my life to cancel out those final few seconds when the van's wheels rolled over him.

And another thing: it's too quiet. There's been no come-back from the night in Hampstead. Surely if you do something truly bad, They'll know? Or He'll know, and He'll send Them to get you? A whole week, and still nothing. I've got away with it (why should I not have?). And yet, as I look out at a sunrise resembling paper that's had raw liver dragged across it, I can sense a change in the atmosphere. Something, somewhere out there, is on the move.

And today, Buddha help us all, at Bel would say, is Kasha's birthday. Technically, it's also my day off. There are however, seventeen eleven-year-olds to entertain for three hours single-handed, fairy cakes to ice, party bags to stuff and tails to be pinned on donkeys. Jim has another meeting ('I'll try and be back early'). None of the other mums are free to help and I can't say I blame them. Actually, these are little Camden girls: they won't be too impressed by donkey tails. Maybe it had better be Robbie Williams' smile or Orlando Bloom's bottom.

Yes, all in all, I do not want to know about today.

Nor does Jim, who has just put the pillow over his head. I prod him in the back. He swears softly, but levers himself blindly out of bed and he stumbles downstairs to make the truck-driver tea he requires for his daily transition into wakefulness. He always brings me some too. In all our years together, I have never found a nice way to tell him that his tea's tannin quotient makes my tongue curl.

Back in our bedroom he's balancing a tray of drinks and cooling cardboard toast in one hand, and holding a big brown-paper Muji carrier bag in the other. It bulges with the irregularly shaped packages we wrapped last night in Kasha's favourite colours: emerald, orange, purple, Pucci pink, sky blue.

Kasha. Twelve years ago today she'd burst upon the world, pale and perfect, eyebrows like crescent moons, a shock of dark silky hair, hands like starfish and an ancient dark blue glaze that speared our hearts. Jim had been so happy. He'd always longed for a daughter and filled roll after roll of film with virtually identical shots of her in my arms, now from this angle, now from that. Then ignoring the nurses' protests, he'd drawn the cubicle's curtains and spent the night in our narrow hospital bed, holding us both in his arms.

And now? Now he's careful not to touch me accidentally and never hugs me in the mornings. However, this morning he's drinking his first cup of tea of the day sitting in bed with me instead of having it in the kitchen, so perhaps... A small figure in pink Chinese pyjamas showing several inches of wrist and ankle wanders in, falling theatrically across the bed, face down. She feels blindly for a hand from each of us and brings them up to her cheeks. We are instantly flooded with love. 'Happy birthday, darling,' smiles Jim, shaking the bag at her.

'Yay!' Instantly awake, she dives in like a Lurcher into a lake. Coloured paper rips and flies. Jim and I beam at each other over her head. At least this is something we can still share.

'Happy birthday, junior,' yawns Tim, shambling in wrapped in Jim's old blue towelling dressing gown, which trails behind him like an imperial robe. He scratches his neck absently and taps a frenzied Kasha on the shoulder, proffering a crumbled bundle wrapped in newspaper and shiny with tape. 'Wow, *thanks*, Tim,' she squeaks, glancing up from some frenzied scrabbling inside a green package.

He assumes his best diffident look. 'Oh, it's nothing really, just rubbish you know.' Kasha looks really pleased because Tim never gets her presents unless heavily prompted, and this, touchingly, looks like it's all his own work. She can't get it open for all the tape, so belts off to get a knife and starts sawing. I glance up to see Tim standing a safe distance away, wearing a faint but discernible smirk.

'Uh, hang on, Kash, let me –' I offer, but it's too late. She's got the parcel open, and is thrusting her hand inside.

There is two seconds' dead silence.

'Aaaagh! Yuck! Eeee-*yew* – *Tim, you bugger...*' The parcel's contents are flung high into the air. Used tea bags, ancient bacon rinds, soggy cat biscuits, fag ends and worse (much worse) rain down upon the floor as Tim flees, hooting, to the bathroom and prudently locks himself in. She is seconds behind him.

'Pig face! Snot-face! I'll get you for this!' she howls, pounding and kicking at the door. 'I'll get you! You'll have to come out sometime and I'll get you – get *off* Daddy – you're going to *die*, Tim Harrington! I've got a big knife and I'm going to kill you, *kill you –*'

'You're repeating yourself,' snickers Tim through the keyhole.

'*So?* Right! I'll just – rub all the rubbish you gave me into your bed and it'll stink, stink, *stink,* just like you do!' she bawls, glancing up the stairs to his loft room. 'Then I'm going to get all your best stuff and – and I'm cutting it up! Do you hear me? I'll throw out all your Nintendo games and carve up your crappy Formula One magazines – and, yeah, I'll pee on your, your *blazer* that's what! Try wearing it to your dumb posh school then –' She kicks the juddering door some more.

We cannot placate her, cannot comfort her. The more Jim reasons with Kasha and demands Tim comes out and apologies, the louder he laughs and the more Kasha screams, eventually disintegrating into tears of pure rage when I remove the bread knife she is now using to slash Tim's prized South Park duvet to ribbons. It's a good job he's going back to a friend's after school.

The tone is set for the day.

The next shock of the morning comes when I'm making my regular call to IT and the nice nurse tells me happily that Mr Lyon has not only regained full consciousness this morning, he's talking.

I receive this news with feelings that can only be described as mixed, and just about manage not to ask whether, perhaps, he is talking about anything special?

Awake and talking. Is this *Thank Christ,* or *Oh Christ?* Spend the rest of the day jumping like a shot rabbit every time the phone rings (it does so frequently, mostly working mothers asking if they can pick their up progeny late) icing fairy buns, and scratching the new eczema rash on my hands.

Four o'clock and bang on cue, the hired minibus bringing Kasha and her friends home from school pulls up outside, blocking out the light. There is a staccato knocking on the front door and a collage of small bobbing faces appears at the sitting-room window, knuckles rapping on the glass to rouse me from contemplating the birthday table which now groans under the weight of cocktail sausages, sandwiches, fairy cakes and a rather squashy caterpillar cake made by self; and it isn't looking half bad. *Girls Aloud* pound out of the stereo. The cats have been cornered, pink bows put round their reluctant necks. Ophelia the orphan hedgehog is trotting around the sitting room on invisible clockwork feet, a gala shower of glitter on her prickles. I scoop her up and put her in the cat-basket on top of the dresser, as like all hedgehogs, she is easily made nervous. There is a life-size poster of Justin Timberlake in profile on the wall, his buttocks cut out. I've even washed my hair. It is party time.

Despite the terror of The Other Thing, I feel a helpless glow of purest mummy-pleasure looking at the amateurish but colourful table, our old birthday banner fished out year after year, the cheerful lop-sided green cake, and listening to Kasha calling through the letter-box. It is no use trying to explain this sort of thing to childless friends because they just think you're being slushy and somewhat too easily pleased. Yet these moments are precious. Parents may not get many of them, but the ones we do have are enough to warm the spirit by for years.

In pours a tidal wave of little girls, squealing like piglets. School coats, denim jackets, fake junior Afgans, outdoor shoes and presents are hurled pell-mell underfoot in the hall. Climbing over them to pay off the young driver, I see he is looking a trifle pale. When I come back thirty-five pounds poorer, they are looking approvingly at the table but standing about stiffly, like staff required to attend the afternoon office party. Kasha is looking anxious. All eyes swivel towards me, alert as a pack of young meercats.

'Right, you lot. Who wants to pin on Justin's bum blindfold for a fiver?' Stampede.

At teatime (seventeen children squashed round a table which seats ten) they ignore the lovingly prepared organic hummus sandwiches and carrot sticks to claw, shrieking and chewing, at mounds of crisps and fairy cakes. As we are all bawling 'Happy *Birthday* to you' and sounding like Ladies Night at Rosslyn Park Rugby Club, the doorbell rings. Streak off to open it. Bless Jim, he hasn't been avoiding his parental responsibilities after all, he's come to help, thank heavens –

But wrenching it open with a 'Darling, you are wonder –' there's a willowy figure in shades of coffee on the doorstep, holding out a small violet package smothered in curls of narrow pink ribbon.

'Where's birthday girl?' coos Lucia, triple kissing me fastidiously and teetering into the hall. 'I felt I couldn't let my god-daughter's big day go by without une petite cadeaux visit.' She stops suddenly, like an ant encountering a lump of coal, in front of a mountainous heap of fashionable junior outerwear. 'Then again, perhaps,' she adds, as a cacophony of yells and giggles reaches her ears, 'I shall return tomorrow. When it's more convenient,' she catches my desperate eyes on her, 'for *you*.'

'Auntie Loo, it's Auntie Loo,' screeches Kasha, intuiting the source of another present and comes charging into the hall with her hordes behind her. They all titter at the name. 'Here, darling,' exclaims Lucia, thrusting the present into Kasha's icing-sticky paws, 'happy days.' She retreats and opens the front door. 'Aw, Lucia, please, I was so glad to see you. I –'

'Darling, you know I just adore your progeny. Adore them. But this sort of thing, it simply isn't me.'

I grab her wrist pleadingly. 'You could give me some moral support. I'll get you a drink.'

Lucia gives me a look reserved for someone who'd just suggested she should travel on the Bakerloo Line in a bikini and backs out onto the pavement, flagging down a passing black cab. It screeches to an obedient halt.

'You cannot turn up at a time like this then just flit off again! '

'So sorry, sweetness.' She drops her voice tactfully, and edges towards the cab. 'It's simply that I find children, all children, bless their innocent little eyes, just so, so –' she opens the taxi door.

'Noisy? Undisciplined? Badly dressed?'

'– *small*. I have no sense of connection with anyone under five foot.'

'Fine fairy godmother *you* are.'

'Arrivederci, darling. I shall ring you tomorrow. *PM.*'

Back inside, a rousing game of sardines is in progress with all the curtains drawn. Olivia Barrington gets stuck in the broom cupboard, someone falls into the six foot potted fig bringing it crashing to the floor, and Veridian is discovered trying to palm one of Kasha's presents ('I only wanted to see if it was like the one I've got at home'). I am just trying to pick the lock of our bedroom with a pair of nail scissors, calling encouragement to Kasha's second best friend Precious Wilson who has locked herself in but cannot get out, when the doorbell goes again. Thank the Lord, this time I know it's Jim, because it's too early for any of the parents and too late for further guests. Racing downstairs, I find Kasha has beaten me to it and is ushering two adults into the wrecked sitting room.

Standing on our worn red Persian carpet surrounded by ecstatic small girls, torn wrapping paper and party popper streamers are a policewoman and policeman. Or to be more accurate, the little terriers have backed them up against our CD player, and are plucking at their uniforms like comic book natives inspecting their first white man.

'Mrs Harrington?' asks the male one, wading through the crush of little girls and trapping me between the sofa and the sideboard.

'Possibly.' My teeth feel too big for my mouth.

'This is just so great, Kash,' whoops Merope Barkworth. 'I've never been to a party where they had dress-up policemen before, not even at Galaxy Johnson's, and her dad's a rock manager – oops, sorry Ophelia.' The hedgehog, released by God knows who, squeaks shrilly under her foot and scuttles beneath the TV.

'Would you like a bit of cake?' offers Kasha, flushed with social success but mindful of her duties as a hostess. 'It's Caterpillar.'

'Is there another responsible adult here, Mrs Harrington?'

'Another one? What makes you think *I'm* responsible? I mean,' I wave a hand at the surrounding carnage, 'look at it.'

Plod regard me levelly. 'We can see it's a bad time, but I'm afraid we are going to have to ask you to come with us.'

'No, thank you,' I reply as firmly as I know how.

'Mrs Harrington, do you know a man called Shaun Lyon?'

'Certainly not. I mean, certainly I do. He's – my husband's business backer.' A vision of Shaun's broken, crash-dummy body wired to a tangle of IV lines scrapes across my consciousness. The one I've been seeing several times a day since it happened. The one that invades my dreams.

'He was. Though now, I'm not sure he'll be in a position to do business with anyone for a very long time,' says the policeman. 'He's not too clever at the moment.'

'Oh dear! Oh no. Poor man! That is to say – er, why?' They are watching my face carefully. 'We can fill you in down at the station. And you never know, perhaps you can fill *us* in on a couple of little things as well.'

'Please, not just now,' I beg, fighting rising nausea. 'Can't you see I'm busy?'

'I'm afraid we really must insist.' It's said calmly, as if they're giving me directions to the nearest car park. 'Just routine you understand, but we just have to clarify a few details.'

'Well of course, if you put it like that, obviously it must be something that needs doing. In which case, we can do it here. How about a nice cup of tea while we're at it?' I move towards the kitchen, but am stopped by a hand on my elbow. The room goes quiet. Britney, now singing that if we want her hot body we'll have to beg, seems inappropriate.

'Down at the station Mrs Harrington. *If* you don't mind,' persists the man, who is looking deeply uncomfortable. 'It shouldn't take long,' cajoles the woman. 'Where's Daddy, dear?' she asks Kasha, whose smile is fading fast. The girls cluster behind me, quiet now, their collective warmth at my rigid back. Two hot sticky hands find each of mine, another one fastens onto the hem of my T-shirt. Someone turns the music off. Kasha looks stricken. She knows there must be some mistake, but she's never going to live this down.

I take one last stab at brazening it out. 'I'm sorry, but you'll have to wait, Sergeant. Parties before business in this house, ha ha. Now come along, girls, we're going to cut the cake. Kash, get the party bags, darling, we must put one piece in each. Veridian, would you separate out the napkins on the table, as cake wrapping? Now – Vienna, isn't it? Do you want to take home the bit with the Smartie eyes, or the liquorice feet?'

'*What the fuck is going on here*?' demands a familiar voice. I wheel round and scamper out into the hall. 'Jim, just the person we needed. You are brilliant, thanks for coming back so –'

'And what are those two,' he jerks his finger at the police who've followed me out, 'doing here? Have you been parking on double red lines again? No, I bet I can guess. It's the TV licence isn't it?'

I grab his hand gratefully and tug him up onto the first floor landing for a bit of privacy. The police wait below in the hall, possibly because they can see they're between me and the door. Everything will be all right now. Here is another responsible adult, who at a pinch might also take responsibility for me as well. Though he doesn't look too keen as he's just taken his hand back, and folded his arms.

'Zoe, I have just had the most appalling day. I'm hot, I'm tired, the last time I ate was a Belgian bun at eleven, I've been in fucking meetings all afternoon and now, on top of it everything else, I come back early as promised to find the place in a riot, the police in my sitting room, and I don't know what else. Listen,' he drags his hands over his face as if trying to iron out its new creases, 'I finally got to speak to Maxwell Fordyce this morning. Apparently, Shaun Lyon is in a *coma*. Been in hospital for a week. No wonder we haven't got our money yet. Some psychopath ran him down in a truck or something. Apart from liking the guy, if anything happens to him, we don't get a penny. And we've already laid out nearly three hundred thousand we haven't got.'

'Darling, please don't shout.' How do I tell him that Shaun did in fact wake up a few hours ago but that he may be less than eager to send a large cheque to anyone remotely associated with me? 'And, look here, as for spending all that money, forgive me for saying this but I never did agree to our house being used as collateral. In fact I –'

Jim interrupts, red in the face. 'Shut up. Just shut up!' he shouts, slamming his fist into the wall and knocking down his picture of the Queen's head on Lara Croft's body. 'Don't you realise what this means? We could lose the house. *FirstPencil* may never get off the ground. We are up shit creek, and someone else has got our paddle. Don't you *understand*? We are, very possibly, bankrupt. Now, I come back, desperate for a bit of support, and I find –' he gestures wildly with both arms to describe both social anarchy and general domestic beastliness. There is a scraping, rattling sound from the other side of our bedroom door. Precious is re-applying herself to the challenge of regaining her freedom.

My husband ignores it. 'And anyway, you never did answer my question. I'm asking you again – what are the police doing here?' As I fight down an urge to throw myself at his feet, a crumpled Ghanaian child finally emerges from our room much disfigured by tears, and stumbles downstairs still sobbing. Then just as I'm trying to cobble together an answer to the most awkward question I've ever been asked, the police-lady rounds the corner of the stairwell, takes me by the arm, and with many reassurances that this won't take a minute, escorts me smartly outside to the waiting squad car.

Jim is left with a broken bedroom lock, seventeen little girls in hysterics and one hedgehog with a broken toe.

The Puppy Stuff

Under chilly, flickering fluorescent lights, a small woman in dark blue trouser suit is shining a torch up my anus. Welcome. Welcome to HMP Highview.

She is business-like but plainly in a hurry until she starts investigating my vagina, catching the sensitive bump of the cervix with her gloved index finger. She has been poking around in there for what seems like an unnecessarily long time. I mean, it's not *that* big. Or do I have a twat like a horse collar, and no one's liked to tell me?

Crouching on the examination couch, buttocks to the ceiling, my skin goose-pimples briskly as she uses wooden spatulas, another tiny medical torchlight and metal probes to check every possible body orifice and part. These include the soles of my feet, the insides of my ears and the roof of my mouth.

The prison officer finally peels off her disposable Latex gloves with a loud snap that could be heard in the Governor's office on the other side of the compound, and drops them inside a metal swing-top bin with a phutt.

We are hidden from the eyes of five other women waiting for more of the same by a green army hospital canvas screen with a couple of moth holes in it. They're sitting uneasily on the other side, trying to cover puffy knees, hairy shins, thread veins and cellulite with identical pale-blue nylon dressing gowns too short for them.

'All right?' whispers a big brunette, as I sit down gingerly in the next chair. She touches my arm awkwardly. 'You'd better get used to that. This is my second time in here, and they do it every month. More, if they want to take you down a peg. You never know when it's coming.'

Next, we get to be processed by the prison doctor. Outside her office under the jaundiced eye of yet another PO, I join another row of women, also in regulation nylon dressing gowns, looking even more demoralised than the last lot. We are forbidden to talk, so sit silently, feet bare, arms crossed for warmth, feeling exposed and disorientated. I would kill for a fag. Hell, a nicotine patch would do. As we shiver and wait, the memory of the motherly DI in her mid fifties who gave me a cigarette last night in Marylebone Police Station floats to the surface of my consciousness, like a corpse that won't stay on a lake-bed.

She's made her offer of a Silk Cut while telling me casually that they'd found 'the assault vehicle' and had proof I'd driven it.

'I'd begin at the beginning, dear, if I were you – you're in very serious trouble. If you co-operate, we'll see what we can do to help (heaven knows you could do with some). However,' she'd suddenly looked rather less motherly, 'we don't like people who waste police time so I really don't advise you to try making up any silly stories. Now then –'

'You ran Lyon down in that van, yes or no?' interrupted her pretty but hard-face little blonde sidekick, springing into Bad Cop role with enthusiasm. 'You were trying to kill him.'

'I was not.'

'Our intelligence says differently.'

I blinked.

'*Oh*, yes. You'd be surprised what local call-outs for information can produce in an investigation like this: a few police signs around the scene of the crime asking if anyone saw anything can work wonders. Especially if there's a reward attached, which there was. Only a thousand pounds, but that means a lot to some, particularly to a homeless person, who, because they are out on the streets at odd hours when everyone else is in bed because they do at least have beds to go to, frequently sees things that no one else does. Yes, some of our best leads come from outreach work with

274

the rough sleeper community. Of which Camden has a more than its fair share. This one was an Arlington House regular but he'd been refused entry that evening for being drunk. For the details he gave us, the reward was a real bargain. He's using it for a down payment on a bed-sit.'

She's just trying to scare you. 'That's nice for him.' *Doing a good job of it, too.*

'Watch your mouth, or you'll be surprised what else comes out of it,' spat Blondie. 'You were on at the Heath that night, weren't you? I said, weren't you?'

'I was not.'

'No? Well it so happens that our Source, having wandered about half the night, had eventually crashed out in the bushes at the edge of the car park because it was at least quiet there, and our boys didn't keep moving him on. And he says he remembers a right row made by some van reversing to and fro in the early hours of the morning in question. First he thought it was just some lads having a laugh, but changed his mind when then he was woken some time later by an ambulance arriving – and just as he was going back to sleep, disturbed yet again by the same van screeching wildly out of the car park. A big white van, Zoe.'

'What's that got to do with me?' *Deny everything, stick to your guns. They've got nothing concrete on you, nothing –*

'Your prints are all over it.'

Jesus. 'I, er, never said I hadn't driven *a* van at some point. I did. That's no secret, I hired one earlier that evening, to, to go and collect a second-hand leather Chesterfield. We really need a new sofa you see, I mean you should see the state of our...'

'Now why ever didn't you say so earlier, dear?' asked Good Cop archly.

'I thought you'd, um, make too much of it.' *Like put two and two together and wind up with 22... or worse.* 'But I never went near the Heath. Why should I? Nor did I run anyone over. And as to trying to kill Shaun Lyon, that's absurd. He's my husband's *backer*, for God's sake.'

'Yes, now why would you do that? Why try to kill a man who's bankrolling your bloke? No one in their right mind would do that, would they?' They both looked at me expectantly.

'But that's exactly what you did do, Zoe. Isn't it?' hissed the little blonde spitefully. 'Oh don't give me the wide-eyed shit, pul-ease. Sofas, my arse. Your place doesn't have a new sofa. Not according to your husband, anyway.'

'No. Well, when I got there it wasn't awfully comfortable you see so I didn't feel it was worth – look, I'd only seen the ad in *Loot* and there's no telling with furniture until you try it out, is there? I mean, there's no point buying something that –'

'Intensive house to house inquiries in your area produced a woman in the next street who'd been up all night with a new baby,' interrupted Bad Cop as if I'd never spoken. 'She remembers a big white van disappearing from the road outside her house for a couple of hours in the middle of the night. And we know it disappeared because *you* drove off in it.'

'See me get in, did she?'

'Shut it, you smartarse little tart, I'm not done yet. Three days ago, one of our patrol cars spotted a vehicle fitting the description parked outside VanTastic – a place misnamed if ever there was one – off the Kentish Town Road. The proprietor confirmed you'd been the last person to use it. So after we'd checked out another related matter – can you guess what that might be, Zoe? – it was the most natural thing in the world to come round yours for a chat.'

'Shame it was in the middle of your little girl's party,' added Good Cop sympathetically. 'They're so sensitive at that age, aren't they?'

Oh no. No, please... and my poor Kasha, this must rank as the party faux pas of the century. 'What exactly is your point?'

'Now I admit,' snapped Blondie, 'that we have no witnesses, as such, to the attempted murder on the Heath –' *I do wish they wouldn't call it that* '– and you'll be relieved to hear that no one has come forward to say they saw you actually drive off, or come back late that night.'

Thank the Lord.

'But we do,' broke in Good Cop leaning forward, 'have something else.'

Something else?

'DNA tests can take a little while to come through. This morning, however, Forensics confirmed that fragments of Shaun Lyon's soft tissue were discovered stuck to the windscreen, back bumpers, wheel treads, wipers (goodness knows how they got *there*) driver's door and passenger door. Which identifies that vehicle, without a shadow of a doubt, as the one that ran him over.'

Iced sweat started trickling down my back. 'What, all by itself?'

'Now, we were hoping you could help us clarify that one.'

'Well I c-can't,' I stuttered. 'And I want a lawyer. I'm entitled to a lawyer, aren't I?' *Dad. Someone please get my Dad... oh God, if I have ever needed my barrister father, it's now. But how can I possibly tell him? He'll want all the facts, the background – he'll want the truth. Which somehow, I don't think he would quite understand...*

'Of course you are, dear,' Good Cop adjusted her white blouse cuff minutely, 'But all in good time, for there *is* another small matter. I don't suppose that you would happen to have *lost* something recently?'

'Like what?'

'Something valuable? Jewellery. A little diamond, I'm talking about. Tiny, but rather prettily cut.'

'I haven't got any diamonds. We can't afford that sort of thing.'

'Not even in a wee earring stud?'

'I don't wear earrings.'

'A *brooch,* perhaps?' interjected Bad Cop.

'Do I look like the sort of person who wears diamond brooches?'

'A ring, then?' pursued Good Cop.

'I've only got one ring with stones in it, that's my engagement ring and I'm wearing it. It has seven little ones, you know, seven for luck –'

'What a nice idea. Traditional. May we see it?'

Suddenly, I didn't want to show her. Not one bit.

'Don't be shy, dear. Just a quick look,' Good Cop leant swiftly across the table, grabbed my left hand in a grasp like a gin trap, and examined the ring minutely twisting it thoughtfully to and fro so the diamond chips caught the light.

'And now we are six.'

'Sorry?' *Why was the woman quoting A.A. Milne?* 'Stop that. Let *go.*'

'Let go? Am I making you nervous? I'm just trying to show you something, Zoe. Something interesting. Now, don't tell me you haven't noticed?'

'Noticed what?' Tugged furiously, but she merely tightened her hold. 'You young women. So casual. That you are missing a stone from your engagement ring, dear. A diamond. And do you know (such a coincidence) the Royal Free Hospital found just such a one on Mr Lyon's person. I do believe it was stuck to his hairline –'

– *shit a brick* –

'– in a blood-clot.'

'Next prisoner.'

I'm catapulted from the memory of what happened next (me throwing up on the interview floor) by the prison doctor. She has frizzy brown hair, a bored expression, and a slightly soiled white coat revealing several inches of maroon pleated skirt. She coughs as she quests and prods where others have already explored today, rattling off questions about whether I have bulimia, nits, am pregnant, on heroin or prescription drugs without once looking at my face. At the word Prozac she appears mildly interested for the first time.

'Sorted you, has it?' she demands, shining a torch into my left pupil. Close up I can see her thumb and first finger are yellowed and shiny.

'Well no, not really, now you come to mention it.'

'Ever felt hopeless, not good enough? Like anything you tried is bound to fail, or whatever you choose is bound to be wrong? Got a voice in your head that keeps telling you you're useless?' She's picked up my right arm now, and is squinting at it for needle tracks and scabies.

'Not as such. Mind you, recently –'

'Got an overly-directive mum or dad?'

I smiled faintly for the first time in ages. 'God, no.'

'Thought not,' she sniffs, dropping my arm dismissively. 'Fucking GPs. Haven't a fucking clue. Treat this stuff like it's a fucking cure-all though it has a very specific psychological profile indication. They're even giving it for exogenous depression in response to bereavement or job loss, and to women with PMS. Be prescribing it for fucking constipation next. Fucking ludicrous. Not suitable for *you*, either. No wonder you're no better –' Her diatribe is interrupted by an emphysemic coughing fit. 'Probably worse, if anything. Am I right? Well, Xanax'll do you,' she wheezes, wiping streaming eyes. 'Specific anti-anxiety medication. Very popular here. I'll tell the screws. You have it for four weeks, you see me again. Take it from there. Well, what are you waiting for? Get your clothes on. I haven't got all fucking day.'

Next stop is the counter of the Check-In room. Two bored-looking POs have been going through my little pile of belongings. They have counted, categorised, and listed (sign please) every last sock, elastic hair tie and crumpled tissue in my overnight case and handbag. The bits I am allowed to keep are handed back in a standard prison-issue Hessian hold-all. I peer inside. 'Hang on, where's the rest of my stuff? And what about that tenner I had in my bag?'

'New prisoners on non-enhanced regimes are only permitted four books, five music CDs, up to three photos from home, one warm top, two pairs of trousers or two skirts, three T-shirts or blouses, three changes of undergarment, three pairs of hosiery or socks and one pair of footwear,' intones the skinny little prison officer behind her large white melamine counter. 'Look in your Orientation Guide.'

'Probably can't read,' sneers her friend. 'Thick as shit, like all the rest of them.'

'I don't have a Guide. And I'd like the rest of my things, if you don't mind.'

'We *said,* sit *down* over t*here*,' growls her mate, who is built like a brick-house door. 'I've got eight more of you to get through before teatime Wing Roll Call.'

'Well, what about my tenner then?' She might be look like a ref for an *Extreme Catfighting* competition in Alabama, but this is barefaced theft. 'And where are my moisturiser, toothpaste and stuff?' Jim had dropped a weekend bag off at the police station late last night. Its contents suggested he wasn't expecting to see me again for some time.

The Large One halumphs like a circus elephant asked to stand on a tub but ducks wearily under the counter, resurfacing with a small brown paper bag. It contains toothpaste in a plain white tube, a black toothbrush and a small cake of cheap white soap with the Queens' initials on it.

'Drugs.'

'What?'

'Your toiletry products need to be checked for drugs. If they're clean, you'll get them back. Eventually.'

'Oh. Well – look here, I'd like my money please.'

'That has to be logged in the book, then recorded onto the office computer. You may have it a bit at a time at your Key Worker's discretion, but you'll need to apply for an appointment to discuss it,' explains the skinny one with satisfaction, adding: 'You can buy anything you need for the moment from the prison shop.'

'What with?'

'You're getting the idea. Good here, isn't it? Now fucking *sit down* before you're made to.'

When I am finally taken to my cell after much locking and unlocking of corridor doors, I can no longer get a word out but simply go and lie, clutching what's left of my belongings on the lower bunk which the PO indicates with a jerk of her head. Curled up in a heap facing the wall, I can feel that my three cellmates are tactfully leaving me be, flicking the odd glance occasionally to see if I am either crying hysterically or clucking with smack withdrawal like many inmates on their first day.

Having introduced themselves as Lally, Marine and Joolz and courteously offered me a half-smoked Marlborough Lite, they resume the conversation I interrupted by arriving. They are talking about nail varnish – which you can't get in here – someone called Mad Val who apparently did it again last night, and which warders are definitely lesbians. I'd like to join in, but this is like being the new kid at a really tough boarding school you'd begged your parents not to send you to. You don't know the routine, the ropes or the people but you've a nasty feeling that unless you get it sorted and quick, you're dead.

And what if any of them are dangerous? Look surreptitiously at the three women, checking for tracks, bruises, potentially self-inflicted cuts, black eyes. *How do I get them to like me?*

Lie very still, battling with feelings of unreality, revolt and impending unpleasantness. This is – ridiculous. I am supposed to be making Tim and Kasha's tea now, helping them with their homework. It's Tim's spelling test night and he needs both cheerleading and bribery to get through that. And I'd stuck hundreds of sequins all over a T-shirt for

Kasha to take to her school play rehearsal next morning (she's Chief Starfish) but she doesn't know where I've put it and she'll be in trouble for not taking her costume in –

Jim'll be home soon. It's about the time of day that I'd pour us both a glass of cheap plonk and have a polite chat about his work. Trying to sew up the rift between us a little more every day with darning wool spun from the homely normalities of life, the odd joke and a bit of food. And, oh please, who's going to be there for the children after school each day? Let it be my mother, not his. But I bet I know who's bloody there now, like a bird on a bun, with her tartan suitcase and her can of Alpine Breeze bog freshener. Am just giving my back teeth a good grind at the thought when one of the women addresses me directly, but I'm so busy loathing Ma Harrington, that what she's saying doesn't register.

'I said I'm busting for a piss,' groans Marine, levering herself to her feet. 'Anyone got any wipe they wanna swap for a piece of Milky Bar?' She's looking at me. 'Think to bring any in, did you love?'

'Wipe?'

'Toilet paper. The Puppy stuff.' I shake my head.

'Shame. Going rate is ten Marlborough for a single roll of Andrex, any colour. Lotsa women put it on the seat an' all. Me, I think that's a waste. I ain't sat down on no bog seats in ten weeks.'

The next time we are let out is supper time: soggy, individual 'meat' pie, baked beans and a scoop of mashed spud eaten off plastic plates with plastic spoons and forks. My cellmates are now treating me with that mixture of tolerance and disinterest shown by a group of teenagers to a tiresome nine-year-old sister. Convulsed with shyness, I am desperate to talk to someone but can think of nothing to say and can only sit, envying the other women their easy brazen back-chat, their air of knowing what's what.

Afterwards, we go to the Free Association Room. Women either slouch in rows on hard plastic chairs watching a TV on six foot aluminium legs tuned into *Who Wants to be Millionaire* or stand backs to the wall, observing the privileged few play table tennis and whispering to each other. It feels like a bitchfight's about to break out but no one else is looking particularly alert. Choose a seat in the back row, stare miserably at Chris Tarrant's toothpaste smile and think about Tim and Kasha who love this show and get viciously competitive about answering the questions. I hope someone's done them a proper supper. Are they missing me? What has Jim told them? I must ask Lally or Joolz how you telephone out of here, or even if you're allowed to. I can almost feel Kasha's warm weight on my lap.

'New girl, eh?' says a voice in my ear. 'Don't worry, it gets worse.' I smile feebly at the speaker, a woman with a platinum crop and nose stud who's passing by my chair.

Chris is just trying to jolly along a nervous-looking bald man in a blue jacket, when a big woman with short stiff black hair, the beginnings of sideburns and a florid face sidles over to my chair. 'You just got in then?' she enquires quietly, six gold rings glinting in the ear nearest me. Oh good, someone to talk to, *finally.* As she lowers herself into the seat next to me, it creaks protestingly under her weight. 'Well, if you want my advice –'

She is still talking when the show ends. Suddenly she lowers her voice, looks quickly around and whispers: 'By the way, got any blow?' I shake my head.

'Brown?' Another shake.

'Rock?'

'No.'

She looks disapproving. 'Christ, didn't you bring *anything* in to pay your way with? Nothing special to come out when you have your first crap?' She tsssks as if I've committed a major social gaffe, like turning up to a house-warming party with no drink and several uninvited guests. 'You might wish you had before the week's up.' My former new best friend heaves herself to her feet: 'Bye-bye, then.' And away she strolls to shrug and murmur with another woman who's been standing nearby all the while, apparently watching the TV. A Nigerian girl who'd been in the prison van with me shuffles past, muttering. I try smiling at her but she looks straight through me.

Thus, the uncomfortable evening passes. By speaking very sharply to myself, I manage to only think about home once every sixty seconds but am already in full blown mourning for Jim. And blown is the word. I think we might just have been beginning to get somewhere, him and me; that our shaky ceasefire was starting to turn into something resembling a tentative relationship with both battered sides at least willing to see how it went. But the last twenty-four hours will have knocked that one on the head, all right. The police have obviously told him all about it and now he'll think he's married to the Psycho-Spouse from Hell. I can just hear the conversation where I try to Explain:

Her: 'But it was an accident. You know what my driving's like, and it was all dark and wet.'

Him *(edging towards the door and checking out the whites of her eyes):* 'Right.'

Oh, what's the bloody use?

Wash time is early here, at eight o'clock. The bathroom contains a long line of cracked basins along the wall in a windowless room tiled like the men's old toilets at St Pancras Station, and an even longer line of impatient women with pungent armpits waiting to use them. There's a plentiful supply of pink prison-issue liquid soap in round metal dispensers with bunged up nozzles, but you need to have your own towel or suffer the consequences: an HMP one with the consistency of a dishcloth and the dimensions of a flannel. A scrawl in indelible red felt pen at the far end of the showers reads *TAMS rule.* 'Tarts & Morons,' translates Joolz, slip-slopping past in tattered pink scuffs, a soggy towel over her shoulder. 'That's us, love.'

Bedtime's nine thirty, and I must be looking suicidal as Marine actually asks if I'm all right.

At nine thirty-one all the lights go out, regardless of whether or not we've finished what we are doing. In the darkness, Marine whispers that I mustn't take on so, that visiting day's less than two weeks away, and that she'll save me a seat next to her at breakfast tomorrow if I want.

I lie awake for a long time. Later, I dream of the children.

We're on a vast empty beach, and I have lost them. The tide is racing in and though I search and search, I cannot find them.

This Ain't Bleedin' Barbados

'THERE ARE ONLY FOUR OUTCOMES OF ACTIVE DRUG ABUSE:
1. JAIL
2. INSTITUTIONALISATION
3. REHAB
4. DEATH.
YOU ARE ALREADY IN JAIL.'

admonishes the large red laminated notice above my head. Pearls of condensation, a fixture in the prison laundry room, are sliding slowly down its surface.

'Fuck a duck, you mean this ain't bleedin' Barbados?' sniffs Marine.

Marine is awaiting her trial for compulsive shoplifting ('I prefer to call it 'aving alternatively acquired possessions') and some truly spectacular white goods fencing ('You should have seen the stuff the wankers *didn't* find'). She has also single-handedly prevented me from going mad these last few weeks and standing in the exercise ground with a slice of flabby white prison bread on my head, shouting at the pigeons to fly me out of here.

We are currently hanging out in here, bored out of our skulls, watching other people's T-shirts go round and leaning against the far wall so we can see who comes in. I hate the imperative of back-watching, the constant mind-jog of never feeling safe, but it's become second nature within the week. Then there's the smothering hand of boredom pressing down day after day after day. There is just *fuck all to do*. This prison is, without doubt, the most boring time of my life. And you're talking to someone who once had a month's work experience verifying Mastermind questions about British Rail routes that pass through Letchworth.

However, the laundry does offer a vital change of scene from lying prone on the bunk in your cell for eighteen hours a day until you are sufficiently desperate to rip off our own head and eat it.

'Zo, when a washer comes free, would ya stick my stuff in wi' yours and keep an eye on it for a bit?' asks Marine, who's been getting more restless by the minute, skilfully edging round the dial the nearest machine so it lurches directly from mid-wash to spin. 'I've gotta wait in line to try calling Kev again.'

'Thought you weren't speaking to him since he flogged your widescreen?'

'I reckon the fucker's got someone.'

'To do what?'

'Someone *else*. *You* know. Anuvva *woman*,' she snarls. 'And if she picks up the phone, well – I'll know then, won't I? Lissen, I can deal wiv the sort of poxy little tart Kev goes for any day of the week. So when I get 'ome...' she trails off, since we both know her trial is unlikely to come up for several more weeks, maybe even months. For thanks to Labour's growing eagerness to remove wrongdoers from Society, there's a backlog in the courts that surpasses even the dog days of Margaret Thatcher.

Marine's pretty, sharp-featured little face crumples and she wipes a swift forearm across her nose. This is a bugger. There was no way you can check up on a potentially cheating partner in here, what with no mobiles (supposedly), long queues for the three wall-mounted public phones, the ban on reverse charge calls, the price of phone cards and lack of spending money. Not to mention other women hanging about in the phone corridor listening to every word you say, the existence of lying relatives and the brick wall of voicemail.

I've left three messages for Jim myself on ours recently in between the daily hello-darlings-how-was-school-today ones for Tim and Kash which I'm not even sure that they got. Two left with Bigge & Willetts' harassed secretary for my solicitor Mr Shannon seem to have got lost too. Maybe this was no bad thing, for our last conversation, about the possibility of bail guaranteed against my share of the house, had not been encouraging.

'I did speak to your husband about this yesterday. He doesn't, er, seem very eager to have you home, and explained in no uncertain terms that the house is (technically, at least) in his name only. Would that be right, Mrs Harrington?' he'd asked politely in his soft Cork brogue. 'I know some men can be a bit economical with the truth where these matters are concerned.'

I started tugging at the telephone cable in desperation, seeing my last chance of getting back to Tim and Kasha any time soon slipping away. 'Listen. That house really does belong to me too. Well, morally it's half mine. I paid for half of everything, Mr Shannon, the mortgage, the bills, all the time except when the children were babies and that was only for a few months at a time... look, couldn't you see your way to –'

'I hear you, Mrs Harrington and I do understand, believe me. But there's another little complication, for I believe the house was collateral for your husband's business start-up. Would I be mistaken, now?'

'No, you'd be quite right. But it's still ours.'

'Not any more. Legally, it's now the property of the man who was backing your husband. The one you are accused of trying to kill.'

Someone is crying noisily in the queue outside the exhausted Liaison Worker's office opposite the laundry entrance. There is the clash of reverberating metal down the corridor as Susie B, epileptic and hooked on barbiturates, takes her displeasure out on a payphone that just cut her off from speaking to her dealer boyfriend twenty seconds before time. Marine jerks her thumb at her fading turquoise T-shirt and grimaces. It says '*I'm a celebrity, get me out of here.*'

The garment reminds me of Lucia on her first visit two weeks ago.

She'd swept in to the Visiting Suite – a long, thin fluorescent lit room with bare walls, pock marked Formica tables and plastic orange chairs – paused till every male eye was upon her, then undulated over to where I was waiting eagerly at my little visitor's station.

Clad in what she felt suitable for a humanitarian visit to a penal institution, she wore a vintage cream silk Jemima Khan tunic (Sotherby's *Fashion for Freedom* celebrity auction for Amnesty International) and a turquoise blob Superglued onto her third eye: every inch Indian designer mutton dressed as nan. She also looked a little older than I remembered.

Mindful of the niceties we air-kissed thrice, though I felt like flinging my arms around her I was so glad to see someone. Bel writes weekly but hasn't yet made it down yet, for the prison's way out the nearest town (Reading) and she doesn't drive. Mum has visited in twice, wearing organza dresses fit for the Queen's garden party and an expression of extreme determination. Dad, who is harassing old barrister colleagues from his Inner Temple days and trying to pull strings, has sent reams of legal advice from his French retreat; Hera, arty postcards of a pierced nipple collages with rousing quotes from French revolutionaries on the back. But no one else has been in touch. Perhaps, I reflect gloomily, as with other difficult subjects such as death, cancer and being sacked for incompetence, they simply don't know what to say.

'I felt the Gandhi look denotes compassion, and full support of basic human rights darling,' breathes Lucia. 'Goodness, you're looking very, ah, practical, today. What do you think of the bindi? Enamel, Jade Jagger, Garrard's. Oh dear – sorry, sorry, sorry,' she adds quickly, looking again at my pale taught face, perfunctory swipe of lippy and plain navy sweatshirt.

We are saved from further embarrassment by an altercation at the visitor's table on our left. A guard has spotted that one inmate in a stone-washed denim mini is not wearing pants. She is promptly frog-marched out amidst some ear-blistering language, leaving her male visitor looking spare and foolish.

'What was all that about?' asks Lucia, roused from her habitual cool by sheer curiosity.

'No knickers, no visitor.'

'Might one ask why?'

'Dope-crutching.'

'Oh, surely not –'

'The male visitors can pass a small packet of Clingfilmed drugs over when they smooch them hello. The girl takes it out of the mouth when no one's looking – the POs can't look at everyone all the time even in here – and slips it up inside. Only takes a second. But they usually wear longer skirts.'

'They smoke it after it's been up *there*?' Lucia's perfect matt-powdered nose crinkles with distaste. 'I do hope it's been properly wrapped.'

'Well!' she tries again, after several more seconds of lumpen silence. 'And what have you been doing this week?'

'Lucia, that has to be the stupidest question you have ever asked me.'

'Ah, yes, I suppose it would be…' She continues to smile brightly, and bravely has another go. 'I was over at your old, ah, I mean your house last Tuesday.'

'Yes? Oh, did you see Tim and Kasha? How did they look? Did they seem –' Lucia hesitates for a moment then surprisingly pats my hands, which are clasped on the table top where the warders can see them. 'The children were rather quiet.'

I say nothing for a moment. The longing to hold them is overwhelming.

'Please, Lucia – how are they really?'

'Now you mustn't worry, sweetness. They're both being *angelic,* under the circs. Though I suppose that Kasha could be said to have developed a weeny bit of a temper of late, plus being a tad finicky food-wise; and Tim's apparently taken the *odd* unscheduled day off school, but that's –'

'What? Where did he go? Is he OK? Not into town, not hanging about in the games arcades –'

'No, no, no darling. He was picked up mooching down Camden Canal at lunchtime –'

'*Picked up*? By who? Who picked him up?'

'Harvey, actually. His advanced juggling classes don't start till mid-afternoon, and of course, you know he stayed on at the barge after Bel walked out to live with a Stopes colleague? *Any*way, he was creosoting that rather leaky roof when who should shuffle past but –'

'What did he do? Did he talk to Tim? Oh God, what did Jim say? And Jim's mum? She must have there – at the house – she's meant to be looking after them...'

'I gather Harvey gave Tim beans on toast, played cards with him – and I suspect, talked to him like a Dutch uncle since Tim admitted this wasn't the first time – then juggler-boy walked your son home at the time he'd usually come back from school. There have been no repeats.'

'Now, what other news do we have?' she flounders on, hurriedly. 'Of course, you do know that your mother-in-law has simply *leapt* into the breech?'

I grit my teeth.

'My dear, your house is, for the first time in its life, quite frighteningly clean and tidy. Did you know she Clingfilms cat food?'

'Yes. Oh, poor, poor Tim, and how lovely of Harvey to... yes, I did. What – what else is she doing?'

Lucia sighs. 'Cooking Jim wholesome little suppers. Ironing his socks, my dear, Rug Doctoring the carpets. Glade in the loos. She's taken over Kasha's room.'

I can feel my rage growing. 'Amazing she's not sleeping in Jim's bed.'

'Doubtless she would if she could. She's also had your old office dismantled, and a compost bin put in its place.'

'She what?'

'Well, she asked Jim if he wanted it done since it was derelict and leaking anyway, and I gather he said OK. Now, let's see, what else did Kasha say? Oh yes, the elder Mrs Harrington's also going through your wardrobe, selecting stuff for – Oxfam, I think it was.'

'My clothes? My clothes? Which I've been collecting for twenty-five years? They may look like tat but they're not, they're cultural history and anyway, I can still get into all of them. Well, some of them. She can't do that –'

'She's ostensibly running the stuff past Jim before she dumps it's but let's face it, sweetie, the only taste in clothes he ever showed was thanks to you.'

My jaw quilts with muscles. 'Anything else?' There can't possibly be.

'Hmmm. Oh, yes. I think Jim may have mentioned that his mother went instead of you to Tim's Parent-Teacher meeting last week because he was working late, and she has arranged for him to have intensive spelling and grammar tuition.'

'There's nothing really wrong with his spelling, it's just a bit individual, that's –'

'– and also for him to be assessed, at her expense, by a developmental psychologist at the Tavistock Centre. She says that if you ask her, dyspraxia is largely a media myth perpetrated by obsessional parents and trendy teachers, and that her grandson would do far better at that military boarding school in Portsmouth where Jim's father went. She says she'll pay the fees.'

She looks sidelong at my homicidal expression. 'When's your trial coming up?' she asks, just as I am about to let loose a filth-studded stream of anti-mother-in-law abuse.

'What? Um, I'm not quite sure. Mr Shannon's being a bit vague. You usually have to wait about three months between a Committal to Crown Court, which I've had (talk about perfunctory, it was barely worth turning up) and actually going to trial. Shannon thinks it might even be heard at the Old Bailey.' An image of Ma Harrington with her smartly shod feet up on my kitchen table floats into my mind. 'Christ, the interfering old *hag*. She can't really get Tim sent to Portsmouth, can she?'

'Anyone offered to stump up bail?'

'Oh – they seem to want about seventy-five thousand. My dad's been trying but the money has to be guaranteed against The Farm, and his branch of the Credit Agricole has tied him up in miles of French bankers' red tape. Jim says he can't. Or more likely, he won't.' I tug at my fringe. 'Has she really pulled down my shed?'

'How long before you get a firm date for that trial?'

'Maybe not that long,' I mumble, echoing Mr Shannon. 'Lou, about Kasha's eating – please could you tell Jim to give her junky favourites for a bit, anything to get her interested? She's never been known to turn down Findus Fishie Shapes, and um, likes those disgusting Happy Potato faces. Then she'll always eat mangos if they're cut up like a porcupine with all the little square bits…'

'Zoe,' orders Lucia, sitting up ram-rod straight, 'concentrate.'

'On what? Oh look, I'm really worried about Kasha…'

'Kasha is by all accounts, eating a perfectly respectable amount, and has merely expressed a disinclination towards her greens. But you – you are in danger of being mothballed. In fact it's happening as we speak. What you need (don't interrupt, darling) is a little positive PR. Max Clifford would have been ideal but he said – well, anyway, you are just going to have to make do with me.'

'That's sweet of you, Lou, but just leave it would you?' A counter-attack would take more energy than I've had in a long time. 'Right now, I – I just wanted to go home I'm sure it will all be sorted out soon.' Ma Harrington however, I would be slow barbecuing at a later date. Military boarding school? I'd see the woman in hell first.

'The way you're allowing things to go, that won't happen for some time. Don't you *want* to tell your side of the story?'

'Who to? Who'd want to hear it? Even my husband doesn't. I don't think my friends do either.'

'The public, Zoe. The public will want to hear it. It's a nice human interest issue. And timing's on our side because news is non-existent at the moment. It's silly season, darling. *August.* Everyone who matters is in Tuscany but newspaper pages still need to be filled with *something.*'

I'm looking over at a mother sitting with a seven-year-old little girl cuddled on her knee and feel my own lap ache. 'That bindi spot's affecting your brain. You should never put metal over your Third Eye. It affects the electrical polarity there and causes the mind to wander.'

She takes no notice. 'I am telling you, things have gone quite far enough. It's time to get some popular opinion on your side.' She gets out her antique Dior compact and, holding it daintily before her face, reapplies Hot Tarte Lancome lippy.

'Lucia, no one else could possibly be interested and anyway, it's hardly anyone else's business.'

'*Which* tranquillisers have they been mashing into your breakfast cereal? Unless you make it other people's business, you are, very plainly, done for.'

'Xanax if you must know, and I'm feeling a lot better for it, even in this place. Look, just drop it, will you? I know you're trying to help, but really, I'm doing fine. And Mr Shannon says my trial may come up in as little as ten weeks.' Ten weeks? *As little as?* What did I just say?

'Sweetie, I hate to be the one to tell you this, but you are about to lose more than a few old clothes.'

'And just what is that supposed to mean?'

294

'Do you know why Jim didn't come and see you last week?' she jack-hammers, swiftly changing tack.

My throat tightens. He was supposed to be bringing Tim and Kash with him too. I'd made them a little card each in Handwork and everything. Two days later, he'd sent a terse message via Throughcare to say he was sorry but something had come up, and that he'd ring. He hasn't.

'He was showing prospective buyers round your house. That's right,' she snapped, seeing the expression on my face, 'your home. Apparently, he got an offer *above* Benham & Reeves' truly inflated asking price immediately: it is Camden Lock, after all, and property's been ludicrous there for years. Your house is being sold to a very proper young banking couple who work for Coutts and wish to buy into some instant Bohemian chic.'

'He can't do that without –'

'He already has. They start renting as from the fifth of next month, while the sale's fast tracked through.'

'I don't believe you. '

'Jim and his mother are so pleased for there was, as I understand it, a bit of a cash flow problem. And my dear, he's got his hands on a two and a half bedroom Peabody flat for a mere hundred pounds a week round the back of your old – I mean just off Ferdinand Street. Top floor, nice little balcony, fearful stairs. Do close your mouth darling, you look like a Koi carp.'

'But there's a huge waiting list for those. How did he manage it?'

'Apparently via some old uni friend of his who's a career leftie with Camden Council.' I try to imagine half a bedroom, and fail. Bet the old friend is Fiona Floyd. Big tits, feet to match, a lip lock on her like a sink plunger (Jim said) and an unread column in *Marxism Today*.

'Well?' demands Lucia provocatively. 'Are you just going to sit there and let them dismantle you piece by piece? Or are you going to trust me a little, tell me your version of what happened, and I'll see what I can do?'

I gaze at her wordlessly.

'Zoe, we don't have much time.'

'Will you – have to use real names?' I blurt, finally.

'There may be a way around that.'

Examining the very limited options, my head clears abruptly. 'All right. We've got half an hour left. I hope your shorthand's good.'

It is. Her notebook comes out and fills up rapidly with line after line of elegant short forms. I have to hand it to her, she never interrupts once.

And once I start talking – very quietly, as the warders are circling nearby like big cats – I can't stop. I leave nothing out. The growing feeling over the last two years that there might be no future for me and Jim, his increasing disinterest in me, Shaun re-surfacing. The fact that I'd never quite got over him. Our affair, the mental disintegration, the Prozac that made it worse, the miscarriage, finding out about Shaun's underage habit. His unexpected and suspicious backing of Jim, my clumsy attempt to discover whether he was on the level, the fear that he'd blackmail us and would flatten Jim whenever he chose. And finally, Star Street, the photographs, the accident on the Heath – and Shaun's appalling injuries.

It was such a relief to just tell someone. No wonder Catholics set such store by the confessional. It's like staggering about with a heavy suitcase for weeks, then someone comes alongside and takes one of the handles.

The ten-minute warning bell sounds just as I finish and the atmosphere in the visiting room shoots up an octave. Men hug their women tight, children climb onto their mums' laps and hold fast, pairs of friends grasp each other's hands.

'I think,' says Lucia quietly, when it becomes clear there's nothing more, 'that we might be able to do something with that.'

'Lucia, no disrespect but something has just, er, occurred to me. You're a fashion stylist, aren't you? Not a feature writer. Not a news journalist. Since when has this been your sort of thing? Or do you know someone?'

Lucia usually Knew Someone.

There is a brief silence. 'I confess,' she admits eventually, 'to being temporarily under-utilized in the style arena.'

'Unemployed, huh?'

'Not exactly. In waiting. A becalm-ment in my little atoll on the designer ocean.'

'Sorry?'

Lucia sighs. 'My book goes out and about, but I don't. I've been around quite a long time now, and these days it seems I'm everyone's favourite second choice. Apparently,' she swallows bravely, 'I'm now considered, shall we say, reliable but hardly cutting edge.' My friend adjusts one of her jacket buttons, then looks into the middle distance. 'I never did make it big. Not really. And now I seem to be becoming popular with – the supermarket rags.'

'Well, so w –'

'Zoe, the truth is I've not had any Ikea or Marlborough ads to style for the agencies yet. Which, in case you didn't know, is the acid test for any stylist. And now I very much doubt that I will have.'

I've never heard her talk like this.

'Come on, Lucia. You're an upper crust creative. Commerce kills creativity, right? You spit on ad agency work.'

'Only because I can't get any,' she admits, with a rare burst of honesty. 'No, those ads (ten to fifteen thousand plus for a top stylist) are what all fash-hags are really chasing. I mean, it's the only reason they put up with the abysmal wages on the likes of *Vogue*. But most of my recent work's, well, cancellation remainders. If it weren't for the *Mirror's* Gossip & Showbiz Editors I'd be severely financially compromised.'

'You're getting paid for gossip?' I'm lost in admiration.

'They've started using me because I get invited everywhere and know a lot of people. I've got the requisite *fabulous* wardrobe. Members-only clubs let me in free all over London,' she adds with a little lift of pride. 'I've never failed to get under a red velvet rope and into an inner VIP sanctum yet. And recently, I've been contributing snippets to the *Mail's* About Town section too. In fact, there were two bits of mine in there yesterday.'

'The *Mail* would never touch this.'

'I wonder? I do know the two relevant features editors. What we have here,' she informs me confidently, every inch an arbiter of newsprint taste, 'is the Classic Noughties Dilemma with a Moral Twist.'

'We do?'

'Hush, I'm thinking. Now let's see –' She fixes half-shut eyes on the top left-hand corner of the room. 'A media mum, a hot-shot pervert lover, a Soho filmie husband. *He* threatens her family. S*he* dumps the love of her life for her principles, and pays with a jail sentence – always the woman who pays. Would you too have the guts? The moral conviction? Yes. It's not right for an 'As Told To' but perhaps as a 'Campaigning Confessional'...? Yes, the tabloids are big on those. Readers might really relate to it,' she enthuses, tucking her shorthand pad into her Louis Vuitton bag. 'And incidentally, those Poloroids. Just a thought-ette, but might one ask where they are now?'

'I, er, burnt them. I felt so bad about running him down and everything, I couldn't bear to keep them.' Actually, they're in our old Tartan shortbread tin, stuffed between the back of my office and the garden fence.

'Pity,' she says lightly. 'Well, we'll just have to run with what we have. I think it may be sufficient.'

'You reckon? But Lucia, you *promise* to keep any names out of it? Just talk generally, yes? This is background PR stuff, not a news feature. They'll throw the book at me if –'

Lucia looks at me with an odd expression, shaking her elegant head. 'You have been a foolish, *foolish* girl. I know you've been poorly, but frankly out of your mind simply does not cover it and for once – I am lost for words. However, fear not. You do have me. And you'd be amazed darling, if you knew who *I'd* got. Should it,' she adds darkly, almost to herself, 'prove necessary to prod them into action.'

'What are you talking about?'

'I am telling you, my dear, no positively assuring you, that I am not going to let them take you down without *the* most spectacular catfight. In fact, certain people may be *very sorry indeed* in the not-too-distant future…' Unexpectedly, she leans over the table and enfolds me in Chanel-scented arms, hugging convulsively – Lucia, who considers a single vertical pat on the shoulder a display of gratuitous public affection. It is over in seconds as she lets go abruptly, more embarrassed than I've ever seen her, brushing herself down and fussing with her handbag clasp.

Everyone is leaving now. A truculent looking lady PO swoops down, removes the chair from underneath Lucia's expensive bottom and ushers her away, still talking.

'You know, maybe it's best for the *Mail*. A pigeon pair of photogenic children, they'd like that. How many bedrooms do you have at home, three isn't it? Four would have been ideal but I suppose three's middle class enough, especially where you live. And fortunately, you're both white.'

'Oooh, I've got another angle,' she calls from the doorway, making everyone's heads swivel in her direction as she watches a sobbing child being led away from his mother. 'The little children separated from imprisoned mothers: the agony, the broken family ties, the child psychology bills –'

'Now don't forget,' she shouts over her shoulder as she is finally bustled away, oblivious to the glares from nearby inmates. 'Watch the post!'

We've Only Just Begun

'Seen that slag Louise?'

It's C Wing's pet psycho, Val McGee. Melon breasted, with forearms like legs of lamb, she's chief bully girl on the block and is big on Respect. Marine and I, watching other women play cards in the Free Association Room, shake our heads respectfully. Poor Louise. A gentle, solitary Eurasian girl who'd been unwise enough to carry a bag of heroin through Heathrow for her boyfriend, Val's had her eye on her ever since they transferred skinny blonde Ingrid to Durham.

'Let you know if we do then, shall we?' brown noses my friend, who has a finely-tuned survival instinct. Val tosses back dyed red hair the texture of sofa stuffing and eyes us speculatively as we slump in adjacent plastic chairs. From the TV comes the interrogatory bark of Anne Robinson intimidating a new contestant. '*Which* famous composer wrote The Planets?'

'Tolstoy?' quavers the big blonde, hopefully.

'Ah, the two little friends,' coos Val unpleasantly. 'Very close, you two seem to be these days. I'd say it wasn't 'ealthy. No, not very 'ealthy *at all*.'

We move apart automatically, wiping all expression from our faces, and wait.

'Yeah, me an' the girls bin wondering if you aren't getting a bit more pally than is good for you.' Val, her brown eyes slitty with malice, hefts a huge breast up a couple of inches and smiles unpleasantly. 'Anyways, our little Lulu. Probably 'iding in the library again, but you let me know if you see 'er before wash time. *Me,* you hear me, not 'er. Stuck up little 'ore. Thinks she's way too good for this place but she oughta be making 'erself useful, and I've got plans. Tell you what. Why don't you two go see if you can find 'er for Auntie Val?'

When we traipse back to our room to collect our wash stuff having tipped off Louise and watched her make a beeline for the PO's office (it's shower night for our corridor, but that's proved more trouble than it's worth so we're making do with yet another pits & paws job) Joolz points at my bunk. 'Letter for ya, Zo. Bin there a while.' It had been opened of course, but otherwise appeared unadulterated. I pounce on it like a tiger on a T-bone.

It contains a single cutting ripped from this week's *Sleuth Eye*.

'In the City

It has come to our attention that Ziggurat Publishing's Shaun Lyon, respected net entrepreneur, publisher and children's charity benefactor, has some novelty items in his bulging portfolio which might give his shareholders pause for thought.

*Imagine our surprise when on a late night net trawl, we came across two hitherto well-kept company secrets – **shagathoncity.com** and **mycreamyway.co.uk.***

Our surprise knew no bounds when we discovered that one was a dogging contact site, and the other a lesbian erotica service (though its pictures took a disappointingly long time to download). Your reporter was agog, especially as the contact details were for JustLegal, a former subsidiary of Ziggurat unaccountably registered in Liberia.

*A quick trip to Companies House reveals that the above sites do indeed still belong to Ziggurat, as do several others not featured in its general shareholders' literature. These include the ever-popular **howbig?**, the perennial favourite **whoppertits.com** and the controversial **tooyoung.***

The latter has subsequently been found to be of interest to Scotland Yard, since many of the models are plainly underage.

Disappointingly, Lyon himself, a media savvy and articulate exponent of his company and no stranger to the plaudits of the financial press, is reportedly, in hospital following a minor car accident. According to the company's spokesperson, this was sustained during a private racing session at Brands Hatch with that other great British entrepreneur, Pritchard 'Beardie' Branston.

*Fortunately Lyon's MD Maxwell Fordyce was available to confirm that the titles for which the thrusting young company is so justly famous still include the mainstream **Riff, Ruck, Wheels** and **Insider**, and that Ziggurat has No Comment Whatsoever to make on any of the above.*

However, further tireless investigation revealed Lyon's connection with several other special interest sites, also of an adult nature. It would appear that together with Ziggurat's thriving phone-line division (Sl. Eye 1026) which also caters for specific tastes, this low-profile sector of the company provided a commendable 68% of its £70m turnover last year.

Sleuth Eye trusts that these revelations will not, in any way, prejudice the proposed buy-out of Ziggurat by the giant Heart Corporation in the US – just when negotiations are, we hear, going so swimmingly.

Eavesdropper ’

Scrawled below in Lucia's favourite violet ink: 'We've only just begun.'

Next morning, eating stale cornflakes with a plastic spoon and looking forward to two hours of in-flight courtesy-pouch stuffing for Fuzz Airlines (eight pounds a week pocket money) the euphoria has subsided. A single story in an albeit fearless satirical magazine famous for its libel bills can't do much, though it may possibly have a small negative effect on Shaun's business interests – which are in fact doing splendidly at the moment. It's not clear whether this is thanks to a sympathy vote for Shaun's accident since word is out that it's more than a little prang, but Shannon says Ziggurat are going from strength to strength. Unfortunately, Jim also reports that there are continual delays on the promised cheque for *FirstPencil* and that so far, all they've had is a goodwill amount of fifteen thousand.

Shannon also tells me that Shaun is not only out of IT, he's been moved to a private room, is doing well with an intensive physiotherapy programme, talking normally, and that there seems to be nothing whatsoever wrong with his mind. Remarkably, he's still insisting that he can't remember anything after the Holly Bush. My first guess is that he'd sooner die that tell anyone what happened to him. But it's also possible that he really did take on board some of what I told him on the Heath that dark, rainy pre-dawn – and could even be trying to protect me, one last time.

And me? My feelings about him have become so tangled that I can no longer see the separate threads. But one thing I do know for sure is that I have made a complete berk of myself, and nearly killed someone I used to love in the process. Oh, and managed to fuck up five lives – his, Jim's, Kasha's, Tim's and my own while I'm at it. It's enough to make you want to go scrub floors in a religious retreat for the rest of your life.

Marine, Lally and Joolz reckon they'll convict me for sure unless I bring up the affair with Shaun, tell them I got pregnant with his child then miscarried, and say that he was blackmailing me to come back by pretending to support Jim's company. 'Well, you fort 'e was,' insists the pragmatic Joolz, pursuing me down the corridor as I do my stint of floor-washing with C wing's stringy mop and the pink prison issue disinfectant that smells of pear drops. 'Same bleedin' thing. The punters on the jury'll love it – oi, mind my feet – and the press'll go mental. They like a bit of sex, and the wimmin'll go all out for annuva girl wot's been taken advantage of by some bastard company suit 'oo's cheating on 'is wife.'

'And you gotta tell the pigs about them underage girls,' insists Marine, coming up behind us. 'That should take the shine off the bugger's respectability. That sort of fing don't go down too well these days. They'll 'ave 'im inside 'stead of you, if you just say the word. Then your lawyer tells 'is lawyer you'll retract your statement if 'e swears it weren't you wot flattened 'is carcass for 'im.'

'What word?'

'*Paedophilia,* you silly tart.'

'Look, I only actually saw *one* who was fourteen or fifteen. And while that's legally underage, you know as well as I do that half all fifteen-year-olds are at it anyway these days –'

'– wiv uvva fifteen-year-olds. They ain't being paid to by blokes old enough to be their dads.'

'True, but I can't use that.'

'Why the fuck not?'

'Because –' *because it would have been a lot better for everyone if it had been him who'd run me over.*

'Because wot? You still soft on the fucker? Listen, it's you 'oo doesn't understand, Zo. You got ammunition there, gel. Better use it, or you'll be eating them shit pies wiv plastic forks for a good while yet.'

Their suggestion offers mitigating circumstances with a capital M. Shannon agrees that with the right jury it might even be enough to get me off altogether, but I cannot do it. If Shaun's really trying to protect me (which I think he may be) and there is no getting away from the fact that I ran him over (which there isn't) I have no right to play that last killer card. Even if it's one that might get me out early.

But re-doing yet another bit of clean floor that's just been walked on by passers-by, I can't help thinking longingly about the children, and about Jim. If I blabbed I'd be able to see them again, and I miss them so much it's making me dizzy. It hits me at odd times, like waking up in the morning to the honking of the prison klaxon and not being able to curve into Jim's back while coming to. Missing the rueful roll of his eyes and the flicker of his indulgent grin when I bring back a new stray animal. Even wanting to hear his latest singing socks acquisition. And the children? I miss every single thing about them, including their furious bickering.

I wish Jim would come. I wish I could just talk to him face to face but there's more chance of pigs flying into Gatwick. Last time, he didn't even send his mother along with the children on visiting day, though he'd promised that they'd be there. Has he any idea of what that meant? To look forward for a fortnight to holding your own children again, then to sit in the visiting room watching other families hug, other kids cuddle their mums and other men hold their women's hands for two whole hours. Alone.

'Bin in Bastard's Corner, lovie?' Ruby had enquired, as I'd shuffled out crying. 'Your bloke not show up, then?'

An exhausted looking little lady, sixty if she was a day with thinning strawberry hair, Ruby is here for running a small family brothel in Streatham. She had fallen into step beside me complaining that her visitor, an accountant son as it happened who was caretaking the business, hadn't turned up either.

'No. Jim said he might not make it himself this time but he *promised* the children would. He promised. Now I'm not due to see them again for – oh Jesus – another two weeks. I can't bear it, Ruby, I love them so much it's like bleeding to death – and, and as for him, well he's only been the once.'

And what a horrible, stilted occasion that had been. It has lasted twenty minutes of the allotted two hours, he didn't know where to look and I didn't know what to say apart from begging for information about our children, home and animals. When I asked him somewhat timidly, if he was all right, he merely shrugged. And when I ventured to say that I had tried, several times, to talk to him about Shaun at the dinner party because I thought he was dangerous but that he wouldn't listen, he still wouldn't.

'Oh, is *that* why you nearly killed him? Because you thought *he* was dangerous?'

That night, the sound of women crying continued long after lights out. 'It's always the bleedin' same,' whispered Marine from the dark bunk above mine. Kev hadn't turned up that day either and her information was that he'd shacked up with some woman from Blockbuster Videos. 'That's girls crying for their kids. Visiting day is a fuck-up, cos it gives us a few minutes of wot we love and can't 'ave no more. The Gov'ner makes sure we get a good dinner the day after. Gives us sumfink positive to think about.'

'So – what are we having tomorrow then?' I asked, miserably.

'Burgers (lamb, right, not that bleeding BSE beef shite) chips that ain't soggy, peas that ain't mushy, jammy sponge, and the only custard of the 'ole week that ain't got bleedin' great lumps in.' She sounded really enthusiastic. 'I'm really looking forward it, me.'

Today, I've got two letters. Two.

One's from Kasha. It contains a pencil drawing of a very small child with spaniel bunches like she sometimes wears, sitting in the lower left corner of a very big piece of white paper, a black castle with barred windows taking up the entire top right quarter. A pathway of small heart-shapes leads, stepping stone fashion, from the child to the castle, and an arrow points to someone's face peering out of the centre window. The building is scribbled over with angry black pen strokes. At the bottom, she has written her signature in her favourite pink gel pen, surrounded by a blizzard of more tiny kisses than you can count.

Lally urges me to look at the other one before I can hang myself with my own bra straps. It contains a folded newspaper cutting, a double page spread taken from the

Women's pages of *The Express,* five days old. I check the postmark. It had arrived four days ago. The prison hasn't exactly hurried to pass it on.

The writer has identified 'an alarming new social trend amongst middle-aged men' and christened it the Mandy Smith Syndrome, or MiSS.

There's a collage of pictures of middle-aged – or let's face it, *old* – blokes including certain seminal rock n' rollers, with girls who look young enough to be, and possibly were, their granddaughters. The writer reminds us of what we all know, that Mandy Smith was fourteen when she and Bill Wyman first got it on.

Round the edges of the collage runs a pseudo-psych quiz to help readers check their man's MiSS potential. Boxed quotes from tame psychiatrists testify to the fact that MiSS is indeed a worrying modern trend. Another warns that 'even the most respected and attractive public figures' can be thus afflicted, often satisfying their horrid desires on the net – and *refers briefly to the bit in Sleuth Eye about Ziggurat.* The spread ends with details of the special new helpline for men, the Lolita Advice Line, offering a 50p a minute taped message from the reassuring Dr Mallory James.

My delight is in no way affected by the fact that the next double page spread my resourceful friend has sent in for a laugh, is entirely devoted to a Tesco Ciabatta that appears to feature Princess Di's profile in burn marks. Apparently, the Church has been notified, and a movement to canonize the woman begun.

Across the top, Lucia has scrawled, this time in bright red: *'Fasten your safety belt. We're off.'*

WAP! Off & Die

Jim actually answers when I ring from one of the prison payphones today. In the controlled but forbidding tones normally associated with narrators of *The Twilight Zone*, he asks me if I know any good reason why my face is on posters all over Soho.

'I don't know what you're talking about,' I screech, having been trying to call him daily ever since Lucia's last visit. 'And never mind that. Why are you selling our house without telling? And what's the big idea not letting the children see me? Are they all right at school? Is Kasha's foot OK? That infection should have cleared up by now, the itchy one between her first and second toes. It could spread you know, so you need to put lots of tea tree oil on it... and I had a drawing she did of herself yesterday where all her hair was short, has she cut it off or something? You didn't let her, did you? And are you giving Tim those fish oil capsules for his dyspraxia. If – if he won't take them, you know you've got to coat them in Nutella first? ...and, and, bloody hell Jim, what's going on at home? *Tell me.*'

There is a long pause. The line hums impatiently.

'And while we're at it,' I shout, oblivious to the fact that the three women waiting for a phone behind me have given up all pretence of minding their own business, 'What right have you to dismantle my office? Or give away my clothes? I'm not *dead.*'

'I've had a few problems,' Jim concedes, eventually.

'*You* have? And what's all this I hear about Tim being sent to some military boot-camp? You must be fucking nuts. Don't you dare do that to him, Jim Harrington, don't you dare. That little school is the first place he's been happy at for years, and a military boarding school would destroy him. I'm warning you: so help me, if you do that to Tim I'll find a way to get out of here if I have to dig under the electric fence with a toothbrush. And when I do –'

'He's not going to Portsmouth, OK?' Jim interrupts hastily. 'I happen to agree with you, over that at least. No, I've had something more pressing occupying me at than changing Tim's school.'

'Like what?' Oh hell, why can't we be a bit nicer with each other. I want to say: come in and see me. Let's talk. I miss you, you miserable great git, I lo – no, can't say that right now.

'I'm bankrupt.'

Bloody hell. 'Are you serious?'

'They've given me the works. Rubber cheques. Frozen bank accounts. Cards swallowed by holes in the wall. Sorry about the kids that day. Mum was supposed to bring them, but felt it would only upset them so she took them to Chessington World of Adventure instead.'

'She had no right to do that! None!'

'I expect it was because we'd all had such a bad time the day before. We were in the supermarket with this trolley full of food, OK, and the check-out refused my Access, Barclaycard, Mastercard and American Express. Then the manager confiscated both my plastic and our shopping, right in front of Tim and Kasha. We had nothing to eat. I had to borrow a tenner off Angel later for some milk, chips, and the Kasha's school dinner money.'

'Oh God, Jim. *Oh no.*'

'Though perhaps it's more accurate to say that *we* are bankrupt,' he amends. 'Seventh Wave paid out for the whole of *FirstPencil's* set-up costs in good faith, as Ziggurat kept assuring the big cheque was on it's way, apologising fulsomely for the delay and blaming it on Shaun's hospitalisation. Fair enough, we thought. Then finally, after coming up with one excuse after another for over two months, they pulled out. No explanation. Nothing.'

'They can't do that. You had a legal agreement –'

'– which they hadn't finished signing. Maxwell asked us to keep the goodwill fifteen thousand as an apology. He was really embarrassed, Zoe, because he didn't understand it either. But Shaun's the boss and what he says, goes. That money's not gone far to pay off our bills because they've amounted, as Jed forecast, for to nearly three hundred and fifty thousand pounds for set-up alone. With Maxwell's agreement, while Shaun was in a coma, we'd borrowed that money from Barclays against the house on the premise it would only be for a couple of weeks, intending that the house would revert to being collateral for Ziggurat again when they gave us the promised money.'

'Oh, *Jim*.'

'Zoe, it looked like a dead cert. We were already being flooded by calls from clients and creatives wanting to use *FirstPencil* and it would have looked very bad if we'd delayed it with no firm start date. We felt we couldn't postpone things any longer. The project had developed a life of its own.'

A double life. 'And what is your esteemed Financial Director, doing about this?'

'Jed can't do anything since he's third-mortgaged anyway, and has been laid off with a slipped disc for the last week –' the fraudulent hypochondriac developed back trouble when Seventh Wave were in schtuck last year too – 'and all his accounts are, it seems, in Maeve's name. So thanks to you, we're cleaned out. And since there's no more cash to pay for the start-up losses (our house was mortgaged too), we've had to shut up shop.'

Maeve's obviously not as hand-knitted as she looks. 'Thanks to me? You never told me about the possibility of our place being put up as surety for Ziggurat until you'd done it, let alone for the bank. I'd never have agreed to it if you had, and you know it. I came back from the Ladies that night to find you half pissed and signing our house away. You were just so damn desperate to close that deal, you'd have given them anything. If you'd only listened to me, you wouldn't have lost Seventh Wave unless you'd gone bust of your own accord (in fact, you were heading that way fast, weren't you?) and at least we'd still have our house. Christ, Jim, could you not have waited just a bit, instead of jumping in like that with both feet? That was pretty bloody stupid, in fact it was more than stupid, it was –'

'All right, all right. No point in going over old ground. I could equally say that if you hadn't run Shaun over – not that I'm saying it was deliberate, because I don't know what to think any more but you've never really explained what you two were doing up there anyway, and –' he changes tack swiftly, hearing me make a noise like an imploding pressure cooker: 'Look: one thing's certain – if you'd left Shaun alone, my company would have its money and its new business. But recriminations won't change anything. The house is gone. That's all in the past now.'

'In a pig's arse it is. Is that all you can say? And as for not explaining what I was doing on the Heath, I've *told* you – he asked me to meet him there, so I thought there was a problem and I'd better go, him being your backer and all. In fact I thought he was going to try and blackmail us or something. Then he turned nasty and I tried to get away and…'

'So you keep saying,' Jim muttered through clenched teeth, understandably not believing a word. 'Look – you asked what's going on at home, and I'm telling you. What's going on is that I've been busting my balls trying to get things sorted out and earn some money. As of last week, I've become a motorbike messenger for Speedbike. You know, that little firm in Berwick Street? We used to use them every day. I'm delivering packages to the all the people I used to have business meetings with.' He laughs bitterly.

'Fortunately, if I keep my helmet on, they don't give me a second glance. Though I'm often tempted to whip it off because if they do see my face, sheer embarrassment might force a decent tip out of some of them.'

I skirt that one. 'Do be careful. The average time before bike messengers have a serious injury is only eight months in Central London.'

'Eight months? I can't think further than next week. And if you want to know the reason why I haven't I been in to see you, it's because I've been extremely busy. You know, a few little details to arrange like somewhere for me and the kids to live –'

I notice he didn't say somewhere for *us* to live '– and it was hardly worth telling you until I'd got something. I mean, there was no alternative, and you're hardly in any position to help, are you?'

I feel hollowed out by a distress compounded of nest violation, powerlessness, and a sense of belonging shot to hell. Our little house, tatty, friendly and warm. The one where we'd all the parties, the babies, the good times and the rows. Twenty years of shared history lost to a couple of bloody bankers buying into some instant Camden cred. I wish them poltergeists, rising damp, dry rot, divorce. There are a few moments' resentful silence, then by mutual unspoken consent we return to the less distressing subject of the posters.

Jim explains that they are quite small – indie band fly-poster size – black and white, but becoming noticeable for their sheer numbers. Apart from a prison-style mug-shot of yours truly with bars across it (I'd love to know where that came from) they also feature the banner shoutline: '**How far would YOU go**?' and underneath: '*Put the Pro back into Active: Contact WAP! 0800 668899*'. Then in small letters at the bottom it says: '*WAP! Fighting the underage sex industry.*'

312

'They're on walls, wrapped round lamp posts and on the black metal rubbish bins,' he elaborates. 'An empty police car got one too, and so did several briefly but illegally parked cars on Dean Street.' This being the neighbourhood he works and drinks in, he adds that it's doing his head in.

'What do you mean, it's doing *your* head in? It's not like anyone even knows who I am, let alone what I, ah –'

'The hell they don't. The media grapevine works fast in this neighbourhood. *Sleuth Eye's* offices are in Windmill Street here, their journalists and freelancers drink in the Soho pubs nearby, and they all like to talk. Their Editor wasn't convinced by Ziggurat's story about Shaun having a little prang while on some racing freebie with Pritchard Branston. He was even less convinced when his deputy saw Branston at some cocktail do at Mosmiman's and the man said he'd never met Lyon in his life. So *Sleuth* sniffs around the Royal Free, pulls in a favour or two at the Met to find out who else is implicated and becomes extremely keen when they discover that the person accused of Shaun's attempted murder is you, that you're my wife, and that porn-site baron Shaun used to be my backer. And now everyone knows.'

'They can't possibly. I mean this is just *ridic –*'

'As most of the nationals pinch story leads from *Sleuth* scoops, of course everyone bloody knows. And it's too good to pass up, especially during dry news season. Oh, they're not allowed to mention you by name. But there's ways round that. The hints are dropping faster than flies sprayed with DDT,' he adds savagely. 'Oh yes, everybody knows, all right.'

Well, sodding brilliant. Why did this case have to come up in August? But the WAP! bit's good news. Vociferous and confrontational, the organisation was set up two years ago by a coalition of refugee charities in response to the Government's apathy over the trafficking of very young girls from conflict zones (especially the Balkans and certain African states) into London. Christian mothers' groups and many of the more adventurous members of the WI had joined the movement, whose initials now stand for Women Against Paedophilia. It used to be Women End Trafficking (WET) but their PR advisors pointed out that the initials lacked impact. To have one of their original red and black *WAP Off!* badges still carries considerable cachet in certain right-on supper party circles.

Trying not to sound as if he cares much one way or the other, Jim adds that this morning, the *Independent on Sunday* had called him for a quote as 'husband of the inspiration behind the campaign.' I can tell that he's not displeased. He's read the *Sindie* for years, and I think he figures that if a newspaper he actually buys wants to write about this, then perhaps the whole thing's not so embarrassing after all. 'But there's something else,' he continues carefully. 'When I say, 'Oh you mean that WAP! thing,' they say no; and refer me to today's *Daily Mail* with instructions to call back when I've read it. So I go down the newsagents, I buy a copy. And what do I find when I open it?'

This sounds less good. 'I'm not allowed newspapers in here. How should I know?'

'An entire colour pull-out supplement on LOCuST.'

'Who?'

Apparently, the *Mail* has not so much climbed as bungee-jumped aboard the bandwagon by launching *Let Our Children STay Kids* (LOCuST Kids), a new campaign against young teens having – or being pressured into having – sex.

It's right up their street. Family Values, Old Fashioned Morality and the Age of Consent combined with prurient tales of underage couplings, the sexual temptation of family men, the beastliness of the net sex industry, the shaming/naming of aberrant public figures, and a bumper-sticker marketing opportunity, all in one. 'I suppose this was your idea?' he asks, his voice a tad higher than usual. He's got to be kidding. I couldn't have thought this up in a million years.

But I bet I know who did.

All of which would make me look like a Crusading Social Reformer with Attitude if only the man I'd nearly killed (and who'd made his millions from big-for-their-age fourteen-year-olds) wasn't my ex-lover, with whom I had no business to be with in the first place. And while the press may be so short of news that they're building me, of all the unsuitable candidates, up into some sort of underground icon, I know perfectly well that anyone would have done as long as they had the right credentials – in this case, been in the right place at the wrong time to commit adultery and attempted murder. And they'll have forgotten all about me in a few days. I mean, last week's tabloids had been full of Wilfred the Water Ski-ing Tortoise; then the week before it was the Mother's Union members who'd done a poledance-athon at Spearmint Rhino for SCOPE.

No, the reality is that like any other female prisoner I am still living for news from my lawyer, a visit from my children, trying to swap Silk Cut for soft loo paper and courtesy-pouch stuffing to earn money for another phone card because that conversation with Jim just blew ten quids' worth. The only real thing that's changed in the last week is that I'm now apparently homeless like forty per cent of women when they come out, unless that half bedroom Lucia mentioned is for me.

Then a couple of days later while on toxic toilet duty, I'm scrubbing down C Block's U bends and trying not to breathe through my nose when Ruby sidles in, her precious little clock radio stuffed up inside her baggy purple cardigan.

'They said you was in 'ere,' she hisses urgently. 'Zo, I may be going senile before me time but I swear I just 'erd somefink 'bout you on the wireless. I'm the only one of the block oo's allowed,' she adds with pride, 'cos I'm on Enhanced. Leastways, I fink it was you but to tell the truth I weren't really paying much attention at the time.' She sweeps a practised glance along the bottom of the loo doors then whips out the little plastic radio and holds it up to my ear.

' 'ere. Better listen to this.'

Glancing about, she turns the volume right down and brings her head close to mine to catch the presenter's voice. Good grief, it's Judy Murphy, the terror of *Woman's Hour*, bellowing about the evils of separating women prisoners from their children and stomping all over a cornered Tory MP for Bath. He has, by the sound of it, just made the mistake of suggesting women's prisons are really a form of holiday camp where feckless females take a break at the tax payers' expense, using it to come off drugs, and have three decent meals a day with IT training thrown in for good measure.

'Utter rubbish! Most of these women should never have been put there in the first place,' snorts Ms Murphy, a bull who's just seen a red rag. 'The Government's own figures show that two thirds of female prisoners are mothers of young children, and that three quarters have committed totally victimless crimes and never hurt a flea.

'Woman like this WAP poster person –' I nearly drop the radio into the nearest bog bowl in excitement '– whom you mentioned before we went on air, are unusual cases anyway. Apparently she's accused of running over a reportedly perverted ex-lover who was blackmailing her young family. God knows if it's true because the business hasn't even come to court yet but if it is, personally I can't say I blame her.'

Ruby also reports that on Radio Five Live, Hannah Rathbone is taking furious calls from parents with her customary calm every day this week. She's set up an ongoing live on-air debate between listeners, and *SoWhat?* a radical pressure group which supports sex between adults and consenting underage partners who've passed the watershed of fourteen. A female games mistress who ran off with a fifteen-year-old boy then went into hiding with him in a Lanzarote fitness complex is one of the star turns of the week, explaining how, if you really love each other, a twenty-eight year age gap doesn't matter. The other is Lucia. And she's playing the part of an outraged best friend speaking up on behalf of a wronged women of principal (me: she's joking, surely?) fallen foul of a manipulative MiSS Man, to the hilt.

'It's a total miscarriage of justice. Total. But I'm sorry, I just can't say who she is as it might prejudice her case. But yes, she might be the one on all those posters.'

MiSS being media flavour of the month, WAP! has seized the opportunity to publicise its crusade against the underage sex industry – prompted, apparently, by the ever-resourceful Lucia – and seen to it that those posters are all over town wherever there's a WAP branch. Blanket coverage has reportedly been achieved in Glasgow, Manchester, Edinburgh, Nottingham, Liverpool, London, Exeter, Cardiff and surprisingly, Tunbridge Wells; which, hooray, must be pissing Ma Harrington off no end.

Lucia does her radio stint so well she's on *Channel 5* next ('My Man's a Secret MiSS') giving, according to an over-excited Bel who was off with stress-induced cystitis and had watched the whole thing, an Oscar-winning performance as the b/f whose friend is serving time because she was being blackmailed by a MiSS Man who'd once been the love of her life and recently come back, er, 'begging for help with his problem.' *The Star,* the *News of the World* and *The Sun* all picked up on this the following week, and are now vying with each other to out minor public figures who may or may not be closet MiSS'ers.

'*How Far Would YOU Go?*' T-shirts and wristbands are positively flying off WAP's website (profits to the charitable counselling services for underage sex workers), bootleg copies of same being sold in Camden Market, and all idle media conjecture has achieved the status of Established Fact for anyone who's not spent the last two weeks locked in a flotation tank in the Northern Greenland.

317

Ten days later it's *The Mirror's* turn. With the surgical precision usually associated with the excision of a cancerous organ, it slashes Ziggurat's reputation to ribbons.

Lucia saves the damning cuttings for me but I don't get to see them till much later. When I do, it's clear that this is the hatchet job of the year. First, the paper rubbishes Ziggurat's attempts to get into bed with the Hearst Corporation. Then it asks hard questions about whether moral fitness is required of men running publicly quoted companies, and if not, why not.

Next, it rakes over the subject of Shaun's more diverse business interests, revealing several buttock-clenching details which even *Sleuth Eye* didn't get. That takes a page in itself.

Then finally, in the name of truth, justice and its circulation figures, the paper lavishes a further spread printing barely-censored extracts from *JustLegal's* underage sex lines plus a large blurred still (with a bar covering the area where one woman's mouth met her female partner's nether regions) from mycreamyway.com. Sales of the edition go through the roof.

'*Ziggurat creamed*' screams the headline.

And so it is.

Court In The Act

Today's the day the case comes up at the mighty Old Bailey, with *The Mirror's* article still fresh in people's minds. It only hit the streets two days ago but is already toppling Ziggurat like a high rise demolished by dynamite.

Shaun's business is history.

Meanwhile Joolz, Lally and Marine have been up since six in the morning. Lally is plucking my eyebrows to extinction; Joolz is spraying my hair with what feels like PVA glue, and Marine is doing my nails pearly white to go with Joolz's bang-on-the-knee powder-blue suit from Principles that's been brought out for the occasion. My friend has also stuffed the armpits with wads of her beloved Andrex. 'Sweat patches says you're guilty. For fuck's sake, don't raise your arms too high or they'll fall out.'

'Got to look the part,' explains Joolz, who has lent the same suit (brought in by her boyfriend) to two other women going in front of juries in the last month. 'Pastels is respectable and feminine, see. But no one nevva wears pale pink cos it looks like they're trying too 'ard.'

'Christ, not *perfume,* you dozy wagon,' screeches Lally, snatching a bottle containing the last millilitre of Rive Gauche from my fingers. 'Specially not flash seventies designer shite. Gives the wrong impression. My gran's sent in some 4711 cologne wipes. Use those.'

I've tried objecting to the suit, feeling like a cross between Peter Rabbit and the Headmistress of a Godalming primary school. 'Can't I borrow Susie B's Monsoon black cotton shift top and trousers? She owes me a favour. I look like that girl from the old Woolwich ads.'

'No. Black says you're a fast bitch; trousers that you're not showing proper respect to the judge, and anyway you can't cross your legs slow and let your skirt ride up when it needs to,' pronounces Joolz, veteran of many court appearances and (unsuccessful) appeals. 'Ere, these fake pearls is from Rubes. Get those round yer Tooting Bec. Fucking A, girl. Per-fect,' she croons, fastening them round my throat and standing back to admire her handiwork. 'Like Princess Di, with dark 'air.'

Oh, terrific. The Adulterous Bulimic look.

'Cry if you can,' advises Marine. 'But save it for when the Prosecution gets really narsty, or for the end just before the Jury goes off to make up its mind. And whatevva you do, don't rub them eyes. That mascara ain't waterproof.'

'If you can't cry to order, just try thinking about the fuck up you've made wiv that Shaun bloke,' cackles Joolz, trowelling on pearlised blue eye-shadow. 'Just look at wot's happened to you thanks to 'im, that should get you sobbing in the aisles. Bloody Norah, you're as bad as me. A pissed off 'usband, no 'ome, no job, can't see your kids. I mean, bleedin' 'ell girl, no man's that bloody good in bed. Cotton wool bud!' she barks at Lally, thrusting out her hand without looking, like a surgeon asking Theatre Sister for a scalpel.

'No point in beating yourself up now, we've all done it,' interrupts Lally, realising why my face has gone mottled. 'Grass is greener, 'an all that. Fact is, the grass on the other side of the fence is usually fuckin' Astroturf.'

'Got an 'andkerchief you can twist?' hisses Marine, as a boot-faced prison officer arrives to escort me away. 'Pity. I'd give you mine, but it's all over snot from Kev's last visit.'

'Cheer up, you miserable cow,' laughs Joolz, pursuing us out of the cell to slap me jovially on the bottom. 'At least it's a day out this shit 'ole. Remember, keep your 'ands folded in your lap and your eyes down. And if you must look at the jury, remember: big puppy eyes but no sexy stuff –'

'Go, girl!' yells Susie B from the end of our corridor. 'Makes a change from another day up the Judge's arse.'

The prison officer marches me off to be strip searched with a thoroughness suggesting there may be a grenade to throw at the Judge parked up my vagina. Shooing me into a prison van with tinted windows and faulty safety belts, she glowers at the two other women who are already in there looking even more done up and respectable then me. One, testing the very limits of credulity, is reading a pocket version of the Bible.

The drive to London takes two lurching, motion-sickness inducing hours before we screech to a halt round the back of the great grey Old Bailey, and are disgorged, blinking like owl-lets who just lost the top of their nesting box, onto the tarmac of the enclosed yard.

The POs begin to lead us downstairs to the bowels of the courthouse threading through the press of people clogging its corridors. Other prisoners being whisked along, often handcuffed to their minders; police officers marching purposefully about, and clots of be-wigged barristers standing with their heads together doing deals as the hoi polloi flow around them like water around river rocks. Nervous-looking members of what appear to be the public are sitting on wooden benches along the walls talking to hyped-up members of the legal profession, and smoking like fiends.

Down in the cells underneath the Court it is chaos. The length of the corridor is punctuated by metal doors with what looks like cat-flaps two thirds of the way up. Through these, prisoners are communicating (well, shouting, pleading, crying, arguing, nagging, wheedling and petitioning) with their solicitors and social workers demanding to see their relatives, partners, have a light, a cup of coffee or permission to go for a leak.

Mr Shannon, stocky but smart in a sharp black suit and recent haircut, arrives with two plastic cups of the best tea

I've tasted in twelve weeks, then stays five minutes. 'Just let Ms Everett do the talking. Do not get lippy with the Prosecution or the Judge under any circumstances whatsoever. Remember: you are a respectable professional woman, forced into a corner by a blackmailing pervert.'

'Right. Will my husband and children be there?'

'They may be along later,' says my defence barrister, a sleek career blonde from the Middle Temple named Stockton Everett, who has already given me a couple of efficient coaching sessions. 'Now remember what we agreed, if the court asks you about your relationship with Lyon, keep it simple and stick to the story we agreed on. An ex-boyfriend appears back in your life as your husband's potential backer and blackmails you into having sex with him in return for bankrolling your husband. You comply, as you know that otherwise your man will be bankrupted, and your family on the streets. But when you find out what's really on some of Lyon's websites, you realise that you must end it anyway, backing or no. That's what people are saying about the case, so we may as well reinforce it. And moreover,' she informs me firmly, 'it is true.'

'Absolutely.' Oh, God.

'As to the night in question, admit only to begging Lyon to leave your husband's company alone, and poor driving skills. You were up on the Heath, OK, because, it was the one place you didn't think anyone would see you that time of night. Lyon agreed to come because it used to be a favourite haunt when you were together.'

I hope I'm not going to get any of this wrong, as who knows how well fiction holds up in the white heat of cross-examination. 'Has he, that is, has Mr Lyon said anything about, er, where he was for the twenty-four hours leading up to the accident?'

'What? No. Oh, don't worry about Lyon. He may be out of hospital and perfectly coherent (if slightly mentally fragile) but he still doesn't want any part of this. As you know, he's always claimed he can't remember a thing after leaving the pub that night, and his neurological reports confirm that amnesia could well be a side effect of the, ah, injuries he sustained.'

'I hear his wife's taken the whole family abroad on an extended beach holiday to Rio, probably so he can recuperate without having to watch his company come apart at the seams,' puts in Mr Shannon, eyeing Ms Everett's sculpted calves. 'But Brazil's extradition treaty with the UK being what it is, there's no way the Crown Prosecution Service can get him back as a witness even if they thought it was worth it.'

They go out together and I am left on my own for an hour, so amuse myself by adjusting Marine's Andrex pads and breaking the cup into tiny fragments after drinking its tar-like contents.

'Your turn, love,' someone shouts eventually through the cat flap. I experience a searing desire for a pee, then as they escort me down the dim corridor and into the well of the court, the scene explodes into dazzling colour as if someone's fiddled with a TV contrast control.

The place is packed.

Shrinking into my seat I risk a shaky glance the judge who with his long red robes and a full white wig, looks like Sir Isaac Newton. He never even glances my way, but watches in silence as the jury files meekly in, most looking fixedly at their feet.

'Lord Pryce-Symmonds, a 'red' judge,' hisses Mr Shannon. 'Tries all the more, er, interesting cases.' The Clerk of the Court gets to his feet, rakes his beady gaze along the box where the twelve jurors are seated, and begins the solemn process of swearing them in. Most place their hand on the Bible, two opt for the Koran.

'Do you solemnly swear that you will faithfully try the Accused according to Law?' he barks at each one in turn. They all do, a row of nodding doggies in a shop window. The

Judge coughs once, then nods briskly at the Clerk who began to read out the indictments in a loud, flat voice.

'The defendant Zoe Harrington stands indicted of attempted murder, and that on the eighth day of June 2005, she did wilfully drive a van over the fallen body of Mr Shaun Lyon with intent to kill him. She has pleaded not guilty and it is your charge to say, having heard the evidence, whether she be guilty – or not.'

The scene is shivering in and out of focus. Look quickly across at the jury to see if any of them look remotely sympathetic. To my surprise, they are all looking back very hard indeed. Two nudge each other. A couple more are whispering together, nodding in agreement.

The judge senses their unease and looks over, only to see them conferring like a team on a tie-breaker in University Challenge. The jury leader, a pleasant looking woman in her fifties with short greying curly hair and a red tailored dress cautiously puts up her hand.

'Is there a difficulty?' enquires the Judge. Balding, broad faced and snub nosed, he has shrewd little brown eyes like Ratty's in *the Wind in the Willows*, and a generous mouth made more for smiling than sentencing people to life imprisonment.

'My Lord, is it not true that in order to be on a panel, the jurors must have no, um,' she struggles for legalese, 'prior knowledge of, or previous connection with, the defendant?'

'It is.'

'Well, oh dear, this is a bit awkward –'

The judge gently moves his hand in the sort of pudding-stirring gesture that Price Phillip uses for waving at the plebs on royal walkabouts, inviting the jury leader to by all means, continue.

'Then we can't do this. You see, we all know her. Or know of her, I should say,' she amends, reddening as she feels the full force of every eye in the court trained upon her. 'You haven't been able to turn on morning TV or open the papers these last weeks without hearing about MiSS men, or the WAP! woman. She's on posters all over the place.' The WAP! ladies rustle appreciatively up in the gallery. 'My daughter's even signed a petition about her.'

'Indeed.'

'We didn't know it was her for sure till we heard her name. Of course, we've not seen it actually *printed* in the papers, but there's all the rumours going around and her name does keep keeps coming up in those… and, um, the trouble is, juries are never told who they're getting before they see the person in court, are they?'

'No, and there are excellent reasons for that.'

'Well, I'm ever so sorry but we can't possibly try her,' concludes the lady, sitting down with a thump, looking rather upset. 'None of us.' The nearest jurors nod supportively, and pat her on the shoulder.

'Your Honour,' the prosecution barrister is on his feet, leapt to his feet, tall, otter-sleek with a Shakespearean actor's voice and snowy white half wig. 'I move that this entire jury stand down,' he looks down his well-bred nose at the panel, 'and the we call in another, who, let us hope, shall be marginally less tainted by the sound-bytes of popular news culture.'

'Proceed,' instructs the Judge, popping a peppermint into his mouth from a small cut-glass dish on his desk. 'And thank you so much for your time,' he says to the departing backs of the first twelve, as they are ushered off by the Clerk.

There is a small commotion when after a sweat-inducing twenty minute wait, another twelve jurors make their way slowly down to the front looking self-conscious. The public and press gallery audience hums and buzzes, shifting in their uncomfortable seats.

'Just how many jury members have they got in this place?' I whisper to Mr Shannon.

'This is the Old Bailey, dear. Fifteen courts, two hundred potential jurors on standby at any one time. Some of them sit on their arses in the waiting room for the standard two weeks then go home again. Never even called.'

I take a quick look round the courtroom as they are still taking their places. Half the Visitors gallery is taken up by black-clad WAP! ladies, several of whom are looking tetchy because they've been made to leave their placards outside. I can't see Jim or the children anywhere, but there's my mum in a stupendous flowered hat sitting next to Bel, who waves and smiles as if she'd just seen me across a room at the pub. Lucia, highly visible in flame-coloured orange and dark frames, is up at the back flanked by two gorgeous looking men in matching dark suits. I'm surprised she isn't in the press gallery, but it hasn't a spare seat anywhere so she must have queued to get in alongside everyone else. And, glory be, there is my dad, bronzed and lined from years of French sun. Ram-rod straight in a pinstriped suit and faded pink shirt with a white carnation in his buttonhole, he is sitting with, of all people, Angel Saint, who's looking serious and stunning in cream. That might explain why my mother is a little put out, since by rights he should be next to her. God, this is just like a family wedding.

'Do you solemnly swear that you will faithfully try the accused according to Law?' asks the Clerk of the Court, beginning the swearing-in process all over again.

'Ah –' says a young black guy in an red shirt and dark tie, eyes darting.

'God, not you too,' mutters the Prosecution audibly.

The Clerk tries again, this time with a middle-aged, pear-shaped but splendid six foot Chilean blonde, asparkle with jewellery and highly visible across the courtroom in a fuchsia jacket and punishingly tight black skirt. Her powerful presence recalls the wives of deposed South American presidents. 'Before you ask, zere is a leetle bit of a problem for me too,' she smiles, flicking a covert glance at the handsome Prosecution barrister, who now has a face like a root. The next two yield similar results.

Why's he so put out? If they had so many jurors to choose from, it's only a matter of time before we got a dozen who never take much notice of what the media says. But up in the public and press galleries, their interest is tightening like a cord. A ripple of nudging and fidgeting breaks out.

'This,' remarks the Judge severely, 'will not do.' And though he has not raised his voice by a single decibel, it carries across the court so clearly that it silences every single person in the room. 'Members of the jury,' he continues, sending them a level look over the tops of his black half moon spectacles. 'I feel that this Court needs to ask you but one question, and that it requires that you answer truthfully and to the best of your abilities.' He pauses for a moment, and leans forward with his chin on his hands. 'Clearly, you too appear to have some prior knowledge of the defendant. But might you also be, truthfully and honestly, capable of putting out of your minds everything you have heard about this woman so as not to prejudice your judgment of the case?'

The jurors look disconcerted and turn towards each other. There is more whispering, frowning, shrugging and shaking of heads. The Chilean blonde is gesturing like a windmill. After a minute or so of this, which seems more like a couple of hours, the new jury leader looks at me for a moment, rigid in the powder blue suit.

'No, My Lord. We cannot.'

I let out a strangled noise, earning an admonishing look from the Clerk. Half the Gallery sits up straighter or leans forwards. An expectant hush develops, like dry ice seeping under a closed door. After a few seconds it has grown so insistent that I can feel it against my back like a physical pressure.

'Permission to approach the bench, My Lord?' requests a voice in the sort of tone that Hamlet might have used to ask what his father's ghost thought it was doing up on the battlements at this time of night.

'That's Alistair Foulsham, QC,' whispers Mr Shannon. 'Top criminal barrister, Inner Temple. Brilliant (well, he thinks so) handsome (if you like that sort of thing). Rarely lost a case. No one in his own Chambers can stand him.'

The judge crooks his pinkie and beckons Foulsham over, who advances with a business-like swish of black robes and a firm stride, which do not bode well for me once he gets me in the witness box. Putting his dark head in its half wig close to the judge's, he talks rapidly for about a minute, once sending me a look of such contempt that I wilt.

The judge listens intently, then motions the barrister back to his place. 'This unusual situation requires a little considered thought. Obviously I am aware of the opportunistic national poster campaign and the irresponsible but sustained nature of the media interest. But so far as I was aware, the picture on these said posters was not an especially clear one and the defendant's name had not been revealed, so I underestimated how much the whole extraordinary business might influence the Court's jurors.

'Naturally, the simplest course of action is to call upon yet another new jury. My initial impression of the Harrington case persuades me that this would be our preferred option. However, though I am minded at this time to swear in another panel, I also believe that time taken in considered reflection is time well spent in the Judiciary, as it is elsewhere. Therefore, the court is now adjourned. We will re-convene after lunch, at two.'

The entire court struggles respectfully to its collective feet as Pryce-Symmonds sweeps off, polished shoes squeaking, in pursuit of balanced reflection and a decent lunch. Both Alistair Foulsham and Everett Stockton spring after him, looking purposeful. Their respective Pupils trot in the barristers' wake with their bosses' briefcases, coats, notes and bottles of spring water; little tug boats following two expensive ocean liners out to sea. The visitors and press galleries empty reluctantly, grumbling, gossiping, and arguing over where to go to eat.

Lunch for me is a glass of weak orange squash and two cheese sandwiches past their peak in a cell downstairs. 'Chin up,' instructs Mr Shannon, clapping me on the shoulder and producing a squashed jam doughnut and a large Cornish pasty from the bottom of his briefcase. I grab them gratefully. 'The craic starts after lunch.'

'It does?'

'Yes, but don't go getting your hopes up yet. They can, and most likely will, go through every available juror member down here. Then if they still don't get any joy, they will almost certainly set a re-trial for somewhere like Manchester or Leeds in a few weeks' time, where the local jurors might not have heard so much about you. I mean, a lot of the publicity was London-based, wasn't it?'

Ms Stockton, making a flying visit but looking like she needed to be somewhere else fifteen minutes ago, nods in agreement and checks her Rolex; wig in her hand and her short, expensively-cut blonde hair glinting in the harsh overhead light. 'I'm sorry, Zoe, I know what you're thinking. But it's extremely rare for a trial to be dismissed because the defendant has had too much prior publicity, OK? Although obviously,' she concedes, 'it can slow the judicial process down.'

My spirits, which have been edging very tentatively upwards, plummet again. 'Look, could I possibly I see my husband or my children now? Please? Just for five minutes? They are probably only upstairs, and I really –'

'I'm very sorry, but it's simply not allowed,' she tells me with a brittle stab at sympathy. 'Anyway, must run. I have a couple of little things to do.' She knocks on the door, is let smartly out of the cell and bustles away, power heels clicking.

An hour later, back in court, she awards me an economical smile from her post down by the bench before composing herself neatly in her seat like a cat on a window ledge, a tactical ten feet away from the Crown Prosecution who is reading casually through his brief and making notes. Jim, Kasha and Tim are still nowhere to be seen.

'The court will please rise,' intones the Clerk, and a Mexican Wave spreads through the assembled company as Judge PS marches back to his post. The Jury panel sits empty. Well, here we go again. Bring on twelve more people who've been summoned from their jobs, homes and former lives to sit in a stuffy courtroom for weeks whether they like it or not.

'Your Honour? Permission to address the Bench.' The cool, clipped tones of Ms Everett Stockton ring out sharp and clear. Foulsham looks up quickly.

'Well?'

She smiles the way women do when they have a secret – and begins.

What The Judge Keeps In The Jar
On His Desk

'Your Honour, I realise that this Court's time is valuable so I shall not mince words but will come directly to the point,' promises Ms Stockton. She then proceeds to mince them for all she is worth.

The phrases 'unprecedented media coverage', 'substantial public sympathy', 'considerable room for reasonable doubt', 'active campaign backing', 'opportunistic media', 'amnesiac victim', 'lack of hard witness-based evidence' and 'support for the prosecution tainted by the teen-porn industry'. ('Objection, Your Honour!' calls Foulsham reflexively) comes up a lot. As do scattered references to touching a raw nerve in Britain's collective moral consciousness, the difficulties of untrained personnel driving large vans, and the unreliability of said van's clutch, especially when it had required replacement for over a year.

'Ms Everett, I'd be most grateful if you *would* get to the point,' interrupts the Judge after several minutes of eloquent tirade, which appear to lead nowhere.

'Jaysus, the mouth on that woman,' mutters Shannon beside me. 'She'd out-talk an Irish boarding house landlady.'

'Very well, Your Honour.' Ms Stockton smoothes her robes and folds her hands demurely.

'In view of the large amount of prejudicial publicity, it is submitted that the waters of justice have been so thoroughly muddied that the defendant cannot be dealt with fairly by any court in the country –' she fusses with the sleeve of her robe for a second or two, then draws herself up to her full height of five feet two inches and looks the Judge right in the eye '– and it is therefore also submitted that this trial should not, under the circumstances, proceed.'

She waits for a moment, before saying: 'Thank you, Your Honour,' into the dead silence that follows, and returning quietly to her seat.

'Your Honour, this is ridiculous, nay outrageous,' yelps Foulsham, leaping to his feet. 'It is also unheard of. Why, it's a simple matter of finding a suitable Jury and we have only assayed this twice. I move that the trial be postponed for six weeks and take place in York. We cannot allow proper Court procedure to be deflected by a few newspaper snippets, derailed by a handful of placard-waving, black-clad harpy extremists, or prejudiced by ignorant popularist hearsay amongst the *Hello*-reading public.'

'That will do, Mr Foulsham,' interjects the Judge, with a slight edge to his voice.

'To drop the case now, at this late stage, will set a dangerous precedent for the media to be set up above the legal and judiciary systems, and for all intents and purposes, to become the estate that effectively runs our country,' rants the QC, failing to take the hint. 'Newspapers and TV stations will become the arbiters of right and wrong, the apportioners, of British justice —' he flicks a quick glance at the press gallery to see if they are taking all this down '— and the Moral Guardians of The Law,' he continues, slowing to let the journalists' shorthand catch up. 'Your Honour, in my humble opinion, to let this matter go would be to establish a dangerous legal precedent. Nay, a slippery slope, whereby sufficient media attention shall come to be offset against the true weight of a crime, given the same legal status as genuine mitigating circumstance, and if present in sufficient quantities, could in theory protect a guilty party from any amount of law-breaking — even attempted murder as is the case here. My Lord, I fear it could be homicide and rape next. Or even tax evasion,' he concludes, with real feeling.

'Mr Foulsham, I strongly advise you not to tell me what I can and cannot do in my own court,' snaps the Judge, who is now looking distinctly testy. 'Well, what is it?' he adds as a quailing flunky sidles up from the left, holding a long white envelope.

The poor man goes as close to the judge as he dares. The jury fidgets and cranes, Ms Stockton re-crosses shapely legs, Foulsham remains standing and adjusts his half wig. The judge listens quietly to the messenger then gives him a stiff nod, whereupon the man retreats backwards to the edge of the room and watches, along with the entire court, as Judge PS opens the envelope. His expression changes not one iota either during or after he reads it. After a few slow seconds of deliberation, he tucks the letter into his robes, takes a long drink of water from his cut glass tumbler, sets it down with a bang and fixes Foulsham, who is still quivering with well-bred indignation in front of him, with a laser stare.

'Case dismissed.'

'What? But My Lord –'

'I *said,* case dismissed,' barks the judge, fishing out a vast white handkerchief and blowing his nose abruptly.

There is two seconds' complete quiet, then I'm screaming and throwing my arms around Mr Shannon. Shouts and whoops break out behind us. Seconds later we are both submerged in an orgy of backslapping, hugging, kissing and hand-wringing by my family, friends (though I am still looking around in vain for Jim and the children) and several dozen people I've never seen before in my life.

Five minutes later, I look up to see Foulsham, who seems to have recovered his good humour remarkably quickly, nose to nose with the big Brazilian blonde; and my father congratulating Ms Everett. My mother is crying, and hugging Lucia. Bel is embracing WAP! ladies, several of whom are cat calling and whistling from the Gallery. Angel is having both hands kissed repeatedly by Lucia's two men in shades, looking smug and ignoring my dad.

'You all right?' Shannon asks. 'You've gone white as a sheet.'

'Ooooh bloody, bloody hell –' I splutter ecstatically, the best I can manage at the moment, mechanically shaking hands.

'I think we've got the fact that Foulsham got right up the Judge's nose to thank for our result as much as anything,' he confides quietly in my ear. 'That is the closest I've ever seen Pryce-Symmonds get to losing his honourable rag. Mind you, Everett told me this afternoon that PS doesn't care for Foulsham. Apparently he was at Charterhouse with the man's father, and he couldn't stick *him* either.

'Sure you're OK?' Nod shakily, trying not to cry. 'Right, then, come with me. It's time to meet your public.'

He propels me out into the bustling, high ceilinged hall and across to the doors leading onto the street. Sunlight is pouring through them, there's blue sky beyond and I want to break into a run then swallow dive into the freedom of the air outside – but all of a sudden, there's a hand tapping me on the shoulder. Quite a firm hand. A hand whose owner is used to people doing what they say.

I wheel round and find myself face to face with Judge PS, minus his wig.

'Before you attempt to thank me, don't.'

'Uh, OK.' *Keep calm. He can't change his mind now.* 'But I'm free, and it's obviously thanks to you. So why not?'

He leans closer. 'Bugger all to do with me,' he says quietly. 'That's why.'

'I beg your pardon?'

'You're a fortunate woman. Because you can believe me when I tell you that under normal circumstances, press coverage or no, there's not a court in the country that would have given you less than two to three years. However, I happen to have received new information today which put a rather different complexion on your case, and furthermore, you have young children, no previous criminal record and

334

hardly seem to me to present any sort of danger to the general public –'

'Gosh, no –'

'– providing you drive nothing more ambitious than a Mini Metro in future and ensure that you are going forwards at all times.'

I look at him thoughtfully, allowing the knowledge of what he could have done if he'd felt like it, to sink in. 'You're, well, even though you look so strict and everybody's scared to death of you, you must be a very nice man underneath it all.'

'Indeed. I have the generous, open heart of a small boy,' he snaps. 'In a jar, on my desk. Good day to you, Mrs Harrington.'

Walking out into the bright October sunshine with Mr Shannon at my side and two policemen at our backs, we find we're facing a sea of people including a pack of reporters, WAP! (whose numbers had grown to over a hundred: the organisers must have been on their mobiles) family and friends. I scan the crowds anxiously for Jim, Kasha and Tim. But as we start down the broad stone steps of the Old Bailey, the media pack below begins to mill and boil, swarming up to surround us. Fight a powerful impulse to leg it as the press converges on us as one: mouths open, eyes narrowed, cameras glinting, microphones bristling, pens aquiver. It's lunchtime in the piranha pool, and we're today's Special. They tense, appear to take a collective in-breath then suddenly, as if on some pre-arranged signal, all start shouting at once.

'John Maguire, Reuters,' bellows a small fat man, pushing himself in between Mr Shannon and myself. 'Apparently no one's ever been let off after being rejected by a mere two juries in succession. You've just made legal history. What do you think of that?'

'We'll issue a statement to the press later on today at, er, six o'clock,' promises Mr Shannon, knowing a good sound-byte opportunity when he hears one but unwilling to see it blown by any euphoric babbling from me.

'We hear you'll be guest of honour at the WAP!'s conference on underage prostitution at the House of Commons next week. What will the thrust of your address be?' demands a bloke in an electric blue suit from Sky, his camerawoman coming in inches from my face.

'How do you feel about our LOCuST campaign?' asks a foxy piece from *The Mail,* who is wearing bright orange lipstick.

'Reckon you'd have been freed without WAP's support?' bawls a bullet-headed bloke from *The Observer.*

'Hi, Mummy!' shrieks a reedy voice.

I whirl round. It's Kasha, jumping up and down like a pogo stick on heat, bearing a huge self-made placard, which says *Hands Off My Mum.* About forty ladies dressed in red and black surround her smiling broadly and waving placards of their own, bearing the legend WAP! OFF in neon-green and black.

'Yo, Mum!' bellows Tim from the other side of the group a clenched fist (complete with red wristband) in the air, and holding one end of a banner which says '*Zoe is Innocent*' with the other.

And who should be on the other end, but Jim.

He catches my eye and gives me a slightly embarrassed 'What can you do?' grin. I wave frantically at them, bouncing up and down on my toes, desperate to get at my children. 'Terrific kids, aren't they?' remarks Shannon, as if he were personally responsible for the whole thing. 'They've been working together real professional with WAP! these last couple of weeks. Many of the placards and banners were made on your kitchen table.'

'Oh! Does that mean that my husband – that is, has, Jim been –' I blather, wishing I could talk properly.

'Yes,' says Shannon with a wink. 'He certainly has.'

Holy Mary and all the saints –

Throwing down their banners and placards, my children burrow through the crowds. The journalistic scrum parts benignly to let them through, eventually lifting them up high so they are virtually body-surfing on a wave of goodwill. Seconds later, Tim and Kasha are hurling themselves into my arms like a pair of rugby prop forwards and we collapse heavily on the pavement in front of the Old Bailey in a tangle of arms and legs. 'Zoe, Zoe, look over here!' 'Keep cuddling your kids and turn this way!' Clutching the pair of them tightly and rocking them to and fro, I disgrace myself by bursting into tears. 'Great, she's crying!' shouts *The News of the World*. There is a frenzy of clicking cameras. 'Fant*astic*: look over here, sweetheart.' 'Hey, give us a trembly smile...'

'Any comments about all the support your husband's given you?' calls the girl from the *Mirror* because Jim has reached us now, tie askew and jacket half pulled off. Thinking of his home-made banners, the Peabody flat and his exhausting, ill-paid motorbike messengering, I have no words but free one arm from the children to encircle him too and we have our first proper hug in months. It goes on for many long moments and his arms feel like home, as the sibilant chattering of fifty rolls of film and digital discs filling up fast makes a sound like whispered machine gun fire.

The family is finally bundled into a black cab, with Tim, Jim and Kasha piling in on top of me. Bel and Lucia's faces appear at the window in front of a mob of press who are still baying questions. 'Lucia, thank you, thank you so much, you're bloody, bloody brilliant,' I gasp, winding the window down still hanging onto Jim and the children. 'In fact, you are a spin *genius*.' My friend is laughing, her sunglasses awry, one arm still round my mum whose hat is gone and whose hair is in her eyes.

'Go home. I'll meet you there,' she calls above the noise. 'Now, Bel: let's tell everyone we can get hold of at short notice that there's a party back at Jim and Zoe's new flat from six this evening. You get there first with the drink, while I take all Harringtons back to my place for a little break-ette. Have you a key she can borrow, Jim?' But it's Tim who eagerly offers up his. New flat, huh. That's going to be seriously weird. Our real home has – dah, *bankers* – living in it.

'What party?' asks Jim, with the expression of a man who's been roughly awoken from sleep and told he has thirty seconds to leave the house. 'No, no, hold on a minute. I'm not sure we can face a party –'

'Oh, come on, Jim.' she wheedles. 'This sort of thing doesn't happen every day.'

'Thank God for that. Oh, oh – all right. Why not? I could do with a drink. Zoe?'

I nod dazedly.

'Zoe! Oi, Zoe! Lean out the cab window and undo your top buttons for us!' calls a man from the *Daily Star*. 'Where are they going now?' he demands, grabbing Lucia by her Versace-clad shoulder. 'Nowhere,' she shakes him off fastidiously while climbing into the cab, 'that need concern *you.*'

Our taxi roars off down the Strand with a lurch that lands Jim and me half on the floor. We disentangle hurriedly, self-conscious as thirteen-year-olds on a first date. The children cluster and snuggle as we bowl up St Martins Lane towards Great Titchfield Street.

'I'm sorry, I'm sorry, I'm sorry I've been away from you for so long,' I whisper to them, holding both children close, their noses against my cheeks. 'But I promise you that I am never going to be away from you again. Not even when you are grown up. Never, never, never. Even when you move away from home, I shall be your mad old bat of a mother in the black leather jacket and the purple crochet hat, who keeps turning up at your flats with apple crumbles and Echinaceaforce in carrier bags.'

'S'cool,' says Tim. 'But I'm never leaving home anyway.'

'Me neither,' agrees Kasha. 'And if I do, I will make sure you come and live with *me.*'

Back at Lucia's, I get straight on the phone to HMP Highview while practically inhaling my first real coffee for months as we gorge happily on Big Macs. Mrs Martin in Throughcare says Marine is just in fact across the hall in the laundry room (again) and do I want to speak to her rather than leave a message?

'You done it, aintcha?' she crows.

'Well, someone did. They threw the case out. It got flushed down the toilet of the media.' Kasha climbs onto my lap and buries her face in my neck. I'd forgotten how heavy she is. And how warm.

'Yessss!' screams Marine. I hold the phone away form my ear. 'We 'ave a result on Block C! I wanna hear everything. 'Ooo was the Judge? Did you get that prat McManners as Prosecution? I 'ad 'im once (vicious cunt), begging your pardon Mrs Martin. Was your man an' kids there? How'd Jools' suit go down wiv the jury?'

After a couple of minutes frantic exchange an awkward silence falls, the first I can remember between us. Kasha feeds me a chip dipped in ketchup.

'Yeah – well. We'll miss you too, you daft cow,' admits Marine, understanding, as she always had. 'But think of the *shopping* you can do for us. Now, me, I'll 'ave three packs of pink Andrex, a navy Maybelline Longlash and a large slab of Milky Bar, you know, economy size. Lallie needs a bumper box of Tampax Super. And being as we just 'eard this lunchtime that Joolz's Phil married someone else yesterday and 'as fucked off to Feringuerola, we reckon the poor bitch could do wiv that book *Bastards Leave Suckers 'Oo Love Too Much.* And if you don't mind my saying so Zo, it mightn't 'urt if you 'ad a read of it, an' all.'

I put the phone down having promised to go see them all as soon as I can get a visitor's pass, furiously aware that the combined time that she, Lally and Joolz have left to do (for crimes which physically harmed no one) exceeds Tim's age in years while the M5 rapist – three victims over one summer – got off with twenty months only last week.

'Cheer up, Mum,' says my son through a mouthful of Hot Apple Pie, putting both feet up on Lucia's elegant green leather chaise. 'Hey, did you know that when opossums play possum they aren't acting, they've passed out through sheer terror?'

'I know how they feel,' mumbles Jim, disappearing into the toilet with his mobile sticking out of his pocket.

'Are you all right in there?' I call, ten minutes later.

There is no reply. But standing outside, I think I can hear him talking to someone.

Anything With A PADI Licence And A Pulse

Our new home is one of the Victorian Peabody flats behind our former house. As Lucia said, fifth floor, no lift, great view. As we enter the quadrangle garden, mostly grass with a small playground area (swing seat still attached to swing chains: there's posh for you round here) Jim leads me over to a bench seat. 'You go on up. Help Bel open some more bottles,' he suggests to Lucia, looking thoroughly awkward. 'I need to have a word with Zoe.'

'What a very splendid idea,' she agrees, smiling fondly at the pair of us. 'Come along, children.' She looks up and points out the brightly-lit windows of our flat for me. 'It appears that your welcoming committee is already in situ.' I'll say it is. Cuban dance music is belting out from the two open windows through which a cheerful crush of people is visible. Suddenly, I feel extremely shy. Shy of my friends, and very shy indeed of this man who is sitting next to me a careful five feet away.

'Alone at last,' I chirp brightly, stomach doing wheelies. Oh zip my mouth, of all the lines, of all the crap bits of repartee, I had to come out with *that?* 'Sorry. Bit nervous. Can – er, may I say something?'

'Not just now.' He's looking even more embarrassed than me. I interpret this as a promising sign, and gesture towards the bench in a friendly, let's-talk sort of way. He sits down cautiously, giving me far more room than necessary.

'Please, I've got to. You've been so brilliant these last few weeks and I've missed you such a lot and I'm so, so sorry about, about everything –' I stammer, all in a rush. 'And er, anyway, I sort of wanted to ask, that is to suggest (not that I

341

expect to necessarily come back and *live* with you, I mean obviously you haven't asked me yet, have you) but please could we try spending a few days together? Just to see how we go? And if you still hate me after that, well, then we can always –' *No, leave it. He's looking really worried now.* 'Sorry. This is all a bit much, I know. Let's just go up to our party and, er, have a drink.' I stand up and try to pull him gently to his feet. He resists. 'Jim? Jim, what's the matter?'

'I'm not coming in.'

'But why not?' *And why isn't he looking at me?*

'Because I have to go now.'

For a few seconds, my brain won't process that one. Then it comes out of reverse and grinds reluctantly into first. 'You have? But where?'

He won't look at me. 'Um, Heathrow.'

'Hang on a minute. Are you trying to say that you're taking a – a *plane* somewhere?'

Jim nods miserably, feet shifting, big hands dangling between his knees.

'What – I mean, how long for? Can't me and the children come with you? We could sublet the flat, take them out of school for a couple of weeks? Hey, that would be *great*. This has all been a terrible strain for all of us. Do us all the world of good to get away bit of sun, sea and, er –' *He's looking at me now all right. Like I'm a bi-polar bag lady.*

'The fact is, I'm going to stay with a mate who runs a little dive shop in The Maldives.'

'Stay with a – since when did you have a mate in The Maldives?'

'He's an old school friend from Highgate,' says Jim, heavily. 'Contacted me out of the blue after that piece in the *Sindie*. I'd told him my head was all messed up and I was desperate for a break. He – he said to come out anytime I wanted, and that he could do with another wet-suit washer, someone to drive the dive boat. He's pretty casual. Anything with a PADI licence and a pulse,' he adds, with a shrug. 'There's a room I can have there, too. Above the office.'

'Oh please no, you – you can't.'

'Zoe, I just can't handle this any longer. What's happened to us all in the last six months simply beggars belief. I've got to get away. I've never known what's coming next with you around, I still don't and I'm telling you, I can't take any more of it. You seem to think we can just pick up where we've left off…'

'No! No, I don't think that at all. I only want to talk to you.' I grab his hand in both of mine, but he frees himself and returns them gently them to my sides.

'We are past talking, way past it. Don't you understand? I've had it. These past weeks I've carried sole responsibility for two traumatised children, seen the best idea I've ever had in my life sent down the pan, gone bankrupt, had to find money and a new a roof over our heads from nowhere, and on top of all that, got roped into springing my adulterous wife from jail by helping run a media campaign that even Max Clifford wouldn't touch when we asked him.' He runs a distracted hand through his red hair. 'And whatever gave you the idea I wanted you back? Thanks, but no thanks. Over the past six months, you've managed to ruin my business, become pregnant by another man, go to prison, then appear at The Old Bailey on a charge of attempted murder. And not content with that, you've made sure every single person in the country got to hear about it.'

So that's how it is. I get slowly to my feet, begging and pleading out of the window. So he's feeling too holy and put upon to even let me talk to him? Very well. He shall hear a few home truths instead.

'Now, just you listen to me. I am grateful, grateful from the very bottom of my heart, for what you did on that campaign. Yet it is also true that you did not get involved until the last couple of weeks. It was not my fault that Seventh Wave went bust, since according to you it was going bust anyway. But I fully admit that *FirstPencil* would probably be still be going if it wasn't for me –'

'Oh, that makes *all* the difference –'

'– however, I would also remind you that I did try, several times, to warn you off Shaun, and you wouldn't listen. And that if you had, you may have found a better backer who'd be bankrolling you even now.' Looking at Jim's clenched fists as he gets up to tower above me and the expression on his face, it seems probable that he won't just be visiting The Maldives, he'll be emigrating there.

'Losing *our* house was *your* fault, OK?' I say slowly and clearly, folding my arms so he won't see my hands shaking. 'Hartland Road was half mine, yet you signed it away when you were drunk, without consulting me. The adultery bit: fair enough. But you were doing the same yourself, remember? In fact, counting back, I reckon that you were at it for far longer than I was.' *And he was the former love of my life, while Bex was merely an opportunistic little cow.* 'Remember also that you even left us to live with her. Back then, we needed to *talk* to each other instead of getting off with other people, so we are both guilty, OK? And don't you remember how many evenings I tried? You used to turn down every attempt at conversation, every invitation go out and be together, and almost every offer of sex, time after time. Though I suppose that having already given Bex of your best, you must have been somewhat fatigued.'

'That's enough! That is totally out of –'

'The fuck it is. And as for taking sole responsibility for your children, struggling get a new a roof over your heads and having to find casual labour to bring in the money, I fully appreciate that it must have been tough. But may I point out that there are millions of single mothers out there doing the same? Only they tend to do so for more three months at a time, and can't push off to The Maldives when they get tired of it.'

Jim lunges forwards and grasps me by the shoulders: 'How would you know about what Tim, Kasha and I have been going through? And as for Rebecca, you pushed me into it with your erratic moods, chaotic housekeeping, your neediness and incessant demands...'

'My what? The house wasn't that bad until I got ill. You want a pristine home with – with *Glade* in the loos? So marry your mother (oh, I forgot, you as good as have these last few months). Mood swings, yes latterly, but neediness? Demands? Since when is asking your husband for sex more than once a month, demanding? Or wanting to hold a conversation occasionally, needy? And – *and if I'm such a horrible person, why did you bother to help get me out?*'

Jim is silent for a moment. Above our heads, Cuban music segues inappropriately into the B-52's *Love Shack*, which gets louder as someone opens one of the flat's sitting room windows even wider 'Mum-eee! Da-aaad!' We whip our gazes upwards. It's Kasha, leaning out of the window at a perilous angle, with Bel hanging onto to her sweatshirt from behind. 'What are you doing? Hurry *up.*'

Somehow, we both smile up at her, and wave. 'Just coming, sweetheart. Save us a sausage roll.' She retires, reassured.

'You really want to know why I helped? All right. I spoke to Lucia. She told me what – what really happened between you and Shaun.' He appears to be addressing the swings, but at least he's talking and he's still here.

'What exactly did she say to you?'

'That you and he once had a big thing, the biggest thing in either of your lives (I presume I was second best after that?). Then that many years later, he came looking for you.'

'What else?'

'That when you wouldn't play, he got at you through me. God, he did a number on me all right. I honestly believed he wanted to back Seventh Wave. That for once, I'd had a really good idea.'

'But he did,' I shouted, wrapping my arms around myself. 'He did, he *did*. He told me –'

'Shut it,' says Jim in an ominously level voice. 'Lucia also said he started blackmailing you after that night at the Grenadier House: put out or I'll pull out. And that you (Jesus, is this true?) kidnapped him, locked him up, took compromising photos of him,' Jim passes his hand over his face, 'and were trying to release him on Hampstead Heath in the middle of the night to find his own way home when he attacked you; then in a panic, you ran him down by accident. Is that really how it was?'

Good old Lucia. 'More or less.'

'Why didn't you tell me? Why didn't you come to me at the beginning? Didn't you trust me?' demands Jim, his voice rising. 'Or did you think that I was too weak to help you, too pathetic to protect you?'

'No, no, of course not. I just thought you'd jump to the wrong, er, conclusion. I mean – it seemed pretty straightforward at the time. A little light abduction, basic restraint tactics, a bit of photography to ensure future good behaviour –' *I must have been off my bloody head.*

There is a long, judgmental pause. 'And you said you were looking at sofas.'

Abruptly, he starts putting on the leather jacket he's been carrying, stabbing his arms into the sleeves, tugging savagely at the zip. 'I'm going now,' he continues, getting his voice back under control. 'As I said, I have a plane to catch. Ade'll come to get my stuff tomorrow, and send it on. If you're worried about money –'

'Money? Money is the least of my worries. No, emotionally retarded and *needy* as this may sound, what's worrying me is that you're leaving us. Again.'

'I was going to say that I'm giving you the bike to sell, OK? It's a bit beaten up but it's worth a couple of grand. BikeNation down the road will probably take it: they do Kawasakis. Mum's offered to pay Tim's school fees for the

346

moment, also for them to come and see me once I get settled this half term. And before you ask, I don't know how long I'll be out there. I don't even know if I'll be coming back.'

So this is how it ends, not with a bang, but with a plane ticket. I can feel my face sagging. Jim finally looks at me properly, exhaustion in his eyes, new lines around his mouth. 'Come on. You don't need me any more. I wonder if you ever really did.'

Bugger dignity, I throw myself at him. 'Don't do this now, not after all we've been going through together, not now we've got this far. I *do* need you, I've always needed you – oh God, please won't you stay just a little while longer? *Please*?'

Jim's face shuts down, blank as a cash machine screen when you've punched in the wrong numbers. 'Together? We didn't really go through anything together, that's the whole point. And we're not a couple any more. We haven't been for a long time.'

I look at him miserably, for I have no arguments left. 'Don't go. Don't –'

'Tell the children I've gone to do some filming in the Islands, and that they're coming out for a week's scuba holiday with me at half term. I explained this morning that it might be on the cards, and now you're back they'll feel secure enough to let me go.'

'Hey, *I'm* not secure enough to let you go and I'm meant to be an adult. What makes you think they are?' *I am not going to cry. I'm not.*

Jim pats me stiffly on the shoulder from a distance of four feet. 'You'll survive,' he promises with a ghost of his old smile. 'You may only be small, but you're considerably tougher than you look. And Tim and Kasha need their mum, Zoe. They've had more than enough of me.'

'But –'

'I promised I'd be there for you when you came out, and I was (let go of my arm, please). But I never said anything about how long I'd be staying –'

'I noticed.'

'– because up until this afternoon at Lucia's flat, I didn't know how I'd feel. Then it hit me. The reason I felt so cornered by the idea of a welcome-home party, was because I couldn't imagine *having* a home with you any more.'

'So you're saying, what? That you have no feeling left for me? None at all? No even a bit?' He says nothing, just fiddles with the zip on his jacket.

'But when you hugged me outside the Old Bailey,' I can feel myself reddening, 'it felt like, well, it felt like the real thing.'

Jim looks, if possible, even more miserable than me. 'It was the real thing. I was – really happy for you. We'd all been working like maniacs to support you, and it had come off. I was very relieved. And like I said, I hadn't managed to come to any, ah, final decisions then.'

'Happy for me. Oh, for Christ's sake. Do you feel nothing else?'

He considers this for a moment or two, looking down at my frantic upturned face.

'No.'

No.

Gently, he prises my fingers off his arm and places a set of silver keys in my palm. 'For the front doors, and the bike. Goodbye, Zoe. I'll be in touch.' Then he turns and walks away into the early evening sunshine, which is making his hair shine like fire and his black leather jacket gleam.

He does not look back.

Background Information

It's late and the flat is silent, the only light coming from a floor lamp creating a soft pool of saffron that's pushing back the shadows cloaking the corners of the room.

The Vicar is curled up asleep on a discarded pink T-shirt of Kasha's on the sofa. I am sitting cross-legged on our old red Turkey rug underneath the picture of Jim with the darts in it, trying to stuff back the contents of a feather cushion the kids have been fighting with and listening to the comforting burble of the BBC World Service on our cheap little radio.

Having been used as target practice every day of the past ten weeks since he left, my husband's picture appears to be riddled with a hail of bullet holes. Bone tired from two months' of fruitless job interviews, washing up/floor mopping lunchtimes at The Stag – bless Awesome Wells, it's four pounds seventy an hour, cash in hand – and trying to think up new ways to serve the baked potatoes and beans we are now living off (never try to enliven with garlic salt, it's disgusting) I've stabbed myself twice with the needle, can't see properly and there seem to be feathers in my mouth.

Just thinking of falling into bed when the doorbell rings, a metallic honk we've never got used to. Instantly on the defensive. No one calls unannounced on a single woman with children after nine thirty at night, unless they are in trouble, up to no good or both.

'Who is it?' I shout through the letter box, trying to sound butch.

'Hello, Zoe.' A man's voice, familiar, but so muffled by our security grill that I cannot place it. Open the door a crack with my foot against it, wishing the safety chain worked. A slice of our visitor's face appears, backlit by the harsh stairwell lighting.

'Oh, holy shit –'

'That's a nice welcome.'

'What are *you* doing here?' I choke, trying to get the last cushion feather out of my mouth. 'I mean, sorry, you caught me on the hop. Er, how – how *are* you?'

'Not bad. Not bad at all, considering.'

'Good, that's – I mean, for God's sake, do you know what time it is? It's practically the middle of the night, it's eleven o clock,' I witter, quite unable to believe who it is.

Shaun says nothing.

'How did you find me? And, look here, what is it you want, anyway?' In answer, he puts his shoulder against the door and pushes. Not as hard as he could do, but pretty hard all the same. Panic-stricken, I push back with my whole weight.

'Look, it's wonderful to see you again, but –' the words die in my mouth, for suddenly, perversely, it is, even though I do wish he'd stop trying to shove that door open and at least wait to be asked in. The image I'd carried of Shaun for so long was of him unconscious, helpless, wired up to drips and monitor lines in the stifling world of ITU. Now he looks strong, well, himself. 'Are you all right? Really, really, totally better? Look, I am so, so sorry about – that is, I never, ever meant – oh, hell, I'm making a right mess of this.'

He grunts in agreement and gives the door a powerful shunt, moving it back a couple more inches.

'Shaun? Say something,' I rasp, shoving my toes at right-angles against the widening wedge and pushing my heel down hard. 'Please tell me what you want. Tell me, then perhaps I can let you in.'

'Just passing by.' His foot's in the door. 'Fancied a chat.'

'Sure. Absolutely. I mean, of course. But does it have to be right now? Can we meet tomorrow, in *daylight*?

Somewhere there's, er, other people? There's a lovely café round the corner –'

'Emigrating to New Zealand tomorrow. Got residency because of Debbie.'

What's he want to do tonight, that he needs to emigrate immediately afterwards? Christ, Tim and Kasha. He goes near them over my dead body, but perhaps the latter's what he has in mind. He brings his face close to mine. 'Paranoid as ever, eh?'

'Yes, well so would you be.' Lean harder against the door, but so does he. 'Like William Burroughs says: paranoia is being in possession of the facts.'

'Well, you're not. So I thought I'd come and acquaint you with them.'

'So I can start worrying properly?' Christ, he's strong.

'No, so you can stop. Ever wonder how you got off?'

'Many times.' Am also wondering if I can reach that lamp five feet away and belt him with it if he tries to come in. But suddenly he stops pushing, catching me off balance so that I lurch forwards, banging my nose on the doorframe.

'You got off because we gave Judge Pryce-Simmons a little background information.' Shaun's eye is pinning me through the gap in the door. 'Thought I should tell you before I left. Debbie says it's healthy to tie up loose ends. Closure, and all that. So here I am.'

What's Debbie got to do with it? My brain scrabbles, a spider in a bath, as I rub the throbbing bridge of my nose. That's going to be swollen tomorrow. 'Hang on, you did what? And who's we? Why would you –'

'My choice' His tone belies a fleeting look in his agate eyes, a look I'd not seen there for, oh, twenty years. I let the door swing open. He comes no further but reaches out and touches my upper arm briefly, the light glinting off his broad platinum wedding band.

'Listen, I know how it must have seemed to you. Believe me, stuck in a hospital bed for months I had plenty of time to think though probably obsess is a better word. That night in the pub, I admit, I was deliberately winding you up. I was really pissed off with you for walking out that day at the flat – after everything I'd said when you first arrived, too (which, just for the record, I'd meant). Nor do I like being lectured. So I thought I'd have a little fun before I – er, let you off the hook. That's the last time I try that,' he adds with a flicker of his old Pan smile. 'Never diss an ex when she's driving a truck.'

'Even now, you can still make jokes about it? Dear God, I nearly *killed* you.'

'If I take the last few months too seriously I'll have a crying jag right here on your doorstep. May I come in, by the way? Thank you.' He steps over the threshold but once inside, he doesn't waste time glancing around, nor march into the flat and take possession of his surroundings in his usual manner. Instead he leans against the wall, taking in my fluffy tartan comfort slippers, white face, and pear-shaped outline created by Tim's nasty puce Kaiser Chiefs sweatshirt.

'Look, I'd never have wound you up like that if I'd realised how vulnerable you'd become, or how much your grip on reality was loosening. Prozac. Jesus, that junk. One of Debbie's friends found herself by her six-year-old's bedside trying to smother the kid after four weeks on the stuff. By the way, are your children asleep?'

I nod briefly and beckon him over to the sofa, asmother with newspapers and cushions. He balances awkwardly on the arm while I sit on the table by the window, feet dangling.

'I know you could have shopped me, OK? I'd been having a few girls at my flat, I admit that. And yes, there had been one other, like the one you saw, who'd been fourteen or fifteen. Fifteen going on thirty-five, but the law's the law. The rest were professionals in their early twenties – and, er, all right, Alicia once or twice. Remember her?'

'Vividly.'

'You can stop glaring, Zoe, I didn't make a habit of that sort of thing. If you must know, Alicia was far more trouble than she was worth and overly ambitious with it. And the two young ones were – well, a major aberration.

'Yeah, major,' he added quietly, almost to himself. 'And not really my thing. Then that Watching business – I'm not sure what all that was all about either. I suppose it may have been something to do with, well, having tried just about everything else in my time; the pressure at work being horrendous (we were haemorrhaging cash) Debbie always on my back to come home earlier (I mean who, running their own company, gets home before nine at p.m.?) or accompany her to see some earnest beard at Relate; *you* having apparently disappeared... hell, I don't know... I think I must have lost it for a bit...'

'You don't have to make excuses.'

'No,' he said tightly with a touch of his old fuck-you arrogance. 'No, I probably don't. But I do know you could have gone to the police about that any time. What with the *Mirror's* sexpose of my websites, if you'd offered to testify that I'd ever used underage flesh myself, the police would have been delighted and you could probably have done a deal. Initially I expected you to do so and thought, sod it, let her try: I'll develop total recall of past events and have her sent down for attempted murder. But you didn't say anything. Did you?'

I stared fixedly at my feet encased in fake tartan fur, unable to meet his eyes. 'People said I should. But I couldn't do it. It would have totally destroyed you, and your family. Look, I was pretty sure you were trying to protect me by saying you couldn't remember anything, so how could I? And I felt so guilty about Jim's company, about having a stupid affair, about having made such a cock-up of everything and about having nearly killed you when I never, ever meant to hurt you. You, of all people –'

Astonishingly, Shaun gets up and puts his arms around me, his heart beating calm and slow, his presence a grounding force. 'I know. You always were (forgive me) an appalling driver. But you stayed in that jail, separated from your home and kids day after day and didn't use what you knew to get yourself out. That was very brave. I know how desperately you must have wanted to go home. I know what that must have cost you.'

'To be honest, I felt like I deserved to be in there, what with one thing and another. There or Rampton, being a bit loony at the time into the bargain.' I hang my head and plait my fingers at the mention of the B-word. 'And it wasn't really –'

'It was, and don't interrupt,' he says softly. 'So when I heard you were up for the Old Bailey, well, I wanted to get stuck in. My lawyer went berserk, but I figured that on top of the media exposure, a few extra details might tip the balance and encourage the judge to throw your case out. If, that is,' he adds off-handedly, 'he happened to feel like it.'

'And just why might he have felt like it?' I wriggle out of his embrace, a comfort I know I have no right to, antenna beginning to wobble.

Shaun grins like a kid who's just stuffed a newt into the prom queen's desk. 'Sent him a letter, didn't I? The one delivered to him in court. It cost a packet to arrange that, believe me (especially since I didn't have much money left by then) but we figured it would have more impact if he got it at the last minute, right in front of everyone. It was written with the help of a contact of mine. The woman who, ah, facilitates introductions to those saucy girls.'

'Facilitates introductions? What is she?'

'She's not a bad sort, actually. And she owed me a favour.'

'Oh?' I find I've folded my arms and developed an old fashioned expression.

'She did, OK? I put a bit of business her way. And she knows that Judge. Knows one or two judges, actually. Like so many of them, he has certain tastes. Sometimes relaxes at the Black Mamba Club, in which she has an interest. Apparently, he enjoys their gimp closets. He told her – what was it, now? Oh yes, that they're the disciplinary equivalent of a sensory deprivation tank only rather more strictly structured, and that it's so restful to be removed from one's responsibilities for a few hours. He also likes the girl who does the post-correctional massages.'

'The what?'

'Don't be naive. Those old guys develop really stiff muscles when they've spent the evening standing in a soundproofed cupboard, all hooded up and chained by the neck. Well, Ms Masseur is very young indeed. Judge PS had no idea how young till he read my note offering to share the information with the Law Society. If, that was, he sent you down.'

'God Almighty, Shaun, you can't go round blackmailing high court judges – what's to stop him using that letter to fix the both of us?'

'Don't be silly,' he sighs, brushing a feather off his trousers, 'I didn't sign it.'

Visions of the diminutive judge relaxing in a black leather helmet and PVC leggings swim in front of my eyes. Did he have pierced nipples under there too? Testicular weights? Post-correctional masseurs. – I should have known the media circus would never have been enough on its own. An expression of gratitude is called for but Shaun has once again demonstrated his ability to turn my world inside out, and I don't know quite what to say. 'Shaun, what you did was – was incredible,' I flounder, hot in the face. 'I owe you a – a huge, vast thank you. Without you, I'd still be in jail.' Actually, without you I'd still have my husband, my home and my old life. *You reckon? Nobody forced you to go back to him, did they?* sniffed my inner headmistress. *And there is such a word as 'no'.*

'But why did Debbie send you round to tell me this? And how come she knows so much about it, anyway?'

'Debbie knows about a lot of things these days, including, after the newspapers had finished with Ziggurat, how her husband made most of his money. Oh stop it,' he exclaims, giving my arm a gentle shake. 'That bit wasn't your fault.'

'But it was. My friend Lucia's been –'

'I know all about her. Made a nice new career for herself on the back of it all, hasn't she? But Lucia had nothing to do with Ziggurat going down. It was Martyn.'

'Martyn who?'

'*Martyn*. You met him at The Grenadier House, remember? My FD. The little shit was selling information to the highest bidder, just like they taught him to at Harrow. The press would never have got anywhere if we hadn't sacked him the previous month for some of the most creative embezzlement seen outside Exxon. Martin's had his manicured fingers in and out of our till so often he's practically got repetitive strain injury.'

'It was *him*? Bloody hell. That's –'

'Yes, and you know something else? The chat lines and net erotica were his idea too. Said they could make up to three times the return of ordinary sites, and he was right. Who was I to argue with figures like that? Our ad revenues were right down, and at least it kept my magazines afloat,'

I need a drink. Slide dazedly off the table, locate the last two clean glasses in our sweatbox kitchen and extract the dregs of bog-standard Bordeaux by removing the wine box bag and wringing it. 'So let me get this straight. You helped me get off because I didn't shop you about that girl, having first ruptured every internal organ you possessed?'

Shaun raises his glass and downs the lot with the expression of someone used to decent vintages but too preoccupied to say so. 'That's about the size of it. Though I think love might have had something to do with it, too.'

Halfway through a slug of wine, I choke so hard that the Bordeaux swills around my nostrils. 'Don't be daft. You can't possibly love me, you can't. Not after –'

'As a matter of fact, I do.'

He doesn't mean that. It isn't possible. As Jim told me by phone when he first got out to his island, no man in his right mind wants a chaotic havoc-wrecking harpy like me fucking up his life. Especially not one who's – oh hell – an ex-con with dependant children and no job prospects.

'But there are lots of different kinds of love, aren't there?' he suggests. Nod violently.

Shaun sits down carefully on the edge of the table by the window and starts fiddling with the jam-jar holding Kasha's gel pens, looking anywhere but at me. 'You can love your children, right? It's unconditional: you'd jump in front of a speeding train for them. That's one kind of love. You love your mother and father (if you're lucky): that's another. People love their horse, their dog, their country, their home, their God, their best friend, their gay flatmate. People may also,' he swings round to look at me at last, 'love someone from their past, someone who's no longer right for them but whom no one will ever replace. Many of us have one of those. We don't want to live with them; if they've gone bald or run to fat we'll no longer fancy them: hell, we may not even *like* them any more. Yet the fireworks and glory you once had together remain like the after-image of the sun when you've been staring at it. And nothing – and no one – will ever change that.' He contemplates his shirt cuff. 'That's the kind of love I'm talking about.'

Run to fat, huh?

'Don't take this the wrong way,' he adds hastily.

I don't. In fact, I can feel a slow smile breaking across my face, a big beam of gratitude for that last sort of love. Shaun looks relieved and surreptitiously adjusts the waistband of his trousers, where convalescence has added additional curvature to his fledgling paunch. I stop looking at it and take his hand instead. 'You're right. Any kind of love at all is precious, and the sort you just described, lasts. It's just that, well,' I squeeze his fingers, 'sometimes, people can, you know, mistake it for something else.'

Stepping forward to give him what I know is our last hug ever, I hold him for a long, long moment, wanting to say something huge, something he'll remember. But all that comes out is a quiet sigh, and: 'What will you do now? You know, out in New Zealand?'

'There's a small magazine company that needs a troubleshooting MD. A client of Deb's accountant brother.'

'Great –'

'Not really. Their portfolio consists of *Total Gerbil*, *Continence Aids Today*; and *GlitterKid*, a failing image monthly for eight-year-olds.'

As I see him out, the fluorescent communal stair-light shows up his thinning hair and fresh facial lines, but he still carries himself like someone who matters. A man less ordinary. Once, all I'd ever wanted was to grow old with him and tell him he had a great shaped head when his hair fell out. But seeing him laughing and blowing up balloons with his wife and children in Smollensky's had been an object lesson in what's real and what's wishful thinking.

They were a family, they belonged to each other, and I didn't. I belong to Tim and Kasha. I also realise, very late in the day that I belonged to Jim as well, even though he is understandably less than eager to exercise his options on that one. Out of nowhere comes the voice of Holly Golightly, crying as she looks for her cat in the rain at the end of *Breakfast at Tiffany's*. 'I'm very scared, Buster. Yes, at last. Because it could go on for ever. Not knowing what's yours till you've thrown it away.'

And fuck it, I have thrown it away. Because I would now give anything to have the right to be there when *Jim* goes bald, loving him and being loved a bit in return even if I've gone tubby and grey. I want to be the one who brings him beers while he works late on his novel, who finds his glasses when he loses them, who snuggles up to him for *Newsnight*, and admires the unnecessary extras he brings back for his bike. I'd even have his mum up for regular Sunday lunches and let her boil all the dishcloths she likes, but it's too late.

Staring out of the window into the dark, I consider Life as our junior tabby comes and butts her head against my leg. A gentle, slightly dippy cat, she's been far better-tempered about her new living quarters than The Vicar (who's taken to peeing in the bath). So: a summary. I have husband who's gone half way round the world to get away from me and I can't say I blame him, insecure children, the bog leaks, the washing machine's on the blink, I look knackered even when I'm not and Tim needs three new pairs of school shoes which will eat the whole of the next quarter's budget for clothes.

So maybe I could write a book to raise some more cash, like all good unemployed journalists? Well, there's one title that's a natural, I think darkly, squeezing out the last half-glass of budget box red, and slumping down on the floor with my chin on the windowsill. How about *101 Ways to Put Men Off You for Life?* Or perhaps: *Take Me Back, I'll Do Anything.* I could dedicate that one to Jim.

It's now one in the morning and I know I can't sleep, not that I ever do much these days. Particularly not after Shaun's visit, the implications of which are still sinking in. Having tucked up and fussed over Tim and Kasha even though they didn't need it, I mindlessly switch on the TV to find Channel Five's showing a Marilyn Manson documentary. Now I've got the pictures of Jim out again. At three twenty, I crawl onto the sofa and lie down with cushion over my head, images of his face scattered all over the floor. Have also found a flat, brown twiggy object. Pressed in the photo album these last fifteen years, it's the bloody rosebud from his buttonhole on our wedding day.

There's something else too, something that makes me want to slit my wrists, tucked into an envelope of photos that never made it into the one album we possess. Two of those pictures show Jim and me with our arms around each other at Glastonbury the weekend we met. He's tanned, beautiful and stripped to the waist despite the drizzle, sporting a six pack stomach and filthy denims. I've got a mud-spattered yellow sarong, muddy Wellingtons and a blissful expression. Despite the fact the shots are blurred and badly composed, our happiness is palpable.

The something else does not, at first, look like much: a soft square of paper, folded and fraying; my writing in faded pencil below a shakily-drawn heart with our initials in it dated 5.5.90: two days after the bike smash he nearly didn't wake up from. I'd slept on the hospital floor beside him for seven nights and taped that paper above his hospital bed, a talisman against death –

Surface next morning with a vile taste in my mouth and a swollen nose to the sound of Tim roaring that the Frosties have run out, and tuts from Kasha at the state of the sitting room. The rose is unrecognisable, a pile of flaking shards in my closed fist.

Tomorrow Belongs to Me

A series of large colour photographs depicting a six foot pile of lambs' kidneys adorned with syringes and razor blades, glistens on the dining table in the August afternoon sun.

I am struggling to write a press handout for the ICA's forthcoming Temporary Organic Art exhibition. By definition, TOA goes off after twenty-four hours so it's a Statement about the fleeting, ephemeral nature of beauty (it says here). I am not allowed to crack any jokes about the exhibition being offally cutting edge, a pointed satire on the current state of BritArt or representing an injection of much needed life into the London creative scene. Unfortunately, that's proving impossible since there is sod all else one can say about it, even on five hundred pounds a day.

Yes, someone is paying me to write crap again. I'd been offered the job during a drinks party at Lucia's place five months ago.

'You *must* meet lovely Pheebs Muller,' she'd trilled, as I'd sat on the sofa surrounded by minor fashionista, trying to deflect questions about what it was really like inside (ex-inmates were terrifically In last season) and mulling over my employment status. 'She's got to go in a moment, but she's chief press officer for the ICA.' Great, I'd thought. Another of Lucia's arty friends, all of whom need retrieving from up their own backsides before you can hold any kind of conversation with them.

Smiling socially, Lucia indicated a small thin woman with a half-inch vermilion crop, tungsten nose ring and a black sheath dress that looked as if it was made of crumpled onion skins but was probably Japanese and horrifically expensive. Having got pissed in record time for medicinal purposes, I found that her face was shifting in and out of focus and stared at her, entranced, but was too ashamed of my washing-up reddened hands with their split and soggy cuticles to shake her proffered paw with its perfectly buffed nails and soft, dead-white skin.

'Loved your piece on vibrators in *Steam* last autumn,' she told me in a flat Milwaukee accent. 'My partner whined so much about strap-on dildo harnesses rubbing that I was close to ditching the bitch. However,' she widened her rodenty brown eyes at me, 'that gel-filled model you recommended with beads in the rotating head is just genius. You saved our relationship, I swear.'

'Oh. Er, jolly good,' I hiccuped, feeling like a girl-guide leader confronted by a lurid lesbian lapse from her past. Hadn't I written that piece ten years ago when I was somebody else? Five minutes of drunken Girls' Best Friend talk later; she offered me a job.

'We have this real hot artist coming up called Bodo. The guy's sensational – psychologically damaged, of course, but, like, *so* creative. He records the pattern of dust motes falling in the upstairs gallery at different times of day, puts it all on computer then generates a digitalized visual soundtrack out of it. He's just so *on it*: I mean, he even wants gallery visitors to sing their own interpretation of what they see to create a personalised pattern of visual melody for the sound of time passing.' I'd felt myself glazing over and wished she'd go away so I could get really plastered in peace. Then maybe I could forget about Jim for a couple of hours.

'We want, like, some press releases and information sheets to go with, plus someone to chase coverage. Trouble is, our man's real picky. Gnomic, taciturn, a lousy verbaliser. But he's been in jail (Florida, 2002, GBH) so I think he might really relate to *you*. Come by Monday, one-ish. We'll do lunch, talk freelance PR. Five hundred a day.' Surely the woman was joking? But she'd pressed her card upon me before teetering off to the next party. A growth-retarded, monosyllabic, homicidal artist who wrote silent music: it was obvious he'd go far on the London art scene.

He did, too. Because despite the whole stupid business being shallower than a paddling pool, practicality came before principles, I took the job and the fickle arts press decided that they couldn't get enough of Bodo. Today, though I still feel pretty sheepish about writing this sort of rubbish, I am also extremely grateful to be asked – for the truth is we're a single parent family, five hundred a day is five hundred a day, and it would take a fortnight to earn that arranging Weetabix.

Not that I'd had the chance to do that recently, since every school-hours friendly store in Camden (including Tesco, Sainsbury's, Iceland and Poundstretcher) has shown me the door on the grounds that my fingers may have got lighter whilst in prison. And since Morrison's had refused to have me back as well, my professional pride (what was left of it) has been binned along with the remains of other disposable items generated by contemporary urban society, Tim has all the new shoes he needs, and TOA is the fifth project Pheebs has hired me to work on. Having instigated this one herself, she is as protective of it as a neurotic mother with a gifted toddler.

'Can't you turn them over, Mummy?' says Kasha, looking up from her homework on the other side of the table at the gleaming shots of indie-art gore. 'They're putting me right off my ag-verbs.'

Stumped for a caption that wouldn't offend The Artist but might interest the press, I tilt the chair back and glance tiredly around the sitting room. The place looks cosy and almost burrow-like in the six o'clock summer light despite the fact it's five floors up. Something to do with a house-full of rugs, cushions, pictures and plants being crammed into three rooms. There seems to be enough space because we didn't bring everything, and Jim's not here. I never realised

363

how much psychological space a big bloke takes up with his sheer presence, never mind all his belongings.

This flat's just the right size for the three of us, I tell myself bracingly at least twice a day, and we don't need a father to be the fourth member of the family. *A sturdy three-legged stool is just as stable as a four-legged chair,* as Bel insists whenever new divorce statistics are announced in the press. Not half as comfortable to sit on, though.

We still miss our old house very much indeed, and take great care never to walk past it. It has been expensively and unsuitably tarted up. Just looking at the tasteful new French Navy gloss door makes us feel shaky, and it hurts as much now as it did when Jim left a year ago. Thinking about him (again) I humph more heavily than a cow in labour. The trick isn't to have what you want, is it, it's to want what you have. *Aw, shit. I must be getting old.* Time for a cuppa, but predictably, there is no milk.

'Kash, Tim, just popping down the garage for some semi-skimmed. See you in a few minutes.' Kasha is out of her chair and over by the door in seconds. 'How long will you be?

'A matter of minutes, sweetheart.'

'I'm coming too.'

'Go on with you, you sit down and finish your homework, yes? You're doing great, I'll test you when I come back, and then we'll have supper,' I suggest, planting a kiss on the top of her silky head. But she's already whipping her cardigan on and getting the money from the penny jar so we potter off down the road hand in hand, her palm warm and seamless a kitten's mitten in mine.

Kasha has been my shadow ever since I got back. I had hoped that spending plenty of time together and sharing a bed would help, but it hasn't. She follows me everywhere, including to the toilet where she stands outside talking through the keyhole.

364

She will not fall asleep unless I lie down with her, though we've made the room as Kasha-friendly as possible by swathing it in purple mosquito netting, hanging her mirrored LOVE wind-chimes in the window and sticking her McFly pictures all over the wardrobe doors. A shirtless Orlando Bloom broods down from the wall above the sagging double bed we share, but once she'd brought her beanie babies, tape deck, tape box, books, extra pillows, old Walkman, CDs and nine favourite stuffed animals, it is exactly as she likes it but there is little room left for her mother. She also keeps a grubby roll of paper secured with a pink hair tie in the dolphin-shaped nightie case under her pillow, transferring it to her school backpack during in the day: the letters and drawings I sent her while I was in prison.

Once, Tim and I tried to persuade her to leave them at home 'where the cats could look after them'. Teeth bared, she'd snatched them back and stuffed them down her sweatshirt. 'Give them back, I said *give them*. It's your fault! It is! I didn't have a mummy for ages, only stupid, dumb letters! And I'm keeping them in case – well, I'm just keeping them, OK?'

Even now, she expects me to be taken away again at any minute. Some days, so do I.

'Hey, Mum?' says Tim brightly when we return, looking up from the floor where he is now sprawled reading an old Formula One magazine. 'Dad rang you when you were taking the rubbish downstairs yesterday.' Time slows, then stops. He's rung every week since he left but it's never me he wants to speak to. 'Yesterday? Why didn't you –'

'Forgot,' he replies cheerfully, sloping off to his room. In deference to his teenage status, and also to the vicious feuding that developed while I was away, Tim has been awarded one of the two little bedrooms to himself (the half bedroom turned out to be a laundry area).

'Did he, er, say anything?'

'Oh, yeah,' says Tim, sticking his head back around the door. 'Something about can he come over to take you out for a drink tonight. At least, yeah, I think it was tonight. I said sure, and that maybe you could ask Hera to babysit. Though I'm not a baby and I don't need a sitter.'

Hera the body-piercing queen of Camden is Ms Stay Home since she got with child. She sometimes child-sits here for free because, she insists kindly, it gets her in the mood for nesting. Being hugely pregnant, she no longer presides over *Divine Agony* in person lest she alarm the customers having their edgy clitori bejewelled. She and her partner have also given up evenings at experimental theatres where the casts spray pigs' blood at the audience, and bondage night at *Apocalypse,* for the *Vicar of Dibley* and the Active Birth Centre couples' classes.

And Tim, as he says, is no baby. Already five inches taller than me, on his thirteenth birthday last month he requested a tube of Clearasil, a Holly Valence poster and a half bottle of champagne. After school, he will only wear black jeans so baggy that they slide down over his narrow bottom, and tattered black sweatshirts that would swamp Vin Diesel. He also has two little zits nestling in his left nasal crease of which he is inordinately proud, and a teenager's resentment of any perceived parental interference which wasn't there when I went away.

Yesterday I'd made the mistake of asking where he was going and when he'd be back as he headed for the door, skater baggies aflap, second-hand blades over his shoulder. 'What's it to you?' he'd dared from the doorway, the look in his eyes saying that he knew he'd gone too far.

'Just want you to be safe and stay out of trouble, darling.' *I will not rise, I will be Firm but Fair.* 'And Tim, I'm not trying to be nosy, but who are you going to meet?' Not Rodway, I prayed, please not Rodway, that six foot fourteen-year-old with the feral face and the dealer dad. Tim had met Rod last month at the local skate-park, and having watched him despatch two other big kids without effort before lining up the rest to buy his mini-spliffs in the park toilets, he now admires the boy's cool immeasurably. 'And who are you to talk about not getting into trouble?' he'd blurted, backing rapidly downstairs.

'Tim! Come back here this minute,' I'd screeched, pounding after him in hot pursuit. 'And don't you speak to me like that.'

He'd fled, shouting up though the stairwell: 'I had to deck this bloke at school today because of you!'

'What? I said come *back* –'

'Some duh-brain who keeps on coming up and going 'Vroom-vroom, I'm psycho-van: where's Mummie then?' bawled Tim who had now reached the ground floor. 'I got detention and extra work, and Mr Webster had a right go at me – he was way livid. But it's happened before, and it's your fault, right? Cos even though they let you off you've been in, in *jail*, Mum; and I'm telling you, right, I'm not letting some dickhead diss you but it's dead embarrassing. So you can't, yeah, go on at *me* about getting into trouble –' His voice was abruptly cut off by the slam of the outer front door as I reached the ground floor. He was back two hours later, trousers ripped, a cut below his knee, and very subdued. We hugged without words for a long time before fishing out the plasters and Germolene, then re-heating the shepherd's pie (mostly baked beans and onions, to save on mince) that Kasha and I had left him from supper.

It must be hell being a teenage boy. All that indignation, fear, confusion and love: all those desires and prohibitions. But it's not easy being the parent of one either, especially if they produce the same unbeatable trump card whenever you venture to suggest staying out of trouble.

An hour later, soaking in our foreshortened brown enamel bath, knees poking out of the water and watching steam fog the window, I'm almost wishing that Jim was here so he could talk to Tim, Dad to Delinquent. But go out for a drink with That Man? Not if I was dying of dehydration. I simply shan't ring him back, that's what. Apart from anything else, I've only recently reached the happy stage where the sound of his voice calling from his Maldavian bolt hole asking to speak to the children provokes neither a bitter tirade of reproach, nor a private storm of weeping.

In fact, I cannot imagine anything worse than a drink with the Rat Who Has Left Us To Rot. Naturally the fact he's had the children out to his place every holidays, been back twice in between to take them down to stay with his mum and writes to them, without fail, each week, is totally beside the point.

No, he can just sod off. For I have a rich, new life. Full of – full of humble pie to eat, pointless press releases to write, early nights to have and dire sitcoms to watch alone on Saturday nights. There's also the small matter of re-locating my self-esteem. I know I must have left it around here somewhere, but I don't seem to be able to lay my hands on it. Rub face with flannel, and slide slowly under the surface.

Fifteen seconds later Kasha is perched on the bath rim shouting something urgent and prodding me in the (rather flabby) stomach.

'What? Ow. *What?*'

'Daddy's here.'

'Christ, where?' Sit bolt upright, clutching the fraying flannel to my bosom.

'Sitting room,' she replies laconically, wandering out and leaving the door wide open. Rear up out of the bath, slam the door shut and go into a frenzy of body drying and hair rubbing. If you're going to tell a man to piss off, you can't do it sopping wet with no lipstick.

Kasha reappears three minutes later, this time bearing clothes. Displaying wisdom beyond her years, she's found my best pair of black jeans, a tight black cardigan, a clean-ish pair of red Converse boots and an amusing little Luella T-shirt blagged by Lucia. In fact, Lucia has been a source of a few designer freebies of late. Since fronting a twelve-episode pilot of the new cable chat-show *EntreNous,* her new career (B-list celeb-schmoozing, scandal-dissection and fashion tittle-prattle) is going like a TGV.

It takes sixty seconds to get dressed, then a further fifteen minutes to pluck up courage to come out of the bathroom. I apply makeup, take it off again because it looks too festive, clean my teeth, get a piece of dental floss stuck between two back ones and have to cut it out with nail scissors; put too much gel on my hair, stick head under the shower to remove it, towel dry and comb it back; slap more foundation onto my now greenish little face, hyperventilate, clean out the bath – then run out of displacement activities and edge into the sitting room. Brought up short by the sight of Jim in the sofa.

He is looking very much at home, playing backgammon with Tim and telling Kasha, who is perched on his knees, yet another *Beano* joke ('What's the fastest thing in the river? A motor-pike') which has her wriggling with giggles.

When he looks up, black patches scud in front of my eyes for I have managed, by ducking, diving, being out at strategic intervals and having my mother or Bel stand in for me during hand-overs, not to clap eyes on him once for the past twelve months.

But now he's here, and he fills the room. He's got a tan the colour of pale sherry which has left white laughter lines at the corners of his eyes, his newly-glossy red hair has grown down to his collar and his long, long legs are encased in faded blue Levis. He looks terrific. I hate him.

How dare he look so relaxed, sitting there on my sofa, in my flat, with *my* children? How dare he suck up to them like that? And where's their sense of loyalty, anyway? Quivering with territorial aggression, I glare at the three of them. They all smile back. I want to be civilised but shock, resentment and something else that I won't admit to even if it kills me, conspire to make me far ruder than I intend. 'What are *you* doing here?' *Hey, steady on. 'Hello' would have done.*

Jim, propelled by Public School Imprint Learning, shoots to his feet and holds out a tentative hand. I ignore it.

'Ah.' His smile evaporates. 'I'm sorry. I thought, er, that is – Tim, you said you'd spoken to mum and that she said she was OK about coming out for, um, a bite to eat. Didn't you?'

'Did I?' says Tim innocently, shooting Kasha a lightning look.

'Well, now he's here, Mummy, you might as well,' suggests my daughter off-handedly adding, one-parent child that she now is: 'It'll save supper money, won't it? Oh, and Hera's here too. She's just lying down in our bedroom for a moment. She says her legs are aching.'

'How – who – and what's *she* doing here?'

'I asked her,' explains my son. 'To save you the trouble,' he supplies, seeing my face.

Fucking hell. Set up by two people who still play Chocolate Monopoly.

'So. What brings you back so soon?'

Jim wriggles his shoulders, tucks both hands behind his back and looks more uncomfortable by the second. 'I've finished my manuscript.'

'Congratulations.' I'm not going to give him any help.

'It's a new one.'

'Is it?' I can feel my jaw clenching, though I long to say: 'Oh good for you! Fantastic!' and throw my arms around him, especially remembering all the rejection letters for the first one from snotty agents who couldn't persuade themselves to love it enough. Yet the words stay trapped in my throat, and cursing my own ungenerous nature isn't enough to stop sheer envy singing in my veins 'Let's hope you can get an agent, then. But I don't expect that anyone decent has room for new clients at the moment.'

'Well actually, I have got somebody,' he mumbles diffidently, retrieving first his rejected right hand, then his left, and hooking the thumbs into his belt loops.

'Jolly good,' I manage through gritted teeth. To complicate matters further, I find I'm looking at his hands. Broad backed but with fine wrists and slim tapering fingers, the sun has burned the hairs on the back a light copper blonde which looks soft and silky to the touch.

'She's with that big Covent Garden outfit which handles a lot of film work. You know, Ed Richter's…?'

'Very nice too. But those large agencies can be so slow, can't they?'

'Well, as a matter of fact, they've, er, already persuaded Miramax to take the film rights. I've been given a bit of development money to help knock up a first draft script, too… it's with Working Title at the moment,' he adds with shy pride. 'Remember, that lot that did *Bridget Jones* and *Love, Actually?*'

Bloody hell. 'Isn't it true that some producers will buy book manuscripts up just to stop them being filmed, because they don't want them to damage other projects they've got on the boil?' I enquire before I can stop myself. *No, no, no. Tell him you're really happy for him, you miserable bitch –*

'Oh, yeah, er, absolutely; that's absolutely right.' He sounds uncannily like Tim for a moment, I think with a flash of pure affection, which gets briskly squashed. 'Look at Douglas Adams' *Hitchhikers Guide to the Galaxy.* Bought by a big studios in the mid-eighties, but the film only came out last year. Anyway, my agent says not to get excited, as apparently I have just officially entered Development Hell.'

'Is it that bad?' I ask, hopefully.

'Ish. Development Hell's the place you go when a film producer's lifted you up, set you on a high place, showed you the world at you feet – then gone off and left you there. When a studio buys your novel it's not really a cause for celebration, though it sounds good. It's more a case of – now no one else can do anything with it.'

Good. 'Well, you never know.' *I wonder if your mouth still tastes of tobacco, and of vanilla lip salve.*

'It's being published as a book, though. Here, in October. That's why I'm over in the UK again,' he ducks his head. 'To do some, er, publicity shots and talk to their press people.'

There is no justice in this world, I think furiously. None. *Oh come on, this man's not my enemy. He may be a deserting, rejecting husband who's got a great tan from sitting on the beaches of the Indian Ocean while I looked after our children in the depths of a dripping British winter, but he's hardly the Anti-Christ.*

'Well, let's go out and drink to your success.' I'm swallowing broken glass, but figure we might as well get this over with. Then I can come home and shred pillows with my bare hands. 'What's the new book about, then?' Not that I want to know. Tim and Kasha are shoo'ing us out onto the dim landing and shutting the door, beaming like Ma and Pa Walton as John Boy steps out with the suitable girl next door.

Jim stops a few steps below me, his face in shadow. 'It's about this bloke who's obsessed with a former girlfriend.'

Suddenly, my feet miss a stair. 'Who – who is she?' It comes out as a whisper. 'This woman, in your book?'

'Just someone I used to know.'

Forget it, girlie. He just needs somewhere to stay tonight, that'll be it. Or he's trying to break it to me gently that the twenty quid a week he's been sending for Tim and Kasha (not much, but invaluable when you were permanently broke with two growing children) will be stopping.

'Zoe, I don't know how to say this, but –'

He's met someone, hasn't he?

'I've, ah –'

He has. He has. And it's only been a year.

He gazes at me with Basset eyes. I'm not just gutted, I am filleted. Because for a second back there, just a second, I had allowed myself to hope. Well, silly me.

'Oh, get *on* with it. Just say it, why don't you?'

She'll be in her late twenties. He probably met her SCUBA'ing, at which she excels. She'll be much cleverer,

372

prettier and funnier than me; have goldfish-bowl tits, no cellulite, a beach house, and think Jim's the best thing she's ever seen.

'I've mumble-ith'd'ou.'

'What?'

'I've mmmmumble-ith'doo.'

'For God's sake, Jim, spit it out. We haven't got all night.' *Later on, I shall drink myself into a stupor. I'll ask Bel and Lucia over. They can help.*

'I said I've bloody missed you. Are you deaf?' mutters Jim, scarlet in the face.

'Who, me? Really. Why?' *Now he's trying to soften me up so I won't be troublesome over the divorce settlement.*

Jim tugs at his hair like a mad scientist. 'Why do you have to make everything so fucking difficult?'

'I'm not. I just don't see why – I mean, this is a bit of a change of tune, isn't it? Bit sudden?' *I know, he's worried about the child access thing. He thinks I'll be difficult. Well, of course I won't. It's just one of those things that he's got some fit little uberfox twenty years his junior and gets to sit on sun-drenched sand with her all day while I wait for busses in the Camden drizzle. I understand completely. And I shall naturally do my small best, not to make things difficult, but to make them hell. Now, where can I start?*

'So who is she?'

'Who? Hey, you're crying.'

'I am *not.*'

'Here.' He produces a nasty bit of loo paper from his back pocket. 'Blow.'

Bugger, I seem to cry every day about something or other these days. I do hope he's not going to take it as a compliment because it certainly –

'Will you please listen to me for a minute? No, come back here,' he reaches out a long arm and imprisons me as I try to retreat back upstairs to the safety of the flat.

'Get *off.*'

'Not until I've told you why I missed you. You're going to hear this whether you want to or – ow!' I've kicked him. His physical proximity (my face squashed against his now unfamiliar chest) is making me panicky.

'You want to know why I've come back?' he demands, rubbing his shin. 'Clearly not, but now I'm here I'm going to tell you anyway. It's not because of the book. They could have done the stuff over the phone and had a local photographer take some shots. No, I came back this time for the express purpose of talking to you because everywhere I went in the islands, you were there too. All over the bloody place.

'You'd be on the end of my bed giving them points out of ten when I'd just slept with someone, and there was no shortage of women there, believe me – lots of holiday girls passing through.' I bristle, but he keeps going: 'When I took the dive boat out, you were often in the back trailing your feet in the water. If I sat down in a beach bar, I'd swear I'd see you walk in. You were at my shoulder in the marketplace reminding me to buy the things you liked to eat. If I went to see a band, I'd catch glimpses of you dancing down the front.

'That's how I knew you were the ghost under my skin – the other face in my mirror. That's how I finally understood that in spite of all the crap, our lives are tangled together for ever like the snarls of coloured nylon fishing line I'd see every day lying on the beach. That's how I knew that because we've been together all these years and had two children, everything I am up to this point is to do with you, and everything you are, is to do with me. No *wait*, I haven't finished,' Jim takes a ragged breath, and ploughs on:

'That day after the court case, you begged me to stay and talk to you and I wouldn't. I should've done but I was confused, exhausted and I just wanted out. Instead, I find I've been talking to you in my head every day for months. Now I've come to do it in person. If, that is, you will listen.'

I stare at him in astonishment for many long seconds. Brain must have finally burst a blood vessel or six. In which case, why aren't I dead? 'Let me get this quite clear. You don't want a divorce?'

'That is the last thing I want.'

I must be hearing things. 'Oh. Oh, right... so are you, ah, trying to say that you love me after all, and you want to start over? Or what?'

'Love? What's that? Hanging in there when the going turns to shit? Being haunted by someone you've gone halfway around the world to get away from? Wanting to take them out for dinner even when they've got red eyes and their nose is running?' He offers me the bit of loo paper again. 'If it's any or all of those, I love you all right. I must do. I've even missed you eating baked bean sandwiches in bed, for God's sake. I've missed hearing you laugh at my *Beano* jokes; nobody else does. There's a great gaping hole in my life where a small, argumentative fruitcake with a body like a pocket Venus who likes stray animals, strange clothes and who makes me laugh before breakfast, should be – I mean, I've never found anyone else who's even coherent when they've just woken up, never mind funny. But as for wanting to start over... well, I don't know about that.'

'So what *do* you want, then?' I'm clutching at the banisters for support, quite unable to believe what he just said.

'I still haven't finished, so zip it.' I keep quiet.

'If we are to begin seeing a bit of each other again – if – some things will have to change around here. You'll have to learn to wait till I've finished talking for a start. And speaking of starts, are you going to come out with me for a, I suppose it's a date, isn't it? Or are you going to hang about up there for the rest of the evening?'

'Out, I guess,' I mutter ungraciously. 'But there's a few things you need change too while we're at it. Have you any *idea* what –'

Swiftly, he claps his hand over my mouth.

'We'll talk about all that later. When we have had something to eat.'

We stand on the stairs, swinging our now clasped hands to and fro straight-armed, beginning to beam with cautious goodwill, adolescently awkward, our tongues smarting from repressed recriminations, smartarse replies, love-words, abuse, rage and relief that prickle and shift just below the surface.

'All right, then.' The workaday words will barely come out and the voice does not sound like my own. 'Tell me where we're going tonight.' *Thank you, God. Thank you, thank you –*

Jim seems to lose some of his confidence. 'Oh, ah, I thought maybe – film and something to eat? Come on,' he says, shepherding me downstairs. His voice isn't quite steady. 'Come on. I've booked us a table at Samurai. Then there's this fantastic Bergman retrospective at The Screen on the Hill which I thought perhaps – I mean, we could – that is, I'd quite understand if you didn't feel like –'

Hot date, huh? Raw fish, a tongue-tied escort, followed by several hours of angst-ridden celluloid from the Suicidal Swede. Yet as I look at his face, my heart starts humming what I could swear was the chorus of *Tomorrow Belongs To Me*.

We.

The very nicest word in the English language.

Acknowledgements

For all their encouragement, support and suggestions:
Sappho Clissitt and Peter La Brooy – THANK YOU

For some invaluable editing:
Lucy Ferguson, Umi Sinha and Hilary Johnson.